Into the Fire

Into the Fire

Linda Davies

HarperCollins*Publishers*

HarperCollins*Publishers*
77–85 Fulham Palace Road,
Hammersmith, London w6 8jb

Published by HarperCollins*Publishers* 1999
1 3 5 7 9 8 6 4 2

Copyright © Lineopus Ltd 1999

A catalogue record for this book
is available from the British Library

ISBN 0 00 225773 4

Set in Aldus
Typeset by Rowland Phototypesetting Ltd
Bury St Edmunds, Suffolk

Printed and bound in Great Britain by
Caledonian International Book Manufacturing Ltd, Glasgow

For my son, Hugh,
with all the love in the world

ACKNOWLEDGEMENTS

I would like to thank the following for their invaluable help.

Peru, for its beauty, gifts and trials. Professor Glyn Davies, economist extraordinaire, diligent proofreader and beloved father; Grethe Davies, raven-eyed proofreader and beloved mother; Roy Davies, bilingual proofreader and beloved brother; Louise Kennedy and Steve Beecham, aikido black belts; Adam Copperthwaite, Julian Hansen, Anthony Culligan and Philippe Bonnefoy, derivatives swingers; Charo Leon, Mix Fix It and Spanish mistress; Lucho Lainez Lozada, intrepid jungle pilot; Kati St Clair, psychological savant; Ernesto Yallico, explorer and guide; Charles and Kate Allen, facilitators; Her Majesty's Ambassador to Peru, H.E. John Illman, squash partner; Adriana von Hagen, archaeologist; Alexander Newman, a boy with some very serious toys; the action men from Bogotá; the curry fancier, and all the others I may not name. They know who they are.

Finally, and most importantly, I would like to thank my husband, Rupert Wise, with whom I walked into the fire, and will do again unto infinity.

Yet all experience is an arch wherethro'
Gleams that untravell'd world, whose margin fades
For ever and for ever when I move.

ALFRED, LORD TENNYSON, 'Ulysses'

Till a voice, as bad as Conscience, rang interminable
   changes
On one everlasting Whisper day and night repeated-so:
'Something hidden. Go and find it. Go and look behind the
   Ranges –
Something lost behind the Ranges. Lost and waiting for you.
Go!'

RUDYARD KIPLING, 'The Explorer'

PROLOGUE

She didn't quite remember when it first came upon her again, this desire to escape. It seemed to creep up on her, with quiet stealth. By the time she became aware of it, it was too late to resist. It held her, quietly goading. At first it had sounded like a voice that whispered constantly in her ear, with increasing volume, in a foreign language. It drove her mad, this insistent, incomprehensible urge. As it grew, it became almost unbearable. Until she decided to give in to it. She would disappear. Escape. Just like last time. Leave home, friends, job and bills. Simply walk away. When the time was right.

Never once did she suppose that her dream would become necessity. But when it did, the lore of the ancient Greeks came back to her: dreams are granted to those whom the gods wish to destroy.

CHAPTER 1

The tube train was packed with bodies rocking to the disrhythm of ancient tracks. It was six thirty. Evening rush hour. Helen Jencks stood in the middle of the carriage, hands free, perfectly balanced. Eight years on a boat and she could keep steady through the worst lurches the train had to offer. Between her feet lay two bulging carrier bags from Marks & Spencer, threatening to spill their cargo with every jolt. One joint of best Aberdeen Angus rolling down the carriage, leaving a bloody trail, pursued by bouncing red peppers and new potatoes, was all she needed. Bodies swayed against hers, some less inadvertently than others. The smell of sweaty cotton and wool mixed unpleasantly with that of the Camembert cheese, oozing in her shopping bag.

She hated the tube. Usually she cycled to work, but her bike had sprung a flat tyre on her overnight. On the rare occasions when she did submit to the underground, there always seemed to be a lunatic on board. Today's version, an evil-looking skinhead, sang loudly, football chants, over and over, the same mindless drone. Helen took bets with herself on how many people in the carriage wanted to kill him. The tube doors opened at Baker Street. Commuters thronged off the train. More forced their way on. The skinhead remained and increased his volume. He was at the other end of the carriage, far enough away, but Helen could feel the hairs rising on the back of her neck. Edgware Road. Tides of people ebbed on and off.

An old man limped aboard. Helen felt as if her heart constricted, just for a few beats, a burn of memory. Mid-sixties, about five foot ten, slightly stooped, thick grey hair, just as her father would have been, could be for all she knew. Something in the wisdom of compassion in his eyes, something in the puzzled gentleness of his smile as he caught her staring at him dredged up the flash of yearning; decades old, would it never go away? Helen wondered with a brief despair. She followed him with her eyes as, with awkward grace, he made his way through the throng, excusing his passing. A City slicker held back from the last spare seat. The old man said a relieved 'Thank you', but before he could sit down, the skinhead had dropped into his place. A few people inhaled sharply. No one said a word. The skinhead took out a packet of Marlboro, lit up a cigarette and blew smoke into the old man's face.

Helen pushed through the carriage till she stood before the skinhead. She stared down at him. He wore jeans and a black leather jacket. He smelled of beer and contempt. Small blue eyes narrowed and looked up at her.

'It's no smoking, and I think you took this gentleman's seat.' Her voice was low, her eyes blazed with a cold rage.

Conversations stopped. The attention of the entire carriage focused on her.

'Oh yeah? And whatcha gonna do about it, *girlie*?'

In answer, Helen reached out, took the cigarette from the man's mouth, dropped it to the floor and ground it out with a twist of her heel. The lunatic leapt to his feet. He stood inches from her. She could feel his spittle spray her face as he spoke.

'Who the fuck d'you think you are?' His face strained down towards hers, veins bulging. A faint sheen of sweat slicked his upper lip. 'Help the Aged? Who gives a toss about some old fart anyway?'

'I do, shitface.'

'You just asked for it, bitch.' The man aimed a punch at her face. With a movement so fast it was almost invisible, Helen stepped out of range. She caught the man's punching hand, turned it back on itself, her fingers inside his palm. The skinhead yelped with pain. He struggled then yelled louder.

'Don't struggle. You'll only make it worse for yourself.' She exerted more pressure on his hand, and began to push him sideways through the carriage. Those in their path backed away, pressing into those behind them. Helen forced the man up to the doors of the carriage. He stood on tiptoes, body rigid, straining away from the point of agony his hand had become. Everyone in the carriage shrank back as if expecting an explosion of violence. There was none, no sound for the next two minutes, save the whimpering of the bully as Helen held him in position. The tube stopped at Paddington, the doors opened.

Helen increased the pressure on the man's hand. She spoke to him in a low, menacing whisper. 'You're a coward, aren't you, like most bullies? See how you like it.'

She hurled him from the train, releasing his hand at the last moment. With a sickening crack, his wrist broke and he sprawled onto the platform. Warily curious, the new passengers got on, while others filed out, necks swivelling. The tube doors closed and the entire carriage burst into applause. The old man nodded to her from his seat down the carriage. There was admiration, a little fear and a quiet sense of avenged dignity in his eyes. Helen gave an awkward smile and went back to her shopping bags. She could feel everyone watching her until she got off the tube at Ladbroke Grove.

A stranger followed her off and came up to her. A tall man in a City suit with a kind smile.

'Well done. That was really impressive. Nice to see someone getting what they deserve for once.'

'Thank you.'

'How'd you do it? It all seemed so effortless. You just sort of held him paralysed.'

'Sankyo,' said Helen. 'It's a particular hold. Move a millimetre, it's agony.'

'What is it? Karate?'

'Aikido.'

'I thought it must have been some fancy martial art.' He held out his hand. 'I'm Jim Haughton.'

'Helen Jencks.'

She waited, and sure enough it came.

'No relation to Jack Jencks, are you?'

Jack Jencks: crooked financier and supposed fugitive. Ex-director of one of the largest privately held banks in the United Kingdom. Two days before Helen's seventh birthday he and a large sum of money disappeared, never to be seen again. Living it up in some foreign hideaway, so thought the press.

'Yes,' she answered defiantly. 'I'm his daughter.'

As always, she saw the quick reevaluation in the stranger's eyes – reflected notoriety, distrust. She heard her mother's voice. *Change your name by deed poll. I'm going to do it. It'll be better, Hel, c'mon.'*

'And you,' asked the man, moving on valiantly, 'what do you do, apart from aikido?'

'I'm a banker too.' She smiled, challenging him. Like almost all the others, he caved in to prejudice. He smiled, knowingly. Yet again she was centre stage of a joke that moved her to rage. After all these years, still the sins of the father ... Did it run in the blood, sedition? Could a climate of distrust nurture it? She almost wished it, but she had never felt like a law-breaker, never saw her father or herself in that role. Even if, as far as others were concerned, she could play it, unknowingly, to perfection.

She walked away from him, losing herself in the crowd, disturbed by thoughts of her father, seeing again the face of the old man on the tube, wondering if in some distant part of the world, some corner she hadn't searched, her father made a lonely train journey, searching the faces of young women for his daughter.

Not once in twenty-three years had she heard from him. Interpol's file lay dormant. There were occasional reports of sightings over the years, but none led to anything. As far as the world was concerned, Jack Jencks was dead. Helen's mother had long ago given up hope, but something in Helen refused to relinquish her father.

She left the station and walked out into the busy evening streets of Ladbroke Grove. She wore a long waterproof coat of the type favoured by Australian cattle herders: brown, stiff fabric, side splits, a slight smell of waterproofing oil. It came down to her ankles, and gave her something of the air of an outlaw. She wore trainers on her feet.

Her walk was athletic, poised somewhere between that of dancer and weightlifter. There was a powerful energy that hovered about her. Her face seemed to have been moulded into life by a sculptor's thumb. Flaring, slightly snubbed, pugnacious nose; full lips, gently curled as if at some ironic amusement of her own; rounded chin; voluptuous cheekbones. Her eyes were dark-blue ovals, deep set,

6

under winged eyebrows which sloped down sharply to the inner corners of her eyes. Two deep, short, vertical grooves cut into her forehead above her nose. Her gathered eyes and brows gave her an air of thought or preoccupation. It was a reflective, resilient face. Her skin was creamy pale, her cheeks rosy, a blood and milk complexion. Her body was strong, compact in its five-foot-six frame. Her breasts were firm and high set, her bottom rounded and high, Africanate. Her leg muscles bulged down to hard, strong knees and ankles. She had a dancer's arched feet. Her natural blonde hair was wiry, permanently tousled, no matter how she tried to control it. She had long since given up and allowed it liberty. It curled thickly around her shoulders, parted off centre, framing her face, with clumps of tendrils curling above her eyebrows. She had a slightly fierce Nordic look, a throwback to the Viking forebears of her Danish mother. Hers was the face of someone you wanted to know, someone who would amuse, intrigue, provoke, rarely complain, never bore. Someone who would be ferociously loyal to those few who gained the intimacy that the furrowed brow seemed designed to repel. She was very much her own woman, with an air of quiet competence about her, as if she could mend your punctured tyre in four minutes flat, and not worry about dirtying her fingernails. There was something else too that only those who got close saw, an incompleteness, a searching, eyes flickering towards the horizon.

She loved this walk home. She could have taken a different tube to Notting Hill, which was closer to her flat, but she had planned a detour via her favourite flower shop, and this longer walk served as a demarcation zone, separating work from home with every extra yard. The route held the familiarity of years, each landmark a comfort: the Afro-Caribbean hairdressers, Have It Off; the video stores; the soaring overpass of the Westway, rumbling with rush-hour traffic; the off-licences better secured than banks; the budget supermarkets; the men with glorious dreadlocks – *God*, that one was gorgeous, he caught her eye and gave her a wink. Where was he in the discos of her teens? Then there were the teenage girls in fashion's thrall, teetering perilously in platforms; the old and the poor, fighting the cold; and the well-wrapped, weary yuppies, intrepidly heading home.

She looked into the window of a streetside flat and caught the eye of an old man, sitting patiently staring out with a look of gentle sadness on his face. She smiled at him. He nodded, and light came into his eyes. There was an unexpected gentleness to her. People often caught her eye, people who didn't want to be living the lives they were, or perhaps were just enduring a bad day in a good life. She had an empathy for the underdog.

She passed a tandoori takeaway, longed to go in, get a rogan josh to enjoy alone with a thriller in her bed. She stopped instead at the Flowered Corner, waiting happily in a long queue, her nose delighting, her eyes gorging on bright orange tiger lilies, brilliant violets, luscious roses, bird of paradise flowers with tangerine beaks. God knows where they came from at this time of year, or what they cost. She went for the birds of paradise which she carried out like a trophy onto the streets. Her present to herself.

She passed the council block on the junction of Ladbroke Grove and Westbourne Park Road where her best friend, Joyce, lived with her husband and three children. She toyed with the idea of going up, giving the flowers to Joyce, playing with her children for hours, sinking blissfully into family life, making herself horribly late for her own evening.

Play fair, Hel, she said to herself, walking on along Ladbroke Grove, up the steep hill, into the gentrified parts of Notting Hill, where the cars and the people were younger and the houses whiter. She skipped home to Dawson Place.

Home was the ground floor of a large, white, stucco-fronted house. Rose bushes flanked the door. A big old oak threw dark shadows over the white steps. The gleaming facade always seemed to welcome her, to offer refuge. The lights of the basement flat blazed and she saw the stooping figure of her eighty-eight-year-old neighbour, Mrs Lucas, standing in the window waving to her. She grinned and waved back. She walked down the steps to the basement flat. Mrs Lucas opened the door with a gap-toothed smile.

''Lo, luv. 'Ow are you?'

'Yeah, I'm well, Mrs Lucas. How're you?'

The old woman gave a thumbs up. 'Not too bad. Chest's playing me up a bit. Can't wait for summer.'

'You 'n' me both.' Helen put her shopping bags on the table.

'Got you some steak. I know it's your favourite. Aberdeen Angus. BSE-free herds, so you won't turn into a mad cow.'

'Oh, get away with you,' said Mrs Lucas, hand on hip. 'Mouth on you!' She peered inside the bag and pulled out the joint. 'You have too. You shouldn't. Costs a fortune that beef.' She started fumbling for her purse. Helen caught the old woman's hands gently in hers.

'Come on, no need for that. I drink my way through enough of your gin. It's already marinated, bits of garlic stuck into it. Just bung it in the oven, three hundred and seventy-five, one hour.'

'Stay and have a bite?'

'I'd love to, but I'm going to a dinner party.'

'Anyone nice?'

'Not really. I'd much rather stay here.'

'Why you going then?'

'Who knows, maybe I'll meet someone gorgeous.'

'If he's lucky.'

Helen bid Mrs Lucas good night, and headed up to her flat. She let herself in to a noisy welcome from her Persian cat, Munza.

'Hi, babe, how are you?' She scooped him up in her arms, stroking his deliciously soft fur.

'Hungry?' She put him down, opened a tin of Kitekat, poured a saucer of single cream, leaned her hip against the kitchen cupboards and watched him eat. Satisfied on his behalf, she arranged the birds of paradise in a tall glass vase, contemplated changing out of her City clothes, decided she couldn't be bothered. She chose a pair of four-inch ankle-strapped stilettos, put them in a plastic bag and headed out to meet her old lover.

She walked slowly down Notting Hill Gate, browsing in the shop windows, continued down Holland Park Avenue, crossed over to Campden Hill Square. She climbed the steep hill, with the square on her left, fenced in by ornate, black railings. The trees cast dark shadows on the pavement. Lights glowed softly in the expensive houses. Shiny cars gleamed dully in the street, the red eyes of alarm systems blinking at her as she passed. The smell of building work and dust tickled her nose as well-maintained houses were subjected to yet another refurbishment by owners tired of last year's interior design.

She aimed for the tall skinny houses that sat upon the brow of the hill. Many of these were adorned with blue plaques, denoting the famous authors or playwrights who used to live in them. Here the square was quiet, the roar of the traffic on Holland Park Avenue diffused by the trees. The lonely did not sit at their windows gazing out here. There was nothing to see, save the darkness or the gleam of a BMW. It was another world, separated by a gulf of millions of pounds.

CHAPTER 2

Helen's old lover, Roddy Clark, moved in all the right circles. He had been for most of his life a child of promise, then a deliverer. His had been a precocious talent; at twenty-eight, following his success in uncovering a major City fraud, he had been appointed head investigative reporter of a major national newspaper, the *World*, a position which he still held three years on. His title sounded good, but the freedom and scope of his job could be a boon or a curse. Uncovering scandals was a patchy business; they never seemed to come in a steady flow and you could spend months chasing fantasies. Roddy had enjoyed one and a half fruitful years, followed by one and a half barren ones. The vagaries of his business contributed to his mercurial personality, and to his moodiness.

He wasn't conventionally attractive, but force of personality made him so. When Roddy was up, he shone. He had thick hair the colour of mahogany, combed back over his forehead, cut crisply short above his ears, angled down, stopping in a razor line above his collar. His eyes were dark, narrowed, set in an almost permanent attitude of scrutiny. His customary pose was head tilted slightly to one side, a half-smile playing on his thin lips. A slight body, clothed fashionably, but beyond that his physical side seemed almost an afterthought. The focus of his being was his mind, alive with intelligence. He had a biting wit, amusing to watch, discomfiting to receive.

The house Roddy lived in was north-facing. Skinny to the point of superciliousness, it peered down the hill over its aquiline features. Six floors including the basement, where Roddy had lived since his uncle died five years ago and bequeathed it to him. It was a good address, but the flat wasn't quite what Roddy would have liked. Basement for a start. On a bad day, it made him feel like a troglodyte, but it allowed him to devote a large part of his salary to a lifestyle that would otherwise have been beyond his means: good food, fashionable clothes, exotic travel, expensive art. A lifestyle that his parents and theirs would have thought shabby, until losses in the Lloyds insurance market and inherited complacency eroded the family money. Roddy had explained many times that this was not quite how he should have been living, until Helen almost felt that she was in some way to blame. Her and her six-figure City salary, as if the more she earned the less he did. Roddy squandered money, she seduced it. Part of Roddy was jealous, another part infinitely proud of her.

He loved her, he said. Wanted to marry her. She enjoyed him, his intelligence, his wit, the sense of edge. He gave her an insight into the arena of news and newspapers, a world she despised and was fascinated by in equal measure. But she didn't want to marry him. Or anyone else for that matter. One day, if the right man came along, but not yet. Four months ago she had left Roddy. There had been no dramatic catalyst, she had merely woken one morning and seen no point in it any more. She was no longer moved by his physical embrace. His ability to transport her had lasted scarcely a year. For the last six months, she had stayed with him merely through habit. There was comfort in that, it helped define the boundaries of a life that had never been rooted, but, after a while, Helen's natural restlessness eroded that solace. Helen had told him quietly and calmly that it was over. Roddy had stared at the veiled sadness in her eyes, a sorrow that enraged him, for he had always known it had nothing to do with him. He had brooded for two months, then regrouped as a friend. Helen was happy to accept him as such. She was still fond of him, and now she could enjoy the habit of seeing him without the claustrophobia of commitment. Roddy would still suggest occasionally that they get married, but he seemed to Helen to be giving up hope graciously. That surprised her. Roddy was notorious. What he wanted, through a mixture of intellect and cunning he usually got. When he failed, he did not like to be reminded of his failure, but he still seemed to crave Helen's presence.

She took out her keys. Roddy insisted she keep a set in case he locked himself out, something which he arranged to do occasionally. She buzzed to warn him she was entering, and let herself in. He was in the drawing room, talking to someone on the telephone. He sat on the arm of a chair, leaning forward, a lock of dark hair falling into one eye.

'Hang on. I said hang on!' He jumped to his feet, strode across the room, grabbed Helen around the waist and kissed her cheek.

'Hi, gorgeous.' He eyed her outfit, down to her trainers. 'You're looking short.' He grinned, ducked out of her way, and returned to the phone.

'Gotta go. Hel on wheels is here.'

Helen pulled a face.

'Heavenly Hel, then?'

They had met nearly two years ago at a dinner given by her boss, Hugh Wallace. Roddy's opening line had been some kind of humorous insult. She had looked beneath the worldweariness and answered with kind words. He had been floored. Each was a novelty to the other; he was a journalist of all things, one of the species which had destroyed her father's name. He was well born, well schooled, a member of the establishment, would have thought himself refined. She was *sauvage*, under-educated, born of notorious blood, but she was compassionate, with an odd, accepting view of the world as if pain and tragedy were not to be fought, but to be wept with and then smiled goodbye. Happiness too. She made Roddy think of the Kipling poem, 'If'. He had said so that first night he met her. She laughed and told him she grew up on Kipling. Her father read 'If' to her every night for years. It was her staple to which he would add Dylan Thomas, Oscar Wilde, Enid Blyton, the Welsh legends of the Mabinogion.

Roddy thought she would have made the perfect Kipling heroine, that 'If' should have been dedicated to a daughter, not a son. She seemed to treat both triumph and disaster the same – with a wry smile, a shake of her head, and a 'let's see what comes next' expression in her sardonic eyes. She was able to mix with his titled friends and with the dustman with equal ease. She gave up eight years at sea, working as a ship's cook, and won herself a job in the City, where every working day she made a heap of all her winnings and risked them on a game of pitch and toss. She gambled her money and that of her employer with equal sang-froid. She wouldn't have cared if she'd lost her slim savings, so they grew and she made enough to buy a half-million-pound flat in Dawson Place while he had to make do with the legacies of other people's talent. He always felt that she was the kind of woman who slept with a packed suitcase at the foot of the bed, so that she could disappear one morning without a backward glance. The prospect of loss was to him exhilarating. Since she had actually left him, part of him would never forgive her.

He was obsessed by sculptures. He had a collection. They filled his flat and lurked in his garden. Helen loved their smooth marble. It seemed to her that with a kiss and an embrace they would stir and come to life. She opened the french windows, walked out into the garden and stroked the naked figure of a man.

'Busy day?' asked Roddy, coming up behind her, watching her hands moving over the marble.

'Average.'

'How much d'you make?'

'Enough. You?'

'Don't change the subject. You have a strange look, like a lioness who's made a kill, debating whether to eat it now or save it for a rainy day.'

Helen laughed. She went inside, sat on the sofa and took off her trainers.

'There was a bit of bother on the tube.'

'What kind of bother?'

She slipped on her high heels. Roddy's eyes lingered over the curve of her calves as she crossed her legs and leaned back on the sofa.

'There was this jerk, causing a bit of aggro. I got him in sankyo and –'

'What in heaven's name is *sankyo*? Explain, please.'

'It's a hold used by the army snatch squads in Northern Ireland. They scan a hostile crowd, identify the ringleaders, then run into the middle of the crowd, get the ringleader in this armlock, and run him out. The pain is *excruciating*. Get someone in sankyo, they'll follow you anywhere.'

14

'Don't need aikido for that. Hey, listen, can I write it up? City diary. It'd be *perfect*.'

'Do that and you're dead, Roddy. You know how I feel about the press.'

How could he forget? She'd told him not long after they started going out. He remembered her cool dispassionate tone as she recounted what the press had done when her father disappeared. He knew that behind her calm lay simmering rage.

'They steal your anonymity, your freedom, they hijack your soul. That happened to my father, and because he wasn't around my mother and I got crucified. Can you imagine how it felt? Almost all of my mother's friends turned their back on her, people pointed and whispered behind their hands every time she left the house. At school all the kids taunted me, until I learned to fight. There were cameras outside for what felt like years although it was probably only months. We had to live in darkness with the curtains drawn day and night. It was like being in prison, and all the time on the news and in the papers, they were saying these things about my father and his face was everywhere, but not where it should have been. At home with us. It infected my whole childhood.'

He could see the speech behind her veiled eyes.

'It's a great story, Hel.' He cursed his sense of loyalty to this girl. She was a walking story. He'd long dreamed of doing a piece on her, and, God, he could really do with a break. *Jencks rises from the ashes of her father's reputation*, a golden little phoenix if ever there was one.

'Yeah, it always is. Print this and forget me.'

'I might occasionally want to kill you, Hel, but forget you? Never.'

'That's comforting.' She glanced at her watch. 'What time are we supposed to make the pilgrimage to Hampstead?'

'Roz said to be there around nine.'

'What kind of sadist gives a dinner party on a Tuesday night?'

'Don't go then.'

'Know thine enemy.'

'C'mon, Hel, you'd eat Roz for breakfast.'

'She'll have called in reinforcements, don't you worry. A committee of lentil eaters.'

15

'You like lentils.'

'Yeah, but I wouldn't dream of serving them at a dinner party.'

'Neither will Roz.'

'Good job. There'll be enough hot air as it is.'

CHAPTER 3

Roz and Justin's dinner party had started late, as Helen knew it would. They finally ate one of Roz's vegetarian concoctions at ten thirty, just as the assembled journalists and architects and Roz, the trust fund baby slumming it as a social worker, were warming to the theme of obscene City salaries. Everyone present at the dinner had one of those jobs that enabled you to get up as late as nine thirty, save Helen and the guest specially invited to 'keep her company', as Roz put it. As if she had no hope of kinship with the others. Roz inadvertently speaking the truth, as she sought to patronise. Helen's 'company' was Reece Douglas, a wry, thirty-two-year-old far-eastern-derivatives trader at Grindlays Bank. Sitting next to her, he'd whispered, 'Indulge them, it's harmless and if knocking us makes them feel a little better then I guess we've fulfilled some social function.'

Helen grinned at him and glanced mischievously at the others.

'*I'm* not a social worker. I can't promise to behave.'

Each member of Roz's coterie spoke out of a familiar mixture of ignorance and envy, attempting unsuccessfully to hide it under the guise of 'conscience'. Helen considered tackling the architects' contributions to the public migraine or the rent-a-view concerns of the journalists, but desisted from some lingering concept of good manners.

'I mean, the thing is, what do they actually do?' asked Roz, as if neither Helen nor Reece was present. 'They just stroll in, shout down the phones and hang around for their million-pound bonuses. I mean, c'mon, it's not exactly rocket science, is it, or saving the world? It's like anyone who could stand to do that for a living'd make out like a bandit. How much d'you earn, Helen?'

'A million's just for failures, Roz; *I mean* the really stupid. If you're just adequately thick you can expect at least two. Pass the wine, would you?'

'And that's the other thing, all this getting pissed at lunchtime. Beats me how you don't lose more money than you do.'

Helen took a sip of wine and put her glass down silently.

'I'm confused, Roz. I thought we made it.'

'Made what?'

'Money, Roz. *Dinero*, moolah, you know, the stuff your trust fund's gobbing with. You know it must be great, doesn't matter one little bit if you're pissed or sober, the old trust fund keeps churning out dosh. You could even be thick, thicker than the most stupid trader that ever existed – and, let's face it, they're pretty thick, aren't they? – and you'd still make money. Now that's really something, that's really impressive.'

She winked at Reece, drank another glass of mercifully good red wine, and sat back to listen to the diatribe that oozed up again. At eleven forty-five, she got to her feet.

'Excuse me, will you, Roz, Justin? I have to go. Got to get up early and start earning my grossly inflated salary.'

Reece grinned delightedly. He got to his feet.

'Ditto. Will you excuse me, Roz?'

Roz nodded, pursed-lipped. Justin looked on, trying to stifle a smile.

Roddy stood up, said his goodbyes. The three of them flagged down a taxi. Roddy slipped quickly into the back seat, separating Helen and Reece. Helen was sleepy, the men uncommunicative. They drove through the streets in silence. Helen got out first at Dawson Place. Reece slipped her his card. She pocketed it wordlessly, a simple act, she thought at the time, without consequence.

CHAPTER 4

The alarm rang at ten to six.

'Shit!' Helen reached out a naked arm, banged about on her night table until she located and silenced the clock. She considered hurling it through the open window, out into the street. Would it give a last, pathetic ring as it smashed against the pavement? She indulged her fantasy for a moment before putting the clock back in its place. She pushed herself out of bed and wandered over to the open window. The breeze chilled her naked skin but she stood there for a while, breathing deeply. She had a thing about oxygen, had to have the windows wide open, even in winter.

She headed for the bathroom, carefully avoiding the mirror. If she was looking half as rough as she felt, it was a sight best skipped. She took a quick, hot shower, followed by a blast of cold. She stood under it long enough for the shock to ease and the sensation to become pleasurable before jumping out and dressing in what was almost her uniform of beige – today a sharply cut wool suit with a long zip-up jacket. She pondered the rows of scent bottles in the bathroom, before choosing Fracas. She sprayed her throat and wrists, her skin tingling as the alcohol evaporated. The smell of tuberose and gardenia seeped up through the steam left from the shower.

On her way out, she couldn't resist a quick peek in the mirror, observing with amusement the elegant, beige camouflage, the career woman in charge of her destiny. The well-cut clothes could not mask the weight she had put on over the past year. She was still fit, but not as lean as she would have liked. She drank more vodka than she used to. Her eyes were slightly bloodshot, as they were so often now, and wrinkles were sprouting around her eyes.

Late nights, alcohol, early mornings and sharp trading did not mix. Her job and her life did not match any more.

She'd forgotten to mend the puncture in her tyre, so it was the tube again. It took almost an hour to get to work, after a half-hour delay at Notting Hill Gate. A passenger on the line she heard. Normally they stuck to the Northern line, as if living in the reaches of Hampstead and beyond were particularly intolerable. A suicide at six thirty in the morning? Why get up and dress up to die? Why not just slink off in sleep with dumbing, numbing tablets in the night, which was always the worst time anyway? She laughed at the morbidity of her thoughts, quickly shook out the *Financial Times*, lost herself in the comforting columns of figures.

She left the tube at Liverpool Street and headed for Birley's. Even at ten past seven, a long queue of hungry traders stood, bleary-eyed, waiting to buy their infusions of caffeine. The smell of bacon sandwiches filled the air. On a good day Helen loved this, but on hungover mornings it was all she could do to wait for her coffee without turning and fleeing for fresh air. She tried to block the smell from her mind, pretending she was on the deck of a boat at sea. She bought a double espresso and two rounds of honeyed toast for herself, a large cappuccino and another double portion of toast for Hugh Wallace, her ever-hungry boss.

Her little paper carrier bags swinging at her hip, she walked out into the chill, wind-blown streets of the City. She cut round into Broadgate Circle, a huge development built in the eighties, where Goldsteins, her employer of the last four years, had their offices. Some of the top merchant banks in the world had their offices here including Grindlays, where Reece Douglas worked. She thought of him with a smile.

The Circle was already busy, peopled by salesmen and traders scurrying from the cold, their faces purposeful and grim.

Thrill and dread, every morning. Part of her would always feel trapped here amid the skyscrapers and ruthlessness, the relentless ritual of work, broken only by the odd exhausting holiday, disruptively liberating, and by the infrequent welcome illnesses that allowed for one extra day, wallowing in bed with a hot toddy and a sailing thriller by Bernard Cornwell. But she loved the adrenaline that came with speculating. She loved to scan a cold eye over information, to weigh and distil, then abandon herself to intuition, a glorious letting go of logic, like being seduced by a stranger. Then the wait. Followed by profit or loss, victory or defeat. That thrill kept her here, even though its power was waning, and the claustrophobia growing.

She was preparing for the day when she would simply walk out, never to return. She knew the City was only ever displacement activity at best. During her eight years at sea, she had searched sporadically for her father. At the end of that time, she couldn't face going on with her search, couldn't face the endless disappointment, and, as more of her life was lived in thrall to an absent ghost, part of her feared finding him. What if he wasn't what she thought? What if he were guilty of fraud? What if he never wanted to see her? So, aged twenty-six, she had given up her search. Now, four years later, the old yearning was still as strong as ever. The City had done nothing to ground her, to answer all the old questions. Now that she had tried the rooted life and it had failed her, she was left more restless than ever.

She walked past one of the many sculptures that decorated the Circle. It was a large horse, possibly winged, with bulging, terrified eyes, that looked as if it was being strangled by a serpent.

She couldn't go into Goldsteins yet. She needed just five more minutes of air, of quiet. She walked slowly around the Circle, gazing up at the rose-tinted towers that surrounded her. Granite, metal and glass, pane upon pane rising up to form giant atria suffused with grey City light. Part of the huge expanse of windows was protected by an external lattice that looked like a giant Venetian blind. Several buildings had narrow balconies from which tumbled a mass of ivy. The plants were no doubt intended to soften the harsh outlines, but they seemed to Helen to lend an air of wildness to the place. They looked like a jungle in waiting, a real, external jungle that could smother the financial one within if left unchallenged. Their roots would crack the concrete, wind in, strangle the computer cables. Perhaps in centuries to come, the ivy-clad mounds would be unearthed by archaeologists from another planet who would hail the discovery of these temples of Mammon. So much power was concentrated here. So much of the global money supply was controlled, invested and manipulated from within these rose-coloured towers. It was as much of an empire as any, and as vulnerable.

Reluctantly, Helen headed into the Goldsteins foyer at twenty past seven. She was hit by a rush of warm, synthetic-tasting air. She said a hungover 'good morning' to the security guards, who greeted her enthusiastically and smiled, sympathising with her bloodshot eyes. She hurried towards the closing doors of one of a bank of lifts.

Skulking in the corner, one hand in his pocket, the other holding onto breakfast in a bag, was Hugh Wallace. With surprising agility, he leapt forward and pushed the button to open the doors.

'Thanks,' said Helen, easing in.

Wallace looked as bad as Helen felt. His suit appeared to have been slept in, his eyes were bloodshot, squinting out at her from under his baseball hat. Coils of hair snaked out from the hat and lay greasily on his shirt collar. His jacket was open to reveal a paunch, surprisingly small considering his diet of take-out food. On his feet, he wore black and white Reeboks. He was breathing heavily. Helen knew he suffered from claustrophobia, was terrified of lifts, but he was asthmatic and chronically unfit, and climbing the seven flights of stairs to the trading floor was not an option. Every day, he submitted to the torture of the lift. Only when it disgorged him and Helen onto the seventh-floor foyer did he look up from the ground. He gave Helen a sideways glance from his apparently gentle brown eyes, and smiled the sweetest smile. His lips were full and delicately red against the pallor of his skin. He looked like a cross between little boy lost and a degenerate Cupid. This time round, his karma seemed to be making money. He was Goldsteins' head derivatives structurer, a job he described to laymen as a bit like that of a bookie once removed. He took bets on people taking bets. He was a mathematical genius, fortified by a PhD in chaos theory from Oxford and an obsessive interest in derivatives.

He and Helen stood still while he brought his breathing back under control.

'Heavy night?' asked Helen. Wallace had recently taken to playing blackjack in the casinos. Borderline addicted, he spent many nights doing what he did all day, but in more glamorous surroundings. The week before he'd taken Helen and Roddy to Les Ambassadeurs in Mayfair. Helen and he had won, while Roddy watched disapprovingly, struck silent by the unfairness of those who simply didn't need it making money as if by accident.

'I was up till three, surfing,' said Wallace, opening the lid on his styrofoam coffee cup, taking a sip, scalding his delicate lips.

'Shit.' He wiped his mouth on his sleeve. 'I was hooked up to these two lesbians, wanted a *three*some. I spent hours trying to convince them that I was a gorgeous, five-foot-ten blonde called Trish.'

Helen nearly choked with laughter as she tried to morph Wallace's five-foot-five, eleven-stone flour dough body into a sleekly muscled goddess.

'And?'

'I was doing really well until they asked me what I did.'

'Oh God, what d'you tell them?'

'Fashion buyer.'

Helen crumpled up with laughter. Most people found it hard to believe Wallace's academic credentials. They often failed to see the humour in his deadpan self-effacement, which they saw as blundering.

'How about you?' asked Wallace. 'Out on the town with Roderick?'

'Dinner with his friends.'

'Not yours, eh?'

'I wouldn't cross the street for them.'

'Nasty girl.'

'Mild really. Here, have some cappuccino and toast.'

'I remembered my own.'

'Have it anyway. Reinforcements.'

'You spoil me, Hel.' He took it, his eyes moved from hers. He seemed sad. Something strange had come over him in the last few months. He had started to behave almost like an adulterous lover, with his occasionally absent eyes.

They flashed their electronic cards, the security doors clicked open, and they walked through onto the trading floor: twenty thousand square feet of white-hot technology and four hundred prima donnas, ninety-five per cent of whom were male – one of the most profitable trading floors in the City of London. Last year's net profits were two hundred and fifty million pounds. It was warming up; Helen could almost hear the clamour that would start soon, almost feel the angry yearning for money, the ambition, cruelty and competition where it was never a fair fight in the open, but always in a plastic conference room, or in the acrid calm of the urinal. She loved it, as if it were the brothel owner who had taken her in off the streets.

They picked their way through the lattice work of desks, heading for the derivatives desk, otherwise known as the rocket scientists' launch pad, or more colloquially, 'if it moves, price it'.

Derivatives were financial contracts just like bonds or shares, but were a stage more complex. They had no intrinsic value, but derived it from something else. That could be anything from soy beans to a share index like the FT100. The most straightforward derivatives contracts were futures. Originally, these were developed to protect farmers against fluctuations in the value of their crops. A farmer could protect himself by agreeing, say in December, the price at which he would sell his harvest the following October. If people asked Helen what she did, this is what she generally told them. Wallace on the other hand, impassioned by his market, could give a historical treatise. He seemed to read almost everything that was printed on derivatives. In his spare time, he was writing a book on the development of the market. The day before he had announced to Helen and Paul Keith, who'd just started on the desk, that there had been a futures market in rice, in Dojima, near Osaka, in the late seventeenth century.

Modern futures markets developed in the 1850s with the opening of the Chicago Board of Trade, but it was only in the mid-1980s that financial futures markets dealing with shares and bonds really took off. Wallace had been there as it happened. He'd grown up with a market that had exploded and now, counting just those products traded on organised exchanges, was worth over six hundred and fifty trillion dollars a year. Wallace loved to quote the example of seventeenth-century derivatives as if age seemed to make the market more familiar, friendlier. To Helen, there was nothing familiar or friendly about the derivatives market. It could rip your guts out overnight, as it had done to Barings, when a lone trader built up a derivatives loss of seven hundred and forty million pounds, breaking the bank. Derivatives were the biggest, most potentially lucrative and destructive market in the world. Wallace was in love with the market. Helen kept it at a distance, respected it as a fearsome adversary.

One hundred people worked on the derivatives desk, with fifty support staff. There were one hundred and forty men, and ten women. All but four of the women were in a support capacity, working in the back office, or as secretaries. Ages ranged from eighteen to thirty-seven, salaries and packages from twenty-two thousand pounds a year to one million four hundred thousand. Qualifications spanned zero to maths PhDs. The group traded interest rate-, currency-, equity- and commodity-based derivatives. They sat, about two feet apart, at narrow rows of desks, each row backing onto another row like a reverse image, cramped traders, desks stacked high with computer screens, panels of direct telephone lines, the smell of sweat and tension, a sea of noise.

Helen sat at a small T-shaped configuration at the end of a long trading desk holding about twenty traders each side. On her left sat Andy Rankin, a specialist in the far-eastern equity markets, and on her right a new console had been added to house a trainee who had just joined the team, Paul Keith. Behind was Wallace's office. Inadvertently, four years ago when Helen joined the trading floor, she'd been placed as near to her boss as it was possible to get. At first she had detested the arrangement, feeling under observation. If she came in late, left early, or skulked around on a bad day, Wallace would see. As time passed, she realised Wallace saw very little, recorded even less, so obsessed was he with dreaming up new and better derivatives. He could happily spend twelve hours locked in his office, blinds drawn, playing with his intricate and alarmingly complex computer models. When he did emerge, he homed in on Helen and Rankin, paying little attention to the rest of the huge derivatives operation. The three of them had become an almost self-contained unit, set apart from the rest of the traders.

Wallace paused now outside his office and turned to Helen with a crinkle-eyed smile. 'It is tonight, isn't it? Dinner at your place?'

'Absolutely. Still on?'

'You joking? I suppose Roddy'll be there too?'

'Better had be, don't you think?'

Every week Roddy and Wallace came round for dinner. It was a routine, broken only by holidays and Roddy's two-month hermitage after Helen ceased to be his lover.

'Would Roddy be jealous if we had dinner alone?'

'Is that a proposition?'

Wallace laughed awkwardly. He wouldn't have known where to begin with Helen Jencks.

Paul Keith looked up nervously at Helen and Wallace. He'd only joined the desk a week ago. Twenty-two, a maths graduate from Edinburgh University, he was spending two months on each of six main areas of the trading floor – a new initiative ordered by Zaha Zamaroh, queen of the floor. 'Cross-fertilisation,' she called it. Keith did not look happy. His arrival had upset the threesome. Helen had welcomed him, Rankin tolerated him, while Wallace had resisted his presence furiously, called him one of Zamaroh's spies, and was uncharacteristically poisonous to him. When Helen chided him, he looked shifty, but persisted in his persecution of the new boy. The bullied bullying. Wallace would have been an obvious target at school. Thirty years on, he was getting his revenge.

'Morning, Paul,' said Helen with a broad smile. 'How are you?'

Miserable, said his eyes. 'Morning, Hel.'

'Hel now, is it?' asked Wallace. 'Only her friends call her Hel, didn't you know?'

'Ignore him,' said Helen. 'He's pining for a couple of electronic dykes.' She gave him a look of reproach. He grinned and shuffled off into his office.

There was a thud in the neighbouring chair. Helen turned to see Andy Rankin trying to shrink down and look inconspicuous.

'Andy, what *have* you done to your hair?'

Andy Rankin's previously thick brown collar-length hair had been attacked by one of the most vicious haircuts Helen had ever seen.

She stretched out her hand towards his head. 'Here. Let me feel it.' The bristles must have been about half an inch long, surprisingly soft. Rankin started blushing furiously.

'Ooh, it's nice and soft. Looks like a nail brush.'

'Thanks a bunch.'

'C'mon, Andy. You didn't do it for beauty. Must have lost a bet.'

He gave a faint, disgusted nod. Helen could imagine the scene all too easily. Andy Rankin let loose for one blissful night to go drinking with his old pals from Epping Forest, left behind when he married a convent-school girl, who styled herself Knightsbridge and whose aspirations did not run to a skinhead for a husband.

'What does Karen say?'

He gave her a hunted look. Rankin, five foot eight and thirteen stone, with bulbous nose and heavy bones, would have looked thuggish enough at the best of times. His redemption was a pair of doe-like brown eyes, warm, kind, easily wounded. Like now.

'Damn it,' said Helen. 'Forgot my cigs.' She gave him a disarming smile. 'Got a spare?'

Rankin smiled back, clearly relieved to be off a subject that would dog him for days on the trading floor.

Don't be self-conscious about it, Helen wanted to say. Don't give the buggers an inch, but any advice would have made explicit his need and awkwardness. He tossed her a packet of unfiltered Camels.

'That should kill off all sugar and spice.'

'I don't have any. I'm not nice, Andy. You should know that by now.'

'Keep saying that often enough and someone'll start believing it.'

She was nice, whatever she said. Beyond those sardonic eyes that seemed to see, smile at and understand human frailty so well, there was extravagant generosity and kindness. To anyone other than her friends, it was well hidden. The focus on the trading floor was money, not soul.

CHAPTER 5

Wallace reappeared at the desk and slumped down in a spare seat.

'All right, Jencks, if you haven't managed to destroy all your grey cells drinking with unsavoury characters, what'll it be this week?' He gave Helen a look half teasing, half admiring. They'd had a bond right from the first. He'd expected to resent the woman foisted upon him when she first arrived on his patch four years ago. No qualifications, no background, just a hardy, streetwise look, an incredible curiosity to learn, and the raw intellect to process what she hoovered up. Her abilities overcame his reservations. What forged the bond was his immediate sense that this was another dysfunctional soul. He could see the shards of pain piercing her skin, could sense the yearning loneliness in her, and he knew that she could see in him his dislocation, his inability to form relationships with anything other than a computer. Until she came along, offering friendship.

Only one thing marred it. He always had the sense that it was just a matter of time until he imploded, until he was destroyed in some way by his own infirmities, while Helen, for all her weaknesses, had about her the grit of the survivor. It was as if he knew that somehow, in the game of life, she would beat him, betray this friendship of what should have been equals. Helen was smiling back at him, seemingly oblivious of the slow corrosion in his mind.

'I don't like the look of things in the Gulf,' she said enthusiastically. 'I think the markets are bored with Iraq, think it's just gonna be a side show, but I reckon they'll need something to scare themselves with soon. When that happens, volatility'll increase, oil'll rise, gold'll fall. I'll give them a few months to brew it up. I wanna buy three-month calls on Brent crude, buy three-month puts on gold.'

She turned to Keith. 'Put and call options give the purchaser – me in this case – the *right*, but not the *obligation*, to sell and buy an index or a commodity at a set level, called the strike price, over a given period of time. If I get the markets right, in three months I'll be able to buy oil at a price below the prevailing market price, on sell immediately and make a profit, or just sell the call option in the options market. It'll rise with the price of oil, and I'll make a tidy profit.'

'That'll be nice,' interrupted Rankin. Helen gave him an indulgent look. She'd made over three million dollars so far this year. Rankin was two million down.

She turned back to Keith. 'If I guess gold right, I'll be able to put, or sell, my gold at my pre-set price which would be above the prevailing market price. I can do this if I choose, and buy the requisite quantity of gold to deliver, and pocket the difference. Or, more simply, I'll just sell my put, which will have risen in value with the fall in the gold price, and take the profit on that.'

Wallace started to drum his fingers. 'If you've finished, Professor Jencks . . .'

'I haven't, so back off. Now, if I guessed wrong and the markets moved against me, I wouldn't want to exercise my call and put. For example, say the price of oil falls, I wouldn't want to exercise my option and buy it at the strike price when I can buy it more cheaply in the cash market today. Make sense?'

Keith pulled a tortured face. 'Yeah. Er, think so.'

'Don't worry. It'll come in time. So anyway, that's the whole joy of options. Flexibility. I can exercise if I choose, but I'm under no obligation to do so. Now, the cost to me of buying options would be the initial purchase price of the call and of the put. We call it the "premium". Premium is determined by, among other things, the volatility of the underlying commodity or index. There's a whole load of incredibly sophisticated valuation models, all derived from something called the Black Scholes option pricing model, developed by three serious rocket scientists in the early seventies. Hugh'll explain it to you, won't you?'

'Not bloody likely.' Wallace ran his fingers underneath his collar and gave it a vicious yank.

'By the way, it's shepherd's pie tonight.'

'If I have time,' muttered Wallace.

'Good.' Helen turned back to Keith. 'The price normally works out at only a small fraction of the value of the ultimate underlying trade. I can buy the right to buy one hundred million dollars of oil in three months' time for an initial outlay of six million.'

'Wow.'

'Yeah. Big wow. It's called gearing. For only a few mill, I can take massive exposure, massive risks.'

'And make a ton,' said Rankin.

'Or blow my premium,' added Helen. 'In this case, I'm long options, but if I'm short, that is if I sell options to counterparties, and have to deliver the underlying, and I read the markets wrong, I lose my shirt. The floor's littered with the corpses of traders who've crashed and burned in the options market.'

'You can hedge your risks, can't you?' asked Keith.

'Of course. Normally you do, but sometimes you want to take a directional bet on an index, and you don't hedge. That's what Nick Leeson did with the Nikkei when he broke Barings.'

Keith looked suitably chastened.

'How much d'you want to trade?' snapped Wallace.

'As much as I can get without moving the price,' answered Helen smoothly. 'We've got plenty of capital, haven't we?'

'Unless the mighty Zamaroh feels like buying up the entire US treasury issue.'

They all smiled. Zaha Zamaroh, head of the trading floor, Iranian princess, with a throne of letters after her name: summa cum laude Harvard, MA Oxford, MBA Wharton. She ruled the floor with all the despotism, passion and bloody charisma of her Mogul forebears. She was the only person on the floor with a brain to match Wallace's. Like most people, he was terrified of her.

'Anything's possible,' said Helen.

'Andy? What're you up to?' asked Wallace.

Every day Helen and Rankin told Wallace what they planned to buy and sell. Recently, Rankin seemed to trade less and less. Helen reckoned he'd lost his nerve after a string of losses earlier in the year. Got burned badly trading Topix futures. Lost two million in three weeks. It was hard to get back after something like that. Got to have balls, got to have faith in your judgement, know when to hang on in there, know when to cut. Rankin didn't seem sure these days. The competition could smell uncertainty like dogs scented fear. They'd take you apart for it. Rankin was thirty-six, getting too old for the violence of trading. There weren't many traders at the sharp end over thirty. Eyes flitting between flickering lines of information on four different screens, one ear on the phone, the other on the cries of colleagues, twelve hours of split-second calculations, judging yourself and being judged on the score at the end of every day. These men and women lived and breathed the market. And outsiders thought they had a chance. She'd always tell people who asked: don't play the markets, stick your money in blue-chip equities and forget about it. It'll grow if you leave it alone, but trying to trade in and out, you'll get hammered by the professionals, and the great queen market herself who'll never forgive your lack of devotion. Leave it to the pros. Not even they got an easy ride. At thirty they looked forty. Many of them seemed to disappear. Where they went to, Helen didn't know. The more socialised of them could rise on up the ladder and become management, watch other people burn out. The rest, if they were lucky, might manage to retire to the country. Helen sometimes wondered what would happen to Wallace. He didn't need to work for the money. He must have made eight million over his fourteen years in the markets. He did it because he was addicted.

Rankin fiddled compulsively with his pen, twisting it between stubby fingers. 'Yeah, I got a coupla things going, talking to a guy,' he mumbled. 'Might do some stuff on the KOSPI.' The KOSPI was the Korean Stock Price Index, a wild market, where many traders had been burned.

'And?'

'Not quite ready.'

Wallace pushed back his chair and got to his feet. 'What do the vultures keep telling you? Write tickets or die. On today's performance you're dead meat.'

'What about you, Hugh, dead man walking?' teased Helen. 'When you gonna invent some juicy new product for us?'

31

Wallace waddled off to his office, hand in the air, middle finger raised.

'That the best they taught you at school?' shouted Helen.

'One of these days you're gonna go too far,' said Rankin.

'Yeah, but when? What's a girl gotta do round here to get fired?'

Rankin gave her a puzzled look. He and Wallace had a private nickname for Helen, 'the hairdresser'. She was revered across the floor for her ruthless ability to cut, or sell out, a position that was going bad. It seemed now she wanted to cut her own job. Rankin felt a flash of panic, mixed with envy. Helen's rootlessness made her free. He was trapped, at work, in marriage, in worse. He averted his eyes from Helen's, and called out to Keith.

'Hey, Paul. Get me a cappuccino and bacon. Here's five quid.'

Keith took the money silently. After six months on the trading floor he was used to being treated as a slave by imperious traders trying to shore up fragile egos.

'Hel, would you like something?'

'No, thanks, Paul.'

Keith wandered off, a disconsolate figure, six foot four, wraith-like. Helen wondered how long he'd survive on the floor.

Helen turned to her screens and tried to spot drama in the columns of figures, an irregularity, a blip, something there that shouldn't be, something that might grow, widen, rip, alarm the faint of wallet, allow her to come in, dollars blazing, buy them out, sit them out, and profit. She was a contrarian, by inclination. She made large and spectacular trades against the market every few months and made, sometimes lost, millions of dollars for Gold-steins. Usually she came out ahead. She had a finely honed sense of intuition. She would watch and wait, sense the markets, look for signs of change, buy in advance, hold, sell when *it*, whatever it was, happened. Sometimes *it* was nothing more than rumour, sometimes it was a Brady plan to bail out the banana republics, sometimes it was a war. But today the figures mocked her in silent superiority. They held true. If there were anomalies, she couldn't see them, if there was a war brewing, she couldn't feel it. Per-haps she wasn't in the mood to look. She was restless, her mind unquiet.

The trading axes she announced to Wallace were pure contingency. Only one thing was taboo on a trading floor: to answer a question with *I don't know*. You always knew, you were always blithely certain of yourself. You always had a view. Hesitation was for losers, equivocation for Oxbridge tutorials. It was buy, or sell. In between was the killing ground of hold. Talking to clients or counterparties, every morning it was, 'What's your *story*?' Everyone spun tales – confuse the opposition, finesse them. But you had to know when a story became a trade, or else you'd end up finessing yourself.

She thought briefly of Roddy and Roz and all the others at dinner last night. They'd still be fast asleep. She recalled Roz's nasal whine.

'Easy money, the City. Just cruise in, cruise out, shout down the telephone and make a few million.' Yeah, Roz, she thought, come and try it, babe. She glanced up at her telephone dashboard to see one of the lights flashing. She pulled on her headset, spoke into the tiny mike suspended before her mouth.

'Yeah, Bernie?'

'What's big and fat and hungry?'

'Bernie Greenspan at 8 A.M.'

'Gonna have to start telling dirty jokes.'

'Think I wouldn't get those?'

'Yeah, right. Scratch that. Doing anything?'

'Not much. You?'

'Sweet FA. Still wanna play Goldfinger this morning?'

'More into massage parlours, Bern.' Traders gave nicknames to just about everything. Massage parlour was code for oil. Helen toyed with the image of parlour patrons being smeared with North Sea Brent.

'What d'you want? Six month?'

'Too long.'

'Three?'

'Maybe. What price three month, put and call?'

'You want a call.'

'Humour me, Bern.'

'Size?'

'Oooh Bernie, big, like always.'

'Yeah, yeah, 'scuse me asking, but what d'you call big this morning?'

'Five thousand contracts.'

'Strike?'

'At the money. Eighteen forty.'

'Call you back.'

Five minutes later he was back on the line.

'1.10, 1.30 call, .97, 1.17 put.'

'I'll buy five thousand calls on three-month crude at 1.30.'

There was a slight gasp. Bernie had been expecting her to go the opposite way and to sell calls.

'Done,' he said sullenly.

'Done,' she responded. 'C'mon, Bern, you angel. I'll buy you a drink.'

'When?'

'Thursday.'

'Promise?'

'It's a deal.'

He began to scream in mock horror at the prospect of another deal with Helen Jencks. Helen took off her headset and laughed.

'Long oil,' she shouted out for Wallace to hear. 'Ninety-two. Three month.' Rankin, three feet away, had heard it all first hand. Wallace waved to show he had heard. Helen wrote out the ticket. Five thousand call option contracts at $1.30, multiplied by the contract size of 1,000 barrels totted up to $6,500,000 in premium which she would have to pay tomorrow. This premium granted her the right to buy, in three months' time, 5,000 contracts of 1,000 barrels each. That amounted to five million barrels of oil, a position worth, at the strike price for Brent crude of $18.40, a total of ninety-two million dollars. On anyone's terms, a lot of oil. She felt the quick thrill of the trade, but, beyond that, dispassion. She had done what she knew to be dangerous, dealt while equivocal about the trade, but she was cruising on luck. She'd had a good run, six weeks. She felt there was a little way still to go.

The desk had gone uncharacteristically quiet. Helen looked up to see Zaha Zamaroh standing to one side of her, peering at Paul Keith as if he were a laboratory specimen. Keith coloured slightly, a doubtful smile flickering on his lips as he stared up at Zamaroh.

Five foot eight and a hundred and sixty pounds of Chanel-swathed goddess, fire-engine-red suit with lips and talons to match. He wouldn't have believed in her if he hadn't seen her with his own eyes. She was like something out of a children's story crossed with an adult magazine: the wicked stepmother meets Jessica Rabbit, with a brain that would blow a mainframe computer.

'Morning, Paul. How're you getting on?'

'Morning. Er, well, thanks. Helen's been helping me.'

'That's a mercy.' She turned to Helen. The two women enjoyed a polite mutual respect, but kept their distance.

'Helen.'

'Zaha.'

'I'm glad to see someone's writing tickets around here,' said Zamaroh, nodding at the blue trading ticket in Helen's hands. 'Profitably, one assumes.' She turned to Rankin.

'Well, look what we have here, a walking lavatory brush. You might hire yourself out, Rankin. You'd make more money than you've made for the desk.' Helen winced. Rankin stared straight ahead, said nothing.

'Couple of pounds an hour would be a contribution,' continued Zamaroh. She came up closer and bent down over Rankin. 'You're two million down, Rankin, and I'm about to stop counting.'

'Makes her feel good,' said Helen, watching Zamaroh walk away. 'Slay a few slaves every morning.'

Paul Keith tried to look invisible. Rankin stared at his screens, a vein throbbing in his forehead.

'She should be put down, that woman. Psychopathic bitch.'

'You might be a bit strange too, Andy, if the ayatollahs had hanged your father,' replied Helen.

Rankin snorted, got up from his desk, and skulked into Wallace's office. The two of them remained locked away for over an hour, trying to salvage Rankin's career, reckoned Helen.

CHAPTER 6

At twelve, Security rang. Helen's best friend, Joyce Fortune, was downstairs. Helen grabbed her coat and bag. Joyce was perfectly turned out as always. She was leaning against a marble pillar, striking a pose and accepting with a nonchalant grin the stream of admiring looks she was attracting from Goldsteins men, young and old. Her perfectly bleached blonde hair was razor-cut in a long bob, topped by a heavy fringe just above dark, arching eyebrows that would have graced a duchess. Her eyes were light blue, unearthly, lit with humour and a suggestion of malice. Her skin was pale, lightly made up with a faint blush on gentle cheek-bones. She'd painted her lips an extravagant red, perfectly outlined with a matching lip pencil so that not a drop of scarlet bled onto the surrounding skin. The effect was a strange mixture of wanton-ness and discipline. She wasn't conventionally beautiful, her lips were too narrow and her aquiline nose, her most striking feature, was too long, but she held herself like a goddess.

She straightened up when she saw Helen.

'Well, if it isn't the beige beauty herself.'

Helen gave Joyce a quick appraisal up and down. She was wearing skin-tight blue jeans, black suede ankle boots and a black fitted leather jacket.

'Got to move with the times, babe. I can see you done up like that at ninety in the retirement home. Could give a whole new meaning to dressed to kill,' retorted Helen.

'Made any money today?' asked Joyce with a malicious grin. She always could tell how Helen had done within thirty seconds of meeting her.

'Barely enough to keep your kids in Reeboks for a week.'

The two women grinned at each other, enjoying a game that had started when they first met, aged twelve, at the local comprehensive school in Holland Park. Joyce had gone there of necessity. Helen had rejected her mother's wish that she attend private school and had insisted on going to the local school where most of her friends went. They both left at sixteen, and although their lives went in different directions, they remained close friends. Joyce went into her uncle's haulage company, graduating from secretary to lorry driver, before marrying, having three children, and supposedly settling down in her ex-council flat on Ladbroke Grove. Whenever money ran short, or the urge to escape the hearth became too strong, she would fit in a week's driving, while her mother stood in to look after the children and Brian, Joyce's husband. Joyce lived a life that seemed to suit her, but to her, Helen's incarnation as a banker, her 'going respectable', seemed to go no deeper than the beige camouflage they always joked about.

'Better get your act together, girl,' said Joyce. 'The twins' birthday's coming up and they're expecting something pretty spectacular from their godmother.'

'Greedy buggers. Tell them they'll get a Mars bar between them if they're lucky.'

Joyce laughed. Helen spoiled her children whenever she had the chance, and, with a combination of charm and intimidation, could turn them into little angels for the duration of her visits.

They headed towards Blomfield Street, and walked down the stairs into Balls Brothers. The restaurant was quiet, but the lunchtime rush would begin in minutes. They greeted Claudio, the manager, who whisked them to a corner table and returned in seconds with two beers. He watched with satisfaction while Helen emptied her bottle in one go. He returned with another bottle and took the women's orders.

'Steak and chips, Claudio. Twice.' Helen turned back to Joyce. 'When d'you get back from the drive?'

'Last night. Was supposed to be this morning, but Brian was pining.'

'Where d'you go?'

'London, Newcastle, Cornwall, London.'

'Big one. How was it?'

'Good. Got chatted up by this gorgeous bloke in a chippie in Newcastle, wouldn't *believe* what he said to me . . .'

Helen gave her a crooked smile. 'Try me.'

Joyce leaned closer to Helen and lowered her voice.

'Said he knew this photographer, they were doing a truckers' calendar together. Wanted me to pose in a red leather bustier with long black boots and a whip, on top of the cab of my lorry. Said I'd make a great dominatrix.'

'He was right.'

Lunch arrived: glorious crisp chips and dripping steaks. Both women ate hungrily.

'How's Dai?' said Joyce, asking after Helen's godfather, the person who probably knew her better than anyone on the planet.

'Fine,' mumbled Helen, mid chew.

'And Munza?'

'He's fine too.'

Joyce didn't mention Roddy. Couldn't stand him. Always tried to pretend he didn't exist.

'Work?' asked Joyce, through a mouthful of chips.

'All right. Wallace's turning into an evil cherub tormenting the new trainee.'

'Bully.'

'Exactly.'

Joyce put down her knife and fork and studied Helen, head on one side. 'What's up, Hel? You're fine on the surface, but there's something going on inside. You're giving off anxsty vibes. I can feel them from here.'

Helen looked up and drew her hair back from her face. 'Oh Joyce. I'm restless, getting more restless every day. All those old feelings I thought I'd left behind four years ago.'

'You wanna leave. Throw it all in.'

'Yep.'

'I don't get it. You work five days a week in a job that you're great at that pays you a damn sight more than anything else I can think of that's legal.'

'You know me. I'm not good at staying still. I want to see what's out there. Beyond the ranges.'

'You wanna look for your father again?'

'I don't know. I never really looked properly for him before. I mean, I never had a plan. Just went wherever the boat took me. Not that I have a plan now. I've just got this feeling there's something out there, just out of reach. I've got to do something, anything, I don't know, just bring it into my orbit, or step into its orbit.'

'Your intuition going again?'

'Yeah, something's coming, Joyce, I can feel it.'

'Good or bad?'

'I don't know. I just know it's big.'

For a brief moment Joyce wanted to urge Helen to change her path, whatever it might be, stay here, where she was safe. But she couldn't put her sudden fears into words.

CHAPTER 7

Helen left Goldsteins at five thirty, pondering what to cook for dinner for Wallace and Roddy. The worst thing about being a professional cook, even worse, cordon bleu, was everybody's expectations. That she hadn't cooked for a living for four years was no excuse. She was qualified, had the rosette to prove it. Fourteen years ago, when she was sixteen and had just left school, her mother thought a six-month cooking course would be a useful accomplishment, better enabling her to make money and, at some appropriate time, find a suitable husband. There was no romanticism to her calculation, just sheer practicality. Although Helen hated to admit it, her mother had been right, although not in the way she foresaw. The rosette had bought her a ticket, as ship's cook, to a ninety-six-foot sail boat called *Escape*, and eight years of cruising paradise. It had thrown James Savage, chief executive of Goldsteins, into her path when he chartered *Escape*. On nothing more than a dare, a gamble, and no little skill, she had won from Savage her chance as a banker. Cook/banker, when it came to dinner, she was a cook, and judged accordingly.

She took the tube, got off at Queensway twenty minutes later and headed for the Whiteleys shopping centre. She walked with a grin into Marks & Spencer. She would play a game of double bluff. No one would expect a cordon bleu cook to serve ready prepared food. She walked round the aisles with a basket slung over her arm, dropping things in with quiet delight: shepherd's pie, ready washed packets of roquette salad, apple crumble, and custard made with real cream. She'd serve her best wines from a selection Dai had given her, splash a bit of brandy in the custard, serve everything up with a garnish on best china, and the boys would be in nursery heaven while under the blissful illusion that she'd been slaving for hours on their behalf. To salve what was left of her conscience, she bought a pound of stewing steak from Dewhurst's and headed home.

She put Billie Holliday singing 'Lady in Satin' on her portable CD player, opened a tin of Kitekat and fed a ravenous Munza. She then emptied the food from the incriminating Marks & Spencer bags, which she hid, put the stewing steak in a saucepan and left it to simmer.

She headed for her bedroom and changed into a tracksuit and trainers. After mending the puncture in her tyre, she warmed up for a run with five minutes of yoga stretches. Then she set out into the falling darkness for Kensington Gardens.

She loved running at night. She loved the power of it, the sensation of skimming over ground, almost silently, screened by darkness. A sole woman was seen by history as prey. Running at night, she felt like the hunter. It must have conjured some ancient memory from deep in her genes. Although she recognised she ought to feel a certain wariness, if not fear, at the prospect of darkness in the park, she never did, nor did she keep to the brightly lit areas. Her aikido gave her confidence, but it was more than that. Years ago, she had learned to love the night, volunteering as often as she could to keep watch, sitting alone above a dark sea, the stars huge and radiant above her. Night had become her friend, not a source of fear. A state where she could expand, where no one could observe her, where she was free.

She ran down towards the lake, empty now of the birds, ducks and geese that had flown away to huddle down for the night. She circled the water and headed off over the grass towards the copper-topped bandstand. The green roof shone in the night light.

The endorphins began to course round her body. She ran off the path and moved into the trees again. She almost felt as if she were running in the country, around Dai's estate in Wiltshire. The sound of the traffic was still audible as a distant rumble, but if she tried hard enough she could almost convince herself that it was the roar of a tumbling river.

She jogged up to her favourite sculpture in the whole of London. Cast in dark, weathered bronze, it was of a horse and rider. The horse was straining against the bit, its gloriously muscled neck reined in, its hind legs stretching forwards in anticipation of flight. The rider, modelled on a classical Greek, had thrown his hand up to his eyes, scanning the far horizon. It was called 'Physical Energy', and it depicted the concept perfectly in the coiled power of the horse and the mastery of its rider. She stopped for a moment before it, then ran down towards the Serpentine. She ran past the sculpture of Peter Pan, wondering what it would be like to be trapped in time, for ever young. Then it was time to turn around, cut back towards the lake. She passed the towering needle sculpture which commemorated a Nile expedition of 1864. It was so acutely elegant in its rose marble, so redolent of foreign lands. For a moment she imagined the hot desert winds washing over her. She felt fiercely then the desire to escape that assailed her so frequently. How could she ever pretend that her wanderlust had left her? Four years in the City had changed nothing, save her ability to travel at the better end of the plane.

She left the park, and the noise and bustle of London reclaimed her as she crossed Bayswater Road. She ducked down the side streets, into St Petersburgh Place. There was a strange anonymity to this part of London, with the rhythms of a dozen languages on the streets and the smells of a score of cuisines. She wished for a moment that she could slip under the cloak of anonymity, step out of her culture, sit down alone in a restaurant she had never been to, and have no one categorise her. To be alien, in an alien place. How wonderful it would be to feel that she had left her baggage in another continent, that she was unencumbered by connections.

She ran on past St Matthew's church: huge, soot-blackened yellow stone; vast, dark windows; and imposing oak doors. She turned into Moscow Road, towards the Greek church with its green copper domes. She could smell the incense as she ran by. As she came to the leafy greenness of Pembridge Square, she slowed to a walk for the last hundred yards round to Dawson Place.

She skipped her stretching routine, in favour of a long hot shower. She washed her hair, fiddled about drying it for five minutes with the hair dryer, before giving up and leaving it to its own devices.

She never spent much time on her appearance. She didn't wear make-up, save lipstick, always tawny natural colours, but she did splash out on those super-expensive wonder creams that were supposed to deal with the wrinkles that had started growing ever since she took on her job in the City. She pondered her array of scent, picked out a bottle of Nahema, and gave herself a generous spray.

She pulled on jeans and a white cotton shirt, sorted out the food in about five minutes, then went through into her bedroom and took out a long leather case from the wardrobe. She laid it on the bed with reverence, opened it gently and withdrew a gleaming bronze-coloured tenor saxophone from the black velvet. The one good legacy of three years with Caz, her musician boyfriend from her teenage years. She wondered what he was doing now. Still picking up teenagers, luring them with jazz nights, smoky clubs and the irresistible attentions of the *performer*. Still beating them up when they grew disenchanted with his daytime world of stale cigarette smoke, cold coffee and post-performance blues. Picked the wrong girl, she said under her breath, remembering the last time she saw him, the last time he tried to hit her.

On his good days, he would teach her tenor sax. When she showed a natural aptitude, he bought her the one she held in her hands. She couldn't cry in those years, couldn't speak of her feelings, didn't want even to try to put them into words. All her pain, her loneliness and her errant joy poured from her lips under the alchemy of the sax and came out as something beautiful. She remembered the tenth-floor council flat in Belsize Park, standing before the open window playing out her soul, while, bathed in the orange glow of streetlights, London slept below her.

She turned out the bedroom light, and moved to the window. She stood motionless for a few moments, holding the sax to her chest, before lifting the mouthpiece to her lips like a lover's hand. The sound flowed from the instrument like a lament. Helen bent back her head and let the music flow through her. She played 'Lily Was Here', over and over, like a lament.

CHAPTER 8

Hugh Wallace, Roddy Clark and Helen sat sipping hot consommé laced with vodka, reclining in the luxuriant candle-lit darkness of the drawing room. Wallace and Roddy displayed the sharp familiarity of old friends, sometime rivals. They'd been at school together, their families knew each other, their lives could have been mapped out along parallel lines, only one loved numbers, the other, words. Wallace lacked Roddy's apparently assured glitter, but then he had money, which Roddy craved. He'd even taken up, and, in his own mind, bested, Roddy's passion for sculpture, buying a piece which he loved as much for its own merits as for the fact that Roddy would never be able to afford it. Wallace's financial superiority maintained a tenuous balance between the two men. Not that Wallace would ever really be fond of Roddy, nor would he trust him. Trust no one. Let no one in. Expect rejection. Sooner or later, it'll happen. He'd learned that from his childhood in the chill house in the Scottish Highlands, an only child to absentee parents, shipped off to school as soon as possible, got out of the way.

Wallace and Helen were gossiping, something about today's trades. Roddy tuned out, and looked around in yearning. He loved this room. He missed the sense that in some, albeit transient, way it had been his to share with Helen. The walls were a deep ruby colour, the sofas and chairs were dark and yielding, the walls and floors were hung and strewn with a selection of wool and silk Persian carpets. There was so much of Helen in this room, so many knick-knacks and trinkets, coloured boxes, gnarled wood carved into snakes, charcoal drawings, all collected magpie-like during her sailing days and thrown together in an exotic mix with the special pieces Dai had given her: the rugs, the silver, some of the paintings. The child hoarder and the sophisticate face to face. Gazing around, he felt a sudden pang, almost a presentiment of further loss, and found himself trying to memorise details of the room, a framed photograph of Helen and Dai playing with Dobermans, a pair of elaborate silver candlesticks, a painting of a felucca sailing down the Nile.

'So, what's new in the scribbling world then?' Wallace's question cut into Roddy's thoughts. 'What's the flavour of the day?'

'Interview with Mrs Stewart Watts,' responded Roddy, coming back to attention uneasily.

'Who on earth is she?'

'Wife of philandering MP,' supplied Helen.

'What could she possibly have to say to you,' asked Wallace, 'save how she'd love to cut off his balls?'

Helen watched, feeling in equal measure the distaste and the fascination that both the scurrilous and the so-called respectable newspapers fed off and encouraged, creating junkies out of newspaper and readers alike, each hooked on pain, humiliation, and the exposing of another's soul.

'You'd be surprised,' snapped Roddy. 'Give someone the mouthpiece of a major national and you'll never shut them up.'

'You mean they take the bait,' said Helen.

'What bait?'

'You tell them it'll be their chance to tell their own story, to have their say, to get the facts across.'

'Exactly.'

'As if there's anything unalterable about *facts*.'

'What're you getting at, Hel?' Sometimes the high moral ground she seemed to take with regard to his profession really pissed him off.

'Oh, come on, you're all experts at twisting the facts, giving them more or less emphasis, cutting in with a comment from another source that makes them seem ridiculous, or naive or deceitful, depending on your angle.' Helen watched Roddy, seeing the annoyance, the guise of professional slight, and the quick, veiled glances he exchanged with Wallace.

'Well?' she challenged.

'Facts speak for themselves,' said Roddy.

'Objective truth, you mean?' asked Helen, trying to contain her derision.

'You're trying to tell me it doesn't exist?' asked Roddy.

Wallace's voice cut in, light, careless. 'I think it was the Duke of Wellington who rather poured scorn on the idea of pure objectivity. "Tell the history of a battle? You might as well ask me to tell the history of a ball", was his take on it, if memory serves me right.'

Helen and Roddy laughed and their glaring eyes softened as they lingered on Wallace, smiling at his little triumph in the name of peace.

'Hungry?' asked Helen, getting to her feet.

'Quite,' said Roddy.'

'Bloody starving,' said Wallace.

Helen left them alone and walked into the kitchen.

Roddy watched her go then got up to pour himself more wine. He downed half a glass, and spoke into the middle of the room.

'I don't know what's got into her. She's so sharp these days.'

'Maybe she's just grown bored listening to bullshit,' said Wallace.

'You mean after a day surrounded by it?'

'It's hardly surprising,' said Wallace, ignoring Roddy's jibe, 'that she sticks the knife in now and again.'

'That she ridicules my profession?'

'Your profession crucified her father.'

'Oh, come on.'

'Have you read any of the stuff they wrote about him?'

'Have you?'

'I have, as it happens. Fraudster, crook, criminal, you'd be amazed at the number of people they trotted out to say they'd always thought him a dark horse, a little dodgy, not quite right, not one of us. He'd never even gone before a court.'

'No, he just did a flit instead.'

'He was never tried, never found guilty, but he was still trashed by every paper in the land.'

'He admitted his guilt, didn't he, the moment he ran? Money disappeared from his bank, must have been about sixty mill in today's money, and the day before the theft was discovered he did a runner. Fact.'

'Conjecture. Who knows the whole story?'

'Who needs to? The press knew enough.'

'Or thought it did,' murmured Wallace, 'which amounts to the same thing. You know, worst thing ever happened to your profession was Watergate. You brought down a president. You're not the fourth estate, you're the first. God help anyone who falls into your orbit.'

'You'd sympathise with any underdog. Classic case of victim psychology.' Dysfunctional, he'd call it if that weren't even closer to home.

'It's called empathy. Add it to your spell check.' Hugh pushed himself up from the sofa, and walked out to the kitchen.

Roddy got up and headed for the bathroom. He always felt as if he needed fortification for an evening with Hugh Wallace. There was something about Wallace's humour he found sly. All that apparent awkwardness hiding behind a wall of money. He and Helen speaking a language of percentage points, betas, volatility smiles, impenetrable idiom that rendered him, the journalist, inarticulate. No matter that he told himself he abhorred the language, couldn't bear what it represented, the soulless exchange of money, a bloodless war waged by financial mercenaries he wouldn't have at his dinner table. Yet here he was with two of them. He could have been Wallace, so close were their backgrounds, were it not for the millions of pounds that separated them. And Helen should have been his.

He locked the bathroom door behind him and leaned against the washbasin. He turned to the rows of glass shelves Helen had put up along one wall. One shelf was devoted to different lotions, the other two to a collection of bottles of perfume. Helen bought them compulsively. She had more scent than she could wear in a lifetime – from the big fashion houses: Chanel, Christian Dior, Givenchy; from the international perfumiers, Guerlain. She had discovered the new, small-scale specialists: Jo Malone in Walton Street; L'Artisan Parfumier in the back streets of Chelsea. She bought scent like other people bought wine. She wore a different one every day, depending on her mood. The result was a bathroom that sent him into transports: honeysuckle in summer gardens, an evening at the opera, jasmine on a hot night in Spain, lime groves in autumnal Greece. Masked in her scents, she was a conjuror of magic. He could chart their relationship by the scents she wore. Violets, it should have been violets now, for remembrance. He splashed his face with cold water and returned to the drawing room.

'Here. You can carry the plates if you like.' Helen's voice carried from the kitchen. Moments later, she and Wallace appeared, carrying through plates full of shepherd's pie and a large bowl of salad. They sat down to eat and drink too much again – a haven from the world. Outside it began to rain, steaming up the windows.

CHAPTER 9

Usually Helen loved to cycle to work, skimming along the quiet streets, lulled by the early morning calm, but this morning she felt an unaccustomed disquiet. The sensation worsened as she neared Goldsteins.

She bought breakfast and reluctantly installed herself at her desk. She dunked a slice of toast, dripping with butter, in her tea. God, she didn't want to be here today. She had a strange feeling that something was going to go wrong. Perhaps her six-week run of luck was about to end. She registered the warning her intuition was giving her, and promised herself she'd trade carefully. Just two days to go. Tomorrow was Friday, the beginning of the long bank holiday weekend she was planning to spend with Dai at his home in Wiltshire. She'd have three free days till she returned to work on Tuesday, three days of peace and nurturing. She just wanted to be out of here, home, free of this sudden sense of oppression.

The line rang for AZC bank in Luxembourg, one of Rankin's regular trading counterparties. Helen had spoken to Carlos, Rankin's trader at AZC, five or six times. She thought he was a sleaze bag, but he was a big counterparty of Rankin's, was known in the markets as a big swinger, and Helen, in Rankin's absence, had no choice but to take his calls.

'Yeah, Carlos.'

'Helen! What an unexpected pleasure.'

'How kind you are. Andy's not here.'

'Ah. Perhaps you'd ask him to call me later.'

'He's off till Tuesday, if you were ringing to trade, which I assume you were.'

'I was actually. Something I need to put on now.'

Helen muted the phone, and shouted to Wallace in his office. 'Hugh, AZC wanna trade.'

Wallace came out of his office. 'Keith. Get me a cappuccino. Lots of chocolate.' He handed over a couple of pound coins and sat down next to Helen.

Keith wandered off with a resigned look. Just his luck to be sent off when there was some action.

'What do they want?' asked Wallace.

'Can I help?' Helen asked Carlos.

'I have no doubt whatsoever.'

'What's the trade?' asked Helen, wondering whether to laugh or vomit.

'Andy had a KOSPI call I might want to buy.'

Helen muted the phone again. 'Wants to buy a call on the KOSPI. Know anything about it?'

'Yeah, we priced it yesterday. Get the details and I'll check it's the same one.'

'Where did he quote you?' asked Helen.

Wallace picked up a handset and listened in.

'Fifteen per cent for a two-year at the money European style in half a million,' said Carlos.

Helen mouthed a silent *shit*. It was a huge trade.

'Dollar?' she asked impassively.

'USD per point,' confirmed Carlos. 'That's ninety-one sixty-five on a strike of six eleven.'

Helen tapped out the trade on a big button trading calculator to confirm the arithmetic, then turned to Wallace. He said in a whisper, 'Do it.'

'Fine.' Helen spoke to Carlos. 'Done. I sell you five hundred thousand two-year six-eleven-strike European calls on KOSPI composite at ninety-one sixty-five, one USD per point, value date tomorrow.'

'Done,' replied Carlos. 'Nice doing business with you.'

Helen cut the line. 'I hate doing that bloody KOSPI stuff. It's not my market. I know sweet FA about it. How come Rankin always seems to be away when that smoothie Carlos comes on with a KOSPI trade? I always get the feeling he's carving me up.'

Wallace turned away and got up from the desk. 'Just the luck of the draw.'

'Huh!' She tore a ticket off the wad and began to write up the trade.

Half a million units at 91.65 US dollars a pop. She did the calculation; 45,825,000 dollars was the overall up-front cost to Carlos, which would be paid into the Goldsteins account tomorrow. In return, Goldsteins would grant Carlos and AZC the option to buy from them in two years' time 500,000 units of the Korean share price index at the money, meaning at the current level of the index which was 611. The price per unit at which Carlos traded was a percentage of that – fifteen per cent – which sounded all right, for all Helen knew. This meant that the KOSPI would have to rise by more than fifteen per cent over the next two years for Carlos to come out ahead. Goldsteins would be in profit as long as the KOSPI index did not rise more than fifteen per cent, adjusted for the time value of money, since they would earn interest on forty-five million dollars over the two years. This kind of trade depended on the two counterparties having different views about the future, or, more complex still, they might just be offsetting an equal and opposite transaction they had written with another counterparty, an exercise known as hedging.

'Shit, that's big,' Helen muttered, out loud this time, feeling a brief flash of nausea. She finished writing up the ticket, checked it, then time stamped it and stuck it in the settlements tray. The underlying value of Goldsteins' obligation was 611 multiplied by 500,000, a gigantic three hundred and five million, five hundred thousand dollars. It would need to buy half a million contracts at whatever price above 611 the KOSPI was in twenty-four months. It would then sell them to Carlos for 611 a unit, so its real exposure was in the difference between 611 and the price two years hence, multiplied by 500,000 units. However you reckoned it, pretty damn huge, thought Helen. They would hedge the transaction. As soon as the markets turned, she, or more likely, Rankin, would buy the position she had just sold for perhaps forty million dollars. In theory. But with a trade this big and risky, the scope for problems and losses was huge.

*   *   *

Helen spent her lunchtime walking the streets of the City, trying unsuccessfully to shake her sense of unease. She'd woken with it, the AZC trade had given it focus. She had a bad feeling about it that seemed to her out of all proportion. Normally ravenous by lunchtime, she'd only managed to force down half a sandwich sitting agitatedly on a bench in Finsbury Circus. Something seemed wrong with the human dynamics of the trade. Carlos and Wallace seemed to be in an almost indecent haste to trade. The logical approach was to quiz Wallace about the trade, but some further prompting of instinct held her back. She needed a third party, someone who knew the KOSPI. The trouble was it was such a specialised market. Then she suddenly remembered Tuesday night, the dinner, Reece Douglas. She was wearing the same suit. She reached slowly into her jacket pocket and pulled out his card.

'Bingo!' She smiled for the first time all day, pulled out her mobile, and dialled.

'Grindlays.'

'Reece?'

'Yeah. Who's this?'

'Helen Jencks. We met on Tuesday night.'

'The dinner party from hell.' He laughed. 'How are you?'

'Well,' she lied. 'Listen, I know this is short notice, but I need a bit of professional advice. Couldn't spare half an hour for a drink this evening, could you?'

It would be simple, quick, a couple of vodkas, reassurance, peace of mind and everything back to normal. Even then, she couldn't quite convince herself.

CHAPTER 10

They sat in the crowded bar of Corney & Barrow in Broadgate Circle. Reece sipped Guinness, Helen nursed a balloon glass of brandy, hoping it would settle her stomach.

'I stepped onto your territory today,' said Helen.

'KOSPI?'

'Yeah.'

'Want to be careful with that one, can be *very* nasty.'

'Yeah.' She glanced around. 'Strictly *entre nous*, I'm a bit worried about it.'

'What d'you do?'

Helen described the trade.

'What price?'

'Ninety-one sixty-five.'

Reece took a long drink of Guinness. For a while he said nothing. Helen could see him playing over the trade in his mind.

'Tell me the trade again.'

'What's wrong?'

'Nothing. I probably misheard you.'

Helen told him again.

'You tell the KOSPI trader where you traded?'

'He's on holiday, but the guy who structures the KOSPI trades was there. He approved it. Why? What's wrong?'

'I did a trade today, pretty much identical, at a hundred and twenty-two.'

Helen silently did the maths.

'You telling me my price was off by more than thirty?' Her stomach lurched.

Reece looked her in the eye and nodded.

'It *can't* have been. Wallace approved it. He'd structured the trade yesterday with the KOSPI trader.'

'You traded five hundred thousand units, yeah?'

Helen nodded.

'That's –'

'I can do the figures.' She raked her fingers through her hair. 'If you're right, we mispriced by fifteen million dollars. Jesus Christ. You have to be wrong.'

'I'm right. You'd better believe me.'

'Wallace doesn't make fifteen-million-dollar mistakes. Neither do I.'

Jesus Christ, this was the end of her career. A small voice in her fear-filled mind whispered that it was more than that.

CHAPTER 11

Helen and Joyce entered the dojo in the Ladbroke Centre. The familiar white-painted walls, the cream tatami covering the floor in two-inch padding took Helen into a different world, designed as a haven. She inhaled cool air scented with bay leaves and tried to calm herself.

The two women changed into their white *gis*, over which they both wore black pleated trousers, the privilege of black belts. Joyce was a first dan black belt, Helen second dan. They left their sandals outside the dojo, facing out, entered, knelt, and bowed to a photograph of O Sensai, Morihei Ueshiba, the founder of modern aikido. Ueshiba had taken an ancient art, whose origins dated back to fourteenth-century Bushido in Japan, and developed a philosophy of life as well as a martial art of the highest defensive skill. Students were taught to subdue an attacker, rather than to maim or kill as in some of the more aggressive martial arts, like tae kwon-do or karate, but some of its movements could be deadly, particularly those using pressure on vital nerve centres. *Aikido* meant 'way of spiritual harmony'. Practitioners were taught to strive to achieve complete mental calm and control of their body in order to master an opponent's attack.

Helen and Joyce joined the class, ten other students and their sensai, or teacher, Dave. Joyce greeted everyone, moving around, chatting. Helen stood alone, off to one side, silent, her two worry lines gouging her forehead. The class began punctually at eight o'clock, and concentration was absolute. They all knew that failure to concentrate could result in serious injury. First they warmed up, swinging their arms, doing standing stretches, summoning their chi energy. Then they moved into Jumbi Dosa, a rowing motion with deep breathing and chanting, designed to row the adherent away from his or her everyday life to the island of aikido. Helen breathed slowly and deeply, trying to allow the outside world to slip away. Next they practised a dozen different techniques, throws and immobilisation holds. First Helen was the ukemi, or receiver of throws and holds, with Joyce the tori, then they switched roles and partners.

'Use your centre,' said Dave, circling the students, taking over as ukemi or tori to demonstrate a point.

'Bring me into you, or go behind me,' he said to Helen. 'Think contact. Yeah. Wherever it goes, you're there.' Helen grabbed his striking arm, caught him in a rokkyo hold and threw him with apparently effortless force onto the tatami. He rolled, came up, they bowed to each other. He prowled the dojo with low rapid strides, keeping up his soft-voiced commentary, eyes flashing energy and smiles.

'Toris, commit yourselves, give the ukes energy to work with. The more he tries to hurt me, the easier it is. Move your centre, keep moving, never be static. He should see you there, then you're gone.'

Bodies wheeled through the air, slammed in a speeding roll onto the tatami. Palms slapped the mat as they came to rest. It might have seemed to an outside spectator that those who fell did so voluntarily. There was no great visible force as they were thrown. Helen had always thought of it as the invisible art. Adherents maintained the impression. They were typically humble about their activities. On the street, there was no suggestion of the great skill with which they harnessed their power.

'Lower your centre, raise your opponent's. Stop dancing,' Dave continued his commentary. The dojo did sometimes appear to be full of whirling dervishes. Helen wiped her sleeve across her face, sweat was streaming down her body. She took a breath as Joyce launched into an attack on her. Helen moved in, and Joyce spun her through the air. Helen rolled awkwardly, her timing off by just a fraction. A searing pain shot through her shoulder. She covered up her grimace, forced herself swiftly to her feet, and bowed to a worried-looking Joyce. Dave wheeled by, almost spitting with cold rage.

'If she's committed herself to an attack, you can't be there. You'll be killed. If you think you're going to be hit, just enter and raise. Your unbendable arm will take the blow. Contact you're looking for, not control.'

After fifty minutes, they finished up with balancing and breathing exercises, taking in fresh chi, then lined up on their knees, bowed to O Sensai, and to Dave, and filed out of the dojo.

After they'd showered and changed, Joyce bought Helen an orange juice and took her aside.

'What's up?'

'What d'you mean?'

'C'mon. Your timing was crap. You were lucky not to get badly hurt.'

Helen let out a deep sigh. 'I don't know. Funny day at work.'

'You were fine yesterday.'

'Something odd happened this morning.'

'What?'

'I don't know exactly. I'm still trying to figure it out.'

Joyce faltered. 'Hel, you look scared.'

'I am.'

CHAPTER 12

The next morning, Helen awoke feeling sick. She put on her tracksuit, packed her suit, shirt and shoes into her saddlebags and set off on her bicycle, trying to pretend everything was normal.

She got to her desk by seven. She stared at her breakfast, picked at it. Keith gave her a worried look.

'Is everything all right, Hel?'

'Mm? Yeah, fine. Just got a stomach ache, that's all.'

Wallace sidled in. 'Hi, Hel.'

She pretended to be engrossed in an article about the labour unions in Hong Kong. She just raised a hand in greeting, waited, gave him time to entrance himself with his computers. All the while, she expected Settlements to approach her, grave-faced, with Zaha Zamaroh thundering down upon her. The black plastic bin bag, five minutes to clear her desk, the disgrace of an ignominious, public exit. Failure. Loser. All the grim drama of a public execution for the chattering crowds. Get it over with. That was if *she* had made a mistake. If she had not, then Wallace and Rankin had mispriced by fifteen million, a mistake scarcely comprehensible on the part of one KOSPI expert, and one derivatives genius.

She watched Wallace settle in his swivel chair, switch on his computer screens, and lean towards them so that his lips appeared to almost touch the screen. He was motionless, rapt. Only his eyes moved over the screen as his fingers ranged across the keyboard. He looked like a snake charmer, playing some electronic instrument, taming coiling serpents of numbers that would have drawn blood from anyone else. She chose that moment. She entered his office with the settlement ticket of yesterday's KOSPI trade. He didn't look up. She dropped the ticket on his desk and began to walk out.

'You couldn't check this, could you?' she said over her shoulder. 'Only I'm not very used to writing these tickets. I'm terrified I'll have written the wrong counterparty in or something.'

He grunted in answer. She went back to her desk, and waited.

It all hangs on this, she thought, on these few moments. Her name and career, Wallace's and Rankin's careers, or their integrity, and, beyond that, the unseen thing whose vague outlines she could only sense, and fear.

She jumped at a sound and looked up to see Wallace walking from his office, eyes down, scrutinising the ticket. She couldn't see his face. Step after step, creased brows, pallid skin, slumping shoulders. With a flick of his wrist, he sent the ticket flying through the air. It landed on the floor beside Helen's desk. Wallace stared down at it.

'It's fine.' He walked back to his office. Helen bent to pick up the ticket. She held it by one corner, as if it were contaminated. Her face seemed to radiate waves of heat. She coiled up the ticket, slipped it inside her shirtsleeve, and got up from her desk.

She walked the length of the trading floor to the coffee machine. It was quieter here. There were plants, a window, a bit of space and light. She stood for a few minutes, sipping her thin coffee, looking out across the floor, seeing it suddenly as if from a distance. An army of traders waging financial war against identical counter-parts sitting in tens of identical floors across the globe. Who won? Goldsteins, or Carlos?

The muscles around her heart felt as if they had contracted. It was as if her body intuitively recoiled from something her mind didn't want to acknowledge. She of all people had a horror of any kind of financial mistake, well-intentioned or not. Reece must be wrong. Had to be. Somehow, she couldn't quite convince herself. The fear stayed with her. She walked over to the photocopy machines, copied the ticket, rolled it up, slipped it and the original back into her sleeve.

CHAPTER 13

Helen met Reece in Broadgate Circle, by the hare. It was a freezing day, harking back to winter. The sky was sheet grey and the wind cut through their suits. Save a few bodies hurrying for their offices, she and Reece were alone. She opened her handbag, pulled out the trading ticket and handed it to Reece.

He took only a moment to look at it.

'It's the wrong price, Helen.'

She stared at him, horror in her eyes. 'Not a word about this, OK?' she said, her voice low.

'What's going on?'

She was turning away already, the wind whipping her hair.

She walked straight back to the office. Wallace was hunched before his screens in his office. Helen slid into her seat and scrolled mechanically through the news headlines on her Bloomberg screen.

Like concussion, two thoughts collided in her mind. Rankin always seemed to be away when Carlos rang up to do huge KOSPI trades. What if it wasn't a mistake? There were only three possibilities: Reece was wrong, Wallace was wrong, or Wallace had deliberately mispriced the trade, arranged for Rankin to be off the desk, and got her to execute the trade. To believe that was a kind of insanity.

How do you act normal when suspicions howl through you like viruses, and every flinch, flicker or blaze of colour is noted by people sitting feet away? How long can you stare at a computer screen? How many news updates can you need in an hour? She skipped lunch, unable to eat.

Wallace came out of his office at three thirty and suggested she and Keith go home. Keith needed no encouragement and skipped out immediately. Helen looked off into the middle distance.

Wallace studied her. 'Everything all right, Hel?'

She returned his scrutiny. For a moment she said nothing.

'Yeah, just a bit tired.'

'Go. See you Tuesday. Happy holiday.'

'Yeah, Hugh. Happy holiday.'

She gathered up her things and turned to go. She began to cross the trading floor, but stopped suddenly and glanced around. She saw Wallace looking after her, standing up straight for once, so that he might follow her departure beyond the rows of desks. He looked strangely observant, his limbs tight with energy. That image would stay with her a long time: the last moments of her old life.

CHAPTER 14

Helen cycled home, parked her bike in the spare room, sat cross-legged on the floor and began to plan her counterattack. She wasn't going to wait for Tuesday. She would not sit back passively, hope for the best, and pretend it was better not to know the truth about whatever the hell was going on. She had always ridden out to meet trouble, never waited for its ambush. She picked up the phone and rang Reece. The line rang and rang. She didn't have his home number. Perhaps he'd gone already. A voice answered.

'Grindlays.'

'Reece please.'

'He's just left.'

'Are you sure?'

'Yeah, I'm sure. I can see him walking towards the lifts.'

'Stop him. Please.'

'And who the hell might you be?'

'Maybe someone with a ton of business to give him.'

There was an agonising wait. Helen could imagine jerkface as he weighed up the bother of getting Reece against the hassle of pissing off some ballbreaker of a woman, who might just have a ton of business.

'REEEEECE. Some woman.'

Helen pitied anyone within a hundred feet of jerkface, but at that moment she could have kissed him. She heard the clang of a handset being dropped on a desk, then there was silence.

'Yeah?'

'Reece. It's Helen.'

'Helen. You just caught me. How are you?'

'Worried. I need your help. Can you meet me tonight?'
For what seemed like an age, he didn't say a word.
'Where, and when?'
'My flat, at ten.'
'I'll be there.'

CHAPTER 15

Reece arrived at five past ten. A slight figure, dressed in a parka and jeans, narrow face, concerned eyes. He was wearing an Aran jersey that looked as if it had been knitted for him. Helen could almost feel its rough strands against her face. She felt drawn to this stranger. In any other time and place, she thought to herself. The one part of her that was always tempted to see life as a cosmic joke recognised a spectacular one now.

There was a strange shorthand in their greeting, in the way in which he came in and took off his parka and seemed to know exactly where to sit, and to wait, not needing to fill in the silence. Helen offered him a drink. He chose whisky. She drank black coffee.

'The KOSPI trade?' asked Reece, looking across at her from under thick brows.

Helen nodded. 'What if it wasn't a mistake?'

Reece took a slow sip of whisky.

'You think Wallace deliberately mispriced?'

'He doesn't make fifteen-million-dollar mistakes.'

'What's he doing then?'

'I don't know. I almost don't want to know, but I've got to find out.'

'How?'

'I've done about eight KOSPI trades over the past year, all when Rankin was off the desk. I want to go into the office now, dig out all those trades, and check the pricing with you.'

He gave an almost invisible nod, as if somehow it were inevitable that he would help.

'D'you have a mobile?' asked Helen.

'Yes.'

'I'll take mine. I'd rather not talk on the office phones and have everything recorded. If anyone happened to tune into the mobiles, they wouldn't know what we were talking about, but we'd better be careful, just in case.'

They finished their drinks, and set off for the City by taxi. Reece dropped Helen at Goldsteins and went on to Grindlays.

The trading floor was dark. Helen flicked on a bank of lights and set the room ablaze. Shiny surfaces, the smell of dust baking in the heat of trading consoles left on, and silence, alien and eerie. Although her presence on the floor could have been perfectly normal – traders would often come in at odd times of the night to put on special trades in some distant market – Helen felt raw, exposed, as if, innocent party though she was, she was about to be caught in the act of some crime she couldn't name. She suppressed a shudder and crossed the deserted floor to the derivatives desk. She unlocked her filing cabinet and searched for her files listing the KOSPI trades, but she could find no record of them. Tried Rankin's desk. His drawers were locked.

'Damn!' She sat back in exasperation, got up, retrieved a steel letter opener from her drawer. Drove the opener into the crack above the top drawer of Rankin's desk, pushed it down, hit it with a sharp blow and splintered the lock. She pulled open the drawer and hunted through books of trade tickets. It took her half an hour to find all eight of the KOSPI trades she had executed on Rankin's behalf, each one on Wallace's instructions. She got up and glanced around the trading floor; a security guard stood by the doors. Helen waved to him and sat down again, hoping he'd go away.

She clicked on her mobile and rang Reece.

'Sorry it took so long, there were reams of tickets to hunt through. I've got eight here.'

'No problem. Give me the details.'

'All right. July the eighth last year, I sold 400,000 three-month calls at a strike of 512 for a premium of 76.' Helen heard the rustling of papers, then the tapping of a computer keyboard. Just minutes, maybe even seconds, then she would know.

The tapping stopped. 'Wrong price. I have 97.'

Helen did the calculation. On 400,000 units, mispricing of 21 put Goldsteins 8.4 million dollars down.

Neither she nor Reece spoke. In that moment, her world changed. It shifted off axis, it began to spin so fast she felt as if she would be flung off everything she knew and had made familiar and would find herself in a vortex.

'Next trade,' Helen managed to say. 'September the twelfth, I sold 500,000 two-year puts at 590 for 88.'

Reece came back. '112.'

Helen did the sums. Twelve million dollars down.

They went on, through all eight trades. At the end, Helen calculated Goldsteins were down a total of fifty million dollars. Fifty million dollars, each one signed away by her signature. Depending on how the markets went, this would either be a loss, or lost profits.

'I want to check some of Rankin's KOSPI trades, at random,' said Helen, fighting to keep her voice level. 'The ones he executed himself.'

'Fine.'

They tested ten. In each one, the pricing was in the same narrow ballpark as Reece's. The only fraudulent trades were those she had executed. She gazed at the ceiling, willing it not to spin.

'What're you going to do?' Reece asked.

'I don't know. I need to think. Go home, Reece.'

'Are you sure?'

'Yes. And Reece . . .'

'Mm?'

'Thank you.'

'For bringing your world down around you?'

'You didn't bring it down, Reece. And don't worry, I'm still standing.'

She hung up and sat hunched in silence. Fear whirled around her like a storm. She cast her mind away, like an anchor. The image came as bidden: she was thousands of miles away, at night, in a boat in the South Atlantic, in a force nine gale, with fifty-foot waves, and the boat doing three-sixties till she no longer knew what was up and what was down, what was life and what was hell.

After that, she could survive anything. Slowly, she brought her mind back, stilling it as it came, until she could think with some semblance of clarity.

She picked up the letter opener, headed for Wallace's office, opened the door and sat down at his desk. One by one, she broke all his locks and started going through his files. She wasn't sure what she was looking for, but an hour later, she knew she'd found it. As she went to force open another drawer, the opener fell to the floor and bounced under the cabinet. Helen got down on hands and knees, slid her hand under the narrow gap between the filing cabinet and the floor. She scrabbled around with her fingers, pulled out a single sheet of paper. Tried again, and her fingertips just brushed the letter opener. Straining, she manoeuvred it out, eyes catching on the piece of paper she had retrieved. Bold type on heavy cream. Expensive.

Helen Jencks.
Account number: 247 96 26 76 2BV.
Account Enquiries, tel: 246 5525.

She picked up the paper. It bore the letterhead of Banque des Alpes, a discreet Swiss bank. It was addressed to her, c/o a PO box number she didn't know she had, and signed by someone called Konrad Speck, a man she'd never heard of. She had no dealings with Banque des Alpes, neither personally, nor professionally. She pushed shut the damaged drawer to Wallace's filing cabinet, and returned to her own desk. Methodically, she took out the fresh packet of cigarettes that awaited her in her drawer, left there at the close of business today, intended to be smoked on Tuesday. She took her lighter from the desk, hand trembling, lit up, took a deep drag, then picked up her mobile telephone and rang Banque des Alpes. A recorded message, speaking first in French, then German, then English, said, 'Welcome to the voice print facility.' Callers using this facility, it explained, could obtain details of their accounts by giving their account name and number when prompted. If the details, and the voice print, matched those pre-recorded into the bank's security system, account details would be released over the phone. Speaking slowly and clearly, Helen said her name. The message came back: 'Sorry, voice print not recognised, please try again.'

She waited a few moments, then answered using her telephone voice, the way she sometimes answered calls at her desk, warm, animated.

'Voice print accepted. Please give account number,' said the message. She recited the account number, and waited.

Back came the tinny voice: 'Balance as of close of business today: US dollars, one million four hundred and ninety-three thousand two hundred and fifty-two.'

She cut the line, reached for the bin under her desk, and retched. She sat, doubled over, breathing raggedly after the vomiting had passed. She spat out the taste in her mouth, wiped her face with a handkerchief and sat back in her chair.

She pieced it all together, the elaborate deception, saw too clearly, the inevitable conclusion: Helen Jencks, guilty as hell. Like father, like daughter. Who would believe her protestations that she had been set up, that she had signed the fraudulent trading tickets in ignorance, that the one point four million dollars in a bank account in her name, activated by her own voice, was not her money, the fruits of her crime? All the documents pointed to her guilt.

So simple, and so irrefutable. She knew what would follow: the yards of newsprint, raking up again what her father had supposedly done. His shame would live again through her apparent guilt. Her mobile rang. She answered it.

'Still there?' asked Reece.

'No,' she lied. 'Just got home.'

'What'll you do, Helen?'

'Nothing. I can't do a thing. Please don't ask me why, and don't ever tell anyone about tonight.'

'Helen, there's some serious shit going down here. We can't pretend it never happened.'

'Just leave it, please, Reece. Pretend you never met me.'

Helen picked up her bag, took the letter opener, and in a sudden spirit of sedition, broke into her own desk, before heading out of Goldsteins for the last time.

CHAPTER 16

Helen poured out a large glass of vodka, drank half. She paced around her flat – elegant, expensive, bought with her earnings. The paintings, the silver, the Persian rugs, some gifts from Dai, others hard earned. Now they seemed to mock her and she saw them through an accuser's eye: lavish fruit of fraud.

She drained her vodka and rang Dai. One AM. After three rings he answered, sharp, alert as always.

'Dai, it's me. I need to talk to you.'

'Hel, what is it? Where are you? I was expecting you hours ago. What's happened?'

'Oh Dai, I'm sorry, I should have called. Something came up, it's . . . I . . . Oh God. Not over the phone.'

'Where are you? I'll come to you.'

'No. I want to come to you.'

'I'll be waiting.' There was a slight pause. 'Drive carefully.'

Helen took her saxophone. It had travelled the world with her. It was as if part of her knew even then that she wouldn't be coming back.

She drove at ninety-five along the quiet motorway. Everywhere she went tonight seemed empty, as if everyone but her had been tipped off and fled, even the traffic police. The bank holiday weekend rush was long since over and she had the lanes almost to herself. Her car, sleek black, moved quietly through the darkness. It had been her father's, a top-of-the-range BMW, now twenty-four years old and much prized by collectors. Dai had bought it after Helen's father disappeared, given it to Helen when she came back from sea. The car smelled of old leather, and tobacco, and when the nights were damp like this, she swore she could smell the faintest trace of the aftershave her father used to wear.

Dai wore it too. Helen always thought of him and her father as twins. They had grown up together in the Welsh valleys. They were both grammar school boys made good. Inspired by one spectacular teacher, an Arabist who had himself gone to Cambridge, they each won a scholarship to Pembroke College, Cambridge, to read Arabic. Helen's father went into the City, building up a large client base in the Middle East. Dai went out to live in Dubai and set up a business trading in Middle Eastern antiquities. He was a brilliant trader, with the instincts of the street and the eye of an aesthete. Thirty years on, he was worth many millions, and lived in a house that was like a treasure trove. He had never married, or had children. He said he did not lead the kind of life he could impose on a woman, and that Helen was all the children he ever needed. But now he was alone and lonely, and Helen knew that the old man regretted the selfishness of youth. Now he paid for the years of freedom.

It began to rain, hesitantly at first, as if the clouds couldn't commit, then suddenly the skies unleashed a deluge. Helen could feel the slight skid as she slowed. She had the windscreen wipers going full pelt, and still it was hard to see through the torrent of water. She stared ahead, grimly concentrating, keeping the car at eighty-five.

Finally she slowed, turned off the motorway, followed a succession of turn-offs, till a narrow lane wound its way towards the long, familiar driveway. High gates barred her way. She stopped the car, pushed a button on a grid and spoke into the intercom. Derek, Dai's butler and old friend, answered and the gates swung open. Helen accelerated through, down along the avenue, a mile long, flanked by oaks, invisible now, save for brief moments of illumination as the moon emerged fleetingly from scudding clouds and silvered the branches.

The car crunched on gravel at the forecourt. Its arrival triggered a bank of security lights which dazzled Helen as she got out. She walked forward, saw the big doors open and her godfather walk out into the rain. His four sleek Dobermans streamed past him. They ran to Helen, pawed her and whined.

Dai followed them down the steps. He wore his usual tweeds, finely cut, soft with wear. His thick grey-black hair was well combed, slicked back, a wave over his right temple. He had high, sensual cheekbones, thick eyebrows, watchful, aware, brown eyes, austere lips. It was twenty past two in the morning but he showed no sign of tiredness. His walk was sure. At sixty-five, he was still attractive. He looked to Helen like an ageing James Bond. Sean Connery in tweeds.

'Cariad.' His pet name for her – *sweetheart* in Welsh. He reached out his arms, hugged her hard, then walked with her up the stairs and into the house.

They went in to his study, sat in sunken chairs of worn cloth. Normally, Helen would stretch out her feet on old Persian rugs, but tonight she sat coiled, hugging herself as if chilled. A fire burned in a huge grate, inflamed by the roaring wind, which sucked and pulled at the trees, hurling stolen leaves through space. The Dobermans lay silent at Dai's feet.

Helen looked across at him. He knew her father better than she. Is this how her father would be, if he sat before her now? Each time she saw Dai after a long absence, she asked herself this, searched his features as if she might find a clue there to her father.

Dai poured two large brandies and handed one to Helen. His face was deeply lined, almost more so than usual. His eyes were worried and compassionate. His lips began to work and then stilled themselves. Helen could see him holding back questions, waiting until she was ready to talk.

She took a sip of brandy, gleaned comfort from its heat.

'I went to the bank this evening, checking on something. If it wasn't for this I almost wouldn't believe myself. I found it under Hugh Wallace's filing cabinet.' She gave him the Banque des Alpes letter.

'I rang the number, recited my name and that account number. A recorded message told me my voice print was accepted, then it told me the balance in that account. Apparently, I have one million four hundred and ninety-three thousand two hundred and fifty-two dollars.'

Dai's eyes widened but he said nothing.

'I never opened such an account. I don't have that sort of money.

Wallace and Andy Rankin have been running a little scheme. They've siphoned off fifty million dollars from Goldsteins. And they've set me up to take the fall.'

Dai watched her as she spoke, took in the forced calm that would have been keeping down a maelstrom of emotions.

'How, in heaven's name?'

Helen drained her brandy. She got up, refilled her glass and Dai's.

'Simple,' she said bitterly. 'Rankin trades something called the KOSPI, doesn't matter what it is, you might as well just think of it as bicycles. I know nothing about the price of bicycles, I trade saxophones, so Wallace and Rankin arrange for Rankin to be unavailable when a client rings up wanting to buy a bike. I take the call, the client asks me how much for the bicycle he discussed that morning with Rankin; Wallace tells me a price, I tell the client a price, we trade. The thing is, the real price of bicycles is twenty per cent higher than the one we sold at. So the client just sells on our bicycle, pockets the twenty per cent difference, then probably gives back half of that to Wallace and Rankin to share.'

'How could they think they'd get away with it?'

'Easy. Not many people on the trading floor know the "real" price for the KOSPI, or the bicycle, and there're so many thousands of different things traded it's easy to hide. Every day there's a printout of Goldsteins' trades, an average of two and a half thousand transactions a day. Bound up, each day's printout is as thick as a telephone directory. How the hell can you monitor that? Let alone check that every price is right. Then they make sure there's no one around when I do the trade. There's this new boy on the desk. Wallace never wanted him there. Zamaroh forced him on us. No wonder Wallace didn't want him. He might have been a witness to him giving me the wrong price. Yesterday he sent him off to buy him a cappuccino just as I was about to do what I discovered later was one of the mispriced trades.'

'Isn't there some other warning system for this kind of fraud?'

'Not really. It comes down to whether or not anyone decides to check out this particular trade and compare it to similar ones. Wallace and Rankin would have been working on the logical assumption that no one would have had any reason to check the trade, and even if they did scan their eyes over it, they wouldn't have known it wasn't the correct price. If, by some remote possibility, someone did check the trade, and realise it was at the wrong price, they made sure I was there to take the fall. It's my name on every illegal trade ticket, my name on a Swiss bank account stuffed with one and a half million dollars, which, incidentally, is designed to be found. Anyone wanting to hide money would never put it with the Swiss these days. They'd stash it in Panama, or the Caymans, or some other thrusting little Caribbean island.'

'How d'you think they got your voice print?'

'When I first recited my name, the recorded message told me that the voice print didn't match. Then I used the voice that I do for answering the phones at Goldsteins. You know, you've heard it often enough, sort of bright and breezy and hyper-confident. That worked. All Wallace and Rankin would need to do was to record me answering the phone.'

'What about the account number? That was in your voice print too.'

'I was coming to that. Rankin came to me one day, 'bout six months ago, said he was so hungover he couldn't even read the numbers on this piece of paper, and could I please do it for him. I remember wondering how the hell he was going to trade that day, because the numbers were quite legible. I remember it clearly.'

'So he could have recorded you reading out those numbers?'

'I'm sure of it. So simple, eh? Then, of course, there's my father. Like father like daughter, both crooks. People believe that of me at the best of times. Now they'd smile in delight and say, "We told you so. Never should have trusted her."' She tugged her hair savagely off her face. 'I don't stand a chance. Oh, Christ. I've never been afraid of a fight, but how can I win this? I'm beaten already. Can you imagine the press? I'll be tried and found guilty by them before I even have my say in court. I'll be crucified. Four years of work, ignoring the sneers, the jibes, said just loud enough so I'd hear, four years' trying to repair the name Jencks. What was it all for? My father screwed it up for me all those years ago, and you know what? I'd always tried to believe he never did it, he was innocent, that he had to run away for another reason, that someone else must have taken the money. I fought anyone in school who said he was a thief. I've been fighting for his reputation all my life, and what for? All he ever did was leave me, and set me up perfectly for Wallace and Rankin.' Stung by her own vitriol, goaded by the fears that even the old comfort of Dai and his haven could not dispel, Helen began to cry. She doubled up, covering her face with her hands. 'The bastard.' Her voice came out as a sob. 'He was a thief all along, wasn't he? And he just abandoned my mother and me when he needed to. I've been fooling myself all my life.'

'Oh, Cariad.' Dai felt the ringing rage in her voice like blows to the memory of the best man he ever knew. Part of him bled as she tore open his friend, as she tried to convince herself that the lies she had rejected all her life were true. The pain almost overcame him. He heard his voice, cracking through the silence. 'No, Cariad. That's not how it was.'

CHAPTER 17

Dai felt his throat dry up in a fire of pain. He had kept his vow; for twenty-three years he had stayed silent. Now he knew he could no longer. His silence could destroy Helen, and the hell of it was, the truth, if he told it, could destroy her too. He needed no reminders of her wild unpredictability, of the tumult of her reactions. She had run away from home, she had run off to sea for eight years, eating herself up with a fruitless search, and when she could stand that no more, she had gambled her hopes on the City career that was now destroyed. But part of him knew that he owed her the truth, that he could no longer protect her from the violence of fate. The use by Wallace and Rankin of her father in setting Helen up meant that she had to know the truth if she could ever hope to fight them. No matter what secrets he spilled, what orders he now betrayed, Helen was all that mattered next to the cold ashes of an ancient loyalty to a cause long forgotten, to people who had never cared in the first place.

How could it be so hard to speak, to say the words, when his memory recalled every moment of that time, as if the decades hadn't passed?

His mind travelled back to 1976, to the windy night in October, when Jack Jencks came to this house, thin and shaking, his face dead. The truth had been buried so deep, for so long, it was almost easier to believe the fiction. But his emotions kept the truth alive. When he thought about that night, and God help him, he tried never to, the emotions sprang to life in all their torment.

Say it, speak, like a child learning to walk. One step, one word. She was looking at him, seeing the pain in his face, watching him with an awful anticipation.

'Your father sat here, twenty-three years ago, same chair you're sitting in. He was forty-two years old, and he had to lose the life he'd lived, lose everything, if he was to go on living.'

'Oh Christ, no.' Helen let out a wail.

'You'll have to hear it now. Every bit of it.' Dai took a long draught of brandy.

'It all started over twenty years before that, in the fifties, when we were at Cambridge. We were linguists, Arabists as you know, we both had perfect pitch. We came to the attention of certain people, and the approach came, to both of us. The Secret Intelligence Service, the Firm. Conversations over tea and crumpets, before roaring log fires, in dusty rooms at Pembroke College. Then in London. We'd be useful. And we were. It was exciting, Queen and Country, and all that, gentlemen's sport. We had no idea where it'd lead. We covered the Middle East, both of us. I used my trading as a cover, and he his banking. He had access, could charm his way in anywhere, and he was good. One of the first western bankers to really make a go of Arabia. I bought up carpets and antiquities, your father sold banking services. We dealt with arms traders, government ministers, terrorists. Passed long evenings lolling with a hookah and mint tea in the Majlis. SIS got him tracking the terrorists, following their money, offering them a conduit. He got close to the PFLP, that's the Popular Front for the Liberation of Palestine, led by someone called George Habash. Almost before your time, Cariad. You were a babe in arms, a toddler, a school kid. All the time he got closer, until one week, twenty million pounds worth of the terrorists' money was stolen. They thought it was your father. He'd been in the wrong place at the wrong time, but it wasn't him. I don't think the PFLP ever found out who stole their money. Perhaps it was one of them. But, without blowing your father's cover, there was no way to prove he was innocent. He had to go into hiding. He came to me. Wanted to take you and your mother, but it was more risky. Your mother wouldn't go, nothing'd make her. I think she was paralysed with the shock of it all. She'd had no idea about his secret work. She wouldn't let him take you, he knew he couldn't ask, though he was crying – God, in all my life I've never seen such pain.' Dai faltered for a moment. He reached down, stared at his dogs. 'He had to go, somewhere far away. We had a friend, another Cambridge man, also part of the Firm, gave him a haven. Another continent. He went to Peru. Press caught a whiff of something, tested the waters with a story of theft of client funds, no one challenged 'em, and they ran with the whole thing. Destroyed his reputation, but he got away. Press never found him. Don't know about the PFLP. Never heard. Twenty-three years ago. I've never seen, spoken to him or heard of him since.'

Helen was breathing deeply, as if each breath were labour. She looked into the fire so he couldn't see her eyes. She remembered the terrible silence on the night when her father disappeared. She had waited for him to return home, listening as she always did for the sound of the door slamming at seven o'clock, then for his footsteps in the hall. She would rush downstairs into his embrace, feeling the hard wool of his suit, or the soft cotton of his shirt against her cheek, and they would all talk together of their day over dinner, her mother, father, and her. But that night, seven o'clock came and went, and the minutes dragged like days in the silence that seemed to have gone on unbroken ever since. Until now. Her eyes clenched shut as if the pain were battering against her eyelids to get out, twenty-three years of pain. Time didn't heal, not this. Time made it bigger, with every missed birthday, every missed step on her way to adulthood, with every missed wet afternoon when the tears dried on her skin.

'Why? Just tell me why he had to go.' Her eyes hung on his, blind with incomprehension.

'Because he had to. It was for the best.'

'How can you believe that?'

'Because it's the only way.'

He went to her, held her. She collapsed in his arms, sobbing silently, her body convulsing, racked by the stillborn sound she couldn't let out.

Outside, the wind roared, rattling the windows; the clock ticked impassively, the dogs snuffled in concern.

She moved finally, slowly pushing back into her chair. Dai stayed sitting on the arm, looking down at her.

'He was innocent, all these years. Oh God.' The idea roared into her mind like a sudden storm in all its violent irresistibility. She knew then she would never have peace unless she followed it. She swept her hand across her face, brushing away her tears.

'Is he still alive?'

'Who?'

'The friend, the one who gave him safe haven.'

Dai saw with horror where she was leading. 'No, Hel, please.'

'I want to go to Peru, Dai.'

'Anywhere on earth –'

'Peru.'

'Your father could be dead, could have died years ago.'

'I've looked for him all my life. Trailed through what felt like every island in the South Pacific. You know, part of me didn't want to find him, I feared he might be guilty, that he might just have abandoned us voluntarily, that he would hate me, reject me if I ever found him. So I gave up. I came home, got my job in the City, tried to forget, tried to pretend there wasn't this gaping hole in my life, and you know what? It didn't work. The yearning never went away. And now I know. I know he was innocent. I know he had to flee for his life, and I know where he went. Jesus Christ, Dai, how can I stay here now? He'd be an old man, maybe he's dying. I have to go.'

She might have been his own child, for the pain he felt possess him.

He got to his feet. 'They're probably dead, all of them, long gone.' His brown eyes were pale, so much paler than she remembered, as if grief had washed the colour away. She stood up and hugged him until it hurt.

'I want to walk in his footsteps, I want to go where he went.' Helen reached out, took Dai's hand and gripped it fiercely in her own. 'I've got nothing of him. I want to see what he saw. If he's alive, I'll find him.'

'If you go, Hel, you confirm your guilt.'

'It's confirmed anyway. How can I stay and fight them now? If I go, just disappear, I have a feeling it'll all be covered up. Goldsteins won't want to be seen as dupes by the rest of the City. If I go, they'll have their culprit on a plate, then they'll want to cover the whole thing up. The press won't have a story.'

'But you're innocent, Cariad.'

'What does that matter, next to finding my father?'

'So you're just going to let them get away with it?'

'No. I'm not. I'll get my revenge on Wallace and Rankin, don't you worry. But first I'm going to find my father.'

CHAPTER 18

Dai and Helen sat in uneasy silence at the breakfast table. Helen looked away onto the distant downs. Sheep grazed the hillsides like still lifes.

'Why did he *never* come back?' she asked, eyes raking back. 'Don't you think he could have? Wouldn't the death threat have waned over the years?'

'Probably, but I think too much damage had already been done. His reputation was destroyed. He probably thought your mother would have moved on, you'd be getting over him, new father, perhaps. How could he come back, smash up your lives again?'

'It would have mended mine, but I don't suppose he knew that.'

'He'd have made a new life in Peru. That would've been hard to leave. Especially the older he got. Once you're in exile it's the hardest thing to return.'

'I hope he made a new life. I hope he's happy.'

'He may have died a long time ago, Cariad. You have to face that.'

'I know.'

'You're still thinking of going?'

'I ran away to sea on a one-minute decision, I won my City job in a game of backgammon. I believe my father *is* alive. I've got to try to find him. If I don't do it now, when will I?'

Dai agonised all morning. There was no right in this situation, just necessity. History turning on a twenty-three-year loop. But there was wisdom, there was caution, there was the case for avoiding pain. Against that, he had seen the will in Helen's eyes. However much he feared for her, he would not thwart that will. It still took him many hours to commit himself, to fight down the unknown fears that rose up every time he thought of Helen in Peru.

Finally, with a heavy tread, he made his way through to his study. He searched through his old box files until he found what he was looking for, a relic of all their pasts.

He turned the pages of the old address book, the red leather cracking. A present from his own father, over forty years ago. All the numbers written with the crisp blade of a fountain pen. The blue ink faded, but still legible.

Victor Maldonado, mother Scottish, father Peruvian, had come to Cambridge to read archaeology and break hearts. Met Dai and Jack at lectures on ancient Egypt, then the trio shared tutorials. Raven-haired, honey-skinned, dark eyes smiling, ready for anything. A circle of friends, the curious innocence of students, only Maldonado was never innocent, had lost his virginity in a Limeñan bordello on his sixteenth birthday, his grandfather in the next room. Seducer, spy and provider of safe havens. Twenty-three years, another lifetime ago.

I can't, Helen, I can't send you to someone I no longer know. Goodish once, what might time and disappointment have done to a man who had it all so young? She would go anyway.

For a long time he just stared at the number, as if trying to read in the configuration some pattern stretching out into the future. The numbers blurred and he felt a wave of dizziness. He shook his head, trying to cast off the sense of oppression that suddenly assailed him.

He dialled. Fate hung on telephone lines.

'Long walk?' asked Dai as he and Helen sat down to fillet of Aberdeen Angus for lunch.

'Think I knackered the dogs.' She nodded at the four black and tan bodies curled up in a heap by the fire.

'I rang Peru. Got Maldonado's brother, said I was an old friend from Cambridge. Wouldn't give me his number, said he'd pass on the message, his brother was a busy man.'

'Oh Dai.' She touched his hand. 'When was this?'

'Just before lunch. Probably have to be a bit patient.'

'With or without Maldonado's help, I've got to go. The whole scam'll come out on Tuesday. They'll discover the broken locks, start an internal investigation. Sooner or later they'll discover the mispricing. Then I bet you any money, my voice print account'll surface.'

'You could fight them, Hel, I'll help you all the way.'

'I know you would, Dai, but in some strange way I don't care about them any more. I just want to get away from the whole mess and try to find my father.'

'Wallace was your friend, Hel. Every week he ate off your plates. What I wouldn't give to get my hands on him now.'

'I'd tear him apart myself, Rankin too. I'd look in their eyes as I did it. Then what?'

'You'd feel better. I can't bear to see them get away with it.'

'They won't. When the time comes, I'll clap my hands. A butterfly flaps its wings and empires fall. I can teach *Doctor* Wallace a few new lessons in chaos theory.'

Night came, and the sound of Helen's sax wailed through the house like the keening of a ghost. On Sunday morning, Helen and Dai lingered over breakfast, surrounded by newspapers, trying to lose themselves in rainforests of print, listening for the phone.

'Tell me about Maldonado,' asked Helen. 'What's he like?' She watched Dai's eyes tunnel back through the years.

'Oh, Duw, it was forty-seven years ago that I met him. The three of us were just boys. Well, Jack and I were. Victor, he was something else. Tall, athletic, well built. This wonderful thatch of hair swept back, big eyes, knowing. Man o' the world he was, and we'd hardly been out of the valleys. A charmer. Charmed us all, men and women the both. Loved life, bit melancholic, like the Welsh. Sentimental.' Dai smiled. 'He was warm, funny, generous. Different character if he didn't like you; if he thought you'd done something against him, God help you. Used to say revenge ran in his blood, conquistador, with a healthy streak of Inca. He'd never have admitted mixed blood back home. Said it was the greatest shame, but I think he was secretly proud of it. Thought he was the descendant of an Inca king, said it was his high cheekbones, barrel chest. He was a good friend, a bit hot-headed, in danger of being spoiled by his looks and his money. Family were fantastically rich at one time, though I think they were running through it pretty fast.' Dai spread his hands. 'That's how he was, but that was nearly half a century ago.'

'Might still be the same. Have you changed?'

'Oh, Cariad,' Dai chuckled. 'I don't know. I feel the same, deep down. Bit more tired, keener on life than ever, bit wiser, perhaps. But I'm still the boy from the valleys, I still love green grass, trees, dogs, cheese on toast, strong milky tea and Dylan Thomas.'

Helen laughed. 'There you go then.'

'That gives me no comfort. He was a friend, a good friend, but not like Jack. I'd have trusted your father with my life. Couldn't say the same about Victor.'

'I wouldn't be trusting him with my life.'

'How can you know that? Peru's a dangerous place. You'd be out there alone, without even the protection of the British embassy.'

Helen felt the unnamed fear flickering at her again. 'I can take care of myself.'

'Aikido's not much use against a gun.'

'Neither is innocence when you've been set up.'

'D'you know what it's like to be chased, Hel? Can you imagine the press on your tail? Say you do go to Peru, you'll be on all the security cameras at Heathrow, there'll be records of your flight. You'll be easy as pie to trace.'

'Would it be better to have the press camped out on my doorstep?'

'They might not find out a thing if you stay.'

'I can't stay now, Dai, not knowing what I do.'

'Well, if you do go, keep a low profile. Stay away from the tourist trail. At least for a while.'

'So I become a fugitive, just like my father.' Her eyes turned ironic. 'I guess that's what's called fighting fire with fire.'

'Yeah, well, better not get burned.'

'Listen, Dai, I'll be careful. I'll be using my common-law father's name. My passport's in his name, my ticket would be too; the press would have to dig pretty deep to find me, the authorities too.'

'Good. But don't go round calling yourself Helen Jencks. Let it be Williams.'

She pulled a face. 'What about Maldonado, if he does ring, if he does offer to help?'

'Same. Helen Williams. Don't breathe a word about who you are.'

'That's crazy. I want him to help me find my father.'

'All right, Hel. We'll do one of your trades. If Maldonado does ring I'll ask him to help you. I won't say a word about any connection between you and Jack. Neither will you. Not for some time, weeks, months maybe. Not until you suss him out. Then, if you feel you trust him completely, you can tell him, ask for his help.'

'What harm could he possibly do me?'

'Tip off the press or the authorities for a start.'

'Why on earth would he do that? What possible motive could he have?'

'People have all sorts of motives for doing all sorts of things. You never see it till it's too late. Just because you can't see evil doesn't mean it doesn't exist.'

The telephone rang. The dogs barked. Dai flinched and walked over creaking floorboards into his study. He picked up the receiver. The voice rolled down the decades.

'Dai, my old friend. Victor Maldonado.'

'Victor. Been a long time.'

'A lifetime. How are you?'

'Not bad, bones ache, every day's a bonus.'

'Always the optimist, Dai.'

'Got to be, no?'

'In Peru? We've had too many betrayals here. We drink caution in our mother's milk.' Still the grandiloquence, better now, built on something.

'You weren't so cautious back in Cambridge, if memory serves.'

'Time of innocence, for us all, no?' Regret in his breath. The ghost of Jack Jencks in the allusion. There was no right way to do this, no clever lead in, like a business proposal. Theirs was an intimacy of friendship and of sorrows.

'Is he still alive?'

A long pause, the seal of silence broken.

'I don't know. I haven't seen him in six years.'

'Why not?'

'We went in different directions. Age changes you, no?'

'It's a wild card all right.'

'What do you need, Dai?' Maldonado asked with the calm confidence of a man used to granting favours, or denying them. Dai had been relying upon the old bonds of friendship. He was surprised by this curt efficiency.

'A haven, for a friend.'

There was a pause, a perceptible charge of energy down the phone lines as history jumped and replayed itself.

'May I ask why?'

'A favour, for old times.'

The Peruvian was involuntarily cast back to firelit rooms, bottles of port and sanctuary on cold nights in Cambridge.

'Oh, Dai. Old times. That was another life.'

'Fair enough then.'

'No, you misunderstand me. You think I wouldn't help you? How long's he need to stay?'

Time snatched in a guess. 'Three months. And it's she. You'll like her.'

'Who is she?'

'A good friend, Victor. An old friend.'

'When does she need to come?'

'Fly today, if she can.'

'She's not bringing trouble with her, no?'

'She's leaving it behind.'

'Has a nasty habit of travelling too.'

'It won't.'

Always does, thought the Peruvian, studying his own hands. Like a contagion.

It was so quick, to unpick a life. Betrayal, discovery, a decades-old story told, a few phone calls, the invocation of ancient friendships, the call upon the honour of a man whose bearing was forged by it. The bathos of a telephone call to a travel agent, the ticket arranged, waiting to bear Helen away.

Dai kneaded his temples, stared into space. He got up and went to the wall safe, concealed behind a painting of the Welsh valleys, the rolling green bisected by coal mines. He took out bundles of notes – sterling, deutschmarks, yen and dollars – putting away all but the dollars. He counted out twenty thousand, relocked the safe, and taped up the money in brown paper.

The walls of his study were lined with books. He knew them like old friends, where they lived, who their neighbours were. He picked out three. He listened to his dogs breathe, waited for the sound of Helen's footsteps. Rapid, athletic, like a dancer's they came, drumming out a rhythm on the stone hall floor. The door handle turned, her wind-blown face appeared. She smiled, forehead creased, sensing the change. He saw her as she was, ten years old, brave little thing.

'You've got your passport with you?'

She nodded. It was a joke between them that she carried it everywhere. Always prepared for flight.

'You arranged it then.'

'You're off. In five hours. American Airlines. To Lima. Via Miami. Maldonado'll put you up.'

'Oh, Dai.'

'Here.' He handed her three Spanish books, phrases and verbs, grammar and a dictionary, all well thumbed. 'Your O-level books.'

'You kept them.'

He got to his feet. She noticed for the first time the effort in his movements. He's ageing, she thought, horrified by the realisation. How had she never *seen* it before? She had fixed him in her mind and not allowed him to change. How selfish we are as children. We do not grant parent figures the independence to change or age without our sanction. They burn, we consume.

'Come on,' said Dai, touching her shoulder. 'You'd better pack.'

He gave her a battered leather suitcase, covered with stickers. In went her sax. Her hand moved mechanically. Unhanging, folding, concentrating on the motion, crushing out all feeling. She carried her case down to the foot of the stairs. Dai came out from his study.

'Like me to drive you to the airport?'

'Better that Derek do it, if that's all right.' Neither of them could bear to prolong the torture of farewell. Dai hugged her. She could feel him holding his breath, so that no sound escaped. She could feel bone where once there was muscle, and she fought back tears. She held him until she grew stronger, until she gave him strength.

'Tell Joycey, will you? She'll understand.'

'Your mother?'

'She won't notice I've gone.'

Dai took hold of her hands. She could feel his effort at cheer, could sense his struggle to keep the pain and anger from his eyes, so all that showed was compassion and love.

'Good luck, Cariad. I'm always here. You know that. You can come home any moment. I'll help you fight those bastards.'

She could feel the will in his words, the strength of purpose that age hadn't tempered.

'I know you will.'

'If you find your father, send him my love.'

'I will. Keep safe, Dai.' She kissed his cheek and walked away.

Part of her yearned to turn and walk back to him, but the other part knew that if she did, she would never be still.

Derek drove her away. The car sped along the motorway, between vistas of green fields alive with spring trees. The faintest trace of mist shimmered over the rivers that twisted in and out of view. It was so gentle a landscape, so allowing. It seemed to open up and accept you. There was nothing harsh or intimidating, no fierce beauty or danger to it, only a comforting softness that gave space for dreams, a haven which spawned explorers, ready for risk, knowing the balm which awaited their return. But she had no such balm. She did not know when, or to what, she would return. She had had no time to say her farewells. She saw the countryside now as one conscious of imminent death, with an anguish of loss, and brilliant clarity.

CHAPTER 19

Jorge Chavez airport. Lima, Peru.

The heat was like honey. It stuck to her skin. After it came the flies. Voices buzzed, limbs swarmed, legs clattering into her path, arms stretching out towards her bags. The air rang with the cries of 'Señorita, Señorita', as the porters clamoured for her trade. She smiled, held her bags firmly, stood still, eyes searching. It was night and the Limeñan sky glowed orange with light pollution. She could see no stars. The air smelled of dust, fumes and excitement. The people were short and broad, with the faces of survivors. She towered above them, pale beside their rich darkness. Some smiled with instinctive friendliness, some totted her up. How many hot meals could she have paid for?

Two men walked towards her, both in their thirties, tall, well built. One in a suit, one in jeans and leather jacket. The crowds fell away from them. Maybe it was the walk, athletic, nonchalant, trained. Maybe it was the hard faces, apparently unseeing, as if there was nothing abroad that could threaten them.

They stopped one pace away.

'Señorita Williams?' asked the suited one, breaking into a sweet smile. He looked as if he worshipped at the gym, muscles bulging through the contours of his suit.

'*Sí?*' answered Helen with a questioning smile.

'*Buenas noches. Soy el chofer de Doctor Maldonado,*' the man answered.

'Ah. OK. *Y Doctor Maldonado?*'

'*No se encuentra, Señorita. Mañana. Por favor, venga al carro.*'

He beckoned towards the car park. Leather Jacket studied her with interest.

Helen gathered that she would see her host tomorrow. She felt a sudden wave of fear, wanted to turn from these strangers and disappear into the crowd. Then logic worked its calm. She allowed Leather Jacket to take her suitcase and she set off after Muscles. He led her to a large, black Toyota Landcruiser. With a gentlemanly flourish, he opened the door for her. She climbed in. The door slammed behind her with a dull thud, as if the whole thing were made of lead. The central locking clicked discreetly. Leather Jacket drove, Muscles, the supposed chauffeur, sat in the passenger seat, looking out into the night.

They drove out of the airport, into the sluggish traffic beyond. The car idled, Muscles drummed his fingers on the dashboard. The car swerved and wove but still slumped into potholes. The crumbling road surface was dimly lit by streetlamps, the night garishly punctured by neon signs for Coca Cola, Inca Cola, Shell, Toyota. Along the side of the road there were heaps of rubbish, patrolled by mangy dogs, haphazard configurations of concrete houses with tin roofs, washing fluttering in the dirty air. Beyond were hills covered in what looked like boxes, clinging precariously to the slopes. Shanty towns.

After ten minutes of crawling, Leather Jacket blasted the horn, swung out into the path of oncoming traffic, cut left, off the main road into a narrow backstreet. Helen could see a gang of boys playing a game of football, the road their pitch. The car's headlights flickered over their running bodies. The players backed into the shadows, glaring with sullen animosity as the car roared through their goal. They turned right, into a much wider street. On either side were high walls, perhaps twenty-five feet, topped with coils of barbed wire. There were no other cars here, no pedestrians, no footballers, just the sickly orange glow of streetlamps, hanging like a pall of radioactivity over the city.

Helen heard her own voice. This is home, girl, better like it. She gazed out of the smoke-tinted windows and laughed silently. This is where your father came. This is what he sees. See it with his eyes. She searched the streets as they drove into a residential area. She found a decaying ramshackle beauty in the peeling ochre paint and wooden balconies, a feathery grace in the lines of mimosa trees spreading their leaves in a lace canopy above the pavements.

The car sped along, horn blaring, periodically ignoring red lights.

After a while, they began to climb. The road wound up a hill, topped by a huge satellite dish. She turned and looked back at the lights of Lima, glittering dimly through a layer of sea mist.

The air was clear as they crested the hill and accelerated down the other side. There were large open spaces, patches of blackness. The houses looked bigger here, what she could see of them. Most were hidden behind high walls topped by electric fences with infra-red sensors whose eyes blinked implacably as the car sped past.

They drove on for another five minutes, then the car turned sharply, approaching at speed a tall gate set in a high wall. The driver pushed a button on a small handset, the gate slid back rapidly, just missing the car, closing swiftly behind it, all in a perfectly synchronised routine. They pulled up, Helen got out and gazed at her new home.

CHAPTER 20

Helen awoke to a Limeñan dawn. She supposed it was the sound of doves cooing that had awoken her, but it might have been the light that filtered in through slatted blinds, lying like stripes of white gold on the floor. Perhaps it was the warm air that had stirred her naked shoulders. She stretched luxuriously, sat up in bed, and loosened the sheets which fell to her waist. Old linen, thick and soft. The bed was hewn of mahogany, intricately carved, with a yielding horsehair mattress, made for dreaming.

Her bedroom was large, wooden-floored. Against one white stone wall stood a wardrobe and a chest of drawers, painted cream, stencilled with flowers. The paint was spidery, cracked by time. Helen moved around like an explorer, naked and curious. Three bedrooms, three bathrooms, kitchen, dining room, sitting room, all cast in shadow. All the windows were covered by shutters closed from the outside.

She dressed quickly in clean jeans and a white T-shirt and opened the front door, onto paradise. A hesitant sunrise, the faintest of mists. Jacaranda trees showered purple blossoms. The faint percussion of banana leaves touching in the breeze. Parrots chattering in flame trees. An eagle circling above, cruising the thermals. Beyond the garden oasis, towering desert mountains – the foothills of the Andes – so close she felt she could have reached through the warm air and touched them.

Flagstones around the pool, warming her bare feet. A feast of trees, drooping with ripening fruit: bananas, figs, plums, pecan nuts, giant avocados. The dawn stirring about her.

She gazed at a huge ficus tree with dazzling emerald- and moss-coloured leaves trembling in the breeze. It made her think of one of the stories her father used to tell her as a child, about a girl who goes walking through an enchanted kingdom where even the leaves on the trees are jewels.

A raucous scream ripped the quiet. She wheeled around, laughing when she saw a bright yellow and turquoise macaw staring at her from atop a large open cage. She walked up to it.

'Hello! Can you speak?'

'Pepelucho,' it seemed to say.

'Pepelucho, huh.'

The parrot edged sideways towards her, walking like a man with his trousers round his ankles. The feathers on its head and neck stood up, it trembled slightly, before belting out another almighty screech.

'So you've met Pepelucho?'

Helen turned. A man stood before her, so close she could almost taste him. He had weathered brown skin, and planed high cheekbones that were almost Mongol. His eyes were like marquise diamonds. It seemed to Helen that he should have been wearing some kind of splendid headdress. He looked like an Inca king.

'Victor Maldonado.' He rolled the r extravagantly. His low voice was thick and slow as molasses, but still she could hear the echoes of Cambridge in it.

She extended her hand. He took it and shook, a firm grip, cool chafed skin.

'Helen Williams.' She caught the 'Jencks' just in time. 'I didn't hear you.'

'The grass is silent.'

'He speaks his name.'

'He can say quite a lot when he's in the mood. Shall we try him on your name?'

'Pepelucho, can you say Helen?'

'Or Señorita Williams.' He paused between the Señorita and the Williams, as if unsure of the combination. He studied her face for a few moments, taking in her sharp, blue eyes, her creased forehead, winged eyebrows, pugnacious nose. He smiled.

'How about some breakfast?'

*　　*　　*

He led her to a wooden table on a large terrace beside the main house. She watched him as he walked slightly ahead of her. He had a heavy, magisterial gait. He pulled out a chair for her and sat down opposite. The skin around his eyes was heavily wrinkled. The lids were half hooded, as if tired by the effort of staying open, but, underneath, the eyes dazzled.

'By the way, we have other animals in the garden you might not find as congenial as Pepelucho. Guard dogs. We let them out around midnight. Best not to roam the garden after that. They're trained to kill.'

'What kind are they?'

'Dobermans.'

Helen hid a smile.

'What would you like? Full English breakfast?' She looked like the kind of girl who enjoyed her food.

'Perfect.'

Maldonado nodded to a short woman in a starched white apron who was busily laying a second place at the table.

'Carmen, my cook.'

Carmen was about five feet tall, with copper-coloured skin and the round, almost Asiatic features of the South American Indians: strong, broad nose, high cheekbones, narrow, intelligent eyes. Fiercely pretty.

'She'll look after you, get you whatever you need. How's your Spanish?'

'Nonexistent,' said Helen, hiding behind traditional British under-statement.

'Better learn,' said Maldonado, pouring coffee for them both from a silver jug. He took a delicate sip, regarding her over the rim of his cup. He replaced it soundlessly in its saucer, his eyes on hers all the while.

'Look, I don't know what you've done, and for the time being I don't care, but just tell me one thing. Why Peru?'

Helen took a slow sip of coffee. Maldonado seemed to be breaking the rules of this new game of hers before she'd even had a chance to start playing it. He gave her no room: the truth or a lie. The truth flashed through her mind. She locked it away. She would have loved just to spit it out, to feel it was the right thing to do, to start the search for her father here and now. For a moment the urge was almost overwhelming. With an act of will, she fought it down. She had promised Dai she would wait and instinct told her a precipitate confession would not be wise. She needed to settle in, formulate a plan, then act, not spill her guts like some ingénue.

'I had to go somewhere,' she said easily.

'But Peru? Deepest, darkest Peru. Why not France, Scandinavia, the States? Somewhere comfortable, somewhere close to home.' He began to cut up a thick slice of papaya, forking it into his mouth, smiling as he spoke. He might as well have been asking after the British weather.

'I don't want to be close to home.'

'Been here before?'

'Never.'

'Just seen Lima then?'

'Mmm.'

'What d'you think?' He took her answers like bites of food, chewed them briefly and went for more.

'Looked like something out of Kafka.'

Maldonado laughed, and shot her a quick look of approval.

'That's fantastic. You're absolutely right. Poor Lima's not a very good advertisement for Peru. They call it the Incas' revenge on Pizarro, but you know, Lima's not Peru. You want to feel a long way from home, wait till you go travelling, if you go. Get into the Sierra, see how the Quechua live, or go to Amazonia, see the tribes. It's a different world. It could be a different century. You want to escape something, you couldn't have come to a better place.'

'That's what I thought.' Beneath the smiling urbanity, there was a harsh humanity about Maldonado, a strange directness in the way he launched straight into questions she had thought would remain taboo.

'But why not Chile, or Argentina, or Ecuador? Colombia even?' he asked.

'Who knows? I suppose I thought Peru sounded more interesting.'

'Wait till you get close. You haven't lived till you've seen the moon rise over the ruins of Machu Picchu, or flown over the jungle at dawn and seen the macaws flying like jewels in the sun, or seen the Seiba in flower, or climbed Alpamayo and stood on the snow summit as if you were on top of the world.'

Maldonado seemed to put himself in a trance. 'There's so much more. I could go on for ever.'

'That's why I came,' said Helen.

Maldonado studied her for a while, his eyes coming back to her from some distant focus. The scrutiny was unnerving, but she held his gaze. After a while he spoke, not with his questions, but in a curious speech that made him seem a strange mixture of professor, priest, psychologist and partisan.

'Listen, Helen. I could say welcome to my home, please treat it as your own, I could say that I and all my staff are at your disposal, I could treat you like a normal guest, and leave it there, but I wouldn't be doing you, or our friend Dai, any favours if I did. Don't get me wrong, you are welcome and we are at your disposal, but you'd better learn a few house rules, for your sake as well as mine. You're running from trouble, that much is obvious. For Dai Morgan to ring me after so many years, you must have done something big. Stop running. Lie low for a bit. Leave your trouble where it is. Don't invite it here. It's obvious you're wounded. Mend yourself, fast. Peru isn't the place to recuperate. It'll kill you if you're weak.' He smiled. 'You think I'm being melodramatic, don't you? Any stranger would, many Peruvians would. It's as hard for us to understand our own country as it is for strangers. But I know it.' He took a deep breath, curling down his lips as if he tasted something bracing and unpleasant. 'I know it. Understanding this place is my life's work. I read archaeology at Cambridge – that's where I met your friend Dai, as you know.' Helen held her breath but Maldonado made no mention of her father. 'But you can't learn about this country from books, you have to experience it.' He got to his feet and his features became soft again. 'Ask me some time, when you've been here a little while, and I'll tell you about Peru.' He said his country's name as he would a lover's: with passion and possessiveness, guilt and deceit, admiration and fear. There was a stubborn sadness too, as if he would see, would take all it had to throw at him in his yearning for under- standing.

'So why do you stay,' Helen asked, 'if it's so terrible, if it can be so brutal?'

'Because it's in my blood, I'm addicted to it. Because it's the most beautiful country on earth.'

CHAPTER 21

The noon sun shining on the white-painted houses of Dawson Place dazzled Dai. He squinted, and manoeuvred his car into the lee of a towering oak. Together he and Derek headed for Helen's flat. They let themselves in. The place rang with her absence, smelled of emptiness. No freshly baked bread, no beef wellington, none of the treats with which she always welcomed them. Only Munza, prowling, tail lashing, who seemed to know in his cat-like inscrutable way that something was wrong, and blamed them. He refused to yield to their outstretched hands and blandishments of cream.

'C'mon here, drat you!' growled Dai. 'Give me a dog any day.'

Munza danced away, bleeding Dai with one vicious claw-stroke when finally cornered.

Dai closed Munza in his wicker cat box. 'Bloody cat. Like to set him on that Hugh Wallace.'

'You 'n' me both,' said Derek.

'Better ring Joycey. Ask her to come round, I think. Can't really talk at her place.'

After two days on the road in her lorry, Joyce was spending the bank holiday Monday luxuriating with her husband, Brian, and their three children, watching videos, eating curry and piecing together a giant jigsaw. Dai's summons was apparently casual, and deeply alarming.

'Just popping out to the shops,' Joyce announced, reaching for her jacket. She kissed Brian's cheek. 'Won't be long.'

She arrived at Helen's flat ten minutes later, her face flushed, her red cheeks glowing against the long blonde hair.

97

'What's happened?' The sight of Munza's wicker box confirmed her fears. 'Where's Helen?' She put her hand to her mouth. 'Oh God, don't say there's been an accident.'

'She's fine, don't worry. She's had to go away,' said Dai, economical. 'She was set up at work. She found out, Joycey, couldn't face it. Gone. Peru. No one's to know. Only you, she said.' He told her the whole story, leaving out only the truth about Jack Jencks.

Joyce went white. She listened in silence. All she could focus on were the words 'set up', and the faces she called up from memory, Wallace, Rankin. She looked around her, at the dining table, where she'd sat with them both.

'Does Roddy know about this?'

'Not a thing.'

'So what now? Will Goldsteins discover the scam?'

'Probably. They'll have to do some investigating when they discover Helen's gone without a trace.'

'And if they do find something, they'll think Hel did it.'

'Yes. Probably.'

'So Wallace and Rankin just get away with it?'

'Looks that way.'

Joyce just stared at him, unwilling to believe.

'Goldsteins'll want to cover it up,' said Dai, 'keep the whole thing quiet. It'll suit them down to the ground to act as if Wallace and Rankin are innocent, even if they suspect they're not. With Helen gone, there's no reason to suspect them in the first place. They can't afford a scandal. A bank lives on its reputation. They'll do everything in their power to protect it.'

'Oh, Dai.' Joyce went to him, hugged him. Her lithe body was hard with anger.

She drew back. 'She gonna let them get away with it?'

'She said she'd deal with them in her own time.'

'So what's she gonna do in Peru?'

'Oh, you know Hel, wander around, throw up her tent in the mountains, look at things.'

'Look for things. Run away to look. Still searching for her father.'

Dai started in alarm, but Joyce was looking beyond him, musing, and showed no signs that she knew she had just hit upon the truth.

'I'd better get back, Brian'll be wondering.'

'What'll you tell him?'

'Christ, what can I say? She's run off to sea again?'

'Why not?'

Joyce pondered this, as if trying out the lie.

'All right. Anyone who asks, I'll tell 'em that.'

'Only Brian and the kids. Anyone else come asking questions, you know nothing.'

Joyce walked home, poured herself a whisky. She finished the jigsaw, cuddled her husband, and cooked supper, carrying off a pretty convincing act that everything was normal. At ten, she changed clothes.

'I'm just off to see Mum,' she told Brian. 'Won't be long, coupla hours.' Brian gave her a strange look, but let it pass. He was well used to her rapid exits, her abrupt cravings for space.

'You look nice,' he said, pulling her against him. 'Like cat woman, all in black. All you need's a mask.' She gave him a long kiss, slipped into the kids' bedroom, kissed their sleeping faces, and pulled a balaclava from the drawer.

She jogged down the fourteen flights of stairs out onto Ladbroke Grove. Exhaust fumes hung suspended in a light fog. Christ, what was happening to the weather, anyone'd swear it was winter? She zipped up her black parka, hopped into her ancient Ford Capri and drove to Dawson Place. She found a parking space just down from Helen's flat. Helen's keys jangled in her pocket as she walked. The spare set, now useful for a contingency neither of them had planned for. She let herself in, shut the door softly behind her.

Light from the streetlamps glowed through the windows. She could see well enough, didn't want to switch on the lights. She searched for five minutes, couldn't find Helen's address book, stopped to think. Always a solution, if you think hard. The computer. Careful Helen would have made a back-up list. Joyce knew enough to explore the machine. Her eldest son, Ian, had taught her on last year's Christmas present. Still it was agonising. Finally technology yielded a list of addresses. She scrolled through, smiled in triumph, uncapped a pen and wrote.

Armed with two addresses, she slipped into her car and drove off into the night, moving fast, cutting through the whorls of fog that might have been designed to give her the invisibility she needed.

Hugh Wallace had spent the entire weekend locked up in his flat working on his book, surfing the net and ordering pizzas. By Monday night he had developed the beginnings of a monumental headache. In his head he heard his mother's voice: fresh air, that's what you need. He pulled on an anorak and let himself out of his flat.

From her car parked opposite, Joyce watched him go. Moving like a cat in her head-to-toe black, she slipped out and went after him. She walked fast, gaining on him. He moved sluggishly, almost wraith-like in the swirling fog, oblivious of the world around him. Joyce pulled on the balaclava. Wallace was feet away. He had no idea of her existence, until she was upon him.

Gently, at first. She just tapped him on the shoulder, stopped still as he wheeled to face her. She wanted to look in his eyes, wanted to see the fear.

This was not what she had trained for. Aikido was defensive, not aggressive, but rage had transformed her. She glanced around. The street was empty. She turned back to Wallace, leaned down and stared into his eyes.

'You bastard. She befriended you and you betrayed her.'

Wallace opened his mouth to speak but his words were lost in a shout as Joyce slapped his face. Even then, she could hardly bring herself to injure him. The little boy lost looked at her as if she'd shattered his world. She hit him twice more. He lunged away, tripped on the pavement and fell head first onto the road. Joyce waited for him to get up. He didn't.

She bent over him, checked his pulse and ran for the nearest telephone booth. She rang for an ambulance, gave them his whereabouts, and melted into the night.

The ambulance arrived ten minutes later. Wallace was taken to St Mary's Paddington casualty unit. He was examined by an intern, who summoned a neurologist. Still he remained unconscious. Wallace was given a brain scan, received a tentative all clear, but only an hour later did he come round. Severe concussion. He would have to spend at least one night in hospital. He lay in bed, throwing up, trying, and failing, to get up and walk.

CHAPTER 22

M aldonado went out after breakfast.
'Off on a dig,' he said. 'I'll be back for dinner. We'll have
something special, a Peruvian treat. Make yourself comfortable in
your little cottage. Ring Carmen on your intercom if you need
anything. She's on extension five.'

Helen heard a car start up, a door slam, then, save the chirping
of the birds in the garden, all was quiet. She gazed around her,
revelling in the warm air which danced against her skin. She
thought of the chill air in London, the metallic rasp of pollution
in her mouth. Here in the garden, the air tasted of jasmine. London,
so immediate in the violence of the discoveries that had sent her
here, seemed a long way away. She was conscious of having stepped
from one world into another. Part of her felt she would pay a price
for the deceptive ease with which she had moved between them,
that the journey from now on would be through an untravelled
world where there were no obvious pathways to guide her, save
Maldonado. She felt the impatience rising within her. This man
was the first signpost she had ever had on her long search for her
father. But she knew instinctively she had to approach him with
caution. She had glimpsed the convolution in his eyes.

She needed a plan. Her mind flickered back to Wallace and
Rankin. She forced it back to Peru. There was nothing she could
do about them now. She'd try to call Dai later, find out if there
was any fallout from her 'crime' and disappearance. Perhaps
she'd go into Lima to do it. She wasn't sure of the wisdom of
making a call from Maldonado's house. Better not take unnecessary
risks.

She put London away, a small compartment in her mind, nothing compared to the roaring in her heart at the prospect of being so close to her father.

She pushed the breakfast dishes out of her way and gazed out into the garden. Her eyes ranged over the contours of plants and flowers, dimmed by the scenery taking place in her own mind. She'd done her deal with Dai. First she had to suss out Maldonado, decide whether she could trust him to tell him who she really was, to ask him to help her find her father. No matter how much she wanted to pretend that he must be eminently trustworthy because she needed him to be, she swore herself to caution. She forced herself to engage her intellect, not decades-old dreams and yearnings. Approach it like a trade, gather all the information that you can, weigh up the risks, then cut or go for it. She knew even then she would never cut, no matter what the risks. This was something she had to chase till the end.

Best to start familiarising herself with her surroundings. Better start with the killer dogs. She armed herself with a couple of leftover rashers of bacon from her breakfast and set off in search of them. She found them in a pen in a far corner of the garden, close to the street.

Bitches, four of them, lined up at the edge of their pen, noses aimed like arrows. She began a low crooning. The Dobermans listened, soft ears flickering.

'There, girls. I'm friend, not foe.' The bars of their pen kept her safe. In a vivid flash of fear she imagined the animals loosed on her. Two of the bitches started to growl. Helen forced deep breaths down, trying to still her fear. As she calmed herself, the growling stopped. She walked slowly towards the dogs, letting them absorb her scent. They could smell the bacon, Helen could see their hunger as their eyes travelled from her face to her hands, and hovered, but they were too well trained to simper for it. Helen waited five minutes, until they showed signs of growing bored with the game of mutual scrutiny. One of them turned away and went to lie in a corner. Another followed. Helen kept talking until the third bitch, then five minutes later the leader, decided she was not a threat and turned their backs on her. Then she bit the bacon rashers in half, and threw in one piece. The leader bitch wheeled round and devoured it with one elegant shake of her head. Helen threw the other pieces in, aiming the rashers so that each dog got a piece. She smiled at them as they stood waiting.

'No more. See you tomorrow, girls.'

She walked round the garden, back to her cottage. She washed her hands, then dug from her luggage a guidebook to Peru she'd bought at Heathrow airport. She pulled up a chair on the small terrace outside, and sat down to read in the shade of a flame tree. Each time she turned a page the faint scent of bacon rose from her fingertips.

She looked up suddenly, her attention caught by movement. A man appeared from round the side of the main house, a hundred yards away. He was walking towards her, swinging one arm, holding a shotgun in the other. She froze, but as he came closer to her, he casually changed direction, moving off towards the far end of the garden. He walked slowly, checking left to right. Another armed man appeared from behind the bushes at the far corner of the garden. The two men nodded, stopped for a brief talk, then moved on. Helen's nerves were eased only slightly by their apparently calm patrolling, the sense that the men belonged. She watched them until they disappeared from view. It took a long time for her racing pulse to slow. Maldonado might have warned her, or were armed guards such a normal part of everyday life here that they escaped comment? Her latent sense of fear began to grow. The garden was a paradise, guarded by attack dogs and armed men. What was the threat? Whom did Maldonado fear, and why? What the hell kind of place had she stepped into?

CHAPTER 23

At eight that evening, Carmen came knocking at the door. She led Helen to the main house. Everything looked so different, so alien. Eyes bright with curiosity, Helen scrutinised the house. She and Carmen walked along a marble hallway, their footsteps echoing through the silence. Low-wattage spotlights in the ceiling cast a dim orange glow on the white walls. There were paintings of thick-set, high-stepping horses with proud eyes.

Closed doors flanked the hall at intervals, but they stayed closed, and Carmen paused only at the final one which was darker, heavier, and more intricately carved than the others. She opened the door, nodded to Helen to go through, and closed the door behind her. The table was laid for two, but Maldonado never appeared. Helen drank, and ate alone. She started with a pisco sour, poured by a smiling butler. It tasted like a serious version of whisky sour, something wickedly strong steeped in lime juice. Went down easily. She had three, grew merrier with each one.

By nine thirty she had finished a three-course dinner of chicken broth, fried pork with crackling, roast potatoes and asparagus, followed by a deliciously sweet rice pudding. She sat for a few minutes after she had finished eating, alone at this foreign table, tipsy, feeling almost amused at her situation. She got up quietly, slipped out of the dining room, and, emboldened by the pisco sours, went exploring. She tried the first door to her left. The handle opened to reveal a marble bathroom, with old, well-leafed copies of *The Spectator* of all things stacked on a small table. She tried the next door. It opened into a study. Helen walked in, flicked on a light, closed the door behind her, and sat on a leather chair behind a mahogany desk. She glanced around quickly, and pulled open a few drawers. Stationery, pens, correspondence, a letter headed Banco de Panama. Helen should have put it away but in some spirit of mischief she couldn't resist studying it. Her eyes flicked over an account number and the balance in the account: four million dollars.

'Shit!' Well, Dai had said the Maldonado family was rich. Her eyes lingered on the letter. Her mind, compulsively hungry for figures, automatically memorised all the numbers. She heard a distant squish-squashing sound of soft-soled shoes walking down the marble corridor. She stashed the letter away, rushed out of her chair, switched off the light. The footsteps passed by and she heard a door opening. She cracked open the study door, peeked out. The dining room door stood open. She slipped out of the study, closed the door silently behind her, then opened and closed the adjacent bathroom door loudly. She walked back into the dining room, humming a tune. Carmen wheeled round.

'Ah, Carmen. *Baño.*' She pointed down the hall. 'Pee pee.'

Carmen nodded in comprehension, then silently escorted her back across the garden to her cottage. She said, *'Hasta mañana'*, and disappeared back to the main house.

Helen fell asleep listening to the rhythmic whirring of the fan and the calling of the night owls, terrifying their prey out into the open to swoop down and destroy them.

CHAPTER 24

Andy Rankin woke groggy, hungry and depressed by the prospect of work after three days off. His only consolation was the bacon sandwiches he planned to devour as soon as he arrived in the City. He kissed his sleeping wife goodbye and made for the street. Dawn had broken, but at 6 AM nothing moved, save a black cat which scurried out of his way. He froze as a black-clad figure stepped into his path.

'Who the hell are you?' He couldn't even tell if it was a man or a woman. The eyes of the balaclavaed face seemed to be smiling at him.

'I'm a friend of Helen's.' The voice was female, savage and low, muffled by the balaclava.

'What the –'

'This is payback time.'

Rankin had a sudden inkling of what was coming, felt a frisson of fear, unbelievably, from this woman. He raised his arm to strike. The black-clad figure moved into him, flung both his arms away from his body to one side, gripped his head and his right arm. He just had time to register the speed, the force holding him, then he felt himself spinning, pivoting over his arm, pain searing up his shoulder. He heard a sickening crack and the pain turned into a flood. His arm was broken before he crashed down on the pavement, head first. For a few seconds he just lay there struggling for breath. Rage pushed him up, made him lash out again.

'Fucking bitch.'

'You ain't seen nothin', big boy.' Joyce jumped out of range. She stood for a moment, watching him, seeing in her mind all the damage she could do, frightening herself with her capacity for violence. Put him out now, quickly. Mark his face. Make them wonder. She waited for him to lunge, caught his good arm by the wrist, doubled it back to the armpit, in sankyo, heard the scream of pain. She held him powerless in her grip, then she threw him, head first, into a parked car. He slumped to the floor, bleeding.

Joyce jogged away. She rolled off her balaclava, turned down a side street, and slowed to a walk in Kensington Church Street. Her breathing eased. A few yards ahead, a smartly dressed man in his thirties clattered down the steps of his house on his stud-soled shoes. Joyce formed her lips into a smile as she passed him. The man smiled back uncertainly. With her halo of blonde hair, her rosy cheeks, and the terrible gleam in her eyes, Joyce looked like a darkling angel.

CHAPTER 25

Paul Keith arrived at the office at five past seven. He set down his briefcase and removed the lid from the styrofoam cup of coffee he'd bought at Birley's. Three days away from Goldsteins had been heaven. Now he was sick with nerves to be back, and had forgone his usual bran muffin. He took a tentative sip of coffee, opened his filing cabinet and reached down to take out Hull's book on derivatives. It was then that he saw the splintered wood of Rankin's desk. He pulled open the drawer, and saw rows of empty holders where files should have been. The bile rose to his mouth as he looked round frantically for Wallace or Rankin or Helen. He checked Helen's desk. Splintered. He checked Wallace's, forced. He sat, in shock, waiting for the others to arrive. Seven thirty came and went and he watched a stream of traders arrive at their desks. At seven fifty, there was still no sign of the others. He wanted to go and warn someone that they hadn't come in, but he knew that Wallace and Rankin would give him a bollocking for letting on to anyone else that they hadn't been there to cover the desk.

The desk's trading lines began to ring. They soon became a braying chorus. He tried to answer one or two but he couldn't keep up.

By eight thirty, his panic threatened to overwhelm him. He began to wonder if the whole desk had done a flit. He took out the Goldsteins home directory, rang Helen, Rankin and Wallace. No answer.

At eight forty-five, the worst possible person on the entire trading floor, the one person in the world he least wanted to see, appeared. He swore he could feel the floor trembling, and the air pulsating with the force field that seemed to surround her, before he looked up with dread to see Zaha Zamaroh sashaying towards him, lipstick gleaming. She took in Keith sitting at the trading desk frantically fielding calls. She stopped and fixed him with a Medusa stare.

'What are you doing alone on the desk? Where are the others?'

Her voice had the natural carrying power of a leader used to addressing thousands of teeming followers in ancient squares. She could shout from one end of the trading floor to the other, but now she spoke quietly, in the perfectly enunciated English taught as a second language in Britain's best boarding schools. A trace of accent remained, a slight hissing on the sibilant letters.

'They're not here.'

'I can see that. Where are they?'

'They haven't come in.'

'Are you trying to tell me that Wallace, Jencks and Rankin are all off the desk on the same day?'

'Er, yes.'

'Where are they?'

'I don't know. I tried them at home and no one answered. I think they went skiing. Glacier skiing. Perhaps the weather was bad. Couldn't get back.'

'They would have rung in then. Keep calling them at home. When traders ring, apologise, say there's no one on the desk yet. Expecting them later. When they deign to show their rancid faces, send them to me.'

Zamaroh turned on a stilettoed heel and strode off. Keith answered the phones, said his piece, eyes searching the floor, praying every minute that the others arrived before Zamaroh exploded.

Zamaroh reappeared at eleven thirty. Paul Keith sat alone at the desk, staring at the flickering screens. The remorseless phones had finally fallen silent as counterparties came to the conclusion that Rankin, Jencks and Wallace had all awarded themselves sickies.

'Well?' asked Zamaroh, as if Keith were responsible for the empty desk.

'Nothing. I've been calling them at home all morning.'

'Not *one* of them is home?'

Keith shook his head.

'And you have no idea where they might be?'

'No.'

'They didn't leave contact numbers?'

'Only Helen and Andy were going away. And they didn't leave numbers.'

Zamaroh's face went rigid with control.

'Stay on the desk. Keep up the story that they'll be in later.'

Keith nodded, stared at the floor, cleared his throat.

'Er, before you go, there's something else.'

Zamaroh took a step closer, towering over Keith.

'Three of the desks have been broken into. And it looks like some files are gone.'

Zamaroh's eyes widened like venus fly traps. The noise of the trading floor drained away. For a few moments, all Keith could hear was the blood pounding in his ears.

'Show me,' hissed Zamaroh.

Keith pointed out the splintered wood.

'Why didn't you tell me about this immediately?'

Keith tried to speak. Zamaroh cut him off.

'Have you told anyone else about this?'

'No.'

'Keep it that way. Total security. Any idea who might have broken in?'

'Er, no, not really.'

Zamaroh gave him a searching look, then turned and stalked back to her office. She picked up her telephone and called James Savage.

'James, it's Zaha. We need to talk.'

'Zaha. I'm expected for lunch at the Bank. Can't it wait?'

'No. It can't.'

Savage gave a sigh of annoyance. 'Come up.'

Savage was gazing out of the huge window of his corner office when Zamaroh entered. As usual, the chief executive was wearing an immaculately cut suit, evidently Savile Row. But there was something rakish, not quite establishment about it. Perhaps it was the richness of the navy blue, unfaded, uncreased, seemingly new, like all his suits, or else it could have been that the pinstripes were just a tad too wide. Maybe it was just the thick silver hair, swept back, Tarzan-like. There was a power to the man that filled the room, even when his attention was apparently directed to the skyline of the City of London.

Savage turned slowly, gave Zamaroh a brief smile. Strange, she thought, Savage's tendency to keep his eyes almost completely closed. It was as if he wanted to keep the world out. Odd in someone who was so tangibly a man of the world; sophisticated, knowing, cynical. Perhaps too cynical, perhaps he'd seen too much. Savage approached slowly, his lizard eyes on Zamaroh. He was one of the few people in Goldsteins who was not intimidated by her.

'What is it?'

'Three members of the derivatives desk didn't turn up for work this morning. A trainee's been ringing them all morning. There's no reply at their homes.'

'Three out of one hundred. Undesirable, but hardly remarkable. What's your point?'

'Hugh Wallace, Andy Rankin and Helen Jencks. They all sit together in a kind of triangle with Wallace at the apex. Incestuous, don't mix so freely with the rest of the desk.'

'Are you suggesting they've defected?'

'Each of their desks has been broken into. Several files are missing.'

Savage winced, stared at Zamaroh through the narrowest of slit eyes. 'Who knows about this besides you?'

'Just the trainee who reported it, Paul Keith. He claims not to know what's going on. Seems shellshocked.'

Savage called to his secretary. 'Evangeline, get Michael Freyn in here.'

The security chief, Michael Freyn, had his office on the same floor as Savage's. The proximity of Security to Execution revealed the new importance of the function at a time when internal fraud, mass defections of key staff, bugging, electronic theft and money laundering were growing threats.

Freyn appeared in under a minute. He nodded to Zamaroh, and

took a seat. His eyes bore the sombre alertness of a man who was only ever called in when there was a problem.

Savage turned to Zamaroh. 'Get the trainee up here.'

Zamaroh dialled the desk's number. Keith answered with a dull 'Special products'.

'Come up to Mr Savage's office. It's on the tenth floor.'

Keith arrived and hovered nervously outside the door until Savage beckoned him in. He manoeuvred his long skinny frame in through the door and, invited by Savage, into a seat. Freyn ranged his eyes over Keith.

'It seems we have a problem,' said Savage. 'Zaha informs me that Hugh Wallace, the derivatives structurer, and derivatives traders Andy Rankin and Helen Jencks, failed to turn up for work this morning.'

Freyn gave a small nod at the last name.

'None of them rang in, and there's no reply at their homes. Paul Keith here' – Savage acknowledged Keith to Freyn for the first time – 'has told Zaha that he doesn't know what's going on, but seems to imply from the look on his face and by the way his hands keep shaking that something is going on, not least of which is the fact that Wallace's, Rankin's and Jencks's desks have been broken into. Several files are missing.'

'When did this happen? asked Freyn, getting to his feet and taking a stride across the office towards Keith.

Keith shrank visibly into his seat.

'I'm not sure. The desk was fine when I left on Friday. When I came in this morning I noticed it.'

'What time d'you get in?'

'Five past seven.'

'Is that when you usually arrive?'

'Usually around that time. Perhaps ten minutes later. Thought I'd get a head start.'

'When did you tell Ms Zamaroh about your desk?'

'Er, I think it was around eleven.'

'You waited four hours?'

Keith took a long breath, almost as if he were gathering himself for some sort of run-up. 'Things were bad enough already, with the traders not coming in. I had to answer the phones. I know I should have said something earlier. I knew it would cause a fuss. Just trying to put it off.'

Zamaroh felt a sudden pity for Keith who looked as if he were about to wet himself. Freyn was one of the few people in the organisation for whom Savage opened his eyes. He was six foot three inches of solid muscle, forty-two, an ex-Parachute Regiment sergeant. Choleric. White skin, thinning red hair.

'Have you told anyone on the floor about any of this?' Savage asked Keith.

'No. Just Ms Zamaroh.'

'Not a word of this gets out. Understand?'

Keith nodded.

'Do you have anything to add?'

'Er, no.'

'Right. Back downstairs. Stay on the desk, be ready to help with our enquiries, but do not answer the phones.'

'You think it's dirty?' Freyn asked Savage after Keith had left.

'Looks that way.'

'Jencks?'

'Could be all three of them.'

'What would you like me to do?'

'Get three men from Security to visit Wallace's, Jencks's and Rankin's homes. If they *are* at home, I want them dragged in here unless they're on their deathbeds.'

Freyn nodded.

Savage turned to Zamaroh. 'Get the head settlements honcho –'

'Kevin Anderson,' supplied Zamaroh.

'Get him to go over the desk's books and tickets and look for anything abnormal. Find out what files are missing. Get a couple of secretaries manning the desk's phones. They're to say the traders are off sick. Not a great excuse, but we don't have much choice.'

Zamaroh and Savage exchanged looks. The spectre of Barings hung over them.

'What about notifying Compliance?' asked Zamaroh. Compliance was the legal department of the bank, charged with policing its probity.

'Let's find out whether this is a compliance issue before we go stirring up a nest of vipers,' said Savage, eyes holding hers, defying contradiction. Zamaroh nodded. The court politics were beginning, the bank's reputation, Savage's job and hers on the line.

CHAPTER 26

Karen Rankin was in the middle of administering painkillers and tranquillisers to her husband when the ring of the intercom interrupted her. She picked up the receiver with a curse and a frown.

'Yes?'

'Mrs Rankin?'

'Who's this?'

'My name's Bill Pittam. I'm from Goldsteins, Mrs Rankin, Security. I wondered if I might talk to you.'

'Look, I'm busy. What do you want?'

'Could you come to the door please, Mrs Rankin? I can't hear very well on this thing.'

Pittam was one of Freyn's ex-Para corporals. Built like a bulldog, gentled by the Pentecostal church, relentless in his duty. He waited patiently. Finally he heard a curse and a dull thud as the intercom went dead, then there was the click-clack-click of high heels on tile floors and the door was thrown open in his face. Karen Rankin stood framed, one hip thrust forward and her face hardened in anger.

'OK. What is it you want?'

'I wondered if you might know where I can reach your husband?'

'Oh, that's just great. He doesn't turn up for work one day and they send a bloody security guard to check up on him. What is this?'

'I'm sorry, Mrs Rankin. I know this is a bit of an intrusion, but I need to talk to your husband.'

'All right then,' she shouted, stepping back from the door. 'You want to talk to him, come on then. See for yourself he's not playing truant.' She marched off down the hallway, up the stairs, calling out as she went, 'Andy, there's a security man from Goldsteins to talk to you.'

Pittam hurried after her, pausing as she turned back to him at the top of the stairs.

'You've got five minutes, then you're out of here.'

He nodded. 'Thanks, Mrs Rankin.'

He followed her into the couple's bedroom, pausing with a start when he saw Andy Rankin lying in bed with a black eye, swollen lips and nose, and a cast on his arm.

'What happened to you?'

'Who the hell are you?' muttered Rankin, his voice faint.

'Sorry. My name's Bill Pittam, Mr Rankin. I'm from Security at Goldsteins. We got a bit worried when you didn't turn up for work this morning.'

'How nice of you.'

'Can I ask you what happened, sir?'

'What does it look like? I got beaten up this morning on the way to work.'

Pittam nodded at the cast on Rankin's arm. 'I take it you've had proper medical attention, sir?'

''Course he bloody well has,' answered Karen. 'I took him to casualty. Broken arm, broken nose, contusions to scalp. Doctors said he was in shock. Had to have complete rest for a few days. Which is exactly what he was getting till you turned up. You still haven't told us why you're here.'

Her husband feared that he might know all too well why the man was here. He turned his face into the pillow and yelped with pain.

'I was told to ask you to come into the office, Mr Rankin.'

'For God's sake.'

'It's all right, Kar,' said her husband. He glanced back at Pittam. 'I think you'd better tell me what's going on.'

'I don't know, guv. All I was told was to come here, see if you was here, and ask you to come to the office. Mr Savage asked my boss and my boss asked me. They said to get you in there unless you was on your deathbed.'

'All right,' said Rankin. 'You've delivered your message. I'm not going anywhere today. I can hardly walk and I keep throwing up. I'll ring the office and find out what the hell's going on.'

'Who did it, sir? Muggers or what?'

'How the hell do I know who it was?' snapped Rankin.

'Right. That's enough.' Karen Rankin nodded at the door, then marched Pittam out of the house.

Andy Rankin stared up at the white ceiling, reached out his arm with a grimace, picked up the telephone and rang the desk. A strange female voice answered. He resisted the urge to ask who she was. 'Hugh Wallace please.'

'Who's calling?'

'A friend.' Rankin had no desire to identify himself till he knew what was going on.

'I'm afraid Mr Wallace isn't in today.' A wave of panic rose up through Rankin's nausea.

'Er, Helen Jencks then.'

'Miss Jencks is off the desk today.'

'Paul Keith?' The panic heaved at his chest.

'Mr Keith is unavailable.'

'Where the hell are they?'

Slight note of disapproval in the officious voice. 'They're off sick, I'm afraid.'

'Andy Rankin as well?' he asked quickly.

'Andy Rankin as well,' the voice answered primly. Rankin put the phone down and collapsed back into his pillows. His wife walked in, and started at the look on his face.

'What's happened.'

'Wallace and Jencks are off work too.'

'That sounds a little odd, but it's hardly the end of the world.'

Rankin shrugged, then winced with the pain in his ribs.

'That's it?' she asked.

'That's it.'

Karen watched him, transparent in his lying, before turning away and leaving the room, sensing that this was one of those occasions when a lie was preferable to the truth, trusting her husband with a few days to sort out whatever lay hidden.

Rankin stared painfully at his wife's back, then reached once again for the phone and rang Wallace at home. All he got was the answerphone.

CHAPTER 27

Helen awoke suddenly. The scent of lemon, mixed with frankincense, blew in through the slats of the shutters. She knew that smell, the tang of aftershave. Her father's aftershave.

She jumped out of bed, wrapped herself in a towel, went to the door, opened it and looked out. The rising sun lit the figure of Maldonado, walking away from her cottage, towards his house. She pulled the door to, watching him through a two-inch gap, until he disappeared. She circuited the cottage once, bare feet damp on the dew. Laughed at the tricks her senses played.

She went back to her bedroom, dropped the towel on the floor, and stood before the mirror, pondering her naked reflection. Her natural curves were made more abundant than normal by an extra ten pounds of fat. Her skin was pale, and her eyes were swollen and bloodshot. She was hungover, and she knew that if she sprinted she would pull up coughing, her chest tight with the tar of twenty cigarettes a day.

But now she was freed of the daily slavery of the office, and she no longer needed to drink to accompany Roddy, or to anaesthetise herself to his friends. She didn't need the balm of nicotine to ease her over a bad trade at work, or to kick-start her in the early morning. Her old props were debilitations, and she had no excuse for them now. She could manufacture new ones easily enough, but the thought of going on like that repulsed her. Her new freedom carried infinite scope for destruction, or the chance to start again, to reinvent herself.

Back in London, she'd been trapped in a persona, even if it was her own, by the perceptions of friends and colleagues. An accumulation of inert objects helped to define her: flat, car, clothes, the books she read, the writing paper she used, each was part of a code used by social observers such as Roddy. Then there were the more vibrant traps such as her enunciation of vowels, crisp and sharp at work, though when relaxed, her voice would go off duty, and a soft laziness would ease to the surface, and fragments of Welsh singsong would dance their way in, relics of her father's voice. Then there was the way she sat, straight-backed and alert. All conspired so that she could not simply awake one morning and put on a new persona, reinvent herself in the latest fashion as she had done, so many times before, with Joyce.

In their teenage years, they had been experts at experimenting with the superficial. She remembered their shopping expeditions to Miss Selfridge, chasing each other round the rails for the latest fashion. They spent hours twisting and preening for the mirror, and for all the other girls in the communal changing rooms. Then they would emerge, finally and triumphantly, with the perfect new image swinging gaily in gaudy plastic bags. After that, if they could manage it, they would sneak in under age for a half-pint of lager in the pubs on Oxford Street to make eyes at the boys, to giggle and to dream.

Later that night they would try out the potency of the new outfits, clothes that always were much more than that: symbols of money, of independence (her mother never would have permitted such a choice), and of womanhood. Robes of magic that transformed and bewitched, and granted the putative women their first taste of the power of their sex. Their beautiful smooth bodies were unmarked, and already at odds with experience. The signs of wear, the cost of living, did not show unless you knew to look very closely at their eyes, or at the set of their mouths. But they had known, had seen the changes, knew the limits of disguise.

Later, at sea, she'd had the chance to reinvent herself, but her scope was circumscribed by her name, which seemed to be known across continents. She'd chosen never to deny her father. Whatever she was or did would be seen as a reaction, more in the way of compulsion than free choice, as if it were inevitable that she be a product of his notoriety, marked and moulded by it, and that presumption of inevitability probably made it so. Until now, she had never deliberately set out to experiment with the hidden contours of personality. With exile came a kind of freedom, lonely, and exhilarating.

She dressed in a swimming costume and shorts, and headed for the pool, tucked away discreetly in a corner of the huge garden. She stood on the sand-coloured stone and stretched, the early morning air flowing coolly over her skin while the sun's rays rose over the treetops and warmed her.

She began her old yoga routine. Her muscles ached and protested, she'd stiffened up badly on the long flight from London, and yesterday she'd not done much save walk round the garden, eat, and sleep. She persevered for thirty minutes until she could move and breathe without restraint. When she stopped she could feel her limbs tingling, as if the blood had just started to flow. Next she did fifteen minutes of floor exercises to build strength. Then, with a quick smile, she stripped off her shorts and took a running dive into the swimming pool.

The water felt wonderful against her sweating skin. She swam thirty lengths, switching between the crawl, backstroke and breaststroke, then she hoisted herself from the pool in one swift movement and stood dripping in the sun.

She gazed at the beauty of the garden, still and harbouring around her. The only sounds were the gentle lapping of the pool and the sweetness of birds singing from the banana trees. As she walked across the garden, back towards her cottage, she was ambushed by the sound of gushing water. It was a wild, inappropriate sound. She walked round a crescent of head-high bushes, narrowly avoiding a pipe pulsing out a stream of water onto the grass. She watched fascinated as a gardener directed another pipe amidst a lattice of tubes which criss-crossed the garden, spewing water.

'*Qué pasa?*' asked Helen, feeling like an extra in a spaghetti western.

'*Inundación de agua,*' replied the gardener; a flood, keeping the garden green. Helen was fascinated by the lakes of water that flowed over the grass, only to be soaked up moments later, as if the ground had a ravenous thirst. She walked closer to the main house and was surprised to find herself ankle deep in water. An entire area, about two hundred square feet, lay sodden, bathing her feet as she walked over it. Odd how the garden didn't drink up here, she thought, wandering with refreshingly cool feet over the little swamp, which ended abruptly with the drier grass.

She headed back to her cottage and took a long hot shower, finishing with a blast of cold. The blood raced around her body, and a hint of colour glowed in her cheeks. She flicked through her clothes – beige, black and cream – her British uniform, mocked by the riot of colours in the garden.

She began to make a mental list of what she needed, expanding it rapidly to what she wanted: shorts, trousers, dresses, jerseys, skirts, face cream, scent, books, everything, and all different. Today she would go into Lima, to ring Dai, to explore, and to buy her new things. She began to feel calmer, restored by her exercise, comforted by the beauty of the garden. The fears of the past few days seemed to be falling away from her.

She put on a sand-coloured cotton dress and, her hair still wet, walked out into the garden. Pepelucho, magnificent in azure and gold, was screaming, for no other reason than the joy of it. She had never before felt outclassed by a macaw. Paying obeisance, she walked up to him.

'How are you, beautiful? You are so gorgeous, d'you know that?' The macaw strutted back and forth along the roof of his giant cage in a manner that suggested he did know. He gazed down his great curved beak at her, an interloper in his domain, appraising her closely, as if unsure whether she should be repelled or conquered.

'Bye then.' In the controlled jungle of the garden, she walked amidst palms, and azucena trees, their white blossoms hanging like inverted lilies, filling the air with a heady scent. Tree fronds, soft as velvet, hung down to head height, and she trailed her hands among them.

She sat down alone to breakfast on the terrace of the main house, which Carmen delivered with smiling efficiency. She had coffee with fried bacon, egg, tomatoes and toast, followed by a great, sweet white fruit she had never seen before, *chirimoya*, according to Carmen. After breakfast, she sneaked round to the dog pen carrying scraps of bacon.

The dogs were lined up along their bars, looking only marginally less murderous than the day before.

'Hey, girls, how are you?' Helen murmured, moving closer.

'You're pets at heart, aren't you? No more psychopathic than I am.' A branch stirred in the warm breeze, brushing her cheek. She pulled it down, held her nose to white star flowers that smelled like paradise. She breathed deeply. There was something almost narcotic about the scent. The dogs watched her, heads cocked. She pulled off the flower and held it out to each twitching nose. She remembered her father telling her as a child that a dog's sense of smell was thousands of times greater than that of a human. The dogs stepped back. They almost seemed to be smiling.

'Blew your minds too, huh?' asked Helen. Bathed in sunlight and the dizzying scent, she stayed with the dogs, murmuring gently. She fell silent when she heard the heavy footfall of someone passing, out of sight. She waited until the sound faded, then threw bacon to each dog.

'There you go, girls. Back tomorrow.'

Then she stopped by her cottage, gathered up her bag with wallet and passport, and walked resolutely to the main house.

Carmen looked up with a start as Helen walked into the kitchen. She gazed up at Helen, towering above her, with an expression of curiosity and distrust.

'Señorita?'

'Doctor Maldonado?'

Carmen shook her head.

'Taxi,' said Helen. Bugger Maldonado and his warnings about the dangers of Peru. Stuff lying low. Carmen looked doubtful, and glanced around as if for help.

'Telephone,' said Helen. 'Taxi.'

Carmen shook her head again.

'*Sí!*' said Helen. She glanced down to the work table at a letter addressed to Maldonado, and quickly memorised the address, finding out, for the first time, that she was somewhere called La Molina. She felt better for knowing that, even though she had no frame of reference for the address, save that it was forty minutes from Lima in the quiet of the night. Helen picked up the telephone and glanced back at Carmen.

'*Número.* For taxi.'

CHAPTER 28

A Volkswagen Beetle, about twenty years old, bright green, streaked red with rust, waited on the road. Helen got in, sat down, and opened up her verb book. In rusty Spanish, she said she would like to go to San Isidro, which her guidebook described as one of Lima's smartest areas, full of shops, restaurants, and offices. The taxi set off with a lurch. The driver drove fast and seemingly wildly, in a rhythm which Helen could not discern, but which must have existed, since they managed to avoid what would have been a series of collisions in London. When the car reached a crossroads, there seemed to be no obvious right of way, merely a system of barging, or nipping through on the exhaust of the car ahead.

They drove up a hill, and Helen recognised the satellite dish on the top from her night-time arrival. Below them, central Lima spread out under a pall of mist. In La Molina, it had been sunny. It was as if she was leaving one country for another, with the satellite dish marking the border.

They drove along wide streets, busy with the bewildering array of traffic seen only in third world countries: packed minibuses plying for trade, ramshackle taxis, some of which identified themselves with a handwritten nameplate in the windscreen, while others seemed like opportunistic drivers picking up anyone who waved his hand. There were huge, decrepit American gas guzzlers from the nineteen-fifties and sixties, which, in London, would have been expensively renovated and deemed the height of chic. Here they constituted not high fashion but necessity. Powering along in the mêlée were sleek Japanese cars, dark blue, with tinted windows, and expensive four-wheel drives. Occasionally a Porsche, invariably black and pulsing with disco music, would speed by.

Every time they stopped at a light, a hoard of street sellers would descend, touting everything from avocados and parrots to maps and books. The title of one rack of books, Helen noticed, was *El Típico Idiota Latinoamericano*. Great. If she'd been in some surrealistic French film, this would have been meant as a message, directly for her.

Tiny shops flanked the road, selling old mattresses, wooden furniture, rattan baskets, then there were the staples seen everywhere – tailors, launderettes, chemists, one of which seemed to be called 'Jesus of Nazareth'. They looked like the kind of shops that had been there for generations, handed down through the family, surviving on unpaid labour and slim profits. Hard goods shops, selling hi-fis, TVs and computers, dotted incongruously amidst the shops catering to the poor, were ostentatiously protected by security guards in brown uniforms and bullet-proof vests, toting pump-action shotguns.

After a while, the roads seemed to take on more order, and the sprawl of buildings knitted down into narrower streets. They passed interior design shops, bookshops, banks. The people were more smartly dressed here, but still they looked cold under the grey skies, and they walked with their eyes on some distant focus, as if they didn't really want to be here. The city seemed to be as unfriendly to many of them as it felt to Helen. This was not the South America she had imagined. There were no blue skies, no bright colours, no vibrancy amidst the walkers on the grey streets. Instead there was the roar of noise, the stink of pollution, and a sense of oppression. No one lingered. Everyone was going somewhere, but there didn't seem to be anywhere worth going. People's faces were blank, as if they could not risk exposure. Christ, where was Peru?

Helen heard, in her mind, Maldonado's sonorous voice: *Lima is not Peru*. Somehow she could imagine him giving her an ironic smile, as he watched her looking desperately out of the windows, scanning the crowds, searching. She almost mocked herself at the thought that she would find so easily. But still she searched for her father on the alien streets.

Suddenly the driver turned in his seat, taking his eyes perilously from the road.

'San Isidro.'

'How much in dollars?' asked Helen

'Twelve.'

'Here's ten.' Never pay what they ask, the rules of the third world again. No doubt she was still being ripped off at ten.

The driver nodded and took the money happily enough. Helen stepped from the car, slung her handbag over one shoulder, across her chest, and walked off down the street. She continued until she found a hotel adjacent to a small park full of gnarled olive trees. She went up to reception and asked in English if she could use one of their phones to call England.

'I'll leave a cash deposit if you like.' She smiled at the desk clerk, a man in his early twenties, good-looking, called Carlos, according to a name badge. 'Here's twenty dollars,' said Helen.

Carlos smiled back and spoke in perfect English. 'It's a bit irregular, since you're not a guest, but we have a conference room free. Five minutes. OK?'

'Great. Thank you.'

'By the time you're back here, I'll have the bill on my computer, and we can settle up then.'

Helen followed him up to a second-floor conference room and sat down to phone. Dai Morgan answered on the third ring.

'It's me.'

'Cariad! How are you?'

'I'm fine. Maldonado's place is fantastic. Somewhere called La Molina, about an hour from the centre. The garden is amazing.'

'How's Maldonado?'

'Seems fine.'

'Where you calling from?'

'A nice little hotel. In the centre. I didn't really feel I could use Maldonado's phones.'

'No. Good. And he's all right, is he?'

'He's perfectly charming when he's there, which isn't much. Any news?'

'Oh, I picked up a little something.'

'And?'

127

'It seems that Wallace and Rankin ran into a little trouble over the past twenty-four hours.'

'What kind of trouble?'

'The kind that lands you in casualty.'

'Oh, Dai! What've you been up to?'

'Nothing to do with me. Joyce. She saw it happen. Apparently. Rang me this morning with a full report.'

Helen burst out laughing. 'Saw it happen, I'll bet she did. That girl is unbelievable.'

'Wallace and Rankin believed it all right. Joyce practically admitted to rearranging their features. I don't think they'll be turning up to work for a day or two. When they do limp in, they'll have a job explaining their injuries.'

'Let them squirm. I can just imagine James Savage wrinkling his nose. You know Wallace is his nephew.'

'He's not!'

'Don't worry. Uncle James isn't one for nepotism, not when it comes to the bottom line, or Goldsteins' reputation. Joyce is a heroine. The muck'll really fly now and some of it's bound to land on Wallace and Rankin.'

'What goes around comes around.'

Helen fell silent.

'Cariad? Are you there?'

'I'm here all right.' Her mind began to race. 'I was thinking. You've just given me an idea.'

'What?'

'You know the money, in my voice account?'

'Yeaas.'

'Well, with Wallace and Rankin out of action for a few days, it seems a bit of a golden opportunity. Seems a shame to waste it . . .'

'I hope you're not suggesting what I think you are . . .'

'You bet I am. I'd like to move the money, to a number of other accounts, you know, in nice sunny places where they don't ask too many questions.'

'You mean steal it? Have you gone mad?'

'How can I steal my own money?'

'Be careful, Hel. Money's never meant that much to you. You'd do better just forgetting about it.'

'It's not so much the money, Dai, though I'd be a liar if I said the prospect of one point five mill didn't appeal. It's a bit of wickedness. I'd just love to see the look on those bastards' faces when they discover the money's gone. Strike one to the bastards for setting me up. Strike two to me, Dai. The beginning of my revenge.'

'I have a certain sympathy with that, but it's not just a question of click your fingers and it moves.'

'I know that.'

'So what d'you have in mind?' Dai felt a sort of enthralled horror at himself as an old sedition awoke.

'You have the network in place. All those offshore structures you've told me about, advising me how to manage my money. I knew all those long lectures would come in useful one day.'

'You listened?'

'Like a disciple.'

'And, let me guess, you'd like to make use of it?'

'Well. If I moved it to one of your banks, then you could move it on for me, wherever you thought fit, making it end up somewhere anonymous, with airtight banking secrecy.'

Dai thought for a while, and all she could hear was his pensive breathing. 'Hang on a sec.' He came back on the line a couple of minutes later. 'All right. I've thought of a way. Got a pen?'

She grabbed pen and paper from her bag. 'Yeah. Go ahead.'

He gave her his account details.

'Now, let's go through the ropes. How do you plan to make the transfer to my account?' he asked.

'Ring Banque des Alpes, now.'

'You've got their number with you?'

'It's in my bag, Dai, together with my passport and all those other little things I hoard. Luckily for me. It's past four their time, but I should get them. I'll give them my account number, recite my name.'

'They'll need more than that.'

'A signature no doubt.'

'Yes. They're bound to have one on file. Possibly in your name, possibly another.'

'I'd guess it's in my name, on the same principle that our friends made sure everything else was nicely documented in my name. They probably just photocopied my signature from my papers at the office, or learned how to forge it.'

'Perhaps. If you're prepared to risk it, we'll work on that basis. But if you run into trouble, if they seem suspicious, or tell you there's a problem, hang up and forget the whole thing. As soon as you give them details of my account, they'll have a paper trail to follow.'

'Compromising you.'

'The account I gave you can't be traced to me, but it could still cause complications. And there's another thing, Banque des Alpes might have been instructed, when your voice account was opened, to forward details of any transactions in it to our friends, via a PO box, perhaps. Records'll be kept, they'll find out.'

'Yeah. There is a PO box number. PO 793 475, in W8. Can you move the money on so there'll be no trace of it?'

'Of course. It'll only stay in the account I've given you for a matter of seconds. Then it'll whiz around the world. Everyone but I will lose track of it, until it comes to rest somewhere for you.'

'Are you sure this won't come back on you?'

'I can make sure. But your phone call has to go smoothly.'

Helen stared out of the window into the olive park.

She said her name out loud a few times to practise, and then dialled the number of Banque des Alpes.

'I'd like to transfer some money from my account,' she told the operator. 'Could you put me through please.' Through to whom, she didn't have a clue, but she used her best, most confident voice, and the operator responded without a qualm.

'Putting you through.'

There was a silence, of perhaps fifteen seconds, then a man answered the line, solicitous, and worryingly correct.

'Konrad Speck speaking. Can I help you?'

'Yes. I'd like to close out my account and move my money on please.'

'A complete withdrawal?'

'The lot.'

'Your account number please.'

Helen recited it, hearing as she did, the faint tapping of keys on a computer keyboard.

'Voice print please.'

'Helen Jencks,' she said with vigour. There was another pause, and Helen imagined the computer system flashing up warning lights. Finally Konrad Speck spoke.

'To where would you like to transfer your balance?'

Was this smooth? Should she give him Dai's account?

'Could you just tell me my balance please?'

'Certainly, Miss Jencks. You have one million four hundred and ninety-three thousand four hundred and fifty-seven dollars, and twelve cents, including interest.'

'Transfer it all,' she said, committing herself, 'to the following account.'

He read back the details she gave him.

'Yes. That's it.'

'Just one thing, Miss Jencks.'

Oh Christ, please, no.

'Your interest . . .'

'Yes?'

'If you wish to withdraw your money now, you will have to forfeit one month's interest of six thousand two hundred and twenty-two dollars, and there will be a three-hundred-dollar administrative fee for closing your account.'

She felt like laughing with relief.

'I understand.'

'When can we expect your follow-up letter?'

Oh shit. 'It might take a while.'

'The transfer will be effected when we receive your letter. Good day, Miss Jencks.'

'Er, just a moment,' she said quickly. Wallace and Rankin would soon return to work, possibly tomorrow. The transfer couldn't wait.

'Can't you do the transfer just on my verbal instructions?'

'Certainly not. We need your signature, and written proof of your intentions. You'll appreciate, for a largish transfer such as this, we have to follow security procedures.'

'What about a fax? If I sent you a fax now, could you do the transfer immediately?'

'Well . . .' She could hear more tapping of computer keys. 'We have operated on faxed instructions before on your account, but we'd prefer not to close it without a hard copy.'

'I'd be grateful if you could go with a fax . . .'

Another agonising wait.

'As you wish, Miss Jencks. If you fax it to me now, the transaction can be processed today. You have my private number.'

'Um, I've got it somewhere, but could you give it to me again, just in case?' She scribbled it down.

'Thank you, Herr Speck.' She hung up, shaking, and called Dai.

'How'd it go?'

'All right, I think. There's just one thing. He says he won't be able to move the money until he has written instructions. I can't wait that long.'

'So?'

'So I said I'd send him a fax.'

'That'll betray your whereabouts.'

'Not if you do it.'

'I can't forge your signature.'

'Yes, you can. I've seen you doodle other people's signatures before. You do it all the time, in your study. You know I've seen you do it.'

'Oh, Hel-len.' He always split her name in a Welsh lilt when exasperated. 'I'll have to fax the instructions on somewhere else and get them to fax Banque des Alpes, otherwise the fax'll be traced to me.'

'Can you do that?'

'Give me the fax number.'

CHAPTER 29

Bill Pittam arrived back at Goldsteins at three thirty and headed straight for Michael Freyn's office on the tenth floor.

'I saw Rankin. Not a pretty sight.'

'Wait,' said Freyn. He telephoned Savage.

'James, I have Bill Pittam here, he's just seen Rankin. Right. I'll do that.'

Five minutes later, Freyn, Pittam and Zamaroh congregated in Savage's office. Freyn introduced Pittam to Savage and Zamaroh.

'Right,' said Pittam. 'I went to Mr Rankin's home. His wife answered the door, didn't want to let me in. Very uppity. Took me upstairs to see her husband. He was lying in bed, looking like a dog's breakfast. Broken arm, broken nose, in shock. Said he'd been beaten up this morning, on the way to work. Missus took him to casualty. I asked him to come in to work, but it didn't look like he could have. Said he was throwing up still. Did look pretty bad.'

'Was he mugged? What happened?' asked Zamaroh.

'He didn't say. I asked him, but he just said he didn't know who it was.'

Zamaroh gave him a disgusted look.

'Mrs Rankin was very forceful,' he said to Savage, ignoring Zamaroh.

Zamaroh gave a snort. 'Mrs Rankin should remember who pays her dress bills. I'll go round there.'

Savage stroked his chin, peering at Zamaroh and Freyn as if they were rough stones and he were a cutter.

'Take Michael with you.'

Zamaroh raised her eyebrows, Savage lowered his. Zamaroh

conceded with a sweet smile. Savage watched her head back down to her seventh-floor kingdom.

'Keep an eye on her,' he said to Freyn. 'She'll do most of the talking, throw her weight about, try to terrify the guy. Give you a good opportunity to watch him. She can be Ms Nasty, and you'll be Mr Nice. I know that's not your customary role, but I really can't see Zamaroh being Ms Nice, can you?'

'How does she get away with it?'

'Because she's good. She understands what goes on down there, she's on top of it, she's a bloody good trader herself, and she's scared of no one. Most managers are scared shitless of the successful traders. Zamaroh knows she's better, brighter, and nastier than them. They know it too. And she understands systems, and settlements. She's totally hands on.'

More like hands round the neck, thought Freyn.

Zamaroh and Freyn shared a taxi, exchanging scarcely a word. Zamaroh spent the entire journey from the City to Kensington talking on her mobile, checking with Kevin Anderson, the head of settlements, if he had uncovered anything suspicious in Rankin and Jencks's trading tickets.

'What's he got?' asked Freyn.

Zamaroh shook her head. 'Nothing. He's probably not looking hard enough.'

'Maybe there's nothing to find.'

'Is that what you think?'

'I think we don't know enough yet,' said Freyn, looking at Zamaroh for as long as he could stand. He finally turned to stare out of the window, wishing he was wearing his nuclear and biological warfare gear.

The taxi pulled up in Vicarage Gardens.

'Million nine,' announced Zamaroh, eyeing Rankin's house. 'That's a bit rich.'

She was enjoying this, thought Freyn. The whole bloody trading floor could be going up in smoke and she'd be dancing a war dance to conquer the flames.

'Time for a little interrogation,' she said. 'Ring the bell.'

'Ring it yourself, or will you break your nails?'

Zamaroh froze in surprise then broke into a slow smile. She gave Freyn a look of admiration, running her eyes up and down the length of his body as if seeing him for the first time. Freyn almost felt himself blush.

'Cocky!' She reached out a purple talon and pushed the bell.

There was a long silence and then Karen Rankin's angry voice.

'Yes?'

'Mrs Rankin?'

'Who the hell is it now?'

'It is Zaha Zamaroh,' she said, icily clipped. 'From Goldsteins.'

'I know who you are.'

Zamaroh pulled a prissy face at the intercom, as if to mimic Karen Rankin. The intercom went dead. Moments later, Karen appeared.

She opened the door, glanced at Freyn, clearly decided he was a side show, and focused her attention on Zamaroh. Freyn stood back and watched the two women. Each eyed the other. The stillness of their gaze and their silence hid mutual microscopic calculations that would have begun with *is she prettier than me, is she better in bed, and does she have more brains?*

They seemed in those seconds to come to some mutual accommodation, as if each knew she was dealing with a fair adversary. Freyn was amazed. Karen Rankin looked tall, thin, fashionable and bitchy. A lady who lunched. Fodder for Zamaroh, but here were both women with veiled smiles in their eyes. He failed to see what Zamaroh could divine in Karen Rankin: the ruthless will and calculation, jaw set as a general's.

'Why don't you come in?' Karen stood back so that Zamaroh could sail through. Freyn stretched out his hand.

'I'm Michael Freyn, Mrs Rankin, head of security.' He saw a faint flicker of worry cross her face. She shook his hand and gestured to him to go in.

'Please wait a moment. I'll go and ask Andy if he'll see you.'

Freyn hid a smile. Hostilities had begun.

'He's extremely unwell, you know,' Karen said over her shoulder.

'Physical assault is generally thought bad for the health,' countered Zamaroh.

'I wouldn't know,' replied Karen. 'I don't go in for it much myself.' She went upstairs to the bedroom to wake her husband.

'Andy.' She spoke surprisingly gently. 'That bitch Zamaroh is downstairs. She's with someone called Michael Freyn. He says he's the head of security.'

'Oh, God.' Andy rubbed his eyes.

'You don't have to speak to them.'

'Yes, I do.'

Karen squatted down beside the bed so that her face was level with his. 'Look, I don't know what the hell's going on here, I don't know what you have or haven't done, but whatever it is, hold yourself together, all right. I'm here, I'm right behind you. I'll do my stuff. You just bloody well do yours. Got it?'

Rankin stared into his wife's eyes. He drank her in.

'Bring them up.'

Zaha and Freyn followed Karen up the stairs. She stood back to let them enter the bedroom and took up position by the door, as if ready to eject them at any moment. Zamaroh considered and quickly rejected asking her to leave.

'Zaha,' wheezed Rankin.

'What the hell's going on?'

'I got beaten up this morning. I'm sure you already know that.'

'You couldn't even pretend at what I know. Do you know where Wallace and that girl Jencks are?'

'Aren't they at work?'

'Are you concussed?'

'Yes, I am. I was thrown head first into a car if you want to know.'

Nice one, thought Zamaroh, feeling a certain empathy with his assailant.

'So, do you know where Wallace and Jencks might be?'

'They're not at work?'

'Quick on the uptake today, aren't we? No. They're not at work. They haven't rung in, and they're not at home.'

Rankin rubbed his forehead with the back of his hand.

'I haven't a clue where they are.'

'Is there anything you'd like to tell me?'

'Like what?'

'Like anything about the desk.'

'What about it?'

'Are you having any problems? Trading problems? Losses we don't know about?'

'Absolutely not. How dare you –'

Zaha interrupted. 'All right, all right, calm down. What about Jencks?'

'No. Not that I know.'

'Wallace, has he been behaving strangely?'

'No, he hasn't. Well, you know, he's always a bit strange. Look, my head is beginning to throb.'

'Sleep it off. We'll expect you in at seven tomorrow.' Zamaroh turned to Freyn.

'What exactly happened this morning, Mr Rankin?' asked Freyn.

Rankin gave an almighty sigh. 'I left the house at six –'

'You always leave at that time?' asked Freyn.

'Pretty much.'

'And then?'

'I'd hardly gone five steps and this woman comes out of the basement next door.'

There was a sharp expression of surprise from Karen, Freyn and Zamaroh.

'A woman?' asked Freyn.

'Yes. A bloody woman.'

'What did she do exactly?'

'Oh, for God's sake. I feel sick just thinking about it. I'll give you a blow-by-blow account tomorrow if that's what you really want. Now I just want to rest.'

Freyn nodded. 'All right, Mr Rankin. We'll continue this tomorrow at the office.'

'What's all this about anyway? What's going on? What's happening to the desk's positions, Zaha?'

'I'm running the positions. Perhaps they'll finally make some money.'

'Listen, Ms Zamaroh . . .' Karen Rankin took a step closer.

Zamaroh held up her hand. 'Sorry. Out of line. Home territory.'

'What *is* going on?' Karen asked. 'I don't appreciate having the head of the trading floor and the head of security paying home visits.'

137

'Missing traders, Mrs Rankin,' answered Freyn.

'Ah, I see. You think it's another Nick Leeson. Well, don't you worry. I can put your mind at rest. My husband is no Nick Leeson. He's a decent man. If he were up to anything, you can bet your bloody bank I'd know about it. And I know nothing of the sort.'

Zamaroh and Freyn could imagine that easily enough.

'It's all right, Mrs Rankin,' said Freyn. 'We'll be going now. Sorry to intrude.' He moved to the door.

Zamaroh gave Rankin a long searching look. 'We'll continue this tomorrow. At seven. I'll send a cab.'

Karen watched them leave. 'She'll send a cab. All heart, isn't she?'

'She thinks I won't turn up.'

'Oh, you'll be there, even if I have to carry you.'

Zamaroh and Freyn headed back to the City.

'What do you think?' asked Zamaroh.

'Sounds like a man who's been beaten up. Groggy, slow.'

'He's always like that.'

'Well, how'd he sound to you?' asked Freyn.

'Too stupid to be up to something.'

She rang Kevin Anderson again. 'Anything?' she asked, without bothering to identify herself. She listened for a few moments. 'Well, look harder.'

Next, she rang Savage. 'Rankin's concussed. Thicker than ever.'

'Could he be up to anything?'

'Settlements haven't found anything yet. I think Rankin's too stupid anyway.'

'Be careful, Zamaroh. You don't have a monopoly on intelligence. What about Helen Jencks? She's hardly stupid.'

'No, she's not,' she mused. She'd never approved of Jencks, beyond her ability to bring in a few million dollars each year. No academic pedigree, just a cool sharpness that she'd evidently picked up on the streets, or on her boats or playing her cards, or however she had misspent her youth. 'Any sign of her or Wallace?'

'No. That's what really worries me. The combination of Jencks and Wallace.'

'They are close. Always joking around. She seems to be the only person on the floor who understands him. She could easily influence him,' suggested Zamaroh. 'And we all know where her family predilections lie.'

CHAPTER 30

At five in the afternoon, Hugh Wallace managed to struggle from his hospital bed at St Mary's Paddington to make a phone call from the pay phone outside the ward. He rang the desk, and, without revealing his identity, got the news that Rankin and Jencks were off sick. The news, combined with the effort of standing, almost made him retch again. He fought to remember Rankin's home number, finally recalled it and dialled.

Karen Rankin answered.

'Karen,' said a hoarse voice she didn't recognise.

'Yes?'

'It's Hugh. Is Andy there?'

'Yes, he's here.'

'I need to speak to him.'

'He's supposed to be resting, Hugh.'

'Why's he resting? Why isn't he on the desk?'

'Why aren't you on the desk? And what's wrong with you, you sound awful?'

'I was beaten up last night.'

'Oh God, not you too.'

'What d'you mean?'

'Andy was beaten up this morning.'

'Oh shit. Look, Kar, I need your help. I'm in St Mary's Paddington. I've got to get out but I can't manage on my own. Barely stand up. Can you come and pick me up?'

'What the hell's going on? What's so urgent? If you're bad enough to be in hospital you should stay there.'

'Kar, listen, I can't talk now. Please, just come and get me.'

With the relentless force of character and brisk efficiency that terrorised and enthralled her husband, Karen Rankin got Wallace discharged by a ward sister who argued vehemently that it wasn't a good idea. It was only when Karen promised personally to supervise her patient's recovery that she relented. By then it was six thirty. Karen helped Wallace into the taxi she had ordered to wait outside the hospital.

Wallace sat down awkwardly. 'I've got to get to work.'

'Oh, for God's sake. And throw up all over your beloved desk. Get real. You're going home and, worse luck for me, it'd better be my home.'

'C'mon, Kar, I'm not that bad.'

'Listen, big boy, your smooth talk might have impressed the sister, but you can't fool me. If I hadn't held right onto you back there, you'd have fallen over.'

'Wait. I need to tell you something.'

'I don't want to know. I have a very nice life and I don't intend to change it. You've got tonight to recover, the pair of you, then you and Andy go in to work tomorrow and sort out whatever the hell it is needs sorting. And you'd better do a bloody good job. We've had Goldsteins' security and the head of the trading floor turning up at the house today.'

'What? Zamaroh came to see you?'

'Shut up and rest. Andy'll tell you.'

CHAPTER 31

At six o'clock, Paul Keith plucked up the courage to ask Kathy, Zamaroh's secretary, if she thought he might be able to go home soon.

'Not until my boss tells me. Then I'll tell you.'

'Might be hours.'

'Might be.'

'Look, I need to buy something for my supper, before the shops close. If I don't know how long I'm going to be stuck here . . . I just want to go to Marks & Spencer.'

Kathy gave him a look, half scorn, half pity. He wasn't the sort of man who gave dinner parties, or who'd know how to cook for himself. Neither could she imagine him curling up with a girl beside the fire and sharing an M & S salmon en croute, a roquette salad and a bottle of iced Chablis. She saw him as a man alone in office-sweaty socks tucking into a steak and kidney pie with a bottle of beer and *Coronation Street* for company.

'Wait a minute.' She rang through to Zamaroh.

'Sorry to disturb you, Ms Zamaroh. The trainee wants to go home. OK, I'll tell him.'

She cut the line and turned to Keith.

'Dream on.'

At six thirty, the head of settlements, Kevin Anderson, rapped on the glass door of Zamaroh's office. He was medium height, with a pared-down marathon runner's frame, wiry black hair and rimless glasses. He had the kind of quiet confidence that came with being good at his job, and a benign disposition, both of which were being eroded by attacks of short temper produced by overwork and contemptuous traders who viewed anyone in Settlements as a parasite living off their genius, until they made a trading error, when they wanted to be your new best friend. Anderson rapped again on the glass. Zamaroh finally looked up and beckoned him in with raptor eyes. He'd been giving her reports by telephone every half-hour. Regular visits to her office would have aroused suspicion.

'Close the door. What've you got?'

'Nothing. Can't find anything that seems off.'

'Well, look harder. I want you on this all night.' She glanced at her watch. 'Disappear in an hour so that your movements don't seem suspicious. Go eat some chips or whatever it is you feed yourself. Come back after nine. No one should notice you. Work until five, go home, get respectable then come back in to report to me at seven. If you come up with anything, here's my home number.' She tossed him a piece of paper. 'If there's something there and you don't find it, you'll be fired for incompetence, without a settlement, without a reference. You'll never work in the City again.'

Anderson stared at her with a look of hatred. She stared back until he was forced to look away.

'It's not that simple. It could take days to find something, if it's really well hidden. There are tens of thousands of tickets out there.'

'You'd better work fast then, hadn't you?'

Zamaroh dismissed him with her eyes and rang Savage.

'Settlements can't find anything.'

'Thank God for that.'

'Don't celebrate. It could be something well hidden.'

'That's comforting.'

An hour later, Zamaroh headed upstairs to Savage's office to brief him. She found Freyn there. She wondered what Freyn had on Savage, why the two men were so close. Savage only had to cough and Freyn would come running with a vaccine. Savage had probably had Freyn dig around and discredit his rivals for the post of chief executive. Savage was the best man for the job anyway, but it never hurt to have a bit of insurance.

'Settlements still haven't found anything dodgy,' she informed them. 'I've told Anderson to go and get dinner and come back when the floor's quieter. I don't want tongues wagging any more than they already are. He's going to work through the night. He'll ring me if he finds anything. Still no sign of the other two?' she asked Freyn.

He shook his head.

'What the hell's going on?' Zamaroh spoke to herself, enraged that here was a problem that neither intellect nor intimidation alone could solve.

'I hate to bring this up,' said Freyn, 'but should we be notifying the authorities?'

Savage shuddered. 'Don't even mention the word.' He got to his feet and walked round his desk so he was standing over Freyn. 'We have nothing to say to them. One trader got beaten up, the other two are probably in bed together having a rampant affair.'

Zamaroh burst out laughing. 'Jencks and Wallace? She may be common, but she's not desperate.'

'Shut up, Zamaroh,' said Savage. 'Her father might have been a crook, but at least he didn't plunder a kingdom.'

'How dare –'

'I've had enough of your act for one day. Shut up and concentrate. Freyn raised a serious point. If we suspect wrongdoing, we're duty bound to notify Compliance and the Bank of England. Now, I'm going to ask you formally, on the record, and your little kingdom down there might depend on your answer. Are you aware of any irregularities that suggest we have a problem with our books?'

Zamaroh had shut down all emotion and looked coldly back at Savage.

'Not as yet. But I can't give you an unconditional no. We might have missed something in the paperwork.'

'Do you think any of Goldsteins' money has disappeared, helped on its way by Helen Jencks, Andy Rankin or Hugh Wallace, or some combination thereof?'

'It's possible. Something's clearly going on. Perhaps Rankin did something to Helen and Wallace, threatened to report something, and they had someone beat him up. Perhaps it isn't even about money or Goldsteins. Perhaps you're right, perhaps Jencks was having an affair with one or both of them. Maybe this is all about sex.'

'And the broken locks on the desks, the missing files?' asked Savage. 'That brings us right back to the beginning, to something to do with trading.' He paused to look meaningfully from Zamaroh to Freyn. 'For the moment, we have nothing to report. To anyone. Is that understood?'

They nodded.

'I don't want one more person knowing about any of this than is strictly necessary,' Savage continued.

'Kevin Anderson's arranged for the locksmiths to come in at 2 AM to repair the desks so that no one sees them and starts gossiping,' said Zamaroh.

'Good. At least someone appears to be using his brain,' said Savage. 'Last thing we want is anything leaking. Christ, if the press got hold of this . . .'

CHAPTER 32

Zamaroh headed back downstairs and released Paul Keith. She watched him go with distaste. He was guilty of something, even if it was only ignorance of the exploits of his superiors. On a trading floor, it was always preferable to be a crook than a fool. The former provoked in many a covert admiration, while the latter induced almost universal contempt.

Keith quit the floor and raced off to Marks & Spencer to buy his chicken tikka marsala and ready chopped carrots and green beans, then he took the tube home to Chalk Farm in north London.

He arrived at his one-bedroom flat at eight thirty and rang Helen Jencks. No reply. Next he tried Andy Rankin. Karen answered.

'Got to speak to Andy.'

'And you are?'

'Paul Keith. I work with Andy.'

Karen had not met him socially, and did not feel inclined to grant him liberties of access.

'Do you now?'

'It's urgent.'

'Yeah, isn't it always? Wait there.'

Moments later, there was a click and a groggy voice spoke. 'Paul, hi.'

'Look, I don't mean to sound pushy but what's been going on? There's a real stew at the office.'

'Where are you?'

'I just got home.'

'Get in a cab and get over here.' Rankin gave him the directions and hung up.

*　　*　　*

146

Keith arrived forty minutes later. Karen Rankin showed him into the sitting room. Wallace lay on the sofa, wearing a borrowed tracksuit, staring out of his wounded face in palpable shock. Rankin sat slouched and battered in a cavernous armchair, the shadows of the room giving a morbid aspect to his face. Keith looked at them in disbelief. Karen Rankin looked from one man to another, then walked from the room as if she'd seen enough. She sat alone at the table in the dining room and stared out of the brightly lit window into the night.

Next door, Keith found his voice. 'What happened to you?'

'It's pretty obvious, I should have thought,' said Wallace, his voice staccato and jittery. 'We were beaten up. What happened at the office?'

'Well, for a start, the three of you don't turn up, and your desks have been broken into.'

'WHAT?' yelled Wallace. 'Mine and Andy's?'

'Yeah. And Helen's. Looks like about six files are gone from Andy's cabinet.'

Rankin didn't respond. Keith thought he looked drugged with his drooping eyelids and almost vacant stare.

'No one else's?' asked Wallace.

'Don't think so.'

'You reported it?'

'Had to, to Zamaroh. She'd already gone apeshit when none of you showed up.'

Wallace groaned. 'What did she say?'

'I thought she was going to turn me into salt when I told her. She went all icy calm and dragged me up to see James Savage and this security guy called Freyn.'

'Shit.'

Wallace's bruised eyelids began fluttering. 'So Helen Jencks didn't show up?'

Lying there, devoid of the armour of his idiosyncrasies, his face swollen and garishly bruised, his voice raw, Wallace seemed to Keith to have been peeled. In their short acquaintance, Wallace had never wasted any charm on Keith, never tried to hide his contempt. Now the balance of power had shifted. Wallace seemed to need something from Keith. Keith hated him for it.

'No. I rang her flat, there was no reply.'

Wallace fell silent.

'What's going on?' asked Keith.

'We don't know. Look, just, just go home, eat supper. We'll see you tomorrow. Er, yeah, thanks for coming.'

Keith eyed him with suspicion for a moment, then got up awkwardly.

'All right. Night.'

Wallace waited for him to go. Karen Rankin showed him out, came back, stood in the doorway of the sitting room, stared straight at her husband, her face unyielding. Wallace found himself thinking of Hillary Clinton, and how, so often it seemed, spouses might be better switching jobs. Karen closed the door and disappeared.

Her husband stared fixedly at the floor.

'I think we're in trouble.'

'The bitch that did this' – Wallace's gesture took in his face and Rankin's slumped body – 'implied it was for Helen.'

'Said the same thing to me,' replied Rankin.

'Six files are gone,' said Wallace, 'Helen Jencks is gone.' He seemed to be doing some kind of manic mental calculation, his eyes flickering with the effort of it.

'D'you think she found out what we were doing?' asked Rankin.

Wallace's face, already pallid, went whiter still.

'Have you got the voice tape?' he asked.

'What? The one with Helen's voice on it?'

'Yes, that one,' spat Wallace.

'I always keep it in my briefcase. I always keep it locked. There's a combination on the –'

'Ring Banque des Alpes, on the speakerphone. Play the message.'

Rankin did as instructed. The voice of Helen Jencks reciting her name and the account number rang like a ghost around the room. Rankin pressed ##1 on the keypad of the phone, electing to hear the balance in the account. The metallic computer voice spoke back to them.

'Balance as of 10.30 PM local time: zero.'

CHAPTER 33

Ian Farrell and Tess Carlyle sat in the glass palace that was Vaux-hall Cross, the new two-hundred-and-thirty-million-pound headquarters of the Secret Intelligence Service. Better known to insiders as Riverside, or Gloom Hall, it was located on the south bank of the River Thames at Vauxhall, from where it gazed imperiously north towards its Whitehall masters.

Farrell was Director of Counter Narcotics. He was fifty-two, well built, barrel-chested. His hair was silver, flecked with black, wiry and inclined to unruliness. He wore a moustache and full beard that gave him the air of a mariner. His eyes were dark brown, intelligent, quick to humour and irritation. In relaxation, they had a pensive tilt, as if he'd seen too many falls from grace. Thick eyebrows burdened his eyelids. He had a boxer's bulbous nose. His upper lip was almost completely hidden by the generosity of his moustache, an effect which gave him a pensive air, an impression added to by the deep wrinkles between his eyebrows. He was prone to ulcers of the stomach, a condition which had forced him, two years back, to abjure alcohol. He still yearned for whisky. Abstinence was a daily penance.

Carlyle was his deputy. Her face was well lined, sallow, slightly ravaged. She was in her late thirties, but there was a strange agelessness to her. Her energy, like a force field around her, was that of a woman in her early twenties starting out in her career, with the whole of the race to run. Her hair was shaggy, chestnut, shoulder-length. Her nose was slightly hooked; Farrell always thought she resembled a bird of prey. Her eyes were cool, clear-sighted. Eyes that had looked and seen and retained their compassion, eyes halfway between saint and heretic. There was in them a glimpse of the wisdom and pain of a thousand lifetimes.

It was Tuesday lunchtime, and Farrell and Carlyle were just finishing their daily briefing meeting, lengthened by the arrival over the bank holiday weekend of copious quantities of reports originating from desks scattered across the world. Carlyle sat in a black leather chair and held up an envelope. It was slim, light, the contents apparently innocuous. Carlyle, for all her sophistication and insight, smiled blithely, unaware of the fates contained within.

'From Favour,' said Carlyle. 'He's just surfaced from a month in the jungle.'

'What's he say this time?'

'Another coded warning.'

'About Maldonado?'

Carlyle nodded. 'A week ago, a joint Peruvian–Colombian–DEA op went down in the jungle in a place called Leticia, on the Peruvian–Brazilian–Colombian border. Something went wrong, the narcos appeared to have been tipped off. All but two of them got away; two DEA, three Peruvians and one Colombian were wasted. And one anonymous "observer". A friend of Favour's it would seem, from his SAS days, only this guy was still in the regiment.'

'Shit. Favour's going to be really gunning for whoever was behind it. And let me guess, he thinks it was Maldonado?'

Carlyle nodded. 'Thinks he tipped off the narcos. It was the el Dólar syndicate. Favour's been suggesting for months that Maldonado's cosy with them.'

Favour was the code name for Evan Connor, ex SAS, now a freelance agent in South America. Favour was run by Carlyle. For the last four months he'd been passing on warnings as to Maldonado's trustworthiness.

'Think there might be something in it?' asked Farrell.

'You have to remember, Favour and his kind like to fight the narcos head to head. He has a bias. He likes to sniff out evil, he would love to destroy it. I'm not so sure he's as comfortable with the concept of supping with the devil as we are. He'd like to tar Maldonado as bad, pure and simple. Of course Maldonado's bad, in part. He's the effective head of counter narcotics in a country which supplies sixty to eighty per cent of the world's coca. He has power, influence and access. He has the power of life. And death. Of course he's corrupt. It's impossible to play our game straight in that country. Question is, has he gone beyond acceptably corrupt?'

'And is he still on our side?' added Farrell.

'Unconditionally, I'd have to say no,' replied Carlyle.

'All right, enough of the moral relativism. Your man warns us not to trust him, think he's right?'

'Favour heard Maldonado was buying up large quantities of Moche artifacts on the black market, spending millions, which, he implied, came from deals with the narcos. For now it's just hearsay. Only time will tell. Maldonado's far too useful to drop in the meantime. Unless Favour comes up with some hard evidence. You want to fight drugs, you've got to deal with Maldonado. Love him or loathe him, we need him.'

'I just wish we could get closer to the man, get a real feel for him. Favour's access is only indirect. He's never met him. We need someone who's right in there with Maldonado.'

CHAPTER 34

'Cigarette?' Maldonado asked Helen, offering her his silver case, opened to reveal a neat twenty all laid out and waiting. Helen looked at the cigarettes with longing. She could feel one between her fingers, see the tip glowing reassuringly, taste the acrid smoke as it seeped into her lungs.

'No, thank you.'

'A drink then?' Carmen waited by his side holding a tray which carried two glasses of opaque liquid.

'Pisco sour,' said Maldonado. 'A national tradition.'

Helen took one. 'I know. I had three last night.'

Maldonado chuckled. 'You're looking remarkably well considering. What'll we drink to?'

Helen thought for a moment.

'Safe passage.'

'For whom?'

For my money, and me. She had a momentary image of Wallace and Rankin's bruised faces, and Joyce stalking away from them. She spluttered with laughter, covering it up with a sip of pisco. She felt a wonderful blaze of recklessness.

'Strong stuff.'

Maldonado smiled. A guard with a gun walked past the window. Helen watched him pass.

'Who is he?' she asked, taking another sip.

'A security guard.'

'I seem to see them everywhere, men with guns.'

'We do have a few, a vestige from our more violent days.'

'So why keep them?'

'Peru isn't London.'

'I've travelled a lot. I've never seen an armed presence like this before.'

He shrugged and took a sip of pisco sour.

'There's a lot of common crime.'

'So much so that you need two armed guards patrolling your garden?'

He put down his drink and studied her with a smile. Meanwhile another guard came into view, like the other brandishing a gun. Helen nodded towards the guard.

'A sub-machine gun?'

'A Heckler & Koch MP5, if you're interested.'

'Not really. I don't like guns.'

'Another routine for you to get used to. As you say, there are a lot of them here in Peru. You can't escape them. It's a breeding ground for crime, a country with such extremes of poverty and wealth. Did you see the shanties on your way from the airport?'

'Yes.'

'Most of them have no electricity, no water, typhoid, dysentery, cholera. Every so often the authorities come and bulldoze the pathetic cardboard shacks, because they're an eyesore.'

'Jesus Christ.'

'That's who we need. Not enough schools, not enough jobs, no way out for the people there. Many of them survive honourably, God only knows how. The others die, turn to crime, or terrorism.'

'Not hard to understand why,' said Helen.

'It's not, is it?'

'So what are you doing about it?'

'Hah!' Maldonado stretched out his hands and studied them. He shook his head and led Helen in to dinner.

They sat down at an old mahogany table. Helen, still wary of Maldonado, felt a keenness for his company that surprised her. He was so charming, this man, solicitous, learned, compelling, like a storyteller, weaving tales about excavations here and there, things he had discovered.

'Nothing beats it, crouching over the soil, brushing away the earth of centuries and you see a treasure lying there, untouched for two thousand years. You touch it, feel it with your own skin.

Ah! It's amazing.' The heaviness that seemed to dog his features vanished when he spoke of archaeology.

After dinner he got to his feet.

'Here, come with me. I want to show you some of the most beautiful things ever pulled from the earth.'

He led her into his study, threw a switch in the darkness, and two shelves lit up, leaving the rest of the room in darkness. She'd missed them on her exploratory foray into Maldonado's study the night before. Now she saw, gazing back at her, about twenty pottery figures, with expressions so humanly real she almost expected to see them blink. Silently eloquent, they told their own stories of grief and joy, illness and childbirth, master and slave. Two of them were mutilated, one was handless, the other appeared to have had its skin peeled off and its eyes pecked out by a winged beast that sat on its shoulder.

'The Moche,' said Maldonado, 'the finest ceramic art created by prehistoric man. They're portrait vessels, so much more compelling than paintings, don't you think?' He reached out and stroked them, one by one, his face softening as if he were touching live flesh. Helen thought of Roddy and his passion for his sculptures, but there was something more than obsession in Maldonado's eyes. There was love, and a yearning sorrow.

'They're my army of private friends. Aren't they magnificent?'

'They are.'

'They're called *huacos*, it means "sacred object". Tens of thousands of them have been plundered from tombs. Mine here are perfect, but you can usually tell the looted ones because they have a hole through their heads. The *huaqueros*, tomb robbers, search for tombs with long thin rods called *sondas*. They say they can tell from the feel of the soil if a tomb's there, so they go round, plunging their *sondas* into the ground, piercing the *huacos* inside the tombs. It's an outrage, all archaeologists despair, but what can you do, there's big money in it?'

'Aren't there curses on the tombs? There are in most cultures.'

'Oh yes, there are curses here. Many people would attest to that, but the *huaqueros* are hungry, they choose to forget.'

'When were they made, the *huacos*?'

'The Moche kingdom lasted from about the year 1 AD to around 700 AD, roughly contemporary with the Maya.'

'What happened to them?' asked Helen, touching the smiling lips of one figure.

'They were wiped out by el Niño.'

'By who?'

'We have a strange weather phenomenon here we call el Niño, the Christ child because it usually comes around Christmas time. Bit of a joke really, because it brings disaster, not salvation. Biggish one comes every ten years or so, with a cataclysmic one every century. Some people say it comes when the warm waters of the Ecuadorian current replace the cold waters of the Humboldt current that normally lie off the Peruvian coast. That's just one of a whole load of theories. It's still a bit of a mystery what causes it. Wreaks havoc. Drought and fires in some areas, torrential rains and massive flooding in others. We think the Niño destroyed the Moche's irrigation canals and they starved to death.' His voice dropped as if he were speaking to himself. 'Tragedy. They were the finest artists Peru's ever seen. Perfectionists, empaths, humorists . . .'

'Couldn't they do anything to save themselves?'

'Oh, they tried, believe me.'

'How?'

'Human sacrifice. One of the most bone-chilling things I ever found was in the Moche Temple of the Moon, the Huaca de la Luna. We found the remains of more than forty men, aged from fifteen to forty. They were lying in a thick layer of sediment which showed they were sacrificed during heavy rains, if not during the ultimate Niño that wiped out the kingdom then during one of its disastrous forerunners. We think they'd been pushed off a stone outcrop behind the Huaca de la Luna. Some of the skeletons were splayed as if they'd been tied to a stake. Many had their femurs torn out from their pelvic joints, several of them were decapitated. The Moche have their very own deity called the Decapitator. We think some of the men were sacrificed to stop the rains, and others killed after the rains had ended.'

'Urgh, God. Brutal.'

'It's a brutal country. Here, let me show you something to make

155

you smile. I don't normally show them to people, but you don't look as if you shock easily.'

Maldonado took a key from his pocket and unlocked a large cupboard mounted on the wall. As he opened the door a light came on. Helen started to giggle. Sitting and lying on shelves inside the cupboard was a collection of pottery figures engaged in a variety of sexual acts. Like the ones on public display, the expressions on their faces were stunningly real. Helen read lust, shock, satiety, longing, confusion. One figure sat alone, grasping its phallus which came up to the level of its own rather startled-looking eyes.

Helen peered at the figures. 'They're hysterical. The expressions on their faces . . .'

'Most archaeologists say Moche ceramics were made for sacred and ceremonial purposes, burials, special rites. Most of them probably were, but I think these were made for fun. Every one of them makes you laugh. They're absolutely real and comic at the same time.' Maldonado gazed at the figures for a long while before closing up the cupboard and locking it.

'You can't stay down long, can you, when you have these to look at?' He led her back into the drawing room. 'Enough of all that. I've talked enough to bore you a thousand times over.' He held up his hand, silencing her protests. 'Tell me about yourself, Helen Williams.'

She remembered James Savage asking her the same question, four years ago. Another world away: *Tell me about yourself, Helen Jencks. Who are you really?* She would answer neither man.

'I'm thirty years old. I've left my life behind. It counts for nothing here, so there's nothing to tell.'

Maldonado laughed.

Helen raised one questioning eyebrow.

'You might have warned me,' said Maldonado, 'that I've a sophist under my roof.' His eyes rested on her, heavy with amusement. 'We could have some fun together, you and I.'

'Oh yeah?'

'You forget. I'm an archaeologist. I piece together lives from fragments.'

CHAPTER 35

Helen sat in the jasmine-scented dark, on the lingering warmth of the stone terrace outside her cottage. She took long pulls from a bottle of mineral water and pondered her evening with Maldonado. The more time she spent with him, the more fascinated and disconcerted she became. He revealed himself in startling glimpses. She had a sense that there was so much she could never hope to discover about the man, that, sooner or later, she would just have to follow her instincts and take a flying leap about trusting him. She longed to start the search for her father, and Maldonado was clearly the starting point; the trouble was, for all that she was drawn to Maldonado's dark charisma, all her instincts were screaming warning. She wished that somewhere she could read a cribsheet, an insight into the life and mind of the man who was her haven. Could she have cast her mind twelve thousand miles back to London, into the secret files of SIS, she would have found one, written by Tess Carlyle.

Victor Manuel Maldonado de la Cruz, to give him his full paternal and maternal names. Age sixty-seven. Born in Cajamarca, in the Andes, on his family's hacienda. Educated at Champagnat and at the Universidad Católica in Lima, then took his second degree in archaeology at Cambridge. In a move which surprised his tutors, he joined the Peruvian army aged twenty-three, rising to the rank of colonel. At thirty-nine, he moved full time from army duties to the Servicio de Inteligencia Nacional (SIN). There he worked as a member, and subsequently head, of Counter Terrorism. In 1989, his two sons, Enrique and Emilio, aged eighteen and nineteen, and his daughter Charo, aged six, were blown up in a car bomb set by the Shining Path, meant for him. One year later, his wife committed suicide. Maldonado pursued the Shining Path until the capture in 1991 of their leader, Abimael Guzman. Then, officially, he retired.

In reality, he continues to work unofficially as an adviser to SIN. For all his unofficial status he exercises more power than most of the officials. It was he who, in 1997, advised President Fujimori to storm the Japanese embassy in Lima, taken over by MRTA terrorists in late 1996 with over five hundred hostages. MRTA released over four hundred hostages in the immediate aftermath, but held the remaining eighty for six months. On Maldonado's advice, spoken directly into the ear of President Fujimori, the Peruvian army, police force and special forces were trained by the SAS and Delta Force, and then set upon the terrorists. They stormed the embassy, liberated the hostages, losing only one hostage and two of the special forces team. All fourteen of the terrorists were killed. In military terms, the operation was a complete success for Maldonado and the special forces.

In Peru, Maldonado is a shadowy, ubiquitous figure, seen as Fujimori's *éminence grise*. His sources are legion, his connections impeccable, both with the high and the low, for all the discernible differences. Nothing so high and so low as the well-fed industrialists whose empires are built on narco money. Maldonado knows who the untouchables are, chases the chaseable, lives the politics of cynicism, fantasises periodically of another way in what seems to be a rebellion almost against himself. He is extremely useful, arguably unstable, and extremely dangerous.

CHAPTER 36

Across the garden, sitting in his study, Maldonado watched the lights go out in Helen's cottage. A man stood by his side, the lamplight draining into his dark eyes. He was slight, about five foot five, with silken black hair, a little too long, covering his ears down to the lobes. His face was dull brown, pock-marked. His eyes appeared to be cut into his face: deep, watchful slits, above high cheekbones, below long tapering eyebrows which rose and fell easily in his expressive face. He would have been pretty as a child, his eyes beautiful even, but now the man wore the marks of omen, as if he had seen too much of the bad the world had to offer, and foresaw only more. He seemed to be forged of resentment. His eyes were mobile, scanning left and right with a hunting, checking scrutiny, as if searching for danger. His voice, when he spoke, was as fast as his eyes.

'Who is she?'

Maldonado turned to his number two, Angel Ramirez Malpartido.

'She's a friend of a friend. I'm giving her a safe haven for a while.'

'Here, of all places? You think you can trust her?'

'No. As a matter of fact, I do not.'

Angel smiled. 'Why?'

'For some reason, she's concealing her true identity from me.'

'Who is she?'

Maldonado smiled. 'She's the daughter of someone I once knew, someone I helped many years ago.'

'Who was he?'

'A refugee from trouble, just as she claims to be.'

'What happened to him?'

'We were friends, we fell out, haven't been in contact for years. Could be dead for all I know.'

'How d'you know she's his daughter?'

'That face,' answered Maldonado with a sigh. 'Those clear blue eyes, the crease in her forehead, the shape of her face, her lips. It was a shock meeting her. I knew who she was immediately.'

'So why's she here, and why'd she lie?'

'She could be a viper, couldn't she, come into my own home? I've enough enemies who'd love to plant one upon me. She just happens to turn up a few days after the Leticia op went bad, when the Brits lost one of their own and the DEA two. I can't afford to believe in coincidence. I think we'd better find out all about Miss Helen Jencks, don't you? CIA, SIS, whatever she might be.'

CHAPTER 37

On Wednesday morning Hugh Wallace and Andy Rankin arrived at work within five minutes of one another. Wallace shuffled in, eyes down, baseball cap pulled extra low, ineffectually screening his bruises. He spoke to no one, sought refuge in his office. Rankin entered the trading floor like a bruiser breasting the pub. Karen had withdrawn his tranquillisers, brewed him two mugs of extra strong espresso for breakfast. Force-fed him a pep talk. He was wired. He tried for his usual saunter, but the broken arm, supported by a gauze sling, impaired his rhythm. Inwardly seething, he smiled and stopped to take small bows, acknowledging with a flourish almost of triumph the shouted questions. No subject was taboo on a trading floor. The players revelled in others' misfortunes. A procession of traders found reason to pass by the derivatives desk, their faces twisted in grinning scrutiny. Wallace hid in his office. Rankin had nowhere to hide. He met his inquisitors head on, flaunting his injuries.

'Glacier skiing. Black run, Val d'Isère. Should have seen it, so steep it disappeared. Caught an edge, hit a rock . . . Must have been doing fifty Ks.' Then a broad grin, comical now in the battered face, followed immediately by a grimace of pain. Couldn't avoid that, exaggerated it.

'But the nurses, shit, you should have seen them. TLC to die for.'

In a chorus of smirks and smut, his inquisitors departed.

Wallace sat in his office and fiddled with his computers, calling up scrolls of information he didn't read.

He stood up and shouted through the open door at Keith: 'Go and get two coffees and bacons for me and Andy. Get one for

161

yourself while you're at it.' He brandished a twenty-pound note and dismissed Keith to his errand.

Rankin waited for him to go and then went into Wallace's office.

'The locusts'll descend in a minute,' said Wallace. 'Gotta act cool, admit nothing. Wait and watch. Get out of this, if you do what I say.'

He looked at Helen Jencks's conspicuously empty desk. Never meant it to come to this, he thought. She was just a contingency, never meant to be used. We were friends. She blew it herself, finding out, breaking into the desks. If she'd come to me, we could've worked something out. But she had to go one better, running away, stealing the money from Banque des Alpes, setting herself up against me. He'd always known that one day, for all their bond, their common loneliness, it would be him against her. It always was, especially with friends. Never trust, always expect the worst. He'd learned that well enough from babyhood.

He had been proven right again, and all his precautions had proved a brilliant contingency. Helen's fleeing was an unexpected bonus.

'The longer she stays away,' he muttered to Rankin, 'the better it is for us. If she were innocent, why would she disappear? She's setting herself up better than even I arranged. If we have to, we tell the truth about being beaten up, by someone close to Helen. Helps point the finger at her, and we have to explain it somehow. Savage won't buy the coincidence. Those bastards' – he nodded to the trading floor – 'they'll go for anything that keeps them amused, doesn't matter if they believe or not.'

'Hah! I was wondering when you'd show your troubled faces.' James Savage stood in the doorway, resplendent in his tailored suit with his swept-back silver hair. He stepped into the office and stood facing the two men. 'I hadn't expected to see them quite so rearranged. Perhaps you'd care to come up to my office and tell me what's going on? Oh, and use the back stairs, you've drawn quite enough attention to yourselves.'

They sat in Savage's office, side by side on the deep green leather sofa that ran along one wall. Savage sat behind his desk, engrossed in a document, as if unaware of their presence. He looked up when the shadow of Michael Freyn fell across him. Freyn, despite his size, slunk silently around the carpeted floors of the bank and was forever startling his colleagues. Savage smiled up at him.

'Do you know Hugh Wallace and Andy Rankin?' He gestured towards the two men, moving his hand through the air as if caressing from a distance their bruise-blackened faces.

Freyn walked up to them. Rankin got to his feet easily enough, although the painkillers were making him feel seasick, but Wallace struggled, and Savage felt a fleeting sympathy for his nephew.

Freyn gave each man a surprisingly delicate handshake, taking his time, scrutinising their injuries with a practised eye. He lingered over Wallace.

'Nasty injuries those. Seen a doctor?'

''Course I have,' said Wallace.

'Sit, please, both of you. In your condition,' Freyn bade them.

'You make us sound like pregnant women,' said Rankin with a grimace.

'What happened?' Freyn's voice cut through Wallace's brain like a gunshot. He looked up at the man standing over him, and anger flared in his eyes.

'Would you mind sitting down, you're literally giving me a pain in the neck, towering up there above me?' Wallace felt his claustrophobia wash over him. He ran his fingers under his shirt collar and yanked at it, as if to free a few more millimetres of space with which to breathe.

Freyn indulged himself for a moment, wondering how long it would take to sort out this crap if he and his Para buddies were given Rankin, Wallace, Jencks and an empty field. Then he turned silently and took a seat opposite Wallace.

'It's embarrassing, a bit awkward,' said Wallace, ignoring Freyn and directing his words to Savage. 'Er, what do you want to know exactly?'

'Whatever you have to tell.'

'Fine. But I feel a bit uneasy. Could be a bit incriminating.'

Rankin studied his shoes.

'Look, Andy's told the boys on the floor it was a skiing accident, and I've said I was mugged. That's not true. We were both beaten up.'

Freyn nodded. 'By who?'

'By a woman.' Wallace saw a smile flicker on Freyn's face, heard Savage give a bark of laughter. 'Andy was too.'

'I know that much, and, apart from its being rather amusing, I fail to see how the sex of your assailant is relevant,' said Savage, turning to Freyn. 'We are, after all, an equal opportunities employer.'

Freyn and Savage shared a quick smile.

'Terribly droll. Remind me to crack a few jokes next time you get thrown head first onto the pavement,' snapped Wallace.

'Thrown onto the pavement?' asked Freyn. 'How, exactly?'

'Ask Andy. She did it to him. I just sort of fell.'

'All right, Andy. Just how did this woman throw you?'

'Christ, I don't know how. She caught my hand, just flipped me, next thing I was flying through the air. Sounds pretty feeble, but there was nothing I could do.'

'Sounds like some kind of martial art,' said Freyn under his breath. 'Tell me more about this woman,' he instructed Rankin.

Wallace spoke up, conscious that he and Rankin had Freyn on some kind of hook.

'Andy and I think it was the same woman.'

'Who was she? Know her?' asked Freyn.

'No,' said Wallace, 'but she implied the same thing to both of us: from Helen.'

Savage and Freyn exchanged a glance.

'Were you aware,' asked Savage, getting to his feet, 'that both your desks had been broken into?'

'Not until this morning,' lied Wallace. 'Paul Keith told us.'

'Two people beaten up, three desks broken into, one person disappears. Would you like to tell me what I am to make of all this?' enquired Savage.

'Christ, I don't know,' said Wallace. He yanked at his collar again in a gesture that was beginning to annoy Freyn.

Savage's lips twisted and set again, almost as if he were tasting his nephew's words, then his gaze turned to Rankin.

'You go back to the desk, hedge or close out your positions, say nothing. Skiing fall. Jencks is on sick leave.'

Rankin pondered this for a while. 'No new positions?' he asked curtly. Cutting off new trades was like starving a junkie of his needle.

'You heard me.' Savage turned to Wallace. 'Lock yourself away with your computers and dream up some new wheeze. Keep a low profile. Stick to the mugging story.'

'And what are you going to do?' asked Wallace.

'Find out what's going on.'

Freyn took an urgent telephone call in Savage's office. He listened in silence, grunted a goodbye, then turned to Savage.

'Security cameras outside the foyer, and on the trading floor, recorded Helen Jencks coming into the bank at ten forty last Friday. She left at twelve fifteen.'

'Why did that take twenty-four hours to detect?'

'I don't like the guy who was on duty yesterday. I didn't want to alert him to anything. He'd have gossiped if I'd asked him to do a search.'

Savage nodded. 'One hour thirty-five minutes on the floor. Plenty of time to break into the desks and steal the files. She'd make a good criminal, Helen Jencks. Got the right pedigree, don't you think?'

'Her own desk was broken into as well,' observed Freyn. 'Bluff or double bluff?'

Savage got to his feet and prowled the carpet, pausing to stare out at the City skyline in his favourite posture of contemplation.

'I don't trust any of those buggers, do you? That's the trouble with traders, good or bad. All of them are obsessed by making money. Doesn't take much to cross the line.'

'Doesn't it?' asked Freyn.

'Someone down there has.' Savage returned to his desk and picked up the telephone. 'I think it's time we called in Breden.'

Freyn kept quiet. At least Savage had said 'we', not 'I'. Dick Breden was Freyn's external rival, and Savage's pet. An ex-spook, who now specialised in private investigations. Freyn took his cue, and stayed.

Breden answered the phone in his laconic drawl.

'Dick, James Savage here. Something's come up, urgent. Could you come around? Good. See you in an hour.'

Dick Breden arrived five minutes early. He had replaced his customary corduroys and blazer with a suit, in deference to Savage's sartorial fastidiousness. His was off the peg, unlike Savage's, but he had no need of a tailor skilled in the art of disguise. His suit hung to considerable advantage on his lean, muscled body. But he posed as a financier well enough to mask his true purpose in coming to Goldsteins. Only Savage and Freyn knew he was a private investigator. They had used him on a number of occasions to investigate prospective clients, colleagues, and rivals, both within and without the bank. Savage's rare respect for his abilities, and their shared secrets, silenced the bully boy in him, and he greeted Breden with the smile of a fellow conspirator. Breden, in turn, liked Savage for his unconcealed ferocity, which Savile Row did nothing to disguise.

The two men shook hands and Breden turned to Freyn. Spook meets Army; they knew each other by type, long before they had met as individuals. Training and susceptibilities yielded grudgingly. There was still something in Breden which looked for surreptitious deference from Freyn, just a flicker of an eye would have done it. Freyn knew it and responded with thinly concealed hostility. But, sweetly for Freyn, he was now the man in charge. It was his department which hired Breden, but, in Breden's favour, Savage was the man who wanted him, so the power lay delicately balanced. Savage could feel the tension between the two men, allowed the faintest trace of amusement to show. Competition and conflict were to the office what guano was to the roses in his garden. Savage spread it around liberally.

Evangeline, Savage's secretary, handed her boss a buff-coloured file, poured coffee and retreated. All three men took their coffee black; Savage for the sake of his waistline, Freyn because he was allergic to milk, and Breden because he liked the harsh astringency of it.

'I need you to find a woman who works here,' said Savage. 'She hasn't turned up for work for two days. She doesn't appear to be at home, and there's a suspicion of wrongdoing. Her name is Helen Jencks.' He slid him Helen's personnel file.

'You should know too that her father is Jack Jencks.'

'The financier who disappeared?'

'Amid rumours of fraud.'

'Like father like daughter?' asked Breden

'Sometimes the simplest explanation is the best.'

166

'Or the most convenient. You want me to find out what she might have done?'

Savage shook his head. 'Michael and I'll be looking into that here. What I want you to do is find her.'

'Tell me about her. Who is she?'

Savage laughed. 'I asked her the same question one night in the middle of the Pacific Ocean.'

Breden raised an eyebrow, sensed a good story, and sat back to draw it out with the easy smile of a man with all the time in the world. Freyn felt he was about to be let into a side of his boss he hadn't known existed, and sat poised in silence.

Savage recounted his story with perfect recall. It was one of those occasions when, even at the time, you are aware of the permanence of a conversation, an encounter. Your brain relishes it with such yearning that it keeps a perfect copy in the memory to replay at will.

'It was January, four years ago. I'd chartered a yacht called the *Escape*. We sailed for two weeks round the South Pacific. We stopped off at Rarotonga, Aitutaki, Atiu, in the Cook Islands; Mopelia, Bora Bora, Huahine and Moorea in the Society Islands. God, it was wonderful. Helen Jencks was ship's cook. She cooked well, kept her distance. She seemed a very solitary person. We all noticed her. She was attractive physically, but it was more than that. You felt her presence. It wasn't altogether comfortable, but something about it was riveting. Some nights she'd play the saxophone. She wasn't playing for us, but we'd all go up on deck and sit by her to listen. She played in a trance like an angel crying. It was as if we weren't there. Anyway, one night I couldn't sleep, so I got up to take a walk around deck. I found Helen sitting cross-legged on the teak playing backgammon with the captain. I challenged her to a game.' He smiled.

'She accepted and the captain went belowdecks, leaving us alone.' As quickly as he said it, his mind cast him back on deck, to a sleek yacht moored under tropical skies, and to a beautiful woman sitting under the starlight.

'What shall we play for?' Helen asked with a smile. 'Be careful what you say, because I don't renege.'

167

'Good, neither do I. What would you like to play for?'

'You're the head of a bank, yes?'

'I am.'

'If I win, I'd like a job. On the trading floor. As a trader.'

He laughed, and studied her for a while. It was an interesting wager, academic, he felt, but revealing nonetheless.

'All right. I can arrange that.'

'And what would you like from me?' She gave him a lazy, wide-lipped smile, her eyes on his all the time.

His eyes travelled down her face, over her lips, down her throat to her breasts, to her crossed legs, brown, smooth and supple.

'I'd like to make love to you.'

She smiled.

'Failing that, I'd like to spend the rest of my life eating your cooking and listening to you play the saxophone.'

She gave a quiet chuckle. 'It's not going to happen.'

He turned to Breden. 'She was so sure of herself. I thought I was quite safe. I won the British Championship eight years ago when I still had time for things other than work.' He smiled abruptly. 'She thrashed me. This pretty little ship's cook thrashed me. I couldn't believe it. We stayed up all night, drinking and playing, backgammon and blackjack, and talking. She seemed so much more than what she was, so I asked her: "Who are you really, Helen Jencks?"'

His mind went back again to the two of them, alone on deck.

'It would be easier,' she said, 'to tell you what I've done.'

'All right then. If I'm to give you a job, it's as well to know something about you.'

'I was born twenty-six years ago in the Welsh valleys, in my grandmother's house. I grew up in London. When I was seven, my father left home and never came back. I lived with my mother till I was sixteen. She moved to Devon to live with a man, and have his children. I stayed in London, alone. I left school, a local comprehensive, when she moved away. She sold the house and gave me money for rent. I moved into a cheaper place and spent the extra money on clothes and drinking and dancing. I got ten

O-levels before I left school, all A grades, then I did a six-month cookery course 'cos it was what my mother wanted. After I finished the course, I moved in with a man, he was a saxophonist, ten years older than me. He played the club circuit, not very well, but I thought he was great, for a while. It ended up that I was sort of trapped. He didn't want me to go out unless it was with him. He didn't want me to dress nicely in case other men looked at me. It sometimes seemed as if he didn't want me to live, and he used to hit me.'

'What did you do?'

'I ran away to sea.'

'And you want to leave all this for a job on the trading floor?'

'I want to try something new.'

'Your life is everyone's dream.'

'I might say the same of yours.'

'We all want our illusions.'

'So indulge mine, or let me discover I'm wrong.'

'Tell me first. I've never seen anyone play like you, and I've never been beaten so resoundingly. Where on earth did you learn to play like that?'

'Here, on board ship. Word always gets around that I can play. One season, the *Escape* was chartered by an old man. He taught me how to win.'

'What was his name?'

'Sandy Goldsmith.'

Savage gave an incredulous laugh. 'Ex-world champion.'

'That's him.'

'Did he teach you to count cards too, or was that a bit of private larceny?'

'I prefer to think of it as skill.'

'Useful on the trading floor, I have to admit. But could you squeeze yourself into a regular working day after all this freedom?'

'I can do whatever I choose to. And you don't understand. Freedom can be a curse to those who don't know how to use it.'

'And you don't?'

'I do, but I want a change. I want to earn enough money to be able to set my own agenda, to be able to tell creeps to bugger off.'

She had other reasons besides, he could feel them, but she didn't elaborate.

'It sounds so nice and safe, doesn't it? But perhaps it's just another type of siren call.'

'No. It's the Golden Fleece, and I want it.'

He laughed when he remembered her words. Subconscious truth in the pun?

Breden's voice drew him back.

'Perhaps that's what she did do? Perhaps she did fleece you?'

'Perhaps. Find her and we'll find out.'

'Did you try to change your mind then, back on the boat, knowing who she was?'

'No. I'd given her my word.'

'Would you give it again?'

Savage didn't speak, but Breden could see the answer in the rare softness of the other man's eyes.

CHAPTER 38

Helen awoke early, filled with a sense of illicit thrill. If all had gone according to plan, just under one and a half million dollars would be speeding her way. Her plan for the day was to go into the Olivar hotel, ring Dai, find out if the money, and her first strike at revenge on Wallace and Rankin, were hers.

She started the morning with a long session of yoga, strengthening exercises and swimming. There was no sign of Maldonado, so she breakfasted alone on the sun-warmed terrace. She finished up, chatted with the dogs, slipped them some bacon, then rang for a taxi, which arrived ten minutes later, another crumpled Volkswagen. She jumped into the back and asked for the Olivar. She didn't notice a battered Toyota estate car start up and swing into the traffic four cars behind her, nor the black Ford Bronco which pulled out three cars in front.

Helen's taxi sped through La Molina and crested the hill topped by the satellite dish five minutes later. Below them, Lima shimmered in the heat haze, stretching out before them until it seemed to disappear into the Pacific. At the Olivar, the friendly desk clerk, Carlos, was on duty again, and the conference room was free. Helen rang Dai.

'Good news, Cariad. You're rich.'

She gave a wild laugh. 'Brilliant. That'll teach those buggers. You're a genius, Dai. Thank you.'

'Oh, I enjoyed myself, don't you worry. I still think we're mad, mind, but there you go.'

They spoke of Wiltshire and the dogs and the coming spring, and Helen said goodbye before she talked for too long and had a chance to miss him too much, then went downstairs to reception to pay for her phone call. She handed Carlos twenty dollars; one of her better investments, she thought. She walked out into the brilliant sunshine, shielding her eyes against the glare. She didn't notice the two men, lounging at the edge of the park across the road, didn't see their eyes following her progress, nor hear their muttered comments into their high-powered walkie-talkies. She flagged down a taxi, and headed back to La Molina, pursued discreetly by the black Ford Bronco.

One of the park loungers put away his walkie-talkie and sauntered into the Olivar. Carlos looked up at him nervously. The casual arrogance of the man and the bulge under his jacket that ill concealed a pistol told Carlos the man was trouble before he flashed his identity card.

'Servicio de Inteligencia Nacional. A moment of your time, *por favor*,' said the man.

Carlos walked quickly into the back office. The man from SIN nodded at a secretary sitting at a desk typing letters.

'Why don't you take a coffee break, Juanita?' suggested Carlos. Juanita glanced quickly at the stranger, and disappeared.

The man sat down at the vacant desk, and lit one of the secretary's cigarettes.

'That woman who walked out five minutes ago, the gringa with the blonde hair. What did she want?'

Carlos stared at the man's shoulder, feeling for him a fear and dislike as strong as the sudden loyalty he felt towards the blonde foreigner.

'And don't tell me she came in here to ask directions,' said the man as if reading Carlos's mind. 'That would hardly take ten minutes, even from someone as pig-shit ignorant as you.'

Carlos knew too well the stories of what happened to those who resisted SIN: the torture chambers, the hospital wards. The morgue.

'She came in to use the phone.'

'And what did she say, on the phone?'

'I don't know. She called from the conference room.'

'For nothing?'

'No. I charged her.'

'How did she pay?'

'Cash.'

'Let me see the receipt, or did you plan to line your own stinking pocket?'

Carlos walked back to reception, and took out the receipt with the computer imprint stapled to the back. He handed it to the man, and stepped out of range. The man read the imprint and pocketed it.

'Has she been here before?'

'One time before, to phone.'

'The receipt . . .' The man held out his hand, palm open.

Carlos looked through his files and brought out the slip.

'Be nice to her, next time she comes in to phone. Make sure there's always a phone available to her. Say nothing of our little chat.'

CHAPTER 39

Angel handed Maldonado two slips of yellow paper.
'One of our men got these from the desk clerk at the Olivar.
Señorita Jencks went in there to make two telephone calls, one
yesterday, one today. Both to the same number, in the United
Kingdom.'

Maldonado studied the papers, then passed them back to Angel.

'Why would she go all the way into San Isidro to make a telephone call?'

Angel pulled a packet of Marlboros from his pocket and lit one.

'Perhaps she's being considerate,' he suggested, his cynical smile
belying his words. 'Doesn't want to load up your telephone bill.'

Maldonado opened his desk drawer and took out a navy-blue
address book. He flicked through until he came to 'M', then he
gave a slight smile and closed the book.

'She rang her godfather. My friend, the one who asked me to
have her stay.'

'Would have been perfectly normal to ask you if she could call
him,' mused Angel. 'What is she up to, this Helen Jencks?'

'We'll find out, won't we? Perhaps it's time I rang Tess Carlyle.
Ask for some intel on Miss Jencks. Call SIS's bluff, if they're
behind her arrival here. See what I can find out from their reaction.'

'Maybe she's just come to look for her father, if he disappeared
like you say.'

'Then why not be open about it, huh? Why conceal her identity,
why not just ask for my help? No, she's up to something. Sometimes I can't decide who's trying to work out whom more intensely,
her or me. And, like I said, timing of her arrival's just too coinciden-
tal to be innocent.'

'So you think SIS are behind it?'

'That's what we have to find out. If they are, we have to play this one extremely carefully, get me? No mistakes.'

'We continue the surveillance?' asked Angel.

Maldonado nodded.

'Expensive. Shall I use the special budget?'

'What's left of it after those fucking *norteamericanos* put in the radar at Iquitos. What with that and lookdown I can hardly take a shit without them knowing.' Maldonado got to his feet and began to pace slowly around his study, pausing to touch the face of a Moche figure.

'Why can't they concentrate on weaning their addicts and leave off molesting us? No demand, no supply.'

'Because some, in their government and ours, want to kill off the *droguistas*,' answered Angel.

'So the gringos should buy Peruvian cotton then, and bid up the price. Give the farmers a real alternative.'

'I don't think the voters in Louisiana would like that very much, do you?'

Maldonado held up his hand as he caught sight of Helen crossing the lawn, her way illuminated by the faint light cast from his study.

'Disappear. I'm having dinner with her in a minute.'

Angel studied the approaching woman.

'Look at her. Look at the way she walks, like a cat, prowling. That blonde hair. I can see her eyes glittering from here.'

'You don't like her.'

'I'd like her, very much.' Angel's tongue flicked out round his lips. He watched Helen approach closer, crushed out his cigarette, and slipped from the house.

CHAPTER 40

Helen cast shadows on the white walls as she walked through Maldonado's house. The air smelled of cigarette smoke and a pungent aftershave. She followed Carmen through the long hall towards the drawing room. Save for the rhythm of their footsteps, hers like the padding of a giant cat on soft paws, Carmen's harsh on hard heels, there was no sound. They passed the dark wood doors leading off the hall. They were all closed. Somehow Helen had the feeling that despite the silence, the rooms were not empty.

Carmen left her alone in the drawing room. Ornate silver vases filled with drooling white lilies dripped scent into the night air. Helen bent over them, breathed in their perfume and slowly scanned the room. She'd been in so many strange places over the years, but always moving, invisible, just a ship's cook, not part of anything more than a boat of dreams. Here she was in this house with a man she knew nothing about. It suddenly struck her that there were no photographs anywhere. There was no history save that of the tortured wood carved by hands long since dead. Every piece in that room was antique, spoke of a past that in the absence of photographs seemed dead. Where were the sepia prints of ancestors? Where were the black and white photographs of parents, or the glossy colour shots of siblings, wife, children?

'Are you looking for something?'

Helen spun around. Maldonado stood in the open doorway watching her.

'Photographs,' she said simply. 'You don't have any.'

Maldonado walked into the room and gave her a light kiss on the cheek.

'I don't, do I?' His eyes were large and dark, utterly impenetrable. 'Would you like a drink?'

They each drank a pisco sour, then Maldonado led Helen into the dining room.

'*Salmón con mango y ají rojo* – that's red chillies. A bit piquant. Not too much for you, no?'

'I love spicy food,' said Helen. 'Curries, Thai, Indonesian. I've got an iron stomach.'

'You'll need it here.'

'I've travelled a lot,' said Helen, thinking of her camping trips in Southeast Asia. 'I think my poor stomach's got used to most of the bugs in the world.'

'So you've been out, exploring Lima again.'

'Yeah. Just a quick wander.'

'Be a bit careful.'

'Why? Apart from men with guns everywhere Lima seems like one of a hundred capital cities. Skyscrapers and beggars, interior design shops and street sellers.'

'Not so similar, perhaps,' said Maldonado. 'Most places don't have the Shining Path or the Movimiento Revolucionario Tupac Amaru. You remember, they were the lot that took over the Japanese embassy.'

There was a strange heaviness to Maldonado's voice that Helen couldn't divine. She watched him closely. 'How could I forget? I saw the storming on TV.'

'There was another attack, not so well known. Close by. MRTA took over a house a couple of hundred metres away, there was a shoot-out, four people died. Better you know what country you're in.'

'I thought terrorism was beaten.'

Maldonado gave a bitter chuckle. 'Not here. Subdued, never beaten. There's too much history to wipe it out that quickly. You see the skyscrapers and the Mercedes and the ladies dressed up for lunch and you think you know where you are but you don't. That's just the surface. The gap between the surface lives most of those people lead and what goes on underneath is huge. It's a chasm, and many people, especially foreigners, never know that they're teetering on the edge. Better that they don't know.'

'What don't I see? What's over the edge?'

'Believe me, Helen, you don't want to know.'

'Don't tell me details then, if it makes you feel better, just describe the outlines.'

'My wife left me. That's why I have no photographs.'

It was a strange answer and at the time it didn't seem to fit, nor explain why Maldonado had no photographs of any other family members anywhere in his house. For a moment there was a flash of mad grief in his eyes, then he veiled it quickly.

Who was this man? Helen wondered. Dai's warning came back to her, wait and watch, don't trust Maldonado till you're certain. But the more she saw, the less she knew him, and the more troubled she became. She had to find something immutable and safe in him, something to trust, but she had a sense which seemed to grow daily that to trust this man would be to trust a hall of mirrors. And, at odd moments, she still felt swirling around her the fear she had hoped to leave behind in London. Part of her longed to be open with Maldonado, to tell him who she was, to ask him for his help to search for her father, but every instinct seemed to urge her to caution. The men with guns, the killer dogs, the lingering sense of danger that hovered in Maldonado's house, and about the man himself, kept her fatally silent about her true purpose.

'Tell me about Peru,' said Helen, trying to weave some truth from the myriad flashes of hints, warnings and emotion.

Maldonado gazed at her, sitting there with the candlelight turning her hair golden, her smile warm, her eyes compassionate. He found himself yearning to speak, to tell someone from outside his world, someone untainted, who might not judge. He saw his fantasy for what it was and felt a flood of bitterness. He took a long draught of wine, leaned back in his chair and turned his eyes full on hers.

'Which Peru would you like to know about? The land of Machu Picchu and the Incas? A postcard for the innocent? Framed contained beauty? Amazonia, quinine, uña de gato, destruction of the rainforest, the old tribes, the Machiguenga, the Pira, jungle warriors guarding lost cities, El Dorado and dead treasure hunters, the *pueblos jovenes* where the people starve, the IMF, the Brady plan and slick bankers, the earthquakes in Yungay, the thousands buried. The Brujos and shamans, white magic and black. The miners five thousand metres up, burrowing under glaciers. The complacent would be Spanish Peruvians, or the true Peruvians – the Indios. The society ladies at the beautician's, chatting with each other on their cellulars, swapping notes on their sons and daughters at Miami State, what are they gonna wear for graduation, or perhaps you'd like to hear about the terrorist training camps in the jungle, the PLO visits, or the narcos, or the people who fight them, or the masked judges so reviled by the editorial writers of the *New York Times* as they sit in safety in Manhattan. There is no Peru, Helen, it's a bastard with many fathers, pick the one you want.'

'Someone must understand it. Someone must see the whole picture.'

Maldonado gave a smile that seemed to span in its curve the spectrum from love to hate. He spoke softly, as if at confession.

'I understand it, Helen.' His eyes glittered with the pride and sorrow of a great sin.

'This country is mad, completely mad. It's like a beautiful woman who's been raped many times. She can no longer respond to a gentle touch. She's been brutalised, but she still has the sensitivity to know it. She knows what she was, what she is, and what was done to her and she takes revenge whenever she can. This country is racked by violence, by acts of God. Earthquakes, volcanic eruptions, landslides, tidal waves, floods, droughts, fires. Go to the high Andes some time, see the violence of the mountains. There's no tame beauty here. Go to the glaciers for the Ice Festival, watch closely and you might still see a human sacrifice.' He pointed at her. 'Be careful it's not you. Every year several people "disappear" into the ice crevices. Go to Machu Picchu, climb Wayna Picchu, climb Ausangate, cast back your mind, imagine you were an Inca girl, beautiful and pure. You'd be murdered as a sacrifice to the mountain gods, promised immortality. But the frozen corpses I've found were fixed in terror, drugged and drunken to ease them into death. Covered in vomit and diarrhoea. They didn't want immortality, just life on earth, and death in its own good time. Death stalks this place. Acts of God, more like acts of the devil. You think I'm an old man who's grown too fond of his stories, has taken liberties with fact. Get out there, and you'll see what I

179

mean. Stay here long enough, behind these walls, and you'll still see it. You think you're safe here, don't you, but you're not. Don't worry, neither am I. High walls, guards with guns, it doesn't make any difference. Stay in Peru long enough and you'll see what I mean.'

'What do you do then? How do you fight it?'

'I'm not sure you can. You invite it. You see too much. You have an imagination, and it will curse you. Nothing you can do, except turn and face it.'

CHAPTER 41

Wallace began his counterattack on Thursday morning.
'We've got to use it,' he insisted, gesturing over his bacon sandwich at a crisp piece of white A4 paper which lay on the table between him and Rankin. 'Bloody Jencks must have got hold of the April statement, can't find it anywhere. That's what must have tipped her off. Still, this'll do.'

'Do you think they'll go for it?' asked Rankin.

'Anything that looks bad for Jencks is good for us.'

'It's just a cat and mouse game. Sooner or later they'll be on to us. Why don't we just get it over with and tell them?'

'Because it's not necessary. What you don't seem to understand is that the longer we're allowed to stick around, the more compromising it'll be if they *do* take any kind of public action against us. Because if we were up to anything, they should've been on to it and fired us immediately. Letting us stick around if they thought we were guilty of something would be putting the firm and their own reputations at risk. All we need to do is to keep damning Helen and keep protesting our innocence. We've got time on our side.'

'You think they'll let us carry on working here?' asked Rankin.

'Yeah. I do. If we play it right. Look, it's us against them, always was, just a bit clearer now. We win if we're smarter and more ruthless than them. Do you understand?' A sheen of sweat gathered on Wallace's upper lip. Rankin nodded. 'Good. Let's go over it one more time.'

They rehearsed in the privacy of Wallace's office before ringing up to Savage, and procuring for themselves a summons.

'Vindication!' said Wallace, walking with Rankin up the back stairs. 'Freedom. Just play. Play the game.'

Rankin flinched and followed behind.

They filed into Savage's office and sat down, Wallace puffing with the exertion of having climbed three flights of stairs. Savage and Michael Freyn waited expectantly. Wallace pushed the piece of paper across Savage's empty desk.

'We found it ten minutes ago,' he said. 'Andy found it at the back of Jencks's filing cabinet, stuck under a drawer.'

Savage read aloud. 'Banque des Alpes. Account number 247 96 26 76 2BV. Account name Helen Jencks. Balance as of March the twenty-eighth, one million four hundred and twenty-two thousand five hundred and eighty-nine dollars.' He looked from face to face but said nothing more.

'That's quite a bit of money for a thirty-year-old banker,' said Wallace.

Savage handed the paper to Michael Freyn, then leaned back in his chair.

'But perhaps not for the daughter of Jack Jencks,' he mused. 'She might have had this money for years. Money in a Swiss bank account doesn't prove wrongdoing. You probably have an account just like this yourself, Hugh. It's not very imaginative if you're trying to hide dirty money to put it in your own name, and leave the details lying around at work.'

'Of course, we don't really know where the money came from,' said Wallace, his bruises now turning blue. 'We just thought you should know.'

'Most considerate. So, let's see what we have. Helen Jencks is a rich woman, who disappears suddenly. So do six files from Mr Rankin's drawer. Then this piece of paper turns up. And let's not forget the joint assault. Would you like to tell me how that fits in?'

'I can't think of a logical explanation,' said Wallace.

'Think of an illogical one then.'

'Helen Jencks never really liked us,' said Rankin. 'Perhaps it was a parting gift from her.'

'That would suggest a level of dislike beyond that which I would consider reasonable and, frankly, I'd be surprised if she counted martial arts experts as her friends. But, if she was behind it, what in heaven's name have you done to make her dislike you both so much?'

They stared at Savage in silence.

'Back to the desk.' Savage dismissed them and rang Dick Breden on the speakerphone.

'Any news?'

'None. To all intents and purposes, Helen Jencks has disappeared off the face of the earth.'

CHAPTER 42

'Maldonado's been in touch,' Tess Carlyle announced to Ian Farrell. 'Sent us a photograph, wanted to know who the woman was.'

'Anyone we know?'

'Records didn't think so. Want to see her?' asked Carlyle, holding out the envelope.

'Why not?'

Farrell took the envelope, withdrew the photograph. Carlyle saw nothing in his eyes, knew that knowledge hid behind the screen of blankness.

Her interest quickened. 'Know her?'

Farrell put down the photo.

'Why'd he want to know?' he asked without looking up.

'Didn't say.'

'Ask him what his interest is.'

'Victor, Tess Carlyle.'

'That was quick.'

'No answer yet. It might help if we had more information.'

'Like what?'

'We have a name, Helen Williams, and a nationality, Brit, but I get the feeling this girl's not in the UK.'

'What difference does it make where she is?'

'C'mon, Victor, we can get the head of the appropriate desk to take a look for a start.'

Maldonado felt the old weariness come over him. Nothing was ever straightforward, everything was a bargain, favours retched up.

184

'Who wants to know?'

'I do.'

'And?'

'Ian, perhaps. No one else.'

'She's in Peru.'

'What's your interest? Drugs?'

'No,' answered Maldonado, listening out for lies or evasions in Carlyle's answers.

'She must have done something . . .'

'She's alive,' said Maldonado with a trace of irony.

That's enough, thought Carlyle, to be alive at the wrong time, in the wrong place.

'Thanks, Victor. I'll get back to you.'

Carlyle stepped next door into Farrell's office.

'She's in Peru.'

'What's she doing there? What's Maldonado's interest?'

'Why shouldn't she be there?' Carlyle bore down on Farrell. 'Who is she?'

'Long story.'

Farrell got up and walked to the window overlooking the slumbering Thames where he stood in profile, looking out. Carlyle waited in silence, feeling in Farrell's self-consciousness the onset of one of the old stories, from the time when the service was peopled by the robber barons of myth, when oversight wasn't even the fantasy of the pimply adolescents who as politicians and civil servants now sweated over the loss of a single paper clip, let alone a fist in the face of an assassin.

Farrell turned from his sidewards contemplation of the water.

'Maldonado's mystery woman. I recognised the photograph straight away, you probably know that anyway. God help anyone trying to hide anything from you. She's in our files. I know of her as Helen Jencks, not Williams. Daughter of Jack Jencks, goddaughter of Dai Morgan. It was twenty-three years ago, I'd been at the Firm seven years.' Farrell paced the room, his face etched with old sorrow, and told Carlyle the story of people he had once known, and events that refused to die.

When he had finished, he sat down and snapped back to the present. 'So the question is why on earth has Helen Jencks gone hightailing off to Peru twenty-three years after her father fled there?'

'To search for him.'

Farrell nodded. 'Has to be. But why now? And why conceal her identity from Maldonado, if that's what she's done? He's the best guide she could have out there. Jencks/Williams, whatever she's calling herself, must have hooked up with him, with Dai Morgan being the link, almost definitely setting it up. Morgan, an old SIS man, probably rings him out of the blue. Maldonado's going to be suspicious as hell, whether or not he knows Jencks's true identity. And if he doesn't yet, it won't take him long. He's on her trail, on a fishing mission with us. No doubt thinks we sent her, that searching for her father, when and if she reveals that to him, makes the perfect cover. And if he knows nothing of that, he must wonder even more what the hell she's doing in Peru.'

'Stupid little idiot. D'you think she has the slightest clue what she's walked into?'

'She'd never have gone, would she, if she knew about Maldonado? Morgan can't have known. He's out of date.' Farrell pulled at his beard and stared over Carlyle's shoulder into the blue haze of the Thames.

'Do you believe in coincidence?' he asked at length.

'No.'

'Serendipity then?'

'Coincidence with romance tacked on.'

'How about a kind of black serendipity?'

'Meaning what?' Carlyle studied him. The light of a new idea burned in his eyes, his smile was grim with resolution. 'Ah, I see,' said Carlyle. 'You want to use Helen Jencks to get intel on Maldonado.'

'Let's run some checks on her first, try and clarify what she's up to, and what kind of person we're dealing with.'

CHAPTER 43

Carlyle reported back to Farrell the next evening. She played with a large, glittering topaz ring that sat high on her bony fingers as she spoke. Farrell rarely saw Carlyle still. The energy that burned within her seemed always to be escaping from a series of different pressure valves, fiddling being one of them.

'OK, here's the story on Jencks,' said Carlyle, eyes bright with enthusiasm. 'City girl, high flyer, taking indefinite leave of absence, according to Goldsteins, her employer. Highly thought-of trader, makes them a lot of money. My guess is if Jencks says she wants a sabbatical, Goldsteins say yes. No point pissing off a golden goose, whom they hope will return to the fold and lay many more millions for them. Checked her phone records. Regular calls to one Roddy Clark, journo, no less, for the *World*. I've met him five times. He came to me, nosing about for stories; I used him twice, fed him some stories useful to us.' Carlyle raised a hand. 'Don't worry. He didn't have a clue he was being used. His ego's too big. He thinks he's the cleverest of them all, also too busy chasing his own ambitions to worry too much about other people's agendas. He's the perfect spout. Anyway, I arranged a meeting, talked about five or six different things, brought up Jencks. She dumped him four months ago. He seems still to harbour strong feelings for her, so he's happy as a bird to sing about her, and, even better, he seems bitter too, so he had no problem with loyalty towards her when I started digging. Apparently, she's been obsessed with finding her father all her life, took a job as ship's cook for eight years just to sail around the world looking for him. Roddy reckons she took her job in the City to make enough money to start looking for him again. He seemed a bit put out that she'd gone. Apparently

187

she just upped and left over the bank holiday weekend, without so much as a goodbye, but he said he wasn't altogether surprised. Said she was always the kind of woman who kept a packed suitcase at the end of the bed. I didn't ring Dai Morgan. I reckoned if we were to use Jencks, no point tipping off Morgan as to our intentions. Also, if he started sniffing around too much, he might just find out what kind of person his old friend Victor Maldonado has turned into, and try to whip the girl out of Peru before we can get started on her. No point wasting potential assets, especially when the weight of evidence seems to suggest that Jencks is in Peru to search for her father. She did seem to leave a bit abruptly, despite what Roddy says. I could investigate that further, if you like, but then it could just be that Morgan told her the truth suddenly for his own reasons, and Jencks chose not to share that with Roddy. After all, she dumped him, she doesn't owe him an explanation. Looking at it from Morgan's angle, he's sixty-five, that's not old, but let's say he's just discovered he's dying, something like that, or just intimations of mortality, perhaps that's what made him decide to tell his goddaughter the truth, while he still could.'

Farrell thought for a while before speaking.

'It's a bit messy, but it's also a gift horse. Jencks is the best way in to Maldonado that I can see, at a time when we dearly need one. How many more dead bodies do we need before we take Favour's warnings seriously?' He paused again before asking, 'Would you use her?'

'Yes. I would.'

Farrell nodded. 'All right then. We go with it. We need the right person to recruit her, someone who's already there, knows the country well, knows the right and the wrong people. Someone who can move easily in society. A man who can charm a woman. Someone to befriend her. A sensitive roughie toughie, if they exist.'

'They exist,' said Carlyle, with a sensual smile. 'Favour's our man.'

'I'm not sure that an extremely efficient man o' war is the best tool here. Don't forget, he could have too much of his own agenda. After all, he thinks Maldonado effectively killed one of his friends. This is an incredibly delicate intelligence-gathering operation, with a number of lives at stake, not least Helen Jencks's and Favour's.

This isn't about his survival and the obliteration of an enemy. I know those SAS men. They're all capable of turning on a coldness that would chill Alaska. They all have a splinter of chauvinism in what passes for their hearts. They regard almost all women as fundamentally weak, can never quite forgive them for being unable to yomp forty miles a day without food. The only women they look at with even a halfway equal eye are those who have the strength to confront them, the intelligence to understand them, and the beauty to seduce them, and they're a pretty rare breed. Unless Helen Jencks is one of them, your guy and she will hate each other on sight, and he'll send her straight back into Maldonado's arms.'

'I don't think so. You've never met Favour, haven't even seen a photograph of him. Let me tell you: five ten, light-brown hair, looks like a rougher, tougher version of a young Robert Redford. The man's gorgeous. And extremely efficient,' she added quickly. 'Don't worry about his own agenda. He's under my control. I'll handle that. And I feel perfectly sanguine about it,' she said, with more confidence than she truly felt.

Farrell gave her a probing look. 'I'll decide to trust you on that. But Favour, the perfect confidant?'

'He read English at Oxford. He loves poetry. He's the perfect combination of rough and smooth.'

'You're putting a lot of faith in pillow talk.'

'Perhaps you don't know his *type* as well as you think, Ian.'

'Perhaps not. You apparently do. He's your best suggestion?'

'We'd be bloody lucky to get him,' replied Carlyle, ignoring his jibe. 'The question is how's he going to feel about nursemaiding Jencks.'

'Get out to Bogotá, soon as you can. It's up to you to persuade him.'

CHAPTER 44

Roddy Clark skipped his morning cup of lapsang souchong, drunk habitually in the tranquil company of his sculptures. He picked up his thin leather briefcase and set off for work. He could scarcely believe his luck. A year and a half without a scoop, eighteen months of being exposed to sidelong glances in the newsroom, to the thinly concealed assumption in colleagues' eyes that he was, if not past it, then on his way out. It was the ultimate irony, really. Since he'd met Helen, his instincts for a story seemed to have softened, as he focused on his pursuit of her. Now that pursuit could be carrying him to a story that would resurrect him. For the whole two years he had known Helen, he'd longed to build a story on her. He'd just been waiting for the catalyst that Tess Carlyle and SIS's interest in Helen had provided. There was a story, and it could be huge. All his journalistic instincts were screaming. No matter what some little voice masquerading as conscience whispered to him, his responsibility was to himself, to his ailing career, not to keeping a little fugitive free of the press she had always loathed, whatever he might have felt for her. She had started it all, freed him of responsibility, when she ran, without a word. If she'd only played it straight with him, none of this would be happening.

He strode across the newsroom floor and into the editor's office. In five garbled sentences he made his case. He was perplexed by Roland Mudd's lack of response.

'There has to be a story in it,' insisted Roddy, his face alive with intent.

'Oldest story in the book,' replied Mudd. 'Girl leaves boy.'

'Oh, give me credit. I can still think like a professional.'

'No one would ever accuse you of thinking with your heart or any other lesser organ.' Mudd drew a doodle of a bleeding heart. 'What do we have? Helen Jencks disappears.'

'SIS sniffing around? You don't think there's a story in that?'

'You need the why behind that and you know it.'

'All right then, listen to the rest. I rang the trading floor, Tuesday after the bank holiday weekend. Normally either Helen, or Andy Rankin who sits next to her, answers the phone. This time it was someone new, sounded like a real grunt. When I asked to speak to Helen he said she was off the desk. I asked him when he was expecting her back, and he said, very awkwardly, that he wasn't sure. I tried a few hours later, but there was still no sign of Helen, so I asked the grunt if I could speak to Hugh Wallace. No sign of him either, and when I asked when he was expected, the grunt just said, er, later, as if he had no idea. Then, on a hunch, I asked for Andy Rankin. Wouldn't you know it, he was off the desk too. I rang again in the afternoon; this time an awkward-sounding woman said Helen, Wallace and Rankin were all off sick. She got all shifty then, asked who I was and could she help me. I said no thanks. That evening, I went round to try and see Helen, but there was no one there, and her flat was dark. I've been ringing the trading floor all week and still no sign of Helen. But Andy Rankin was there. I suddenly got this thought that perhaps Helen was there, and they were covering for her, so she wouldn't have to speak to me.' Mudd had a sudden flash of sympathy for Clark. 'So I decided to go to Goldsteins yesterday afternoon, wait in the foyer, see if Helen appeared. Traders leave work early so I was there by quarter to five. No sign of Helen, but I did see Wallace and Rankin coming out of the lifts together.' He gave Mudd a satisfied grin, as if finally delivering what was to Mudd's mind a long overdue punchline. 'They both had black eyes. Rankin had a broken nose too. And a broken arm. He was a real mess.'

'You talk to them?' asked Mudd.

'Of course. They were really surprised to see me, looked a bit shifty, not that you could tell easily with Wallace, he always looks ill at ease, but I went to prep school with him so I know what's going on underneath. They said they both got mugged, within twelve hours of each other.'

'It happens,' said Mudd, getting up to straighten a watercolour he'd painted on his holiday in Tuscany the year before. He peered at the cypress trees for a while, then returned to his seat with a smile. 'Perhaps they fought each other, or were together somewhere they shouldn't have been, got beaten up at the same time.'

'No. They were lying, I'm sure of it, or covering up the truth at any rate. I asked them where Helen was, said I couldn't get hold of her. Then they looked distinctly dodgy. Wallace just grinned and said he thought she must have eloped with me. When I pushed him, he just said she was having a few days' leave, and gave me a sort of knowing sympathetic look, as if the truth was that Helen had run away from me for a while.'

'It could just be that,' said Mudd gently.

'She left me months ago,' shouted Roddy. 'This has got nothing to do with that. For God's sake I'm not stalking her. We're friends, she still likes to see me. The idea that she's disappeared just to get away from me is ludicrous.'

'All right, calm down.'

'Can we just focus on the details?' demanded Roddy.

'Yeah, focus, great idea.'

'Why were Rankin and Wallace mugged? Why was the desk so defensive about where everyone was on Tuesday? Where has Helen Jencks gone and why? And why the hell is SIS sniffing around?'

'Does sound a bit odd,' conceded Mudd. 'All right, Roddy. Chase it, but if I suspect for a second you're trying to make any personal capital out of this . . .'

'Roland, for God's sake, will you drop that? There's a story here. I can smell it.'

'What about your friendship with Wallace? He won't exactly be thrilled if he finds out you've gone nosing after some story involving him. And Helen, of all people? How's she going to react if you start digging round after her?'

Mudd caught the look of determination on his journalist's face. For Roddy Clark, ambition was infinitely more powerful than loyalty.

CHAPTER 45

Roddy walked up the urine-stained stairs, feeling intrepid and disgusted. He paused before the brilliant yellow of Joyce Fortune's front door, then rapped out three knocks.

'Saints preserve us, if it isn't wanker number one himself.' Joyce stood, hand on hip, lips pursed in distaste. Two identical black-haired children of about four ran into the doorway and stood flanking her. They seemed to pick up their mother's vibes and glared at him ferociously.

'Hello, Joyce. Nice to see you too.'

'Why don't you all just go away?'

'All?' Roddy smiled. 'Who else is looking for Helen then?'

'Better men than you,' said Joyce, trailing her eyes up and down his body, finishing him off with a contemptuous smile, before slamming the door in his face.

Cheered by Joyce's disproportionate hostility, Clark set off for Goldsteins' offices in Broadgate. The press officer, Monica Coldburn, agreed to see him with the hearty cheerfulness that convinced him she had something to hide. She kept him waiting for ten minutes, just to show she wasn't craven, then admitted him with a breezy, 'Hi there, the *World*, right? You must be new, yeah? I thought Freddy Monro was the financial man.'

'Roderick Clark,' he said, extending his hand. 'I'm news. I write the front pages, not the back. Like Barings you know, financial stories that blow up?'

'Hey, I'm sorry. We haven't got anything like that at Goldsteins. I can tell you about all the deals we're doing, we've got some great new business over the past few weeks, but we're a bit short on scandals.' She spread her hands in mock apology.

'I'm interested in the trading floor.'

'Mmhm.' She smiled, eager to please. 'They've been doing *particularly* well.'

'The derivatives desk?'

'What about them?'

'Perhaps you could tell me what's happened to three of the people on that desk. They all seem to have disappeared on Tuesday.'

'Look, Roddy –'

'Roderick.'

'Roderick, I'm sorry. You must know we don't comment on personnel issues, and really, are you that short of stories you're trying to make one out of Goldsteins' staffing issues?' She glanced at her watch, just indiscreetly enough to be sure he saw.

Nice try but not good enough.

'I'd have a word with whoever's in charge of the trading floor,' Clark said conversationally. 'They ought to get their story straight. Whoever was answering the phones on Tuesday didn't seem to know his arse from his elbow. Kept muttering that the traders were off the desk, or that they'd be in later. One of the traders, Helen Jencks, seems to have just disappeared. Oh, and then there's the joint mugging of Hugh Wallace and Andy Rankin. Both had their features rearranged within twelve hours of each other. Sounds a bit odd, don't you think?'

'Look, Roderick, I'm sure you're trained to have a suspicious mind, but to those who don't understand the financial markets lots of things probably sound odd.'

'Ah, outsiders don't understand, therefore let us regulate ourselves, and get on with our frauds nice and quietly. That one's wearing a little thin, don't you think?'

'I think whatever fishing trip you're on is a waste of time. Waste yours, by all means, but if you'll excuse me . . .' She got to her feet.

Clark nodded and got up to go. 'I'll be in touch.'

She didn't smile as he left. He had succeeded, at least, in cracking through the saccharine, and they both knew it. As soon as he'd gone she rang Zamaroh.

Traders tend to terrify everyone else in the firm. They're sharp and aggressive by necessity, if not by inclination. To non-traders they always give the impression that any conversation is a waste of time when they could be on the phone with their own kind, making money. Monica rang Zamaroh with double trepidation.

'Zaha, it's Monica Coldburn, here. Press office. I need to talk to you.'

'The markets are busy. It'll have to wait.'

'I'm afraid it can't. If you can't see me I'll need to talk to James Savage and I'd rather talk to you first.'

Monica sat in Zamaroh's office, seeing the contempt in her eyes, but pretending not to notice. She took a quick pleasure in passing on her problem.

'I've just had a visit from a journalist on the *World*. Not a financial journalist, but someone who writes the front page stuff, like Barings, he said.' She saw the muscles in Zamaroh's face contract.

'He wanted to know what was going on with the derivatives desk. He told me that you guys should get your stories straight.' She told Zamaroh verbatim what Clark had said. 'And frankly,' she concluded, 'it does sound rather odd to me.'

'What did you tell him?'

'Well, it would have helped if I'd been told what was going on so that I could have prepared an answer. I made do with telling him that we didn't comment on personnel issues, and that, frankly, he must be short of news if he was trying to make a story out of our staffing policy.'

'Good answer.'

'In the circumstances, but he'll be back.'

'Why?'

'I get the feeling something not quite right is going on. You can lie to me if you choose,' Monica continued, colour rising, 'but for God's sake make it stand up, and actually, if it's all the same to you, I'd prefer the truth. It makes my job a little easier.'

'The truth,' said Zamaroh, her voice dripping derision, 'is that one of the traders is on holiday, and that the other two probably got pissed in a bar, upset someone, and got taught a lesson. Now, I know that you're too busy taking people out to lunch to have any inkling about life down here, where we make the money that pays for your lunches, not to mention your salary, but allow me to fill you in. Most traders are thugs. It's hardly news that two of them got into a fight, nor that one's on holiday.'

Monica gave a tight smile. 'Maybe not, but a *World* journalist clearly thinks it is.'

Zamaroh rang Savage. 'We've got a problem.'

She was summoned immediately to the tenth floor. Savage and Freyn were awaiting her.

'What now?' asked Savage.

'A journalist, from the *World*. News page.' Zamaroh watched Savage's eyes flare. 'Fishing around our PR, Monica Coldburn. She seemed to handle it all right, if her story's to be believed, but the journo frightened her.'

The press were, Zamaroh knew, Savage's great tormentor. He loathed them. They were independent, out of his control, and their interest ran not in writing about success but in slavering over failure or improprieties, real or imagined. They were like a court jester who had ousted the king.

'I want you to tighten everything up,' Savage said to Zamaroh. 'Brief Wallace and Rankin and that ape Keith on what to say and what not to say if the press approach them. Got to have consistent stories. Tell them to keep their mouths shut to everyone else. Whatever the hell's going on here, we don't stand a chance if we can't keep the lid on it. Speculation breeds speculation. We give the press a morsel to feed on, they'll be ripping the flesh from our bones next.' He nodded in dismissal and Zamaroh left.

'Still no sign of Helen Jencks?' Savage asked Freyn.

'Not a whisper. But something'll come up, sooner or later, don't worry. Everyone makes mistakes, even her.'

CHAPTER 46

Roddy Clark indulged himself with fishcakes at Sweetings, the fish restaurant at Mansion House. He sat alone at the window, gazing unseeing at the passers-by, thinking of Helen. Half of him was traumatised that she could have gone off without saying a word, the other half was thrilled by the possibilities it suggested, and by the way it liberated him from any inconvenient sense of loyalty towards her. She had dented that loyalty when she finished with him. When she disappeared, she ripped it apart. He was more convinced than ever that a great story was looming. When he returned to the *World* at three o'clock, he was wired. He hurried across the open plan floor and nearly collided with Mudd, as the editor came striding out of his office with the look of a man whose patience had finally expired.

'What's up?' asked Roddy, falling into step.

Mudd, clearly enjoying the prospective outing of his temper, didn't pause or look around, but maintained his trajectory for the fashion desk.

Camilla Wardgrave, the fashion editor, looked up with a start.

'Will you never learn?' shouted Mudd. 'I do not want to pick up my paper and browse through my cereal and be confronted by another terminal stick insect. Does it give you pleasure to feature anorexic thirteen-year-olds whose ribs should be declared an offensive weapon?'

'It's the look,' replied Wardgrave, lips pursing as if she wished to fire darts from them.

'It's the emperor's new clothes. What's wrong with Cindy Crawford, women with bodies, women who look as if they might just belong to the same species as our readers?'

Wardgrave looked at a point beyond Mudd's right ear. Mudd, robbed of an opportunity for comeback, sighed with exasperation.

'Why don't you do a spread on gorgeous women who like to eat three meals a day?' He stared pugnaciously at the silent Wardgrave and spun around to walk off. He paused and shouted over his shoulder.

'Next week, put it in.'

Wardgrave and Roddy watched him go.

'His wife's put him on a diet,' explained Roddy.

He waited five minutes, then found Mudd in his office, viciously pounding a mound of executive stress plasticine.

'What?' snapped Mudd.

Clark took a seat, wound one long leg over the other. He had on what Mudd called his 'praying mantis' look.

'Helen Jencks. I *know* there's a story. It's coming. Too many denials, friendly and hostile.'

'Any facts?' asked Mudd, calming visibly as he decapitated the bulbous figure he had created with the plasticine.

'There will be.'

'Present tense, Roddy. Or you're just another bloody fisherman harping about the one that got away.'

Roddy spent the rest of the afternoon away from the paper. Research, a special kind, in a shop in South Audley Street that specialised in the sale of surveillance equipment. Expensive, but if Mudd wanted facts . . . That night he paid a visit to Helen's flat. He parked his car, a racing-green 1970s Jaguar that consumed outrageous amounts of petrol, directly outside, rolled down his window, slouched back on the leather bucket seat, and waited. The windows were dark, stayed stubbornly black. He didn't know what he expected to see. Perhaps seeing nothing would help him accept that Helen had gone. He felt like the bereaved robbed of a corpse. At twenty-five past ten, he sat up, rolled up his window, and drove off.

He drove down Ladbroke Grove, towards Elgin Crescent. With one hand on the steering wheel, he reached into his jacket pocket with the other, drew out his mobile and tapped out a number.

'Hey, Hugh. Not sheen you for ages.' He deliberately slurred his words. 'How 'bout a drink?'

Wallace sighed. 'It's ten thirty, Roddy. Sounds like you've drunk enough for two.'

'Ha ha. Very funny. I'm almost passing you now. I've got a bottle here with me. Come on, just a quick one?'

What man has ever been able to refuse that line? thought Wallace, acceding gracefully.

Roddy was in and out in an hour. All it took was for Wallace to make a quick trip to the bathroom, and out came the adaptor plug, into the wall, and wired for sound. A trip wire that would catch them both.

CHAPTER 47

Victor Maldonado was sitting on the terrace taking breakfast when Helen emerged dripping from the swimming pool. She hadn't spoken to him for several days, although she'd seen him occasionally, in the distance, moving through the garden, framed in a window of his house. In her mind he was beginning to take on the characteristics of a phantom. She wrapped her towel around her waist, making a kind of miniskirt, and walked up to him.

'Good swim?' asked Maldonado, his eyes lingering over the water trickling like wet kisses down her arms and breasts.

'Mmm,' said Helen, holding his gaze so that he was forced to keep his eyes on hers. 'Lovely. So where've you been then?'

'Oh, up north.' He gestured with his hand.

'Had a good time?'

Maldonado sighed and suddenly gazed at the sky as if seeking an answer there to a question she wasn't even aware of asking.

'Is everything all right?' she enquired.

'Everything's always all right, isn't it?'

Helen brushed a drop of water from her face.

'You're a strange man, Doctor Maldonado. I can't quite make out what goes on behind those eyes of yours.'

He laughed genuinely, as if delighted to be taken by surprise.

'Why should anything be going on?'

'Because an intelligent man doesn't have such a closed face without having something to hide. A stupid one, yes, but I'm sure in your life you've never been mistaken for that.'

'Don't overestimate intelligence. It can sometimes be a mixed blessing, wouldn't you say?'

'No. I wouldn't. It can be uncomfortable, yes, when you perceive unpleasant things, but I'd rather that than be blind.'

'Would you?' he mused. 'I don't think so. Perhaps only someone with the luxury of a first world upbringing can say that.'

'What have you seen then that's so terrible?'

He looked at her for a moment, and in his eyes she saw a strange pain.

'You want to see? You want to see what I've seen, here in Peru?'

'You make it sound like a threat.'

Maldonado waited while Helen ate a quick breakfast. He watched her devour three slices of toast and two cups of coffee with professional speed. No languid toying with her food, no delicate picking. She reminded him of soldiers, chowing down while they had the chance.

He took her to his car, gave rapid-fire instructions to his driver, Muscles, Helen noted with a smile, and his sidekick, Leather Jacket; the same team who had collected her from the airport. Another man joined them. Helen had seen him in the garden, talking to the guards. He sat in the back seat, between Helen and Maldonado.

Maldonado gazed out of the window as they drove along. It felt good to have Helen with him, buzzing with silent curiosity. He liked her silence, her self-containedness. He wondered how she saw his country, if she was capable of loving it. Bastardised country that would never leave him alone. When he had gone to Cambridge as a young student, the liberation was intoxicating. He even convinced himself it would give him for ever a piece of freedom to carry around; a space in his mind and in his heart that was neither claimed nor contaminated by Peru. He had forgotten how rapacious his country was. Whether in joy or in sorrow, it would claim him, possess him for ever, caught between love and the bitterest hate. He feared his hate. Like a mental illness, outside his control, it would come and ambush him, make him do things that would haunt him when the rage had passed. His solace was the Moche, the treasure he was about to lay before Helen.

The Landcruiser pulled to a halt on a dusty side street in the northeast of Lima. They stepped from the air-conditioned quiet of the car, into the humid noise of horns and traffic. Leather Jacket went ahead of them, walking quickly, alert, glancing around. Muscles followed behind, walking backwards, scanning the direction from which they had come. The third man stayed with the car.

'Jesus! You expecting an invasion?' asked Helen. She wondered again who the hell Maldonado was that he needed such protection.

'Insurance.'

'How do ordinary people manage?'

'They're not kidnap targets. I'm a rich man. Come on, let's not talk about all that. I'm going to show you something wonderful.'

The morning sun gleamed against a whitewashed house tucked inside a large courtyard. The sounds of the city receded, and Helen felt she could have been in old Spain. Pots of red geraniums blazed against limed walls. They walked under the bows of a jacaranda tree spilling its purple flowers onto the grass, up a winding stairway, into the outer halls of the building. Leather Jacket approached a wizened old man sitting at a small desk and took out what looked like an identification card. The man jumped up. His eyes darted to Maldonado, rested briefly on Helen, and from that moment, they never left the ground. Helen glanced at Maldonado. He didn't appear to notice the man in whom he had instilled such unease. His face was impassive, betraying nothing that might have been the origin of the man's reaction.

'So, what is this place then?' asked Helen lightly, as the man led them through a set of tall double doors.

'My favourite place in the whole world,' said Maldonado. 'The Rafael Larco Museum.' In his eyes was the beginning of rapture. 'If you know how to look you'll see the whole emotional history of Peru here.'

It took a few moments for Helen's eyes to adjust to the gloom. Before her, stacked from the floor to the ceiling twenty feet above, were rows of faces. They gazed out at her: brave, confounded, afraid, gloating, sadistic, penitent, petrified, comic, stoic, waiting for the disaster that glowered in the eyes of their rulers, that bent their necks ready for the axe blow.

'The greatest collection of Moche *huacos* in the world,' said Maldonado simply, his hands hanging by his sides as he gazed at the pottery figures. 'There are five thousand faces here. The Moche craftsmen captured every human emotion there ever was, every expression there could ever be.'

Helen looked up at Maldonado. There were no tears in his shining eyes, but she could feel them in the reverberations of his deep voice, hushed with awe, straining slightly as he tilted back his head to gaze up at the figures.

'Look at them, can't you see it? Everything one human being ever did to another, it's all there. Two thousand years ago. Nothing will ever change.'

'That sounds a bit defeatist,' said Helen.

'Realistic.'

The *huacos* seemed to power their way into Helen's mind. Smooth, ebony-coloured faces; rough terracotta; Negroid features – broad noses, thick lips; Asiatic faces – slanted eyes, dark, appled cheekbones. Faces to make you smile, and laugh out loud at their impish audacity, faces to gaze on, rich with compassion and understanding, faces to make you weep, fired with suffering. But there was something intensely comforting and reassuring about this massed humanity with all its woes and glories. Whatever you felt, it had been felt before. You were not alone in your pain, or in your joy. It was almost impossible to believe that a soul did not reside behind the eyes. Perhaps the Moche potters had left a splinter of their genius and destiny in each of their creations.

'They're amazing,' said Helen.

'Aren't they?'

'Which one are you?' asked Helen, looking at a smiling face next to one carved by tragedy.

'I'm all of them,' said Maldonado, as he came out of his reverie for a brief moment. 'So is Peru. If you stay here long enough, you will be too.'

'That sounds halfway between a curse and a promise.'

'You've seen the faces. You know the answer to that.'

CHAPTER 48

Colombia. The Cordillera Oriental, east of Bogotá

The Paso-cross-Arab horse seemed to dance its way up the mountain. For over a mile now it had climbed, flicking out its hooves, agile and elegant, almost gliding over the rough terrain. Evan Connor sat low in the saddle, his body scarcely moving, so smooth was the horse's gait. When he came to the scrubland of the *páramo* he reined in and gazed about him. Little grew at this altitude, but in the valley below, grass, trees and flowers flourished. Above him, two miles to his right, was the high sierra, grey rock, peaks of ten thousand feet. He was safer in the valley, but the beauty of the sierra always drew him higher: the cool, clear air, the vastness of the empty plains, the power of the jagged mountains. The sky was huge here, the horizon distant, beguiling and dangerous. The guerrilla hid in these mountains. Connor had hunted them often enough, knew their ways, hideouts and disguises. Usually they dressed like the army, but they always differed in some small detail – green gumboots instead of the regulation army boots. Knowing the difference could save your life.

The guerrilla were an unholy mixture of ideology, avarice and murderousness. Their aged leaders were Maoists. Their followers included children as young as ten. Their stance on capitalism did not inhibit their business interests. They provided protection for the drug cartels, and they ran a lucrative sideline in kidnap and ransom.

Connor would make a reasonable target, a highly prized one if they knew what he did. But it was the oil workers or the employees of the big international mining companies who were the most sought after. British Petroleum contracted and paid for five thousand Colombian soldiers to protect its personnel and installations, as well as employing a private security force armed with helicopter gunships. They could start their own war if need be. The company ran a billion-pound-plus local operation. That upped the value of its employees. In terrorist hands, they could be worth millions of dollars. The guerrilla were abetted by the local peasantry, or toughs from Bogotá. They knew the prices of the different multinational workers as if they were supermarket items. Prices started at around a hundred thousand US dollars for a low-level Colombian employee of a foreign company, rising to five hundred thousand for a high-level Colombian. An expat would fetch between five hundred thousand and two million dollars. The toughs did the kidnap, delivered their captives and were paid off. The randomness of it all made protection and detection a nightmare, and added considerably to the danger.

Connor passed a thin stream where a peasant sat fishing. A peasant, or an observer who might be reporting to the terrorists, the authorities, or both. It was just possible he was a man trying to catch a trout. Connor smiled at him and moved on at a canter. Soon the smoothest part of the plain was before him. He loosened his reins, and gave the horse a gentle squeeze with his legs. The animal responded, jumping into a gallop.

They sped through the emptiness, the only sounds the roar of the wind and the wild drumbeat of hooves. Connor slowed his horse as they approached rougher ground. The animal came to a halt and stood blowing hard, its nostrils flaring, as exhilarated as its rider. Connor stroked its soaking neck, then moved it on, taking a different route back down the mountain, to the farm.

The horse and the farm belonged to a friend of Connor's who rarely visited it, and allowed Connor to use it as his own. The friend, known as Peters, sold executive jets, and had a thriving business throughout Latin America.

Connor reached the finca two hours later. He was met by two of Peters's dogs who lived permanently at the house, half pets, half guard dogs. They barked, leapt in the air, and ambushed him when he dismounted. Peters's groom, Pepe, appeared, summoned by the noise of the dogs. Connor handed him the reins then played roughly with the adoring animals. They followed at his heels as he walked through to the kitchen and took a beer from the fridge.

He went out onto the stone terrace to sit and gaze at the richness of the valley floor below him, and the mountains fading to blue on the horizon. He finished his beer and walked out to his car, a black jeep. He had been planning to spend the night here, preferring the cold mountain air to the pollution of Bogotá, but on impulse he decided to return to the city.

He drove quickly along the rough track from the finca, then swung out onto the tarmacked road. He drove fast but expertly, well prepared for the eccentricities of Colombian drivers, who regularly cornered on the wrong side of the road, and overtook with scant regard for the oncoming traffic. The passing landscape always seemed to him like a cross between Wales and Switzerland: the towering mountains, the green slopes, and the wooden chalets, Swiss; the slight higgledy-piggledyness of some of the smallholdings with sheep grazing next to car engines, Welsh. But the illusion was hard to sustain. He rounded a corner and glanced up a side street. A tank loomed next to a house. The army on one of its anti-guerrilla sorties. The soldiers milling around would not expect to find the guerrilla this low down, but attached to the house was a little shop which sold provisions, and the owner might know something. The guerrilla needed to eat. Provisioning made them vulnerable.

Connor drove on. As he neared Bogotá, he was overtaken by a succession of powerful four-by-fours roaring along the road, intimidating all the smaller traffic, and most of the lorries. A Toyota Landcruiser with music and horn blaring meant one of two things: a narco, or a wannabe. Most people gave way. Connor waved them past with an amused smile.

The message light on his fax machine blinked at him as he walked into his flat on Transversal 1A. He tapped in the code of his secret mailbox, and the fax printed out.

It was from Carlyle. She was arriving in Bogotá that night.

CHAPTER 49

Tess Carlyle gazed out of the window as her plane began the descent into Bogotá airport. Miles below her, the plastic roofs of acres of greenhouses glittered in the moonlight. The greenhouses contained fresh flowers, one of Colombia's lesser-known agricultural exports. Third in the ranking of the country's leading revenue producers after coffee and oil, before cocaine which came fourth. Over 120,000 people were employed in the flower business in the savanna of Bogotá alone. She felt a fleeting sympathy for them. Externally, the flower exporters suffered a bit of a credibility problem. Internally, many of them suffered a bit of a logistical problem, for the narcos often asked them to make room in their consignments for a little of their own product. Carlyle pondered long-lasting flowers.

The plane touched down and Carlyle disembarked. She passed quickly through the airport, travelling light with only carry-on luggage. The night air was cool as she stepped from the airport into a taxi specially ordered for her, a precaution against kidnap. She set off for the Charleston.

Bogotá sat in a small bowl, at eight thousand feet above sea level, with mountains to the east rising another two thousand feet. Carlyle could see the houses sprinkled along the hillside like fairy lights. A city in so beautiful a setting had no business being so violent.

In many ways Bogotá did not look violent to Carlyle, at least not along the route the taxi took. There were no mean streets. Instead, there was almost a suburban prissiness in parts. Rows of red-brick net-curtained houses, shops selling four posters draped with pink lace, inoffensive, well-dressed men and women waiting at bus stops. As far as she could see, there was no gleaming ostentation, nor extreme poverty. But, as she neared the centre, there were the familiar armed men. Some of them were police, others private security guards, others army. They stood alert, eyes raking the traffic, carrying their weapons of choice. Carlyle recognised the hardware. Galil 7.62 assault rifles and Uzi 9mm sub-machine guns. She was amused to see one of the army boys clad in his tight-fitting camouflage uniform, leaning nonchalantly against his armour-plated personnel carrier, wearing a camouflage-patterned cowboy hat.

The taxi swerved off a main road and snaked along potholed side streets flanked by glorious tall trees. A further bump and lurch and it swung round a corner and came to rest outside the Charleston.

'Welcome to the Char-les-ton,' said a smiling receptionist, long brown hair and dark eyes glistening as she registered Carlyle under the name of Elisabeth Armitage. The Charleston was the best hotel in Bogotá: small, discreet and expensive. Carlyle had a large room on the fourth floor facing the street. She opened the window to let in fresh air. The sound of animated conversation from the street below drifted up. She took a long shower and put on a coral-coloured long fluid wool skirt and a matching heavy silk blouse. She slipped on high heels, brushed her hair, and sprayed scent on her neck.

She walked downstairs to the foyer. A grand piano stood ignored next to display cases for gold jewellery and Colombian emeralds. She studied the emeralds, her favourite stones, then walked past reception into the bar. The light was subdued, the patrons hushed, and there was an air of intrigue mingling with the musky smell of the mahogany panelling. She ordered black coffee and a Cognac and sat back to wait for Connor.

She sensed his presence before she saw him. She looked up to see him coming towards her with his easy, loose-limbed walk. He was wearing fawn-coloured corduroy trousers, outrageously tight, showing off muscular legs, and, no doubt, from the look on the waitress's face, revealing an attractive rear view. He walked up to her table, leaned down and kissed her cheek.

'How are you, Tess?' he asked quietly.

'Very well.' The light mellowed her eyes and for a moment she looked becalmed.

'You?'

'Not bad.' Connor beckoned the waitress and ordered a mineral water.

'You look well,' said Carlyle, her eyes dropping to his chest.

'Just been riding in Guasca, up in the sierra. I was going to stay the night, came back here on impulse, got your message.'

The waitress brought a glass of mineral water with a neat flourish and a deep smile. Connor nodded and drank back the water.

'Shall we go for a walk?' he asked.

'Sure.'

Carlyle called the waitress, paid cash and walked out with Connor. Midway, Connor stopped abruptly, his gaze riveted by a display of flowers.

'God, that's amazing.'

They both studied a wild display of sunflowers and long-stemmed violet flowers about three feet high.

'Looks like a miniature jungle,' said Connor. They walked out onto the street.

'We'll be safe enough in this area,' he continued. 'It's pretty quiet, lots of security.' He nodded at three armed guards standing outside a large shopping centre.

'A lot of the narcos have flats here in the Zona Rosa. Their wives and kids like the shopping.'

He took Carlyle's arm and they walked for a while in silence.

'So, much as I'd like to think you flew all this way on the spur of the moment just to see me, I have to suspect you've got something else in mind.'

Carlyle stopped and stood in Connor's path.

'We want you to go after Maldonado.'

Connor stared up at the outline of Monserrate and for a moment wished himself up there, alone in the distant mountains.

'With an H & K?'

'With a girl.' Carlyle handed him a file and two photographs of a woman. The lamplight cast a glow over her features. She had pale blonde hair and dark blue eyes, ironic, sensual.

'Who is she?'

'Helen Jencks.'

'Jencks . . .'

'The daughter of Jack.'

Carlyle took five minutes to give Connor a short history of the life of Jack Jencks.

'What do I want with her?'

'You're to befriend her. Get her to talk to you. Use her blind, recruit her, whatever works best. Drop everything else.'

Connor watched Carlyle with a look of disbelief, half amused, half outraged. 'You're joking!'

CHAPTER 50

Connor arrived at Bogotá airport in the middle of the morning rush. He dealt firmly with the check-in girls who invariably found some problem with his ticket or visa, quickly solved by the expenditure of cash. This constituted his corruption-adjusted cost of travel. In this part of the world, his expenses claims could only rarely be backed up by receipts. He smiled at his first triumph of the day, then loaded up with Colombian coffee beans. With the rich burnt smell of the beans seeping from their box, he took out a biography of Emma Hamilton, sat down and prepared himself for a long wait.

Much to his surprise, his flight took off only two and a half hours late, so he arrived in Peru in good spirits. His home in Lima was a two-bedroomed flat on the twelfth floor of a modern white apartment building, overlooking the ocean on Malecon Cisneros. He rode up in the lift, hungry for the view that awaited him. He let himself in, crossed the floor in loping strides, opened the french windows to his balcony and stood outside, bracing himself with arms outstretched, hands grasping the rail of the balcony as he gazed out into the infinite blue. He stood that way for five minutes before returning inside. Sometimes one minute was enough. Sometimes it took hours. It was the first thing he did whenever he arrived, whether he had been away for two months or two hours.

He moved efficiently around his high-tech kitchen, making coffee from his fresh beans. He had time to check his radio equipment and to study his map and work out a basic plan by the time Augusto Maralconi and his brother Toni arrived. The two brothers nominally worked for the same travel company as Connor:

Adventure Latin America. ALA, as it was invariably shortened to, had a network of operations throughout the region, and provided cover for various intelligence and special forces personnel. Augusto and Toni were short, wiry, and immensely strong, equally adept at undercover work and leading a pack of aspirant, unruly Indiana Joneses through the jungle.

Connor passed round beers and caught up on gossip about the latest tourists from hell. The brothers chatted away animatedly, eyes wide with curiosity, waiting. Connor drained his beer.

'We've got ourselves a surveillance job. Not straightforward. I have to make accidental contact with the target, so we have to establish her routines, if she has any.' He spread out a map of Lima on a table. 'I'm making an informed guess here, but I think she's either staying at an address in La Molina, or at least visiting occasionally. Anyway, it's our only lead, so that's where we'll start.' He pointed to the street and then handed out photographs of Helen. The men scrutinised her appraisingly.

'Pretty lady.'

'Isn't she? I don't know how old those photographs are, or if she'll be disguising herself in any way, so use your eyes. We'll need two cars. I'll be in one with Toni; Augusto, you go in the other. I'll use my old Beetle and put a taxi sticker in the window. Augusto, you use a smarter car. You can pass yourself off as a chauffeur.' Augusto gave his brother a one-up grin.

'Anyone watching will think we're drivers waiting for our ladies. I've got the gear all ready and checked.' Connor nodded to three black handsets. 'Motorola UHF P10s.' He walked over, picked up two and threw them to the brothers, who caught them like cricketers, with one hand.

Connor briefed them for another fifteen minutes. 'Right. Let's do a recce. If it's kosher we begin surveillance straight away. Now here I have to warn you. This is a very delicate job. We use utmost caution, at all times. If we mess up, if we're detected, we die.' The brothers looked at Connor in momentary shock. He had never warned them like this in the past. The caution, and something in the tone of his voice, almost a threat directed against an unseen person, chilled them.

*   *   *

They travelled in silence through the heaving streets of Lima. Forty minutes later Connor's blue Beetle taxi drove past Maldonado's house and parked a little way on. 'That's the house,' said Connor, pointing back. 'Number 96.'

Toni noted the high walls and electrified fence. Most of the houses in that area were well protected, but Maldonado's walls and fences towered above the rest.

'Serious security. Who lives there?' he asked uneasily.

Connor had saved the best bit for last.

'Victor Maldonado.'

'Holy shit. God help us, and Helen Jencks. Whoever she might be.'

CHAPTER 51

Helen finished a late, solitary lunch, fed the dogs some leftovers, then set off in a Beetle taxi for San Isidro, following her vague instinct to explore. She didn't notice another Beetle pull out and tuck in two cars behind her, and if she had done she would have seen nothing sinister in it, so ubiquitous were the little cars.

She asked the taxi to drop her outside the Olivar. For a minute, she contemplated ringing Dai, but decided not to. Talking to him would only leave her with a nagging loneliness as soon as she hung up, and she didn't want to worry him. She knew she would be unable to conceal her growing disquiet about Maldonado from him. She turned and walked off towards the olive park. She didn't notice the foot pursuit.

She walked amongst the groves of gnarled olive trees. Their branches reached out, dust-grey, aged, beautiful. She passed benches where lovers sat, coiled around one another, glancing proudly at curious passers-by. She stopped to gaze at a pond, ripe with giant goldfish gliding beneath white lilies. At the far end of the park, a man in shorts and bare feet practised t'ai chi, swayed by an invisible breeze.

Back on the streets, the noise and exhaust fumes of the traffic engulfed her. She walked past lighting shops, garishly lit, by shopfronts full of sinuous alpaca jerseys. She tried to imagine these streets rocked by terrorist bombs in the early nineties. The people carried the memories of terror in faces turned away with preoccupation, in their tense walks, in the absence of smiles. These people didn't trust life.

She stopped outside a sports shop, her attention caught by a sign flashing over the window, announcing 'Fitness'. On impulse she walked in. The little kiosk sold sports shoes, and aerobics shorts and leotards, all designed in outrageous body-revealing cuts and vibrant colours. Helen smiled to herself and bought three changes of outfit, all garish and exhibitionist, then she walked downstairs, following signs to a gym. The pulse of a disco rhythm rose to meet her, the music so loud she could feel it beat in her chest. She turned a corner and came upon a large wooden-floored studio with mirrored walls. A class full of women glanced between their reflections and the teacher who stood sentinel, hands on thighs, leaning forward and shouting instructions. Helen had tried aerobics a few times and decided it wasn't for her. The class structure, the leader and followers, the strivers and slackers, the almost messianic zeal of the teacher, all made her think of organised religion. To the right of the studio, to her relief, there was a large selection of weights machines and free weights.

She asked, in Spanish, if she could use the gym and how much for one visit. A smiling receptionist asked her for ten dollars, handed her a key, and led her to the changing rooms.

Helen stepped into a pair of green and purple aerobics shorts which just about covered her bottom. Over those she pulled on a thong leotard which emphasised her curves. She studied her reflection. By her standards she looked a little overweight and weak, but not bad. Revelling in her exhibitionist garb, she walked out into the gym and began to limber up. Most of the scrutiny she provoked, and certainly the less subtle, was female. The Limeñan women worked out delicately, without breaking into a sweat. With few exceptions, they wore a uniform of minuscule body-hugging shorts and thong leotards, just like Helen's. Their skin was brown, their hair was big, and their eyes were hopeful. Many of them lounged on the machines in calculated poses, talking to each other, eyeing up women with a frown, and men with a smile. After their initial scrutiny of Helen, they deemed her unworthy of further analysis and turned their attention back to the men.

Satisfied with her own perusal of the gym, Helen gave her attention to the equipment, starting off with the step machine.

Evan Connor waited five minutes, then dug around in his car boot. He found his sports bag which contained a very stale gym kit he'd worked out in about a month earlier. He threw the bag over his arm, nodded to Toni, and headed down the stairs into the gym.

Helen became aware, through the sudden enhanced posturing of the women, of a frisson of excitement. The women had turned their attention to a European-looking man who had just walked in. Of medium height, powerfully built, he was wearing a tatty pair of shorts and T-shirt which in no way detracted from the lusciously muscled body underneath. The features of his face were well carved, handsomely symmetrical, glazed with a hardness that seemed to rise through weathered skin the colour of desert sand. A scar traced upwards from his right temple. He had light-brown hair, layered in a short cut that swept back over his temples, around his ears, stopping just above collar length. He seemed purposeful, self-contained, his eyes did not flicker idly around the gym, but there was a sense of extraordinary alertness about him. Helen recognised the look from the aikido dojo, quiet confidence, a kind of whole body awareness. He moved with the grace of an animal. He looked to Helen as if he should have been prowling through jungle, or climbing a mountain. The other women watched him avidly as he chose a mat and loosened up. Helen felt a quick flash of amusement when he chose a machine next to hers and turned to her with a smile.

She did a set of leg presses, got up and kicked over a bottle of lemonade the man had placed by her feet.

Helen righted the fallen bottle which now contained only a dribble of lemonade. 'Oops!' She raised her eyes to his, looking anything but contrite.

'Don't worry,' he replied in English, smiling warmly. 'I can buy another.' He nodded to a small bar at the edge of the gym.

'I should get it,' said Helen. 'It's only fair.'

'If you really want to make amends to me, you can share a drink with me after your workout.'

'Perhaps you'll finish before me,' she mused.

'We'll see, won't we?'

Helen smiled, and walked across to the free weights. Connor watched her go.

It was normally women who pursued him. With his peripatetic life, it had been easy and convenient to succumb. He would have liked to choose a girl and have the time and freedom to pursue her. The easy conquests had long since bored him. He supposed he was now passively looking, but he hadn't found anyone and he chose not to fill the void with the ephemeral women of his past. It would have surprised his male friends who teased him enviously about his evident allure to know that he spent much of his free time alone, reading, or riding in the mountains.

He watched Helen discreetly as she applied herself to the weights, and the running machines. He couldn't help but admire her body. She was slim, well rounded, and strong. She worked out hard and rigorously, till the sweat soaked her minuscule aerobics shorts and leotard, and ran down her legs. As she pumped weights, her muscles swelled impressively.

As he turned away from her, a series of rapid-fire impressions of her stayed with him: agility and grace as she moved around; a flash of her eyes like sun catching on glass; a watchful, pretty face; long, wavy blonde hair; a powerful attraction that both intrigued and bothered him.

After fifty minutes, Connor watched her begin her cool-down stretching exercises. Her suppleness surprised him. She slid easily into the splits position, stretching out her long, muscled legs. She sat there, erotic and still, with the sweat glistening on her back. Connor felt to his consternation the beginnings of an erection. He diverted himself with a gruelling set of chin-ups, then walked casually across to her.

'Finished?'

She looked up at him with a smile. 'More or less.'

'I'll see you upstairs after showering?'

Helen studied him for a moment. He was gorgeous, she didn't exactly have anything better lined up, and some instinct made her accept.

'OK then. I'll be about ten minutes.'

She took twenty, but that was as he expected. She smelled of soap, shampoo and clean hair.

They walked out into the afternoon sun. It shone low in their eyes, making them squint. 'By the way,' said Connor, with a smile, 'just in case you worry about having a drink with a stranger, my name's Evan Connor.'

'Is that supposed to comfort me?' she asked airily. 'What's in a name? You could be anyone.'

'As could you.'

'I'm Helen Williams.'

Connor stopped and offered her his hand. 'Delighted to meet you, Helen Williams. Here, this way.' They crossed the street and ducked through a low entrance and down four stone steps into a narrow bar. There was just one small window at the back, veiling the sunlight. Lit Tiffany lamps hung like clusters of jewels from the ceiling. The walls were panelled with ancient mahogany, dark-ened with time, carved ornately, still bearing the faintest forest smell. In the far corner, two pairs of old men played chess, watched by a patient Alsatian dog, who flicked his tail in hope every time a piece was moved. A fat man in a tight blue sweater polished glasses behind the bar.

'What'll you have?' asked Connor, as they sat down at a round table.

'How about a pisco sour?'

'*Hola, amigo,*' he called to the barman. He ordered two pisco sours in machine-gun Spanish.

'Do you live here?' Helen asked. 'Your Spanish sounds pretty good.'

He turned back to her. There was a penetrating clarity to his blue eyes. It might have been discomfiting. Helen found it interesting.

'I move between here, Colombia and Bolivia.'

'Doing what?'

'Guiding expeditions, treks through the jungle, the mountains, all over.'

'Must be fun.'

The piscos arrived, froth-covered and evil-looking. Helen took a sip.

'Whoa! Delicious!'

'Best piscos in town,' said Connor, raising his glass to hers. 'It *is* great fun,' he went on. 'Pretty irregular – sometimes I work four months nonstop, other times I get a month with nothing.'

'Why so irregular?'

'It's all organised though this friend of mine in London. She says it's just the way the market is, I reckon it all depends on how much she feels like going in to work on a given day.' He shrugged. 'It's no great hardship, having enforced holidays.'

'On one now?'

'Yep.'

'So you know the lie of the land here pretty well then?' The vague outlines of an idea began to form in Helen's mind. This man knew the country, perhaps he could help with the search for her father if she decided to do it without Maldonado. She banished the thought quickly. You've only just met him, she admonished herself.

'Well enough. Why?'

'Oh, just idle curiosity. I was wondering how safe it is, here in Lima,' she said, inventing another justification for her question. 'My host discourages me from wandering around on my own.'

'So why are you?'

'I'm a big girl. I can't imagine it's that dangerous.'

'Depends on your luck, and on what you compare it with. There are places you shouldn't go, just like in any big city. But then in London you needn't worry about the possibility of being kidnapped for ransom.'

'Does that go on here?'

'A bit. More so in Bolivia and Colombia. It's staple income for the terrorist organisations, and there are plenty of common criminals at it too.'

'What do they do? Come up to you with guns?'

'Sometimes. Or they stop people in their cars. They're attracted by a certain kind of car.'

'What kind?'

'Nice, big, glossy four-by-fours.'

'What, like Toyota Landcruisers?' asked Helen, thinking of Maldonado's car.

'That's one of their favourites,' replied Connor.

'Why would anyone want to drive a car like that then?'

'A lot of government ministers have them. They're good and solid and can get you out of trouble with a bit of rough driving. The narcos like them as well, for the same reason.'

'Narcos?'

'The *narcotraficantes*. They like 'em so much that four-by-fours are known as narcomobiles here.'

219

Helen stored that away with a frisson of interest. 'Anyway, I got here in a battered taxi. I don't think anyone'd want to kidnap me in that.'

'That's not necessarily true. You should be a tad careful taking those things. It's better to book taxis through a reputable firm than hail them off the street.'

'God, why does everyone try to make this place sound so dangerous?'

'Do they?'

'Mmhm.'

'Perhaps because it is for someone who doesn't know the ropes. Listen, don't get upset, but you're obviously a gringa. You look a little uncertain. You probably don't stride confidently from A to B, because you're not quite sure where you're going. Any kind of uncertainty is seen as an invitation.'

'I know that,' Helen answered quickly. 'That's true in London.'

'Yes, but you're probably not unsure of yourself in London, and you probably are here.'

She sipped her drink and regarded him thoughtfully. 'Yes. I'm unsure of Lima. I've never been in a place that's so hard to read.' She thought of Maldonado's unseen precipices. 'I suppose that makes me unsure of myself.'

She spoke slowly, contemplatively, watching him for his reactions, speaking in a slightly detached manner, as if ready to withdraw. 'I'd always thought,' she said, 'that confidence was something you either had or you didn't. I didn't think I'd leave mine behind at Heathrow.'

He smiled. 'Like most things, you take it for granted until it's gone.'

'I don't think it's gone. I think it's hiding, waiting until it thinks it's safe to come out.'

'And then you won't need it.'

'True. Why is it we have things when we don't need them, and when we do they're gone?'

'Must be something repellent about need.'

'Bit of an unfair trick that one, don't you think?'

'I think it's a combination of "to them that hath shall be given", and "fortune favours the brave".'

'Bit of a robber-baronish philosophy.'

'Why?'

'The strong take what they will.'

He smiled.

'It can be. Depends where you're sitting.'

They looked at each other in silence.

'So, tell me,' he asked, deliberately, not allowing her to be the one to move away, 'what brought you to Lima?' He sat back to wait for the lie. He knew enough of her story. Carlyle had briefed him well. Part of him recoiled from an assignment which turned Carlyle into a pimp and him into a tart. But anything that got him closer to Maldonado was worth pursuing, and, as he looked across the table at Helen Williams as she called herself, the resistance began to ebb. Her attraction pulled at him again. She was lovely. He could see in her face a strange mixture of defiance and warmth, and he could sense the loneliness that made her accept his invitation.

She lowered her eyes to her drink, swirling it in her glass like a wine taster. Then she looked up at him.

'I came to see what it was like.'

'And?'

'It's early days.'

'Do you like what you've seen so far?'

She finished her drink and gazed back steadily.

'I think it's dangerous, but not altogether unappealing.'

CHAPTER 52

One week was a long time on a trading floor, and Hugh Wallace was beginning to think he might just be getting away with it. Beating Helen, beating detection, beating the system. His lifelong conviction that he was, deep down, a loser, seemed in danger of being wrong, and it filled him with a strange thrill. He mustered something of his old fifty-million-dollar waddle, crossed the floor with a smile and a wave of his baseball cap and made for his office. His bruises were fading, along with the terrifying feeling of physical vulnerability. Over the weekend, he'd invented a stonking new trade. When he showed it off, he would be Wallace the winner again. Maybe his nickname would come back into the trading floor lexicon: Huge Stash. He grinned to himself; if only they knew.

Rankin appeared with a breakfast bag. Wallace scooped one arm through the air beckoning him into his office. Rankin trailed in, the musky smell of bacon sandwich following him.

'For God's sake,' hissed Wallace. 'You look as guilty as a pervert in a playground. Don't you get it? Every day's a victory for us. You should be euphoric. We're getting away with it,' he mouthed, glancing around quickly. 'Go and see a hooker, lie on a sunbed, act like you're glad to be alive.'

'The day I need your advice on how to live I'll top myself.'

'Why wait around?'

'Why don't you go fuck yourself?' said Rankin, biting off half the sandwich. 'You know, you really don't have a shred of conscience, do you?'

'I have a skin to save. So do you. Get out there and play your part.'

Survival had done bad things to Wallace's ego. It was as if he was on a massive dose of Prozac. Rankin found his ebullience profoundly depressing. He considered giving Wallace the finger, ran it through his thinning hair instead as he left Wallace's office.

Wallace drank his double espresso and went through his e-mail. The telephone rang.

'Yeah?'

'Hugh, come by my office, would you? I'd like to have a little chat.'

Zaha Zamaroh in molten chocolate form. Wallace jumped up from his slouch. 'Yeah. Er, on my way.' He wondered if he should keep her waiting, decided against it. Instinct told him he was in for a stroking, not a whipping. He wandered off across the floor and arrived at Zamaroh's office three minutes later.

She was wearing vermilion nail polish and a lime green suit which on a pale skin would have looked terminal, but on her it glowed like phosphorescence on a dark sea. She reached out the pointed talons. Harvard, Oxford and Wharton would have gone to horrible waste, but Wallace thought, not for the first time, that Zamaroh would have made a hell of a madam.

'Hugh, please, sit down.'

He gave her a quick wolfish grin, and curled down onto the white duck-down sofa.

She smiled back, rested her chin on bridged fingers and studied him for a moment. Wallace felt an equal mixture of excitement and discomfort.

'Well done,' she said.

'Thank you,' he answered, hiding his puzzlement.

'You must be really pleased.'

'Er, yes, I am.' Wallace decided to take the initiative. 'We've really shifted some product.'

'So it would appear. What's the tally now?'

'Up eighty mill. Four 'n' a half months' work.'

'That all?' asked Zamaroh, eyes widening stagily. She got up from behind her desk, and smoothed down the front of her skirt. Her hand formed an arc as she did so. Wallace had a quick image of the voluptuous flesh beneath.

'Zaha, I'm hurt,' said Wallace, daring flirtatiousness.

223

Zamaroh came around from her desk and half sat on the edge so that her thighs splayed magnificently in a burst of lime. She was now no more than a foot away from Wallace. She leaned down towards him. He caught the scent of tuberose, cloying, intoxicatingly close.

'Hugh, what are you doing tonight?'

For a brief moment Wallace was paralysed by fear, a kind of primeval male terror from the collective unconscious about goddess consumers of men. He must have been gawking at her because his mouth suddenly seemed to snap shut, ripping from Zamaroh's throat a deep peal of laughter.

'I thought perhaps I could pay you a visit, at home, say about seven?'

Wallace's brain seemed to be playing some kind of word association game, spinning through his consciousness: sexual harassment, uncle and refuge.

'Fine,' he said weakly, rising to his feet, fighting the temptation to back out of her office.

CHAPTER 53

Wallace arrived home at six fifteen. He shuffled into his bedroom, stood before the full-length mirror built into a wardrobe, and wondered whether to change from his work suit into something less formal. He cursed himself for wondering. What difference did it make what he wore? Why was she coming anyway? Surely not to seduce him. Why come to his home then? Why not meet him for a drink at the Ritz, or whatever watering hole she preyed at? She'd had a strange look in her eyes when she cornered him in her office, like a cat about to pounce.

'Buggery!' shouted Wallace, and poured himself a double vodka.

He stayed in his suit. By the time the doorbell rang at seven thirty, he had consumed two more double vodkas, and his liver had begun to protest.

Zamaroh strode down the hall, eyes flicking left and right at the artwork on the walls. She entered the drawing room and froze before a sculpture that dominated the centre of the room.

'What in heaven's name is that?'

'It's called *Conception*. It's by Philippe Baudoi. It was conceived in 1966, and executed in 1969.'

'Conceived? Executed? It's a pile of bricks.'

'One hundred and twenty, firebricks to be exact. Five inches high, one foot ten wide, nine foot and half an inch long.'

'How much did it cost?'

'Two hundred and fifty thousand.'

'Dollars?'

'Pounds.'

'Are you mad?'

'I think it's beautiful. It's very strong, grounded. I love it.'

'I was wondering how you spent your money.' Zamaroh turned around from her contemplation of the sculpture. 'That's if you spent it at all. Some people would argue better not to, for a while anyway.'

'I'm not sure I follow,' said Wallace, unease pummelling his liver. He sat down on a straight-backed yellow plastic chair.

Zamaroh eased herself down onto a strawberry-red sofa.

'How much do we pay you?' she asked. 'Around one mill, all in, I seem to remember. Not much is it, if you want to build an' – she paused, lip curled in contempt – 'art collection? Never quite enough, is it? No matter how much it actually is. That's part of what this is all about, isn't it? Salary's for spending. Bonuses you save, but that's a slow process. You're like me, when you want something, you want it now.' Zamaroh got up and bent down over Wallace. Her breasts were almost touching his face. She reached out a finger and stroked his cheek. Wallace couldn't disguise his recoil.

'Look, I'm not sure this is a good idea.'

'No,' said Zamaroh, showing her teeth in a smile. 'I think it's an excellent idea, and, let's face it, you don't have much choice, do you?'

'What?' Wallace got up, moved out of her reach and began to pace around the drawing room. 'I don't believe it. If this is what women have to put up with . . .'

Zamaroh let out a roaring laugh.

'Oh God, it's almost been worth it, just to see the tables turned.'

Wallace, through his anger, found it extremely difficult to imagine anyone ever harassing Zamaroh about anything, but decided not to say so.

'You little idiot, do you think this is about sex?' asked Zamaroh.

Wallace spluttered. 'What else?'

'Oh, my dear little boy, it's not your body I want.'

'What the hell is it then?'

'How old do you think I am?' asked Zamaroh.

'I have absolutely no idea,' said Wallace warily.

'I'm thirty-nine. I've worked for thirteen years in that shithole, and if you think what I did just then was bad . . . Have you any idea what it's like being a woman in this business? The patronising, the harassment, the prejudice, the disbelief of one's abilities so you practically have to ram them down people's throats. The commandments: you shall be white; you shall be thin; you shall wear Chanel and nice make-up and tights at the height of summer. God forbid you show a bit of skin, let alone brown skin. How tacky, how inflammatory, how very secretarial, although God only knows why the secretaries haven't organised a revolution yet. Then there's *you shall not have a private life*, because you're supposed to be *committed*. Tell me, am I supposed to fuck my work, fall asleep with my arms around it, cry on its shoulder? I yearn for all those things. You don't see it, do you? All you see is the ballbreaker. You know why that is?'

Wallace said nothing, awed into silence.

'Because I wouldn't last a day otherwise. All you fucking Anglo-Saxon males would trample over me with a smile if I didn't look like I could do it ten times better to you without even noticing. So, you know what I want, you little pretender? I want to get out, retire, have my houses and my staff and my cars, and enough money not to have to think about it ever, not to have to take shit from people like you. Don't you think I can feel the knives out, every day? How many little aspirants like you are vying for my job? Huh? How much poison d'you spread about me?' She walked up to Wallace, bent over him, nose to nose. He could feel her breath.

'How much did you make, Hugh? I knew something wasn't right – not straight off; I bought Helen Jencks like the rest of them, but after a while it didn't *feel* right. So I waited and I watched and the more I saw of you, the more I felt sure. You've been back to your old self these past few days, haven't you? Wallace the winner. Back on form. That's what did it for me, and that bloody self-satisfied smirk of yours. Do you know how it makes you look?' Wallace shook his head. 'Like the man who got away with it.' Zamaroh went back to the red sofa, where she sat with all the patient sadism of a medieval judge. 'I've been working over the weekend, did some all-night shifts. I had a good excuse, another problem somewhere else on the floor. No one suspected I was going over the old tickets on your desk. I have to admit, it took me a while to bone up on the pricing of Korean equity options. But I

227

pulled it all together, your dinky little scheme. Helen Jencks was the perfect fall girl, wasn't she? Easy to shaft a girl, right? But you didn't count on me. You must have cleared fifty mill, maybe less, depending on what you shared with AZC.' She paused and smiled. Her teeth glittered like bullets. 'I think I ought to get a nice big chunk of that.' She got to her feet and headed for the door. 'Think about it. I'll give you twenty-four hours. Then I'll go to uncle.'

CHAPTER 54

Evan Connor waited for Helen thirty yards from the gym on Calle Victor Maurtua. He had arrived fifteen minutes early, as training dictated, to check, to observe. He stood outside on the street, leaning against a wall in an apparently casual pose, smoking a cigarette and gazing gloomily at the fog that had swept in overnight to lie like a curse over the city.

Helen appeared from round a corner and walked towards Fitness. Connor scanned the street. He felt a quick stab of adrenaline as, ten paces behind Helen, he picked out two men, thick-set Peruvians, whose eyes followed Helen as she disappeared into the gym. They paused; one of the men went after Helen, the other took out a two-way radio, spoke into it briefly, then idled towards him. The man hadn't noticed him yet, so Connor, veiling the fact that all of his senses had switched onto operational mode, quickly laid out his gym bag on the pavement, unzipped it, and rifled through it as if checking that his kit was all there. He rezipped the bag, and straightened up as if satisfied, just as the man slowed and stopped to lean on a Ford Mustang, one car away. Connor felt the man's eyes rest briefly on him, then he walked towards the gym with a long, leisurely gait.

Why the hell was Helen Jencks being surveilled? Surveillance meant she was compromised. Any idea of her neutrality blown away. Someone in the upper echelons of the pervasive secret world in Peru – and his guess was Maldonado – thought Helen Jencks was a danger. That put her, and anyone connected with her, in peril. Connor could choose now to abort the mission, walk away, and remain outside whatever storm was encircling Helen. Or he could follow her into the gym, be observed with her by the watchers, enter the storm, and pray his cover was secure. He felt a momentary rage at himself. If the watchers had been in place yesterday, and there was no reason to suppose they hadn't been, he had failed to see them. If they had seen him watching Helen, then that compromised him. He walked closer to the gym, imagining the watcher's eyes on his back. He had five paces to decide. He smiled to himself, and whispered under his breath: 'Who dares wins.' He had never been able to resist the lure of chaos, and besides, he had a score to settle with Maldonado, so he walked down the stairs to the gym, and into the storm.

Helen was standing at reception, paying for her session and a bottle of lemonade. The heavy-set man was pretending to read notices pinned to a board. Connor memorised every detail of the man, while appearing to ignore him. He approached Helen and smiled warmly. She grinned back in genuine pleasure at seeing him. He kissed her cheek, paid up and went to change.

They worked out for an hour, Connor noting how Helen lifted weights far in excess of those which her rounded frame would have suggested her capable of. His eyes wandered over their fellow exercisers. The heavy-set man did not put in another appearance. But when he and Helen strolled out into the night, one and a half hours later, showered and changed, he saw a movement in the shadows as the watchers resumed pursuit.

He took Helen to Sushi Ito, three minutes' walk away.

'Wonderful,' she said, taking a seat. 'I adore Japanese food.'

'There're some great Japanese restaurants here. Fishermen came from Japan last century, looking for tuna. The coast is teeming with fish. A single tuna's worth so much to the best restaurants in Japan, just one catch can keep a Peruvian fisherman and his family going for a year.'

Evan ordered sake, and poured for Helen as she lost herself in the menu. Appetites rampant from the gym, they ordered miso soup, sashimi, prawn tempura, and side dishes of rice and fried vegetables.

'You got home all right last night?' asked Evan.

'Yeah, fine, thanks. It beats me how some of these taxis manage to keep going. The one I went in last night must have lost its suspension some time in the fifties.'

Connor didn't smile. 'Like I said, it's not always a good idea to hail taxis off the street at night. It might be better if I drove you home this evening.'

'It didn't bother you that much last night. Why the sudden concern?'

'It just struck me after you went last night. These aren't London taxis.'

'I know that, but how else do I get around? I'm not going to stay cooped up at home all the time.' She took a sip of sake.

'Maldonado, my host,' she explained, 'says I can use his driver if I want to go out, but he's not always available, and, besides, I like a bit of privacy.'

'Don't you get that at home?'

'Not really. Carmen, his housekeeper, is forever tidying my things, picking up after me, wandering around silently like a dis-approving spirit. She's always rearranging my stuff. She knows what I have and what goes where better than I do.'

'That's what maids do.'

'I know, and I sound ungrateful, it's just that she seems a bit more zealous than most maids. But it's not just her.'

Evan waited.

'It's all the security. Two full-time armed guards, patrolling with sub-machine guns. I've seen a lot of guards around the place – on the streets, guarding shops and hotels and so on. But two guards inside a garden protected by a twelve-foot wall with another two feet of wire fence and spikes on top seems a bit excessive. Every time I take a swim or a stroll around the garden I run into one of the guards, and they're not exactly the friendly type.'

'Does sound a bit over the top.'

'It is.' Helen sometimes felt that everyone seemed to be watching her, not doing anything, just watching. She began to loosen up. God, it was bliss to talk to someone who, even if she didn't know him, seemed familiar, felt as though he might think the same way she did.

'What's this Maldonado character like?' asked Evan, topping up Helen's sake.

'Charming, interesting. Passionate about his country. But he can be quite veiled. I can't make him out.'

'In what way?'

'I don't know exactly. There always seems to be something going on behind the charm. He's not exactly a happy person. And he's very curious.'

'He probably just likes talking to you.'

'No. It's more than that.' How could she explain, without giving herself away, that he always seemed to be trying to catch her out? Their food arrived. Helen raised the bowl of miso soup to her lips and took a long, comforting drink.

'You can drive me home tonight, if you feel it's safer. I'll just have the third degree tomorrow. Did I have a nice evening? Who was the nice young man who drove me home?'

'How would he know?'

'Oh, he always seems quite aware of my movements, even if he isn't around. Carmen tells him, I suppose. She watches me leave, so do the security guards. They have to let me in when I get back.'

They travelled home together in Connor's car. Helen sat beside him, glancing at him discreetly. She noticed his hands as he held the steering wheel; they were large, the skin well tanned, leathery, as if he did manual work. She remembered Roddy's pale soft hands, which only ever did battle with the keys of a word processor. She remembered them moving over her skin, and she shuddered involuntarily, suddenly repulsed by the memory.

'All right?' asked Connor, turning towards her.

She looked from his hands to his face and smiled. 'I'm fine.'

He turned his eyes back to the road. She watched his profile. The streets, the traffic and the car horns were held in abeyance by his beauty.

His face was sensual in repose. His lips seemed to smile faintly, and his eyes were gently contemplative. Helen became aware of the sure physicality of his movements, of the musculature of his chest and shoulders through the white T-shirt he wore, and the curving strength of his biceps and forearms. He had a powerful but understated masculinity, a quiet confidence as if he did not have to try, but merely be. He stopped the car, engine running, outside Maldonado's house.

'Thanks for the lift.' Helen stepped from the car, and walked back into Maldonado's kingdom.

*   *   *

Connor turned the car around and drove home. He emptied his mind of Helen, and concentrated on losing the tails, who were now following him. Normally it would have been relatively straightforward, but he didn't want to reveal that he'd spotted them, nor that he knew how to evade them, so he had to lose them as if by accident. He preferred that they did not know where he lived.

Two hours later, he arrived home. He walked out onto his terrace, and stood for fifteen minutes in the dark, listening to the lulling ocean, his eyes resting on the dark mass of the sea. He switched on his scrambler and rang Augusto.

'You pick up the tails?'

'Bastards were there all afternoon, since she left Maldonado's place. Four lots of two, pros, but not as good as us.'

'D'you think they picked you up?'

'No. I'm sure they didn't.'

'What about yesterday?'

'Nothing. Don't think they could've been on then.'

'Let's pray they weren't,' said Connor, curtly.

He hung up and rang Carlyle. It was 6 AM in London, and Carlyle answered after five rings.

'This better be good.'

'It is. I've made contact. The first bit of good news is she's staying with Maldonado.'

'Is she now? And the second?'

'She's being tailed, professionally.'

'What? By whom?'

'Maldonado, I'd guess.'

'Shit, he must be suspicious as hell about her. What on earth is the little idiot up to?'

'If I had to take an educated guess, I'd say she is searching for her father. I don't pick up any ill intent.'

'She might not have any but she's still walking trouble. The watchers, they didn't see you watching, did they?'

'No, they didn't,' said Connor with more assurance than he felt.

'And when you spotted them, tell me you backed off, aborted the mission.'

'No, I didn't. I made contact.'

'Jesus, Evan. Jencks is compromised, a dangerous asset at best, possibly lethal, to herself and you. She could be DEA, CIA, under-cover for a rival narco.'

'She could just be an abandoned daughter digging up old secrets.'

'Secrets Maldonado might wish would stay dead and buried.'

'All the more reason for me to pursue her then. If Maldonado's so worried about her, she must know something worth my finding out.'

'At what cost, Evan? What the hell d'you think you're playing with?'

'If anyone's going to be burned, it's Maldonado.'

'How can you be so sure?'

'I can't, can I? I take risks, Tess. It's what I do, it's what I've always done. You want intel, it comes at a price. If I could get it by scrolling down a computer screen I would.'

'Bullshit. You want Maldonado so badly I can taste it from here, and you're willing to walk into the middle of hell to get him.'

'And that's exactly why you chose me for the job, isn't it, Tess? Don't go all squeamish now that the prospect of blood is that bit closer.'

'Dear God, Evan. Closer! You could be swimming into a sea of it.'

CHAPTER 55

Maldonado and Angel lounged in armchairs, smoking cigarettes, in an attitude of contemplation. Angel came every night to brief Maldonado on the day's events. Less and less could Maldonado bring himself to go in to his office in Calle de la Crucifixión. Angel brought the world to him, brought the squalor of outside in. The windows of Maldonado's study were thrown open to an unusually balmy night, and coils of smoke eased into the garden as if in thrall to the dark. Maldonado found his mind wandering. He looked sideways at Angel. The man was dressed entirely in black, save a lilac-coloured shirt that would have been bad taste in a brothel. He wore black shiny shoes with almost no discernible heel. Thin rubber soles, the kind that facilitated a silent approach. Angel appeared and disappeared like an evil spirit. Maldonado realised with a quiet horror that Angel probably knew more about him than did any other living person. Knew more about him, knew what he did, which, like a sickness spreading, now defined what he was.

Maldonado felt life had tricked him. He had felt so confident when he embarked on what he thought of as a little balancing of fate's damage that he could keep the separate parts of him distinct, keep the bad from infiltrating the good. He thought it would be an exercise of the intellect, subject to the mind's control, but evil was an emotion as much as it ever was an action. Like all emotions, it leaked. Now he sat in companionable silence with an atrocity, a man with a pock-marked face and eyes that had once been beautiful, a man with a name like a benediction, and a putrid soul. A man who could talk only of life as a series of commodities to be traded, suffered, lost or stolen depending on the balance of power. Freedom, imprisonment; silence, information; fortune, destitution; entrapment, deliverance; life, death. The legacy of the coca leaf. Their brief had been to fight that estate, not to perpetuate it, but the finer objectives had long ago been swept away by the river of money that flowed from the jungles where the coca leaf grew, through their hands, into Colombia, where it became a sea that could wash away the world.

'Any news from London?' asked Angel.

'Carlyle rang today. Claims to have nothing on Helen.'

'You believe her?'

'Of course not.'

There was a knock and Carmen appeared at the doorway.

'Sí?'

'She was driven back, by a man in a Volkswagen taxi.'

'What's so unusual about that?'

'He wasn't a taxi driver. He was a gringo.'

Maldonado nodded and Carmen backed out of the room.

'You've got a good team on her?' he asked Angel.

'The best.'

'They'll no doubt be able to tell me who he is then, the gringo.'

'I'll ring them as soon as we've finished here.'

'Did they pick up anything yesterday?' asked Maldonado.

'I had to take them off in the morning. There was the emergency with el Dólar. The shoot-out with Vaticano's men. We had to clear up the mess. I didn't want anyone I couldn't trust poking around, asking too many questions. I had to use the tails. They're some of my most trusted men. I had no choice.'

'Damn.' Maldonado wiped his fist across his mouth. 'Curse el Dólar to hell!'

'Are we going to help him?'

Maldonado heaved a great sigh.

'Why couldn't he just play it cool? He had more than enough. Why go after Vaticano's territory?'

'He wanted it all,' replied Angel, with the simplicity of truth.

'Now Vaticano wants to destroy him,' replied Maldonado, 'tries to blow up his operations, gives the DEA all they need, and I'm supposed to arrest him. How can I? He'll sing against us, and why not? If he goes to prison, even we won't be able to protect him. Vaticano'll blow up the whole place if he needs to.'

Maldonado got up and walked to the open windows. He breathed in the night air, heavy with jasmine and tuberose. When he turned back to Angel he was smiling.

'We could arrest him, hold him, and allow him to escape.'

'Not so easy if we hold him at Canto Grande,' said Angel.

'We won't. We'll hold him here.'

'Here?' Angel tried to conceal his disbelief. 'And how's he sprung?'

'A firefight,' said Maldonado. 'We appear to lose. We satisfy the DEA, Vaticano, and el Dólar. So we lose him later, no one's perfect.'

'What about the girl?' asked Angel.

'We'll sell her a story.'

'She's in the way.'

'I know,' snapped Maldonado. 'What can I do? I have to believe she's been sent by SIS. And if she is a plant, I can't chop her down, that'll give SIS all the proof they need.'

'Proof of what, that you're a killer? They know that.'

'Not that. If I have her killed, they'll know that I'm afraid, that I have something more than usual to hide from them. Killing her would be like a declaration of war. D'you think they'd just walk away? They'd gang up with the DEA, and the US justice department. The fucking Yanks'd try to extradite me, just like they did Noriega from Panama. You think I want to spend the rest of my life rotting in some underground bunker?' Maldonado's breath was coming fast and ragged. He jumped up from his chair and paced wildly around his study. After a while, he slowed and sat down. Gradually, his breath came back under control. 'And if I'm wrong, Angel, if by some outside chance Helen Jencks is just an innocent in the wrong place at the wrong time, here to search for her father and nothing more, then she doesn't deserve to die. I don't want innocent blood on my hands.'

You're dripping in it already, thought Angel. 'She deserves to die for being stupid enough to come here. And there'll have to be casualties, or the firefight story won't stack up.'

237

'Come on. We can't just . . .' Maldonado didn't finish.
'Tell me a better way and I'll do it,' said Angel.
Maldonado turned back to the night.

CHAPTER 56

Roddy Clark had always loathed mornings. This one was gold dust. He was in the office at seven fifteen, waiting with almost insane impatience for Roland Mudd to arrive.

The editor appeared at eight. Roddy pounced on him, brandishing a tape in the air.

'You won't believe what I've got here.'

'Morning to you too, Roddy. Looks like a Maxell ninety-minute cassette to me. You'll get sick if you don't stop that pirouetting.'

Clark did another. Mudd had a sudden thought about drug testing his employees, ruled it out immediately amid a nightmare vision of having to write and put to bed an entire paper alone.

'Sit down, you're making me queasy.'

'Got a cassette player?'

'Over there, on the shelf.'

Clark danced over to it, put it on the table and inserted his tape.

'Fasten your seatbelt,' he whooped.

Mudd listened to a voice that could have ruled empires, to a passionate speech, to the sweetest, coolest blackmail. His hands lay still in his lap, his entire attention focused on the words flowing from the tape recorder, electrifying his office. He jumped to his feet and began to pace back and forth the moment the tape clicked off.

'Shit. Who's the woman?'

'Zaha Zamaroh, head of the trading floor at Goldsteins.' Roddy followed his pacing. To the journalists surreptitiously watching from their work stations, it seemed as if the two men were engaged in some elaborate mating ritual.

'How in Moses' name d'you get hold of the tape?'

'Sources,' said Roddy, tapping his nose.

'Bugger off, Roddy. I'm not a bloody judge, and this isn't a court, so save your grandstanding.'

'Hugh Wallace's flat.'

'You bugged it?'

Roddy gave a dazzling smile.

'How'd you get access?'

'Wallace's a friend.'

'Silly me. Friend. Of course he is.'

'When did this conversation take place?'

'Last night.'

Mudd stopped pacing and stared at Roddy as if recognising him for the first time.

'Shit! This is hot.'

Roddy stared back. 'Didn't I tell you? We can run a story, go with that. I'll write another piece about Helen Jencks's disappearance, tag on crooked Jack's story, get everyone thinking like father, like daughter, both fraudsters, both disappeared; got to watch the lawyers, sure, but I can finesse it, suggest just enough, stop short of libel. God, it's a great story. I've always wanted to do a piece on Helen.'

'For Christ sakes, Roddy, rein yourself in. You heard the tape. Jencks is the one person who seems to be innocent in all this. That Zamorah woman describes her as the perfect fall girl. She's been set up by the sound of it. Why the hell go after her?'

'Why'd she disappear if she was completely innocent? I know what's on the tape. I listened to it all night, I could practically recite it to you. Come on, Roland, no smoke without fire. She must have done something.'

'Perhaps she found out about the set-up; that scared her, made her run.'

'Could be. Either way there's a story and Helen Jencks is in that story. We've got to find an angle to write about her. We can't afford to sit back, let someone else scoop us.'

'What you mean, Roddy, is you can't afford it. You're so desperate for a scoop you'll sell out your own girlfriend.'

'Ex-girlfriend. She dumped me, remember.'

'And now you want your revenge. Well, let me tell you something, pal, you won't get it like that, not on my bloody paper. The story's promising, but it's not enough. It's threats, accusations, nothing more than hearsay. There are no facts, no proof. I need transaction details, bank account numbers. Details. No way am I going to run a story on what you've dug up so far. I can live with your own bent motivations if you've got an iron-clad story; until then put your desire for revenge on ice and get corroborating.'

'Shit, Roland. Don't go cold on me now. What the hell's wrong with it? It's an awesome story and you're saying it's not enough? Where the hell am I going to get the kind of detail you want?'

'You'll find a way.'

Roddy burned out of the office and sat down on a bench on the Embankment. He gazed at the dull-grey waters of the Thames, eddying by. Slowly, he cooled down, and worked out his next plan of attack. He returned to the paper half an hour later, and got to work on the telephone.

It wasn't too difficult to track down Dai Morgan. A call to his Wiltshire house was answered by Derek, who said curtly that Mr Morgan was in London. After that, it was simply a question of getting into position and waiting.

Roddy parked his Jaguar in Dawson Place, sat back and was rewarded in less than two hours. As soon as he saw Dai appear he was out of his car with his camera poised and his Dictaphone running. Dai walked slowly down the steps to the street, face aching following a visit to his dentist earlier.

Eyes downcast, carrying an armful of letters, he didn't notice Roddy, standing to the side.

'Hey, Dai!'

Morgan spun around. Roddy caught his expression of surprise.

'Looking after Helen's flat, are you? Then I suppose you know where she is.'

Roddy imagined the rage burning across Morgan's face when he saw the article he was going to write about his beloved Helen. He anticipated with glee the old man cracking, losing his temper, waving his fists in the air. Eighteen months of silent disapproval he had endured. Dai took a step towards him.

'Hello, Roddy.' His voice sounded the same as always, distant, vaguely troubled as if by an unpleasant smell in the air. 'What are you doing loitering around here? I thought Helen had ditched you.'

'Nice try, Dai. Let's get back on the subject, shall we? The way I see it, Goldsteins have lost some money, and Helen Jencks has disappeared. Sounds familiar, doesn't it: like father, like daughter.'

Morgan took a step closer.

'If it weren't so pathetic, it'd be funny,' he said slowly. 'The truth isn't terribly interesting, is it? Girl dumps boy, and, by the way, not a moment too soon, but that's another story. Boy can't swallow the blow to his ailing ego, so he tries to strike the only way he knows, with his brittle little pen.'

'You flatter me. I deal with facts, not imagination.'

'Oh, how clumsy of me, I meant to expose you.'

Dai turned away and headed towards his car.

'So that's it then, is it?' asked Clark, pursuing him. 'Nothing to say on Helen.'

Morgan turned round slowly. 'Nothing at all, and if I were you, I'd find a real story to write about.'

'You're not threatening a member of the press are you, Dai?'

Morgan burst out laughing. 'You pompous bastard. You really are a hollow man, aren't you? Take away your press card and there's nothing to you.' He paused beside his Range Rover. 'You lot remind me of priests in the Middle Ages. You use the press card like they used the cross. Flash a press card and everything is sanctified, and justified. Anyone who challenges you is a heretic. You think a press card gives you the moral justification to rummage in other people's lives, and all the while it's just a cover for your own twisted agenda.'

'News is its own justification, Dai. It's irresistible. Not even you can protect your blessed Helen. The last word'll be mine, and I'll have a readership of millions for an audience.'

CHAPTER 57

At eight fifteen that evening, Zaha Zamaroh drove her black Mercedes 500SL into Elgin Crescent. Wallace let her in. She walked through into his drawing room and sat down on the brick sculpture. Wallace turned pale.

Zamaroh made him think of violence and avarice and a cat's evil pleasure in toying with its prey. He began to wonder what had made her like this, until she got up and came to him, so close that he couldn't think at all.

'Let's get it over with,' he muttered.

'I take it that's a yes?'

'What else? You made me one of those offers it's impossible to refuse.'

A perverse part of him almost relished this: his genius seen and appreciated by another. Crime could be so lonely.

'Drink?'

Zamaroh looked momentarily surprised, to Wallace's intense pleasure. She had expected to script the entire encounter.

She gave him a lazy smile. 'What the hell? Vodka. If you have it.'

Wallace went to the kitchen and returned with a glacial bottle of Stolichnaya. He removed the top with a flourish, poured out two glasses and handed one solemnly to Zamaroh. They looked at their glasses, then at each other. There was something so surreal about it all that Wallace began to laugh and within seconds they were both bent over, gripping their stomachs, giggling like children.

'To easy money,' said Zamaroh, through gusts of laughter. She thrust her glass in the air, and then drank, her neck open like a swan's.

'Another?' said Wallace, approaching with the bottle.

'I'd rather not.' Zamaroh got up abruptly as if conscious that she'd been too nice. 'Let's get down to business, shall we?' She opened her handbag and took out a piece of white paper on which a long series of numbers was written. 'CILD bank in Antigua. I'd like fifteen million dollars. Electronic funds transfer. Early next week.'

The merriment was gone now and suddenly it all seemed too real to bear.

'You're insane.'

'Would you like me to save your neck, or would you prefer I hand it on a plate to your loving uncle?'

'Who d'you think you are? Salome?'

'If I have to be. You'd make a better Judas than John the Baptist though. Setting up Jencks. Look upon this as the cost of betrayal.'

'It's too much.'

'How much did you make, Judas? Must have been at least forty million, probably fifty.'

'It was split.'

'Between whom?'

'You can't go chasing round after everyone.'

'I can do anything I choose. Let me guess, the counterparty, obviously. He would have channelled a portion of the illegal gains back to you, and then who else? Make it easy on yourself. The more I collect from other people, the less I need from you.'

She gave him a minute. 'You really don't think I figured it out? Andy Rankin would have known the correct price. He wouldn't have dreamed all this up, he's much too stupid for that, and timid. But he would have gone along with you. He'd have followed you off a cliff. So, say twenty-five for the two of you, split fifteen to you, ten to him. Is that fair?'

Wallace turned away.

'Good, then fifteen to me. Ten from you, five from Rankin.'

'You can't go to him.'

'Why ever not?'

'He'd collapse at the thought of you. This whole bloody investigation. He's terrified. I'm worried he'll crack.'

'Don't worry about the investigation. They're still trying to find

Jencks. I can handle that. You handle Rankin. Get the money from him, or pay it yourself. I don't care how you split it, but by the end of the week, I expect to see fifteen million dollars in Antigua.'

CHAPTER 58

Wallace returned exhausted from work the next evening at seven. He dropped his suit on the floor, pulled on a towelling dressing gown, padded out to the kitchen and made himself a triple espresso. He took a hesitant sip, and carried it through to his study. He sat down at his desk, stared at the telephone with weary regret. He felt sick, thinking about what he was going to do. Piss away the money that was his. His reward for ingenuity. His triumph in the only kind of battle he was ever likely to win. He wasn't going to find a wife and be happy. He would never be worshipped by a woman and children. He would never be at the centre of anybody's life. He had put money at the centre of his and it was all the justification he had for the way he lived.

He pondered for one brief moment of hope the possibility of telling Zamaroh to go to hell, but he had no doubt that if he did, she would go straight to James Savage, expose him, and destroy his career. Savage was the only semblance of family with whom he had any connection, but he felt no prospective shame on behalf of his family. The distant spectres of parents, cousins, the whole social milieu to which he supposedly belonged, he couldn't give a toss about letting them down, besmirching the family name. The shame was in being caught, not that he had committed a crime in the first place. Being caught meant that someone else was brighter than him, that he had cocked up, and lost. Being caught meant that he would never work in the City again. If Savage couldn't keep a lid on the fraud, getting caught meant that he would do time in some open prison, crowded in day and night with other people. A wave of claustrophobia washed over him and he fought for breath. But if he handed over his money to Zamaroh, he could survive, pound by precious pound, build up his fortune again. Learn from his mistakes, find a bigger and better way to beat the system next time.

It was early afternoon in Gran Cayman. Wallace picked up the phone, rang the number, spoke to his account manager, managed to say the words.

'I'd like to make a transfer.'

'Your money's on fixed three-month deposit; you'll lose interest if you don't give notice.'

'Forget the interest. Move fifteen million dollars into one of your nominee accounts. Then I want it moved to another nominee account in another bank, I don't care which one, and then on to a specific destination in Antigua. Can you do that for me?' Wallace read out Zamaroh's bank details.

The classic paper trail shuffle, thought the clerk.

'Yes, sir. We can do that.'

'How long'll it take?'

'The money'll be in the final destination by the end of the week.'

'You can't do it sooner?'

'We could, directly, but when we have to involve other banks, we're at their mercy.'

Just as he was at Zamaroh's.

CHAPTER 59

The garden was as silent as a ship becalmed. The heat seemed to hold sound prisoner. Helen was beginning to develop a mental claustrophobia at her lack of progress with her search for her father. She resolved to decide, today, whether or not to level with Maldonado, to enlist him in her search. She had a strange sense of events speeding by her, yet here she was landlocked in the garden. The desire to act was almost overwhelming, yet still a voice of caution spoke a warning in her mind. She knew she was capable of precipitate and unwise action in her fractious state of mind.

She jumped to her feet and telephoned for a taxi. She would go to San Isidro, ring Dai from the Olivar. She had to talk to someone, and he was her only confessor. He might dispel her unease about Maldonado with wise words of counsel. Perhaps there was nothing really sinister about Maldonado. Perhaps it was just that her claustrophobia was making her neurotic, and that Wallace and Rankin's set-up was making her paranoid. She knew the signs of cabin fever, how loneliness, alienation, the absence of a confidant right there by your side, could strip a personality of the mirror it needed to flesh it out into healthy balance. Her years at sea had made her familiar with the phenomenon, but that didn't make it any easier to resolve, and she had never suffered from the need for secrecy as she did here, nor had she been in a country that seemed to seep alienation into her blood with every dawn.

Carlos, the desk clerk at the Olivar, seemed preoccupied when she appeared.

'Hi! How are you?' she asked with a smile.

He looked at her as if he didn't know her.

'I'm fine.' He nodded curtly.

Must be having a bad day, she thought.

'Any chance of using the phone?'

Carlos shook his head with more emphasis than seemed necessary. 'No. Conference.'

So he did remember her. 'Oh, well.' Helen wondered what to say next. He seemed to be waiting for something.

'Better not to come back here,' he said quietly.

'What?'

'I think you heard me.'

'What are you talking about?'

Carlos glanced around and then spoke very quickly. He seemed frightened.

'Last time you came, a man came in after you, wanted to know who you were, who you rang.'

Helen felt a wave of her own fear. 'Go on.'

'I had to give him the receipt, with the number you rang. He said if you ever came in again, I was to call him.'

'What did he look like?'

'Short, dark, moustache.'

Helen ruled out a momentary suspicion of Evan Connor.

'Who was he?'

'SIN.'

'SIN! What in hell's name is that?'

'Servicio de Inteligencia Nacional. They're spies, Señorita. Some people would say they run the country. Believe me, you don't want to cross paths with them.'

'Looks like I already have.' Helen hurried out of the Olivar, all thoughts of ringing Dai, of trusting Maldonado, of trusting anyone in this country, destroyed.

She walked on to Fitness. She resisted the almost overwhelming urge to look left and right, to stop and check behind her. She looked into the eyes of the people who walked up to her and passed by, searching for guilt, conspiracy, a knowing look, studied disinterest, something that shouldn't have been there. She saw nothing. The ordinary had become ominous. Even the blue sky around her, the air of normality, seemed sinister. She'd been in enough storms to feel them coming from a long way off, to know that sometimes the worst ones, the most life-threatening, were those that raged from a blue sky, turning it, in what seemed like seconds, to black.

Connor was waiting at reception. He kissed her cheek. 'How are you?'

'I need a workout.'

Helen exercised until her muscles trembled. She tried and failed to exorcise the spectre of SIN.

Connor prowled across the gym to her. Sweat blackened his grey T-shirt. 'Had enough?'

She stretched into the splits position, touched her head and chest to the floor, stayed there for twenty seconds before sitting up and lifting her face to his.

'Yeah, just about.'

Fifteen minutes later they walked out into the street.

Helen was glancing about her, almost nervously. Connor wondered if she knew she was being tailed. A sudden impulse to protect her made him want to get her off the street and into the comfort of his home.

'How about I cook you some dinner?' he suggested with a gentle smile.

He knew that would mean SIN discovering where he lived, but, he reasoned, he couldn't keep them off his trail for ever, not without them discovering how skilled he was in evasive tactics, and, by implication, working out that he was some kind of operative. Anyway, he'd made his decision to wade into chaos. This was just another step.

Helen studied Connor for a moment. With SIN following her, she wasn't sure it was fair to drag Connor into it. They would trail her to his home. But then he was innocent, he had nothing to fear. She looked into his boundless eyes and felt that somehow, in a way she couldn't define, he was involved with her and her problems already, and, more than that, if anyone could take care of himself, he could.

'You cook too?'

They sat in silence as Connor drove his beaten-up Beetle across the city. Helen studied him out of the corner of her eye. She could tell he knew something was wrong, and yet he didn't push her. There was a quiet acceptance to him, almost as if nothing could shock him. There was a readiness to him, a confidence that suggested he could deal with whatever life threw at him, or else go out fighting. Part of Helen longed to open up to him, the other part refused to breathe life into suspicions and fears by speaking them. Why should she let a stranger into her life? She'd done very well keeping men at bay emotionally since she went to sea. She wasn't about to declare vulnerability now, when she could afford it less than ever.

She yearned for a kind of oblivion. Maybe the kind that comes from falling into another person's arms and drowning in pleasure for a few hours. And then? asked a little voice. Do it all over again, came the answer.

Connor turned onto the seafront. Through the open window, Helen could smell the briny ocean. After five minutes, Connor slowed and swung his little car down a ramp to an underground car park. They got out and took the lift up to the twelfth floor. Connor unlocked his door, walked in ahead of Helen, and, in an act that surprised her, seemed to scan the room before he encouraged her to step in after him. She walked into a white-painted hall, hung with enlarged photographs of desert dunes in different lights from pale gold to burnished red. There were more photographs in the sitting room: Arab horses, manes and tails streaming in the wind as they galloped along endless stretches of beach beside a glittering sea. Stacks of books piled high, spilling over. Good Persian rugs were scattered on the floor. A hookah pipe was propped in a corner. Helen wondered at Connor's connection with Arabia, feeling strange stirrings of fate in the discovery that the totems this man had chosen to decorate his life with were hers too.

Connor reappeared from down the hall and led her out onto a long balcony, overlooking the ocean. They stood, side by side, each gazing out at the slumbering sea, silvered by the light of a sickle moon. Neither spoke. There was a strange intimacy in their silence. Helen felt herself being drawn further into Connor. She turned abruptly, breaking the sensation. Connor turned to her with a smile. 'Come on, I'll give you the best risotto you've ever had. Comfort food.'

251

'Do I look like I need it?'

'We all need comfort, Helen, no matter how tough we look.'

'Even you?'

'Even me.'

They walked into his kitchen. It was huge, visibly well stocked with a large variety of cooking utensils. Helen looked at Connor in surprise.

'Can I help?' she asked.

'You can sit and keep me company.'

She watched as he chopped onion and garlic. Soon the rich tang of frying garlic filled the air. He added chopped bacon, then threw in several handfuls of rice.

'Now a little something I prepared earlier,' he said with a smile. He added a splash of beef stock. The sizzling mixture sighed, and bubbled slowly, while he added white wine and the juice of two freshly squeezed limes. He opened a cupboard filled to overflowing with sachets of herbs and spices.

Helen peered over his shoulder. 'You could open a restaurant.'

He took out four sachets, and shook generous quantities into the mixture. 'Salt, cumin, cardamom and jalapeno.' He stirred them in and covered the pan. After a few minutes he opened it to check. A delicious aroma filled the kitchen.

'Good. Few more minutes and we're there.' He washed salad, tossed it into a bowl and put it on the table. He opened a bottle of Chilean white and poured out two glasses.

When they sat down to eat, Connor let Helen start, waiting to see her reaction.

'Delicious. Where d'you learn to cook like that?'

He shrugged. 'I taught myself. I used to be in the army.' That much was available for public consumption. He wasn't going to specify SAS.

'When you're on an operation it's very important. Not just for survival, but morale too. It can get depressing eating the same thing for months on end. Tiny luxuries, like a bit of spice in your food, make a big difference. A lot of the guys carry little sachets of spices around with them.'

Helen smiled at the image of a load of rough tough men holed up in the mountains, carrying along with their paraphernalia of death little sachets of curry.

'I'm not used to men like you,' she said, unexpectedly.

'I don't really know any other kind. I've gone to school with other types, and university, but I didn't really fit in. I learned to act it, you have to sometimes, but it's not me.'

'You're a funny mixture of rough and smooth.'

He laughed. 'Am I?'

'You've got a lovely voice, nice and deep and smooth, and a pretty face.'

'Oh God, pretty?'

'Yes,' she said slowly, her eyes moving over his smiling lips, the curve of his cheek and his fathomless eyes. 'But it's hard too, the planes of your face. There are no jowls, nothing like that.'

'I'm thirty-seven, for God's sake.'

'Lots of thirty-something men in London have jowls. I was surrounded by men like that in the City, who work all day and drink all night and look ten years older than they are.'

'They can't all be like that.'

'No, there're exceptions, some lovely ones, but it's not much of a place for male beauty.'

'Is that what you're looking for?'

'No. But it helps.' She took a swig of wine, her eyes moving away from his. 'Were you born there?'

'Where? England?'

'Mm.'

'No. I was born in the Yemen, in Mukalla. My father was a colonial man. I was born in our house on the beach. God, it was beautiful. Forty miles of empty beach. I was given a donkey when I was three and I used to spend all day riding along those beaches and swimming in the sea.'

'Alone?'

'Yes. My mother died when I was born.' His eyes held hers and she saw the stubborn unwillingness to show pain. 'I grew up with my father, and Harigoo, my amah. She looked after me. My father had to travel a lot. Sometimes he took me with him, but I was on my own a lot.'

253

'Wasn't it dangerous?'

'There was a bit of terrorism. My father taught me to shoot when I was five. There was a guard at the house ... But I was more worried about sharks than terrorists.'

'There were sharks there?'

He nodded. 'You learned not to swim in dark or turbulent waters, I sort of developed a feel for when it was safe and when it wasn't. But you couldn't always get it right. I was in the sea once on one of the more popular beaches. There was a woman bathing ten feet from me. She was only waist deep in the water, and suddenly she started screaming. There was this great tail lashing, and a dorsal fin. Her husband rushed in to pull her out.'

'What happened?'

'Half her leg was gone. She died on the beach, from shock I think.'

'Oh God. How old were you?'

'Six.'

They were both silent for a while, Connor remembering, Helen thinking about a child brought up with death.

'That must have marked you.'

'It did. What about you, Helen, what's marked you?'

'Am I marked? Is it so visible?'

'Who isn't?'

She smiled. 'Who indeed?' She felt torn again by the conflicting urges to keep her silence and to open up to this man. Where would she even start? Connor seemed to read her mind, made it easier for her.

'What's the best thing you've ever done?'

'To run away,' she answered without a pause.

'What happened?'

Helen took in a long breath, then let it out in a shuddering sigh. Her yearning to talk to this man who had opened himself to her was now overwhelming. With each of his words he had brought her closer to him. For all of that time, he had banished from her the spectre of SIN. She thought about them now, briefly, then, with the power of the memories she would put into words, she pushed them from her mind. She kept her eyes on Connor, making the act of her opening up more intimate still.

'I was eighteen. I was living with a musician, a saxophone player. We'd been together since I was sixteen. About a year after I moved in, he started to hit me. Not often, only when he was drunk, and . . . oh Christ, here I go again explaining it away.' She stopped and Connor could see her eyes glistening with rage. 'Anyway, he hit me, and for whatever reasons I put up with it for about six months. I could defend myself,' she added, as if in mitigation, 'so he never managed to really hurt me. But one night he came home, picked a fight, tried to slap me. I went to jump out of the way, but it was late. I was tired. I tripped over a stool, fell and smashed my head. I was lying there and I could feel my head hot and bleeding, and he was just standing there above me laughing. Something inside me snapped. I got up, I was going to go, just walk out, but he lunged for me, tried to hit me again. I caught hold of his right wrist, twisted it back until it snapped. He passed out with the pain. He was out for half an hour. I packed a case and left.'

'You ran away?'

'Yep. First of all to Devon, Dartmouth, where my mother lives. When I got there I couldn't face it. She would have been OK, put a brave face on it, but her boyfriend would have treated me like some kind of delinquent. So I stayed in a bed and breakfast. The next day, wandering around town, I saw an advert in a newsagent's for a ship's cook. I applied, got the job. Two days later I set sail for Jamaica.'

'Not a bad place to run away to.'

She looked wistful. 'It was bliss. I spent eight years at sea, slipping anchor, sailing out into the dawn. New horizons every day. I've never been so scared or so excited in my life. I crossed the North Atlantic. I sailed the South Atlantic, just me and the crew when we were given six months off; I cruised the Pacific, saw things you wouldn't believe – huge waves the size of houses breaking on us, whales swimming alongside us at sunset, these huge black shiny backs arching through the water. Silent mornings when the sea's as still as a mirror and there's complete silence. The whole world seems to have stopped turning.'

She gave a smile of yearning and of joy.

The air was thick between them. Connor yearned to take Helen into his arms, just to hold her, to rock her to sleep.

They fell silent. It seemed to Helen for a moment that Connor might have been squatting cross-legged in the empty quarter of Arabia, with no more than a crackling fire for company. He had a facility for silence that only those who spent long horizons of time alone could master. Dai had it, she had it. All her life, she had searched for someone with whom she could be silent. In the distance, the sea rolled and rumbled. The night seemed to grow darker.

Some time later, Connor spoke.

'What would you like to do now?' he asked.

Helen looked into his eyes. She was silent for a few, long moments. She didn't want to break this intimacy. She wanted to take one step closer to this man. She smiled slowly.

'I'd like to dance with you. Somewhere dark and dingy and wild.'

They drove downtown through abandoned streets to a warehouse. The ground thumped as they walked in. Helen noticed a bar, a band and dancers. She smelled dope, sweet and heady. It all flowed away as she and Connor cut through the dance floor swaying with bodies and began to move.

Fast salsa, a wild tempo, like stampeding horses, high stepping, whirling till dizziness came and sweat ran down her breasts and thighs and the heat seeped through her whole body. Then the tempo slowed. Connor stepped nearer, took hold of her. She felt the contours of his body blend with hers. She felt they had left dry land and were swimming in a sea of music. It filled the air around her, flowed through her. They moved in the same currents and for those hours everything else was washed away.

CHAPTER 60

Roddy Clark clattered down Campden Hill Square towards Holland Park Avenue, the studs on the soles of his shoes beating out a war tattoo. He grinned to himself, showing gleaming teeth. He could feel his return, see his prodigal boyish charm working in the eyes of the women he passed.

He faced the newsroom like the principal actor entering centre stage. He could feel the buzz, the excitement with which the brokers of news spun their product into gold. For the first time in eighteen months he was King Midas. He felt within him a surge of beneficence towards the more engaging of his colleagues, a 'fuck you' arrogance towards the others, who constituted the majority. He was tripping once more on his own talent and, God, it was good.

He rapped on the glass door to the editor's office.

'Hey, Roland, have I got something for you!'

He'd caught his boss in a good mood. Mudd pursed his lips, camped it up.

'Come on then, pal, show me what you got.'

Clark almost seemed to dance around the tape recorder as if it were playing the most sensual tango. He took long dramatic strides back and forth as the voices filtered out into the air-conditioned citadel of Mudd's office. Zaha Zamaroh giving Hugh Wallace orders to move fifteen million dollars of his illegally earned money into an offshore bank account of hers, then Hugh Wallace giving instructions over the telephone about moving the money, reciting Zamaroh's bank account details.

'Details, numbers, hard facts,' spat Roddy in excitement. 'Enough for you now?' he asked, clicking off the tape, pocketing it. 'Corroboration or what?'

Mudd smiled slowly. 'Go with it. You got page one. Top left. Have it ready after lunch. I'll get the lawyers in for three.'

'Can I do a piece on Jencks too, her disappearance, hints, nice and subtle?'

'All right. Do it, you bastard. You're so hungry for revenge I can hear your stomach churning from here, but you're right, Jencks is part of this story, we'd be fools to leave her out. Write a nice little teaser, bring in her old man. But subtle, got it? She's supposed to be innocent. Just hint that she's involved.'

Clark wheeled around. He was already almost out of the office when Mudd's voice stopped him on the threshold.

'Well done, Roddy. Nice piece of work. I've a feeling this is only the beginning. Who knows where it's going to lead?'

Roddy nodded, stared almost unseeingly at Mudd. He walked out, strangely silent, his urgency stayed. It was as if he'd had a forewarning of the consequences of his story. He crossed the newsroom, sat down at his desk and stared at his blank screen for a long while before finally calling up the words, summoning the furies.

CHAPTER 61

Helen woke late. She was conscious of drifting from about nine on but couldn't drag herself from her dream world. She and Connor had danced until 5 AM. He'd brought her home, they had stood, hands by their sides, sweat cooling in the night air, and said their goodbyes from a safe distance. A kiss would have been a match to a touchpaper, and they both knew it.

Part of her felt that she was dancing still, the slightly intoxicated sensation she always had after a long sea voyage, disgorged onto dry land. But there was a sense of sick trepidation too, a hangover of fear. It took only a few seconds to remember that SIN was real. She skipped her yoga and went straight for the pool. She dived in and broke the surface, still as a glass. Pearls of water glistened over her skin. She swam for nearly an hour, trying in vain to clear her head of the lurking spectre of SIN.

Finally she gave up. She stopped in the deep end, pulled herself up, rested her elbows on the warm tiles. She gazed out across the garden, trying to order her thoughts. The smell of chlorine mixed with the scent of the hibiscus flowers that blew from the trees, garlanding the water around her with amethyst stars.

The way she saw it, there were only two possible explanations for SIN's interest in her. Something to do with Wallace, Rankin and Goldsteins, or something to do with the fact that Dai, her father and Maldonado had at one time all been secret agents. It didn't make sense that Peruvian Intelligence would be following her on Goldsteins' or on the British authorities' behalf. If the long arm of the British law were reaching out for her, surely it would do it through the Peruvian police? And if it had nothing to do with London, that meant that, for some unearthly reason, Peruvian

Intelligence had some business of its own with her. What had she done here to invite interest? Stayed with Maldonado, that was all. SIN must be interested in him. She stepped from the pool, shuddering. The other explanation, which chilled her with an almost premonitory fear as she came to it, was that Maldonado himself was SIN, that in coming here to search for her father she had inadvertently walked into the heart of a secret world. Perhaps that explained the electric fences, the dogs and the armed guards. That would explain the odd touch of paranoia she thought she glimpsed in Maldonado's eyes, and would warrant his threat that not even behind his guarded walls was she safe. Dai had warned her about Maldonado, had cautioned her that, twenty-three years on, he might have changed, and not for the better, but Helen began to think that not even Dai with his innate caution could have foreseen the change. Maldonado had been a friend, he was supposed to be a haven, not a kind of predator, preying on her every move with spying eyes. Why did he mistrust her? Now that she was thinking this way, it seemed he had been ambivalent about her from the first. Almost every time she saw him, he issued a warning of some kind. She had never thought he might be warning her about himself. His words came back to her, verbatim. *Death stalks this place. You think you're safe here, don't you, but you're not. You invite it. You see too much. You have an imagination, and it will curse you. Nothing you can do, except turn and face it.*

CHAPTER 62

Helen met Connor that night, at Too Too Tango. Argentinian tango played on the juke box: slow, insistent, wildness just a beat away. Connor was sitting at the bar on a high stool, muscled legs in faded jeans. He held a glass of beer in his right hand. His left lay idle on his thigh. He was in profile to her, eyes apparently resting on the crowded bar. She could almost feel him dreaming, longed to see what his eyes conjured, wanted it to be her. His beauty stopped her for a moment, and she just looked at him. In that pause, she began to crave him. She forgot her fears as she imagined his hands on her skin, the taste of his mouth, him lowering his body onto hers, looking at her with his eyes of dreams. He turned to her and saw. He looked a question at her, savage, yearning. She went to him, and he smiled. He slid off his bar stool and kissed her lips. His hand found hers, their fingers laced together. Something inside her did a dance of joy. Another part tried to run. Some men could come and go, leaving no imprint. This man was danger. She knew she could not remain unchanged by him. Something in him could cut right through her, through the barricades she had built over decades.

'How are you?' he asked.

Reeling, yearning, excited. 'Fine. You?'

'Not bad. What will you drink?'

'Vodka. Very cold.'

She knocked it back, then another. Goosebumps rose on her arms.

'You cold?'

'The air conditioning.'

'Here, have my jersey.' He peeled it off. He wore a white T-shirt underneath. She could see the curve of his muscles. She could imagine the feel of his skin, smooth, marble, like Michelangelo's David; a sculpture of perfection, with the eroticism of life. He draped his jersey around her shoulders. Her nerve endings burned with his fingerprints. She became preternaturally sensitive. The bar seemed to go quiet. The rhythm of the tango insinuated itself into her veins. Now she felt hot. She let Connor's jersey slip to her waist. Her body felt strong, glowing, it longed to fight him, then take the delicious surrender of yielding to him. She looked into his eyes and gave him a smile of challenge. He looked back, steadily, sure of himself.

'Shall we go?'

Connor left a twenty-dollar bill on the counter. They left the bar together, not touching, not speaking. They walked the two blocks towards where Connor had parked his car.

'Damn,' said Helen, stopping. 'I left your jersey in the bar.'

'I'll go back to get it, don't worry.' Connor handed her his car keys. 'Car's just round the corner, just in case there's an identical blue VW there, the number plate's VX 264.'

'VX 264. Got it.' She watched him run back towards the bar, then she turned and slowly walked towards the corner.

The streetlights cast a dull orange glow on the faces of the men who seemed to loiter on every street. They never seemed to do anything, they just stood, murmuring to each other, and watching. Helen walked by them, skin tightening.

Connor emerged from the bar with his jersey just in time to see two men turn the corner at the end of the street, following at a slow jog the direction in which Helen had gone. He broke into a sprint, cursing himself.

Helen was aware of the sound of footsteps, fast and insistent. They came out of nowhere in the dark street. There was something callous in the rhythm they drummed out on the dusty pavement. She knew immediately that they were bearing down on her. Every woman's nightmare.

All her instincts screamed at her; she desperately wanted to run, but they were too close now. She kept walking slowly, as if unaware of their intent. She resisted the urge to look around. She took her hands from her pockets. All her training came back to her, summoned unconsciously. *Breathe, summon your chi, timing, commit.* She readied her body and her mind. At the last minute, she spun around, her hand up in the air, palm facing the two men.

'KIAI!' she roared. *The way of breath. Cure the angry spirit of your opponent on contact. Or capture it.* The men stopped in shock, just for a moment, feet from her. The one closest recovered first. He lunged towards her. She drew back her hand, shot it out again, arm straight, struck him just below his jaw with the inner blade of her hand. He reeled over backwards, head crashing down on the pavement. Then he lay still. *Keep your body moving, never be there.* Helen wheeled around. *If you think you're going to be hit, just enter and raise. Your unbendable arm will stop you being hurt.* She raised her arm, rigid with her chi, and shielded the punch of the second man. *Think contact, wherever it goes, we're there.* The man punched again. Helen moved in, caught his hand, turned it outward towards his side, placed the knife edge of her other hand at his elbow, propelled her energy upwards and threw him up and backwards. *Sumiotoshi.* He crashed down on a parked car, his head breaking the glass on the windshield. He groaned, grabbed his back, tried to move. He raised his bloody head from the shattered windscreen, and slipped down over the bonnet, onto the pavement. Helen stared down at him, her eyes blazing. She turned back to the first man, who lay prone, eyes shut. She made a scissor motion with her hands, over the bodies of the two men, then she turned and came face to face with Connor. He stared at her burning eyes, took in the scene behind her. Without a word he took her arm, they both ran for his car, jumped in, locked the doors.

Connor drove off at speed, wheeling through the traffic, jumping the red light on Conquistadores. He watched Helen out of the corner of his eye. She had her head turned away from him, and was staring fixedly out of her side window. Her chest rose and fell quickly with silenced breaths, and her hands were clenched into fists which she jammed under her thighs as if to hide. He checked his mirror. He couldn't see the tails, but that alone gave him little comfort. To Helen, he seemed like a man possessed, racing through the backstreets, taking one-ways the wrong way, going round in circles. She watched in silence.

*   *   *

263

They stood side by side on Connor's balcony. For a long time neither of them spoke. Connor seemed, like Helen, to be doing his own form of meditation.

They both turned to each other together.

'What happened?' asked Connor.

'Got a cigarette?'

Helen lit up and exhaled heavily, her words coming out with the smoke.

'They were coming up behind me. Running. You know anyway, by instinct. I knew.'

'You floored them, both of them?'

'Yeah. I think I might have hurt them quite badly.'

'If someone's going to get it, better the other guy. What d'you do to them?'

'Disabled them.'

'Where d'you learn that, Helen?'

'What's it to you? Why d'you sound so suspicious?'

'It's a bit unusual. You have to admit that.' Carlyle's words came back to him; *she could be CIA, DEA, she's lethal.* Not just in the way Carlyle had meant. Connor had seen enough on the street to know that, with her skills, Helen could kill. His radar flashed out a warning to him, but, in some perverse way, that only made Helen Jencks more attractive. He'd thought that the storm was swirling around Helen, maybe the storm was Helen herself.

'What's usual?' Helen was saying. 'Welcome to the twentieth century. Girls do stuff like that now.'

'Stuff like what? Jujitsu, tae kwon-do? To that level?'

'Aikido.'

'What are you? A black belt?'

'Yes. I'm a black belt. Second dan.'

Connor whistled through his teeth.

'Nice girls don't live in a nice world any more,' Helen snapped. 'They can't, or don't want to sit around waiting for a nice man to come and bail them out of trouble.'

'So you bailed yourself out,' said Connor softly. 'What made you feel you needed to learn? What happened to you, Hel?'

As Connor watched Helen, her eyes became distant. For a long time she said nothing.

'I started aikido when I was seven, just after my father left. My mother encouraged me. It was very clever of her. I was angry, full of rage, and I felt so useless. Aikido got rid of some of the anger, and as I got good at it, I began to feel pretty useful.'

'I'll bet. You almost seem to be thriving on it. It's as if you've gone up ten gears. Your face is glowing, you look fantastic.'

Helen laughed. 'I've always thrived under adversity. My friend Joyce says I have an edge, and I need to sharpen it otherwise I go dead. She's right. For four years I've been back in the City and it's been civilising me, dulling me. Look, if you want an idea of what I'm really like, there's nothing I love more than standing on deck, roped in, slamming through the sea with a force eight gale behind me and thirty-foot waves. I love that, got it? So, two little shits having a go at me, whoever the hell they might be, don't faze me. It's not the first time I've had to defend myself. I met some real bastards when I was at sea. In dodgy ports and on deck. What I want to know about tonight is why?' She raised her hand suddenly. 'Cancel that. Forget I ever asked. They were two yobs, out for the main chance.' She could see disbelief in Connor's eyes. She didn't believe herself either. It seemed to her to be another warning, perhaps personally delivered by SIN, a possibility she didn't want to have to deal with.

Connor got up to get a bottle of whisky.

'Best single malt.' He poured out two large glasses. 'Perhaps it's time to go home, Helen,' he said softly. 'You were lucky tonight. Those men might have had guns. Aikido'll never block a bullet.'

She smiled. 'That's what someone else said.'

'Who?'

'My godfather.'

'He sounds like a wise man.'

'He is.'

'So will you go home?'

She studied him for a while. She could almost feel him circling around her, the way she was him. So much hovered in the air between them, not just desire, but an awareness of danger, a sense he knew more than he was saying, and a feeling that just as she had her hidden agenda, so he had his.

265

She shook her head. 'I'm not going anywhere.'

'Why not?'

'I haven't done what I came to do.' She gave a half-smile. Implacability lay beneath. 'Don't ask.'

How many times had he said those words? Just as she said them. It was like listening to an echo. Connor watched her. He could feel the chaos stalking her, perhaps walking with her, seeping out of the unreadable eyes she turned on him. He wanted to warn her, to reach out and pull her to him, to banish the danger he knew surrounded her, but the part of him that was an agent felt compelled to stand back, to wait and watch as her fate played itself out. In the deepest part of him, untouched by training or mission, he vowed to stand by her, as close as she would allow him, ready to pull her out just before the fatal moment. That it was coming, he had no doubt. Extreme danger had stalked him, and that instinct, once felt, could never be forgotten.

Helen felt the weight of Connor's eyes upon her. The desire that the attack had killed began to rise in her again, but now it was muddied. She fought it down. She had too much to deal with. She knew her days at Maldonado's were numbered. She felt a sick foreboding at the prospect of returning to his house, but all her things were there, her money, her passport, and, more than anything, she had a sense that she had a last chance to discover something that would help her search for her father.

'You'd better take me home,' she said to Connor. She could see him struggling with some internal dilemma, but he said nothing, just drove her home, occasionally glancing at her with worried eyes.

He kissed her good night, stroking her cheek.

'Be careful.'

Grim and efficient, the security guards let Helen in without a wasted word or smile. She crossed the garden to her cottage.

She glanced around her bedroom, as if uncertain what to do next, then she slowly took off her clothes and got into bed. She sat up, resting her forearms along her thighs, trying to still her mind, to weave out fears, to blank out unreason. Half an hour later, she had made up her mind. She would stay one more night, somehow get into Maldonado's study, and search it. Then she would leave, enlist Connor's help, and start searching for her father.

CHAPTER 63

The next morning, Maldonado watched Helen taking breakfast on the terrace from his vantage point in his study. He wheeled round to Angel.

'She doesn't have a mark on her. What the hell happened?'

Angel paced around the room. 'I organised everything, *jefe*. Two of my men went for her.' He glared through the window at Helen's back. 'She beat them up.'

'She did what?'

'Broken ribs. Unconscious. Concussion. Left them bleeding on the street.'

'Who were they? Amateurs?'

'They were good, *jefe*.'

'Get rid of them. A girl beats them up.'

'No ordinary girl, *jefe*. No ordinary house guest. The trap worked. Though it hurt them to say it, my men said she was awesome. Every mark on their bodies betrays her for what she is. They said she probably could have killed them if she'd chosen. She was incredibly powerful and skilled. Do you still have any doubt that she's an agent?'

Maldonado ran his hand through his hair. The thick grey rippled over his fingers. He sat at his desk, facing Angel.

'Surely, if she were an agent, she'd have been intelligent enough to spot the trap.'

'She had about five seconds to think about it, then it was instinct. An agent's instincts have been trained to fight. It takes a hell of a lot more training to cover up your training.'

'So, she's an agent,' said Maldonado, slowly, unwillingly, as if he were passing a sentence of some kind. 'One able to kill with her bare hands.' For a long while he just stared at Helen's back before speaking again.

'Everything's ready with el Dólar?' he asked, voice grim.

Angel nodded. 'He's on his way. Officially, we'll arrest him this afternoon 'round three, while he's having lunch with his mistress. To show how seriously we're treating the arrest, we'll announce that we've taken him to the private quarters of a senior member of SIN – everyone'll know it's you – for detailed questioning. The shoot-out'll start about midnight. We make it look as if el Dólar gets away, although in reality, we keep him here, underground, with your private collection of Moche. Two days later, we spirit him away to Colombia.'

'Leaving a trail of bodies behind tonight,' interrupted Maldonado. 'Perhaps we could solve two problems at once,' he said, almost in a whisper. He rubbed his hands over his face. 'What choice has she left me?' He got to his feet, crossed the room to the window. He gazed out at Helen. 'How could she do it? She's so beautiful, the daughter of a man I once loved.' He looked inside himself and knew that the small part which kept him from falling over the brink into insanity still loved Jack Jencks. That love had made him, against his better judgement, allow Helen Jencks to remain in his care as the evidence against her escalated. With her incandescence, with the blood of her father pumping so visibly in her veins, she had brought life and hope to his atrophying good. And all the while, she was spying on him. Betraying him. Her destruction in his eyes killed a little bit more of his scant resources of good. The pain in that was extraordinary. It surprised him; he had thought his capacity to feel pain had long ago died. He gouged away at it. It reminded him that he was still human, still felt like a man. A wave of bitter despair and futility engulfed him. What was left of his finer feelings changed nothing. He would go on, like he always did. He was too far gone on his bloody voyage to turn back now. No one could swim against that river of blood. It struck him as the ultimate irony that, despite his much vaunted power, he had long since lost his freedom. All his actions seemed to him pre-ordained. He tried to console himself with the argument that, as an agent, Helen knew the risks, knew the consequences. He doubted that she could have discovered much that would have harmed him during her stay, but he could not be sure of that, and, in any case, the real danger to him was the fact that she had gained entry to his house, possessed as she was of the ability and opportunity to kill him. Word of that would seep out. The agents of his myriad enemies would take encouragement from Helen's example, the attempts to kill or destroy him would escalate, unless he took the necessary measures to restore his credibility. Part of him admired Helen for what she had done, as much as he damned her for committing him to action. He wished to God she was innocent, but wishing changed nothing. The only thing he yearned for these days was that his own death, when it came, would be swift. He had agonised for years with his desire to hasten his own death, but the survival instinct in him was too strong, and he seemed cursed to live on, moving relentlessly down his bloody path, while around him others fell.

He turned back to Angel. 'Have her killed tonight. Get a professional. No mistakes this time.'

CHAPTER 64

Helen waited for her chance to get into Maldonado's study all day. She walked around the garden, as close to the house as casual strolling would allow. She swam in the pool, trying to shake the tension which stalked her. It seemed the house too was in the grip of some unnamed suspense. Strange men appeared. She could hear their voices, low and urgent, in conference with Maldonado in his study. Maldonado stayed there all day, and when he moved to the dining room for a brief lunch, Helen heard the low murmur of the strange male voices seeping out of the study. As twilight faded, her frustration grew, along with the sense of unease that had plagued her all day. She felt that time was against her, that the spikes of some hidden mechanism were grinding on relentlessly, counting down the seconds that were dripping from her fingers like blood. She shivered in the growing night, resolved to try one more time.

At eleven, as she peered from her windows across the garden, she saw the lights go out in Maldonado's study. She took her pinpoint torch from her sponge bag, pulled on trainers, slipped out of her bedroom window, and stole across the garden.

She slipped down against the wall beneath the open window to Maldonado's study. She waited for a couple of minutes, just to be sure no one was inside, then she glanced around quickly, before hoisting herself through the window. She dropped into a crouch inside the room, heart pounding. She waited until her eyes grew accustomed to the darkness, and then she began her search without using her torch. She pulled at the desk drawers. All of them were locked. She scanned the shelves, her eyes coming to rest on a series of box files beneath the shelf of tortured Moche. She pulled down one box, opened it, turned on her torch, and began to flick through the reams of paper. She found nothing. She replaced the box file and pulled down a second. She was halfway though when she heard voices. She flicked off her torch and hunched down under Maldonado's desk. Her body gave a racking convulsion of fear as the voices came nearer. She struggled to still it, horrified by her response, which seemed to be beyond the normal spectrum of fear. It was as if her body knew something she didn't. She imagined hands upon her, saw in her mind the men from last night, shuddered again as the voices drew level with the door, then passed.

She waited until she heard a door open and close, choking off the voices, then she crawled out, and straightened up. She wanted to flee. To hop out of the window, run from the house and the garden, keep on running. A stronger yearning kept her where she was. She had a sense that this was her last chance, that somewhere in this room lay the secret of her father's whereabouts.

The second file was as useless as the first. Full of reports, clippings, articles, nothing that could be remotely relevant to her father. She pulled down the third file. Fifteen minutes later she consigned that to the shelf. She glanced at her watch, luminous in the dark. It was nearly midnight. She was haunted again by the feeling that somehow time was running out. With trembling fingers, she pulled down the fourth box file. Something inside it rattled. She opened it to find a series of old diaries and address books. She started with the address books. She flicked through until her fingers were dry. Her eyes were beginning to ache and she nearly missed it.

Arturo Leon, then in brackets after the name, *Jack Jencks*. Her fingers trembling violently, Helen scrabbled for a pen from the desk. She wrote down the address on her hand: 268 Calle Choquechaca, Cusco. She was replacing the contents of the file when she heard voices again. Maldonado's, harsh and low, seemingly issuing some kind of order. She pushed the file back up on the shelf, the voices coming closer every moment. She wheeled around, headed for the window, and swung herself out. She dropped to a crouch and angled herself along the wall just as she heard the door to Maldonado's study open. She suddenly remembered her torch. She'd left it lying beneath Maldonado's desk. She cursed herself, and tried to suppress the sudden shuddering that coursed through her body. She heard footsteps inside the study, then Maldonado's voice, so close. He must have been standing by the window, looking out. Helen tried to quieten her breath. It seemed to be coming in rushes of sound she felt sure he must hear. She knew she couldn't stay where she was, exposed against the lit wall of the house. The guards would be making their rounds with remorseless regularity, but if she moved she risked being heard. She waited, seconds drilling into her brain as she imagined the guards getting closer. She heard Maldonado's voice dull as he must have turned away from the window. She edged along the house, made a low, crouching run for the nearest bushes. She paused, glancing around, then ran again to the next bush, and on in a series of wild dashes until the adrenaline threatened to choke her. She reached her cottage, slipped through her bedroom window just as the first guard rounded the house. She saw his outline, silhouetted against the stone, as he patrolled the garden, passing just feet from where she had been crouching less than thirty seconds earlier.

Inside her cottage Helen rolled on the floor, catching her breath, trembling, and stilling her desire to laugh out loud from the elation of her discovery of her father's address, and from the sheer narrowness of her escape. As she thought of escape, she sobered. She had a sudden sense of being trapped. Now she had her father's address, the desire to flee was overwhelming. She looked at her watch. Five past midnight. The dogs would be freed now, roaming the garden. Even if she could, by some miracle, quieten them, persuade them not to rip her to pieces, she would have to take her chances a second time with Maldonado's patrolling guards. She reckoned that she wouldn't be so lucky as to evade them twice in one evening. But, God, she wanted to go. Her legs were trembling with the suppressed urge to run. She got up and paced in the darkness.

The sound of a gunshot ripped through the night. Helen froze. She could feel the sound in the echoing silence that followed. Another shot rang out. One of Maldonado's guards was probably just checking his rifle, something like that. But then a third shot ripped through the night, raw and close. She stared around, as her mind began to race. Before she could gather her thoughts, another shot cracked the air, and another, then a chaos of shots, and the drilling of machine-gun fire, in short sharp bursts, like a mad conversation with everyone trying to speak at once. She dropped to the floor and crawled into the sitting room. Her blinds were drawn, she could see nothing. All she could feel was terror and confusion. She was running towards the bathroom, the shots still blaring, when another sound wailed through the air: an alarm, shrill and insistent. It came from across the garden, from Maldonado's house. Even that wild sound was silenced for a moment by the roar of an explosion, deep and vibrating so that it shook her chest and seemed to force the air from her lungs. Then, as the sound died, leaving her ears ringing, the alarm in her own cottage went off, which meant only one thing: someone was trying to get in, might be in already. She ran for the kitchen, towards the only weapon to hand. She took a carving knife from the kitchen drawer, ran to the bathroom and locked herself in.

She waited, knife poised. Still the gunfire raged. That was the only sound. There were no shouts, no spoken words, all she could hear were the sickening explosions, and her own breath. The knife shook violently in her hand. Her whole body trembled, her breath came in shallow gasps. She had never felt pure terror before, never been at the centre of what sounded like blind, insane chaos. She imagined men walking on silent feet, through the cottage, guns poised, seeking her out. She imagined them going through every room, until they came to the locked door of the bathroom. She was trapped, with only a knife and her aikido for weapons. In the wildness of her thoughts, Dai's words, and Connor's, came back to her. *Aikido's not much use against a gun.* The fear ripped through her till it felt as if her whole body was vibrating. Her body and mind were operating on a level she had never before experienced. It was a wild, live mayhem. Part of her wanted to run out, to search for the intruders, to see their faces, to do something. Her fear didn't paralyse her, as she had read it did to many people. It gripped her, goading, and her body shook as if to break away. She listened for sounds in her cottage. Nothing. She unlocked the bathroom door and cracked it open an inch. She looked out, waited, eased herself out. She seemed to be following some unspoken instinct to move. She ducked below the shuttered window and crawled towards the main door. A sound stopped her. A key in the lock, the sound of it turning. The rage of panic threatened to blind her for a moment. In three silent strides, she made for the wall, flattened her body, waited. The door inched open. She could smell someone, the stench of sweat, of sexual excitement. There was a faint sound of breathing, of movement. The door opened wider. An arm protruded, holding a revolver. Helen's mind went silent. Her training alone spoke to her, guiding her body. She placed the knife by her feet and waited until the man took a step forward, until his whole body was inside her cottage. Then her right hand shot out and caught the man's right hand, the one holding the gun. She wheeled round one hundred and eighty degrees, placed her left elbow over his right elbow, and threw all her force down upon it. His elbow cracked and he plunged face first to the floor. Helen grabbed the gun from his flailing fingers, moved back and pointed it at him. He was wearing a black balaclava with a slash for his eyes. She could see in his look of wild implacability that he wouldn't back off. He was so close she could almost touch him. He pushed up from the ground, reached down towards his ankle. Helen saw a glimpse of a black nylon ankle holster, a flash of stainless steel, the barrel of a revolver. She aimed for the man's shoulder, and fired. The sound of the pistol roared in her heart. The shockwave of the explosion hit her chest. There was a blinding flash of burning yellow edged by white, with red at the centre. She blinked rapidly, for a few moments she couldn't see, then her eyes picked up the figure of the man, staggering backwards, falling out through the open door into the garden. Helen grabbed the revolver he had dropped. The man looked at her for a moment, at the two weapons she pointed at him, then he struggled to his feet, and ran away into the darkness.

Helen slammed the door, locked it, dragged the dining room table out into the hall, rammed it up against the door. Her ears rang piercingly. Her hands were shaking violently. She stuck them under her armpits, went to the far end of the room, squatted down on her haunches, the guns by her feet, and stilled the wailing scream that was gathering in her throat. The man had come to kill her, and something in her knew that others would follow, and probably in minutes. Outside the gunfire still raged. She could choose to stay and wait, or take her chances in the mayhem. She crawled back to her bedroom, peered out of the window. The garden was strobed by spotlights. Low figures ran in bursts across the garden, machine guns blazed and she heard screams. She leapt up, pulled her window closed and sank down to the floor. It would be suicide to run out into that, but she knew too that to stay in the cottage was sure death.

She would rather die running than trapped in a corner. She grabbed her sports bag, threw in the two guns, her passport, the bundles of money Dai had given her, and her walking boots. She zipped it up, crawled back to her bedroom window, and, inching her way up, peered out. The shots outside sounded as dull thuds, growing sharper as her hearing gradually returned. As she watched and listened, the shots grew fewer till she could hear them individually, and then they stopped, leaving an awful silence. Her ears hurt, she seemed to be able to hear her heart beat and her lungs move. She began to shake more violently, knew that now was the time to run. She picked up her bag, peered out of the window again, and saw only stillness. She pushed open the window, raised her leg over the sill, and froze, as she heard a voice calling her name.

'Helen! Helen, are you there? It's Victor.'

He was at the front of the house, maybe twenty feet away. His voice was subdued, but insistent at the same time. He called her again and again, the sound growing louder as he walked around the cottage towards her. She heard him speak again, what sounded like instructions. She eased out of the window, her muscles spasming with stiffness. She glanced around, then loped towards a clump of bushes twenty feet away. She crawled into their dense interior, branches scraping her face. Once hidden in their midst, she froze. She heard Maldonado calling her again, then he appeared, a blurred outline through the thorns. Four men followed him, all carrying sub-machine guns. They stopped by the open bedroom window. Maldonado barked out instructions and two of the men climbed into the cottage. They emerged after a couple of minutes and spoke to Maldonado in low voices. Helen heard him curse, and in the instructions she heard him speak next, she picked out the word *perros*, dogs.

She crouched in the bushes, watching the dim outlines of

Maldonado and his men as they walked back towards the house. Some minutes later – she had no idea how long it was, as time, like any of the realities she had known, seemed to be suspended – she forced her way out of the bushes, glanced around the now empty garden, and ran towards the next clump of bushes ten yards away. She paused there, heart pumping, then ran on, dropping down behind a thick cluster of heliotrope. She could see the dull purple of the flowers glowing in the ambient light that beamed still in the illuminated garden. The scent of the flowers filled her nose, mingling with the smell of cordite, legacy of the gun battle.

She heard a sound and wheeled around. The Dobermans were approaching at a run. She crouched down, making herself as small as possible.

'Hey, girls, it's all right, good girls,' she whispered. Her breath made her words ragged. The Dobermans slowed, approaching at a stiff walk. They stopped about five feet from her, legs angled back, necks straining forward, teeth bared, growling.

'You've been trained, haven't you, to attack anyone loose in the garden when you're let out, anyone except Maldonado and the guards?' She forced her breathing into a deep, slow pattern, trying to take the edge off her fear. 'There, it's all right, I'm no threat, you know me, remember, ssshhhhh, quiet there.' She could see their eyes soften fractionally as she spoke, her voice low and rhythmical. She kept her words flowing, a stream into their unconscious. She spoke quietly, knowing there was a chance the guards or Maldonado would hear her, knowing too, that if she couldn't becalm the animals, she was dead anyway. She knew what they could do. In seconds her throat could be torn out. She forced the image down, replaced it with one of sitting with Dai and his dogs beside the fire. She must show no fear or they would smell it.

'There, come on, come to me.' She reached out her hands, very slowly, gently. The growling eased to a low rumble, then stopped altogether. The lead bitch came right up to Helen, sniffed her outstretched fingers, then licked them. Helen rolled onto her back with her throat exposed and the three other dogs came up and licked her face. She wanted to giggle with a kind of wild relief, and their tongues were tickling her. 'All right, girls, good girls, good dogs, I'm gonna get up now, OK. It's all right, don't be alarmed.' She got up very slowly, stroking the dogs as she straightened. 'Got to go, girls, bye bye.' She glanced around, then walked slowly across the garden, forcing her rubbery legs to keep to a slow, smooth rhythm. She couldn't run now. In three paces all the Dobermans' training would be reawakened by her flight. The bitches watched her go, nut-brown eyes gleaming in the dark.

Helen glanced left and right. There was no sign of Maldonado or the guards. They had probably retreated inside, to Maldonado's study, where the light glowed, complacent in the knowledge that the dogs would succeed where the assassin sent to kill her had failed.

The perimeter area burned with light. There was nowhere to hide. Helen paused, staring at the thirty feet that separated her from freedom, from life. The urge to live was so strong. She fought down the terror which gripped her, stepped into the light, crossed the glaring border, and reached the door to the street. She stood in the full beam of a spotlight, slid back the bolts, opened the latch, and walked through.

CHAPTER 65

Evan Connor was awakened from sleep by the insistent ringing of the intercom. He peered at the luminous dial of his clock – three fifteen. He felt the stab of alarm always produced by abrupt night-time awakenings. He swung out of bed, padded through his darkened bedroom to the intercom. Helen's voice rose ragged from the handset.

'Evan, are you there?'

Two minutes later the lift brought her to him. He had positioned himself to the side of the elevator shaft, waiting, a six-inch carving knife in his hand. When he saw Helen was alone, and the lift doors had cracked shut behind her, he dropped the knife to his side and pulled her into his flat. He locked the door behind him, flicked on the light. Helen stood before him, terror illuminated in her bloody face. He opened his arms and she fell into them. He carried her into his sitting room, laid her down on the sofa. It was only when he had tended to the thorn scratches on her face, and made her a mug full of heavily sugared tea that he spoke to her.

'What happened?'

Below them the huge, deep rollers of the Pacific crashed onto a darkened shore. Helen could almost feel them, imagined herself floating on the white spume, in a yacht fully rigged to sail her away. She took a long drink of tea. The bitter sweetness coated her tongue. The mug burned her lips. She seemed supernaturally aware of every sensation.

'Someone tried to kill me. I was in my cottage when a shot rang out, then another. All hell broke loose, this massive gun battle. The alarms went off, in Maldonado's house, in my cottage. There were these explosions. I could see lights sweeping past my window,

I hid in my bathroom, then something told me to get out of there. I let myself out, moved towards the door when the key turned in the lock. The door opened, a hand reached through, holding a gun. I waited, then this man stepped into the room. I went for him, got him in rokkyo, broke his elbow, threw him to the floor, took the gun off him.'

'Jesus Christ. What happened then?'

'He reached down to his ankle. He had a holster there. He pulled out another gun. So I shot him.'

'Kill him?'

'I hit his shoulder. He staggered away.'

Connor stared up at the sky and blew out a breath.

'Shit.'

'I've got the guns here.' Helen nodded at her bag.

Connor opened her bag and took out the larger revolver with his right hand, pushed the catch forward with his thumb, and flipped out the cylinder with his fingers.

'Smith & Wesson .357 Mag. You fired one shot?'

Helen nodded. 'Deafened me.'

'Yeah, it's a bit of a monster, especially if you're not expecting it. He ground off the hammer spur,' mused Connor, examining the weapon. He pulled out the second revolver and proved it.

'Smith & Wesson 640. Nothing fired. This was his second gun, yeah?'

'The one in the ankle holster.'

'Yep, he was a pro.' Connor took a handkerchief, wiped both guns clean, and put them into a plastic bag. 'I'll have to get rid of them later. God knows how many jobs they've got on them.' He turned back to Helen.

'What happened next?'

'After a while, the shots stopped, there were voices calling out. Maldonado came for me, calling me. I didn't go to him. I hid in the bushes. They searched for me, couldn't find me, so they let the Dobermans out. I'd befriended them some time before, so when they came for me, I managed to quieten them.'

Connor shuddered.

'I crept through the garden, walked through all these blazing spotlights, managed to get away. I walked for an hour and a half before I found a taxi. I got him to drop me about a quarter of mile from here.'

Connor took hold of her hand.

'It's a miracle you're still alive. Christ, Helen, that was about as close as you get. Pretty heroic stuff getting out of there.'

Helen smiled. Connor stroked her hand, turned it over in his palm, saw the smears of red ink. Helen followed his gaze and screamed. She pulled her hand from his, and stared at the blurred writing.

'What is it?' asked Connor.

'It was my father's address. Oh Christ, it's gone.' Her eyes were wild with despair.

'It's not gone. You saw it, you wrote it down,' said Connor urgently. 'It's there in your memory. We'll get it back.'

'Cusco!' she shouted. 'Somewhere in Cusco.'

Connor got up from her side and returned with a small guide-book to Cusco. He flicked through the index, reciting street names. The words glazed over Helen until she suddenly sat up, bright with recognition.

'That's it. Calle de la Choquechaca. I remember now. It sounded like "shock and shakra". Got it. Number 268.' She grabbed Connor's hand and squeezed it with all that remained of her strength. She began to weep tears of relief. Connor held her, watching her. As the tears abated, he saw the plan forming in her eyes.

He got up and began to pace before her. 'Helen, you can't even think about looking for him now. We have to get you out of the country as soon as possible.'

She looked back steadily at him.

'Nothing's going to make me go.'

'Not even saving your life?'

'I just saved it.'

'It'll always be in danger as long as you stay in Peru. I don't think you have any idea what you've walked into.' He squatted at her side, his face grave.

'Listen to me, Helen, then decide. Do you know who Maldonado is?'

'An amateur archaeologist. Someone who tried to kill me.'

'Not just someone. Probably the most powerful and blood-soaked man in this whole bloody country. He's the head man in Peruvian Intelligence. He runs counter narcotics at SIN.'

Helen began to feel a strange madness tear at the fringes of her mind.

'Why did you come here, Helen?'

The questions whirled in the storm in her mind. Did Dai know? He couldn't have known. Why were SIN following her? Did they know about her? Why should they care? Why had they tried to kill her?

'Who are you?' she asked.

'What?'

'You heard me.'

'Why d'you ask?'

'My host, whom I thought was an archaeologist, turns out to be some great spy master. Who the hell are you?'

'Do I have to be anybody?'

'You're like someone who's waiting, one of these people who apparently glide through life, then suddenly something happens and you see a completely different side. You're not just this calm man who leads adventure holidays and works out at the gym in Lima.'

'And you're not some tourist who's come visiting because she likes the sound of the country and just happens to be staying with the head of counter narcotics.'

They glared at each other, and then something seemed to rise up in both of them, something essential, that had nothing to do with circumstances, and kept them searching each other's eyes long after the anger had died.

Connor decided at that moment there was no more room or time for concealment. He would tell her what she had to know, breaking his cover, breaking all the Firm's rules of engagement for this operation. But the Firm wasn't here. The Firm hadn't fought their way out of a murder attempt three hours earlier, and the Firm didn't know Helen Jencks. He stared at the woman lying before him, the defiance mixing with the fear in her eyes, the yearning for her father glowing through all the while. It conjured feelings he didn't know he possessed. He felt his own yearning, a furious tenderness for her, the overwhelming desire to protect her, and something that must have been the birth of love but which scared him so much he refused to name it. His wariness, the congenital and learned distrust that had saved his life many times, he confronted in that moment and set aside.

'You first,' said Helen.

Connor looked away, thought for a while, then blew out a long breath and began to speak.

'I'll understand if you hate me, but I didn't meet you by accident. I met you to befriend you, so that I could use you to find out about Maldonado.' He saw her face harden and he wanted to stop, try to win her round with a word or a touch, but he carried on relentlessly.

'I work for the British government. Counter narcotics.'

'I see.'

She turned away from him and Connor thought he had lost. He watched the line of her neck and the rise and fall of her breasts as she breathed deeply. Then she brought her eyes back to him. She said nothing, simply lay on the sofa and looked at him.

Many times in the SAS Connor had needed medical attention. Occasionally he had to see the doctor simply for a check-up. Strip naked, cough. The woman doctor with her cool, appraising eyes. Helen looked at him now, not with a glance, but with a long, unselfconscious weighing up that made him feel she could see into his bones, feel for their integrity, know how many times they had been broken and where they were weak, as if she knew how his blood flowed, what slowed it, what made it speed.

Her words when they came dripped like blood from an open wound.

'Why exactly were you asked to befriend me? What did you want to find out about Maldonado?'

'Some of us have our doubts about his integrity. What's happened to you shows we were right.'

'Why did he want to kill me? What the hell did I ever do to him or his henchmen?'

'Beat them up. There was nothing accidental about those men on the street, Helen. I started to follow you last week, the same day we met in the gym. The second day, we picked up another tail on you. SIN was following you. I don't believe in coincidence. Those men had to be Maldonado's. They picked their time. They had about two minutes when I was away from you, when the streets were empty, and they moved right in.'

'Why would Maldonado want to have me beaten up?'

'To test you. To see if you were some kind of specialist, agent type. There aren't many men, let alone women, that can do aikido to your level, but agents can. I know of a couple who could give you a run for your money.'

'Any time.'

Connor smiled. 'When you floored his men he got his answer. Next thing, someone's walking through your door with a pistol. Makes sense in their warped world. Maldonado couldn't afford to take any more risks with you. If word got out that an agent had insinuated herself into his household, which is supposed to be so secure, that an agent had befriended the man who's supposed to be able to see through everyone's cover, it'd be open season on him since he has so many enemies. A man like that maintains his position by fear, mystique and sheer bloody ruthlessness. You threatened the mystique. His only way out was to kill you.'

Helen thought back to her arrival in Lima, how she had walked into mayhem disguised, in the form of Maldonado's garden, as a paradise. Unwittingly, day by day, while thinking she was merely marking time, she was setting up her own fate, walking towards her own murder.

'You know, you'll probably think I'm mad, but I can't imagine Maldonado wanting me dead. There's a hardness to him, sure. I can imagine him ordering a trigger pulled on a bitter enemy, but he seemed to treat me like a friend. He seemed to need that. There's a loneliness to him, a tragic side.'

'You saw what little was left of his good side. You saw only what he wanted you to see. But you're right about the tragedy. His two sons and his daughter were blown up in a car bomb the Shining Path set for him. His wife killed herself a year later. He probably decided he had nothing more to lose. That was 1989. I reckon he turned then.'

'Oh God.' Helen thought of Maldonado's house, empty of photographs, sick with ghosts. She thought of his face as he showed her the Moche. Every emotion ever felt by man. He must have felt them all.

'Before that?' she asked. 'What was he like?' Now that Connor was lifting the veil of mystery that had obscured her vision ever since she had arrived in Maldonado's house, Helen wanted to know every detail. It somehow made her survival more real, the more she knew about the man who had tried to have her murdered.

'He wasn't entirely uncorrupt before. He was what we'd call acceptably dirty. Inevitably dirty. We could work with that.'

'How d'you mean?'

'Long story. You need to go way back, to understand where he came from, what shaped him and his country.'

'Tell me, I want to know.'

'His family used to own a number of huge haciendas, but they were all nationalised in 1969. Not before time. One estate was the size of Belgium. Anyway, Maldonado's family squandered what was left of their fortune. So Victor, as a junior army officer in the early sixties, didn't have a lot of money, but he had a lot of history, the sense that he mattered, that he was owed. He wanted to reclaim his family's position of money and power, so he got himself posted to the jungle, to a place called the Huallaga Valley. Most postings last about two years; Maldonado was there for seven. In case you didn't know, and there's no reason why you should, something like forty per cent of the world's cocaine originates in the Huallaga. Coca's grown there, and flown as basic paste to Colombia for processing into cocaine. There're hundreds of tiny airstrips dotted throughout the Peruvian jungle, not just the Huallaga, but a place called Manu too. Pilots get paid around fifty thousand dollars a pop for a narco flight, about a thousand times as much as they'd make on a legal stint, so there's no shortage of planes. We're talking thirty to forty flights a day before lookdown. Satellites, the spy in the sky,' explained Connor. 'Anyway, the point is, many drug consignments go from army-controlled airstrips, or else the army and air force just turn a blind eye to some of the private strips. The officers in charge take a massive cut. Maldonado was the man in charge.'

Helen thought of the Banco de Panama letter. Her mind, with its hungry facility for numbers, conjured it perfectly for her: the account number, the four million dollars.

'How can the army get away with turning a blind eye to drug trafficking on that scale?' she asked.

'They don't turn a blind eye, they sponsor it. They can do it because there's no one to challenge them. People who did, whether locals, or journalists, tended to end up dead. More journalists have died in that region than anywhere else apart from Vietnam during the war. It's not the place to go asking questions, and for most of the eighties it was controlled by the Shining Path and the MRTA. The government was either too busy profiting from drugs, or too busy trying to take on the Shining Path elsewhere to worry too much about the Huallaga. Fujimori's just started fighting the narcos, he's beginning to make some progress. He's banned Peruvian airforce and navy vessels from leaving Peruvian airspace or waters – that cuts down on the trafficking actually carried out directly by the military. But even if the military were straight, they wouldn't stand a chance against the *droguistas*. The narco business is worth probably four hundred billion dollars a year worldwide. That's about eight per cent of world trade, more than the trade in either iron and steel or motor vehicles. Just to give you a little example, there are two thousand drugs police in the Policía Anti Narcóticos in Colombia, which is a much richer country than Peru, and they're armed with twenty-two fixed-wing, single-engined aircraft, and sixty-odd helicopters. Stack that against the Colombian narcos who make at least twenty billion dollars a year from drugs, equivalent to eight per cent of Colombia's GNP. Imagine how many of them there are, what kind of gear they can afford and you begin to get an idea of the battle. There was one big Colombian narco, Parafan, arrested in Venezuela not long ago. He's being extradited to the US now, every narco's nightmare. Anyway, he alone had over twelve billion dollars in his private bank accounts. The whole continent's awash with drug money. About thirty per cent of the Colombian economy is driven by drug money. Just about everyone in its path gets corrupted. Maldonado too. He grew rich in the Huallaga, and very powerful, and soon carved himself a career within SIN. He was on the take, we knew that, but we thought he could balance his loyalties, provide us with the intelligence we wanted, hand over some of the biggest narcos, particularly in Colombia. Then his family was destroyed and I think that balance went with it. That's who we're up against. That's who you elected to stay with when you came to Peru. Why did you come here, Hel?' To find her father, that much he felt sure of, but he wanted to hear it from her. 'And why stay with Maldonado, of all people?'

Helen shook her head. 'I can hardly take it all in. I thought I was getting out of the frying pan, and all I did was walk into the fire.'

'Into an inferno.'

Helen gave a wry smile. It was easier to talk now. This new world she had walked into was so far from London. Surviving a murder attempt in Peru had somehow immunised her against what had happened to her back home. That held no fears for her now, and in the same way that Connor had obviously decided there was no room left for concealment, so did she.

'Maldonado was supposed to be a haven. I needed to get away from London. There was all this shit going on around me –'

'Like what?'

'The details don't matter. I work in the City. I was set up, I looked guilty as hell. Then I found out something, the answer to something I'd been searching for all my life.' She looked away from him, suddenly nervous of going further.

'Tell me,' he said with infinite gentleness.

She looked back at him.

'I found out my father had come here. I came here to find him. He disappeared when I was seven. I've never seen him or spoken with him since.'

'What makes you think he came here?'

'I know he came here. Which bit of the government do you work for? If you are who you say you are, you must know about him.'

She knew that Connor, the man, wanted to tell her. The operative, or whatever he was, struggled to the surface and fought for silence.

'You've already decided to tell me. I know it goes against your rules,' she said gently.

'The Secret Intelligence Service. You'd know it as MI6.'

'I know it as SIS, so far as I know it at all, which I didn't until a few weeks ago.'

'Then what happened?'

'I learned the truth about what happened to my father. The truth you must know.'

'You want to know what I know?'

She nodded.

'I know that your real name is Helen Jencks, I know that your father is Jack Jencks,'

'Go on, say it.'

'Suspected fraudster, fugitive.'

'And the truth?'

'He worked for us, we made him disappear. To Peru. To Victor Maldonado.'

'Has SIS heard from him? Since?' Helen's voice was raw.

Connor shook his head. 'He didn't maintain contact.'

'You've never heard from him in twenty-three years?'

'That should be the way it works. For the relocation to be successful, all traces of the old life have to be erased.'

'A wife and child too,' she said bitterly.

'But you decided to come after him twenty-three years on. Why? Why not stay in London and clear your name first?'

'I told you, I was set up. In case you haven't figured it out, I make the perfect fall girl, with a name like Jencks.'

'You could still have tried to fight.'

'It's easy to say, isn't it? The obvious thing to do. I worked for a big bank, I was there on sufferance with some of them. They kept me on because I was good at my job, I made them a lot of money, but there were plenty of people uncomfortable with my pedigree. I was up against the chief executive's nephew. They did a real number on me. I'd never have had a fair hearing.'

'You seem too strong to run away.'

'It wasn't running away. It was the opportunity I'd been looking for. I'd been searching haphazardly for my father all my life. When I was at sea, I'd search for him in every port. Part of me didn't want to find him; perhaps I thought he didn't want to be found. Anyway, when I discovered he was here, there was no room for evasion any more. And I discovered I'd been right all along, that he was innocent, that he had been forced to flee, he hadn't abandoned us voluntarily.' Her voice became ragged again. 'Besides, he would be sixty-five. Not old, but not young any more.' She glanced away, struggling to maintain her composure. She turned back to Connor, deliberately changing the subject. 'So what about you? What brought you after Maldonado? I get the feeling it's almost personal with you.'

'It is.'

Helen could see the shadow of anger in his eyes, and the pain.

'There was a big operation against the *droguistas* a few months ago. Someone tipped them off. One of my mates was killed. You know the rules. You can die any time. But to be set up . . .'

'You think Maldonado was behind it?'

'The same way he was behind what happened to you. The only difference is you're not dead. Who arranged for you to come to Peru, Helen?'

She glared at him. 'He knew nothing about this, got it?'

'Come on, you have to tell me or we don't have a chance to work out what's going on here.'

'It was my godfather,' she said slowly. 'He and Maldonado and my father were all at Cambridge together, best friends. My father and Dai knew each other from the Welsh valleys, practically since they were born. What else d'you want to know? Go on, ask me a question, or do you know all the answers already?'

'I want to know if you're going to let me help get you out of here.'

'I'm not going, Evan. I came here to find my father. I've been dreaming of this all my life. I'm going to go to Cusco to look for him.'

'You're mad. Don't you understand the risks?'

'Yes. I do.'

'And you're still going ahead?'

'It's my life we're talking about, Evan.'

'Maybe your death.'

'Maybe.' Her face was thoughtful, sombre, and he was relieved to see that at least she was affected by his words and didn't push on, wilfully blind to the danger that until a few hours earlier would have been so alien to her that it would have been easy for her to pretend it didn't exist. The inexperienced often took risks that those who have lived with the consequences would run from. Helen was no longer inexperienced, and while Connor could see his words had chastened her, he could still see her resolve.

'Haven't you ever shut yourself off in your own world and ignored everything else? Haven't you ever just wanted to go for something, regardless of common sense, or the risks?' she asked.

'Quite frequently.'

'When you do a military exercise, I suppose.'

Connor nodded. 'You put everything else from your mind, or you try, and sometimes you do things you shouldn't, not according to the rules, or to common sense. Survival instinct kicks in.'

'I suppose I'm really doing it because I love him, I've loved him all my life, and there wasn't a day I didn't bleed from the loss of him. I know it's mad, I know the risks. I suppose you could say all's sane in love and war. Do you know what I mean?'

Connor gazed at her across the room. 'Oh yes.' He'd known about war, not until now about love. He turned away, reeling from the sensation.

Helen misread his gesture, seeing in it, despite his words, a rejection of what she had said. 'That's what I want to do. Don't think for a minute that I'm going home. I'm going to look for my father.'

'Have you thought that perhaps it might be an old address you have?' asked Connor, his voice gentle as he turned to look at Helen.

'I know what you're saying. You think he might be dead.'

'It's possible.'

'I still have to go. I have to try.'

'Oh God, Helen.' Connor stared at her with despair.

'You can't change my mind.'

'Bloody hell. Then I'll have to come with you.'

'Why should you?' Helen shouted. 'You don't have to be my knight in shining armour.' She bit her lip as she saw his face, the anger mixing with something she couldn't fathom. Why couldn't she say what she felt? Why couldn't she tell him that she would go alone if she had to, that she would survive, but that she yearned for him to be with her, that every moment with him was charged, filled with a wild joy, that she felt so unbearably, wonderfully alive, even through all this?

'D'you want me to spell it out?' he asked. 'I don't want to but

I will if I have to. I've looked all my life for a woman like you. I'm not going to lose her before I've even started with her.'

Helen pushed herself up from the sofa, crossed the room to him and touched her lips against his. She breathed in his breath.

'You'd better come along then.'

Connor let out a long sigh and moved away. He seemed to move back into himself, caught between instinct and calculation. She could see consequences in his eyes, could see the passing of black visions like clouds in a blue sky. For just one moment, he looked naked, unprotected. She could see right into him, past civilisation, artifice and all defences. She could see a twin to her, who thought like her, chose like her, was free of fear, was not mind, but clean heart. Then the moment passed, overridden by the man of consequence and calculation.

Connor knew he would go with Helen. He had long ago committed himself to the path of chaos. All his life he had sought out the incomparable excitement that came with the dance between life and death. He had plunged into that intensity of living and ordinary sensations had become dulled for him. He had long ago fallen in thrall to fear, and in Helen he had found someone who could electrify his moments of peace. Now he would follow love, just as Helen was. He was going way outside the bounds of his professional remit by deciding to go with her on her search for her father; it was the man deciding, not the agent, but the operative in him thrilled to the risk, to the hovering war with Maldonado, who would, he knew, seek them out. Connor would be waiting, the memory of his dead friend fresh in his mind, vengeance in his heart.

He got to his feet and walked across to the balcony. He gazed out at the darkened ocean. After a while, he felt Helen's silent presence by his side. He turned to look at her wild eyes.

The wind almost blew away the words he spoke so softly.

'Time to go.'

CHAPTER 66

They flew up, through the fog, into the dawn, on the 6 AM AeroPeru flight to Cusco. After five minutes' flying, they entered a different climatic region, and the sun shone down on rolling golden desert. As they flew further inland, heading southeast towards the spine of the Andes, the desert rose up into mountains, some snow-capped and streaked with mist. Helen gazed down. She could see a village square squeezed into a narrow valley. The sun glinted off the rooftops like flashlights exploding. It looked to her like a landscape riven by a terrible fury: folds of mountains, narrow gorges gouged by an invisible river. The earth turned red in the sun, she could see houses dotted around like tiny sheep. The Andes were a young mountain range. She could see the unformed element to them. They had the anger of young men: wild, uncontained.

Helen turned to Connor. 'D'you think Maldonado will try to find me?'

'Yes, I do.'

'He'll be able to track us to Cusco then. My name'll be on the passenger lists.'

'Not quite. If you check your ticket you'll see I got it issued in the name of Chell Willems. Close enough to Helen Williams to get you on the plane if anyone kicked up a fuss, but hopefully different enough to fool any computer or manual checks they run.'

'How did you manage that?'

'I'm a travel guide, remember. I know the ticket sales staff. I misspelled your name to them, they didn't even want to see your passport.'

'Inventive.'

As they flew on, the rocks became craggier and the wisps of mist that circled their peaks thickened. The earth was reddish-brown now, streaked in places with red as if some mad artist had hurled powder paint at the summits. The pilot flew low through the ranges; it almost seemed to Helen that she could reach out of the window and touch a passing peak. The mountains turned chocolate-brown, capped with heavier snow that looked like icing. The landscape changed again and they found themselves flying over an arable valley, with quartered squares of cultivation, and hillsides dotted with trees. The mountains seemed lower here, tamer. They curved like rippling silk, blowing in the wind. They had turned spongy green, with moss and fir trees growing from the red earth. Row upon row of green peaks rolled away into the distance like crested waves in a choppy sea. Beyond, on the far horizon, like an encircling fortress, were snow-shrouded mountains and towering peaks.

The plane came closer still to the mountains. In the valley before them, as they began to descend, Helen could see red-roofed houses blending into the earth. She gazed down at them, almost trying to see through stone, imagining her father sitting at a rustic wooden table, eating breakfast, drinking the strong coffee he had always loved. She felt her excitement rising, and with it a terrible fear. It was almost impossible to grasp that her father might be here, that after twenty-three years she might see his face again, hear his voice. She cautioned herself. As Connor suggested, he might be long since dead. Maldonado's address book was obviously old, an out-of-date one filed away. He might have moved away. Or he might be horrified to see the daughter he had abandoned just walk into his life. Helen tried to imagine his shock. Part of her wanted to turn the plane around, fly away, never to confront his presence or absence, but beneath that ran the certainty that she was following the only path she could.

She felt Connor's hand on hers.

'Cusco!' he said. 'Beautiful, isn't it.'

'It is.'

'The name means the belly button of the world.'

'Why on earth call it that?'

'The Incas believed the navel was the source and centre of life.

This was the heart of their empire.' He smiled at her. 'Welcome to Tawantinsuyo, which means the four quarters of the earth. Cusco was at the centre; to the north lay Chinchaysuyo – northern Peru and Ecuador; west lay the Condesuyo – the south central coastal regions; south lay the Collasuyo – the *antiplano* of southern Peru and Bolivia; and east the Antisuyo, the unconquered Amazon jungle. The word "Andes" comes from the "Antis" who lived there. A fierce lot, brought the Incas no end of grief.'

Helen smiled. Connor's erudition she knew was designed as distraction, to lighten her spirit.

They swooped down to land.

CHAPTER 67

Calle Choquechaca was a narrow, steep, cobbled street, flanked by two-storey stone houses decorated with ornate wrought-iron balconies painted sky blue. As Connor paid off the taxi that had driven them from the airport, Helen stood on the street beside the two rucksacks Connor had packed at his flat. She gazed up at the facade of number 268. She could hardly breathe, and she knew it had little to do with the fact that Cusco lay at eleven thousand feet. Her heart felt as if it was vibrating with fear. It seemed inconceivable that she had reached the end of a voyage of twenty-three years. Aged seven, she had vowed that she would find her father. She had sailed just about every one of the seven seas to search for him. Now all she had to do was reach out her hand and knock on a door. Her fingers formed a fist. She knocked twice.

A stout Indian woman in a red skirt answered the door. Helen stared at her in shock, unable to speak. Connor addressed the woman in some strange language that wasn't Spanish. The woman looked at him in surprise, wary at first, then, as Connor smiled, gestured and spoke some more, she seemed to soften a fraction. She let forth a torrent of words. Helen stood immobile, watching the exchange, her brain running through ten different interpretations a second. Every moment seemed to stretch into eternity. Suddenly she was conscious of her own voice, shouting.

'What's she saying, goddammit, where is he?'

Connor and the woman fell silent. Connor took both Helen's hands in his. Tears were pouring down her cheeks, each one burned a trail. Her skin felt as if it was on fire.

'He was here, Hel, until yesterday. He left in the morning.'

'Oh God, we've lost him.'

'We haven't lost him. Listen to me. I found out where he is, where he's going. In five days it'll be Inti Raymi, the winter solstice. There's always a big ceremony at the Inca ruins of Machu Picchu, but this year, there's something called Cosmic Convergence. The solar configuration's supposed to be very auspicious. They're holding this big party, archaeologists from all over the world'll be there. Your father left yesterday to start the Inca Trail, to trek into Machu Picchu. He's an archaeologist, apparently. He's been invited to the ceremony.'

The tears stopped as Helen gazed into Connor's eyes.

'He's alive?'

Connor smiled and gripped her hands tighter.

'Yeah, Hel. He's alive.'

Connor thanked the housekeeper who was watching the scene with a bemused expression on her face, and led Helen into a café down the street. They sat down at a table and Connor ordered two coffees. Helen felt a wild elation filling her head, almost drowning out all sound.

'You know what I want to do, don't you, Evan?'

'You want to do the Inca Trail. Follow your father to Machu Picchu.'

'Will you help me?'

'Hel, there's something you need to understand. I meant what I said back in my flat. There are two of us on this journey now.'

She smiled at him, and he wondered whether he saw in her eyes the flicker of love.

'So,' she said, her voice low, 'tell me about the Inca Trail. What is it, exactly, and when do we start?'

'First I ring a friend of mine, and he'll help get us provisioned up. Hopefully, he'll manage to get hold of a jeep for us. Then we drive to Chillca, that's about seventy-odd kilometres from here. Then we start the Inca Trail. Depending on fitness, it's usually three and a half days' trekking, four nights' camping. It's about fifty kilometres in all, and it is *magical*. If we don't catch up with your father on the Inca Trail, we'll find him at Machu Picchu.'

'How? What if I don't recognise him?'

'Don't worry. I've worked with most of the porters on the Inca Trail. They'll help. They're like an intelligence service in their own right. And we'll really need them. The whole place'll be crawling with tourists and archaeologists because of Cosmic Convergence and Inti Raymi. It'll be hard to seek out any one person in the mêlée.'

Connor saw Helen's dispirited look.

'We'll find him, Hel, don't worry, and the crowds will work to our advantage. They'll camouflage us. The Inca Trail'll be a great place for us to hide. And if there is trouble, we can trek into the mountains and disappear.'

'You're sure Maldonado'll come after us then?'

'His credibility's at stake. Your escape made a mockery of him and his men. He doesn't know how much you found out about him. Remember, in his eyes, you're an agent. You've been spying on him from inside his own home for two weeks. He's paranoid. He's not like you and me, Hel. He's seen so much bloodshed, his children being blown up in front of his eyes, his wife shooting herself, he's had so many of his enemies executed. He has a different perspective on life and death. Murder is just another daily weapon in the war of his own survival, in the exigencies of state security, call it what you like. You're his enemy, you're an enemy of the state. I've no doubt he'll try to finish what he started.'

'Don't try to frighten me.'

'I'm not, just giving you the facts.'

'How will he find us? Perhaps he won't?'

'It's a question of time. He's the head of intelligence in a country filled with spies. Sooner or later he'll find us. It's us against him now, a kind of war. Forget the world you knew. The nice safe life. There is no London any more, no court of appeal manned by impartial judges. There is no safety net for us. Only three things matter. We survive, we find your father, and we get the hell out of Peru, alive. We have to be stronger, faster, more ruthless and more cunning than Maldonado's men. You see that, don't you?'

'I see it. So what room does that leave me? I find my father then I have to leave him and flee?'

'I can get you both out. I know someone in the jungle who could fly us out to Colombia. From there we go to the embassy. They'll help us fly back to the UK.'

'You make it sound so simple.'

'No, it won't be simple, it'll be hellishly complicated.'

'What if he won't come?'

'That's a risk you have to face.'

Helen turned away and looked resolutely out of the window. She wondered then, if she survived this, whether in years to come she would look back and think she must have been mad. Perhaps she was, but she had started something which now seemed almost ineluctable. With every extra minute, every extra metre of distance covered, she felt she was further along a path she was determined to follow to its end.

CHAPTER 68

Connor rang his friend Ernesto from a booth in the café. An hour later, a slight man of about thirty picked his way through the tables towards them. He had a drooping moustache and gentle eyes that gave him a sad countenance. Connor jumped to his feet.

'*Hola*, Ernesto!'

Connor's friend looked to Helen like a thinker, of the pessimistic variety, who could foresee the end of the world all too easily, and thought, too, that trying to save mankind probably wasn't worth the effort. He came forward and Connor introduced him to Helen.

'Ernesto, this is my friend, Hel.'

She shook his hand. He gave her a doleful smile. '*Encantado*,' he said. 'Shall we go to my house? You said you were in a hurry. I've got together everything you asked for.'

They drove through streets that made Helen think of Renaissance Italy. On the way to her father's house she had gazed out of the window and seen nothing. Now she took in vistas of domes, arches, disappearing alleyways, traffic-polished cobbles that gleamed in the sun, red-tiled roofs, walls coloured white or chocolate, pigeons fluttering on the ubiquitous churches.

'Cusco was the Incas' sacred city,' said Ernesto suddenly, 'until the morning of November the fifteenth 1533.'

'Pizarro?' asked Helen.

'Pizarro the illiterate pig farmer. The first conquistador,' said Ernesto, emerging from his pessimism and spitting out the words like a curse. He swung the car round a corner and out into a large square.

'The Plaza de Armas, and the Cathedral,' he said, turning around, taking his eyes perilously from the road.

'It's magnificent,' said Helen.

'It should be,' said Ernesto. 'It was built on what was the palace of the Inca Viracocha. If only we could see it, the splendour of the Inca empire. You know the Inca wore a cloak made of vampire-bat skins?'

'You're joking,' said Helen.

'Never.' He drove on around the square and into a side street.

'That's El Triunfo.' Ernesto pointed to another church. 'It was built to celebrate the Spanish victory over the Indians in the great rebellion of 1536, when Cusco was under siege for many months.' He swerved into another street.

'And this is probably the greatest of all the conquistadors' triumphs.' He took both hands off the steering wheel and held them out in a gesture of bitter supplication towards an imperious-looking church, built in high Spanish colonial style.

'The church of Santo Domingo. The conquistadors built it on top of the foundations of the Corincancha, the Inca Temple of the Sun. It was the most magnificent complex in Inca Cusco. Its walls were covered in seven hundred sheets of gold, studded with emeralds and turquoise. Its windows were built so that the sun would enter and shine on the gold and jewels. It was so bright, you could have gone blind looking at it.' Ernesto spoke as if somewhere in his mind he could see the dazzling reflection, as if he had seen it yesterday. Helen could feel the spirit of the Incas alive in this man, in this place.

'The conquistadors built over that?' asked Helen.

'They built a church on every Inca shrine and temple they could find. They destroyed everything they could, and what they didn't destroy they shipped back to the coffers of Spain.'

They drove in silence, the car shaking violently as they sped down cobbled streets. Ernesto swung the car into a succession of spectacularly narrow side streets then stopped before a wide wooden door. He jumped out, opened the door with a key, hopped back into the car and drove them through.

They were in a courtyard of dust and stone. In the centre was a fountain long run dry. The three closed sides of the courtyard were made up of a two-storey stone house, with ornately carved wooden balconies. It was quiet in here, the sounds of the city muffled by thick walls, shielded out by steep eaves.

They got out of the car. A dun-coloured dog ran towards them, barking enthusiastically. Ernesto ruffled his fur, then turned to Helen and gave a little bow.

'Welcome.'

'This is all your home?'

'Not just mine. Parents, grandparents, brothers, sisters, cousins. There are forty of us here, or there were at the last count, but that was six months ago and there will have been babies since then.'

He led them into a low-ceilinged whitewashed room with a huge open fireplace in the far wall. The fire was lit and the air was heavy with woodsmoke. Stacked in the corner was a pile of provisions: dried fruit and nuts, tins of meatballs, packets of rice, powdered orange juice.

'Everything you asked for,' Ernesto said to Evan. When Helen was looking the other way, he handed over a pistol concealed in a plastic bag. Connor took it off to the lavatory to check it. He returned with it tucked into the waistband of his jeans at the back, concealed under a loose shirt.

'You can return what you don't use,' said Ernesto. 'I've got the jeep ready. You can leave it at Chillca. Give the keys to Edda, she's in the shop closest to the bridge.'

Connor took the keys. 'Thanks, Ernesto.' He got to his feet. 'We'd better be on our way.' He gave Ernesto some notes and began to pack away the provisions into his rucksack. He gave Helen the bare minimum, enough to stave off hunger pangs between meals. Her rucksack was heavy enough already.

'You'll be at the ruins for Inti Raymi?'

'Possibly. We might go off camping in the mountains.'

Ernesto looked from Connor to the woman. There was something between them; she was not just an ordinary tourist he was guiding. They were both quiet, restrained, yet there was an unspoken excitement too, stronger than the tourist's thrill. He seemed to be protecting her, but his eyes, when they lingered on her, showed fascination and a strange wariness. Ernesto got the message. He wasn't to know where they were going, nor was anyone else. Fine. Perhaps

301

she was married, the lady. He hadn't taken Evan for a plunderer.

When they walked out into the courtyard, the skies had blackened and it had begun to hail, huge stones bouncing off the ground, stinging Helen's cheeks as she turned her face to the sky. She started laughing, threw her rucksack into the back seat, kissed Ernesto goodbye and jumped into the jeep. Evan jumped in next to her. The windows began to cloud with the steam from their bodies.

Helen cleared the windows while Connor reversed out from the courtyard onto the street. He beeped a goodbye to Ernesto, who closed up the courtyard behind them. Connor wove through the narrow cobbled streets filled with the flotsam of a thousand university campuses: young, unformed faces, challenging in their blank authority, uncrossed by life, and sublimely confident. Helen wondered if she had ever been like them. Ten years ago? She had never been sure or safe. With faint contempt, she envied them their certainty.

Evan sensed her mood, reached over and touched her arm.

'All right?'

'I was just looking at all these kids.'

'Yeah, Cusco's becoming a city of beautiful young things.'

He saw her teasing look.

'They're a bit young for me. I lost interest in blank canvases years ago.'

He turned into a wide street that wound its way up the hillside out of the city. They passed a group of women walking downhill in rapid procession. They wore fire-red hats over two long black plaits, the ends joined in a loop, and big swirling black skirts dotted with embroidery round the hems. Helen looked down into the bowl of Cusco below them, and beyond to the mountains opposite. Rising up to twenty thousand feet were the snowfields of Ausangate. Halfway up, the ends of a double rainbow seemed to plunge into the snow.

'Wow, look at that,' said Helen. Connor followed her eyes.

'Amazing. You'll see loads of rainbows here. The Incas lived in a rainbow kingdom. They worshipped water, saw symbols in rainbows.'

'Pots of gold?'

'No. Inca women were wary of rain, especially rainbows.' Connor didn't add that to the Incas rainbows were seen as an omen of evil.

'Why on earth fear a rainbow?'

'Because, legend has it, the rain can impregnate you. There are still some *campesino* women, countrywomen, who don't like going out in the rain alone, and would never risk urinating beside a stream.'

'What about a double rainbow then?'

'Doubly dangerous.'

'Thanks for the warning,' said Helen. She rolled down her window. The hailstones had finished, the air was cool with mountain breezes, fresh with the smell of the eucalyptus trees that flanked the road, their leaves silver in the sun.

They crested the hill. Below them gentle plains, green and yellow with crops, stretched off towards the blue horizon of distant mountains. They passed farmsteads of adobe dwellings with thatched roofs. Black piglets rooted around by the roadside, donkeys grazed contentedly. The corrugated iron roofs of distant buildings gleamed like mirrors in the sun.

They drove in silence, Helen awed by the beauty, Evan alone and untouchable in his thoughts. After an hour's driving, he spoke up.

'We're coming into the Sacred Valley now. The Incas called it Vilcanota.' Below them, fifteen hundred feet down, the Vilcanota river powered through the landscape.

At the western end of the Sacred Valley they entered a large village marked by gnarled trees and ancient hillside fortifications. They stopped in the village square, lined with women in red sitting on the kerbside, provisions spread out for sale on their brightly striped blankets. The men were resplendent in their red ponchos, dark eyes smiling, discussing the tourist crop, which was good.

'Emergency provisions,' said Evan, swinging out of the jeep. 'Back in a sec.' He ducked into one of the shops which lined the square. Helen got out and stretched. The sun warmed her face, while the air was crisp and cool like water. She could hear Connor's laughter coming from the shop, and his machine-gun Spanish. She looked around the square, which seemed to be blanketed with serenity. She tried to imagine men with guns coming for her and Evan. She pushed the thoughts from her mind.

Connor came out then, with four bottles of beer and four *empanadas*. He opened two of the beers and handed one to Helen. She took a long thirsty swig, her eyes lingering on a huge statue at the side of the square: a warrior, carved in bronze, his muscles sinewy and flaring, his cheekbones high and imperious. The fire burned even in the stone of his eyes. She walked up to study him closely.

'He's magnificent. Who is he?'

'He's called Ollantay. The town's named after him – Ollantaytambo.'

'Was he some kind of king?'

'Sadly for him he was just a general. He had the bad luck to fall in love with an Inca princess. He wanted to marry her but the Inca king, her father, forbade it, so they ran away, took refuge in the fortress here. The old Inca loved them both, but he couldn't permit the marriage of a royal to a commoner, so he hunted them down, banished his daughter, and had Ollantay put to death. The Incas say he came back to life as a hummingbird, and she as the mountain flowers.'

'That's beautiful,' said Helen, turning away with sudden tears in her eyes.

Connor touched her arm and together they walked back to the jeep. They sat on the bonnet and lunched on *empanadas* stuffed with mincemeat and thyme, washed down with the last of the beer.

They drove on towards the village of Chillca, moving deeper into the ancient Inca kingdom, with every mile more beautiful and wild.

In a field beside a thundering river Evan picked a campsite, ringed by towering peaks. A collection of brightly coloured tents sprouted from the grass. Excited trekkers milled around, with porters in attendance. Connor studied them. Helen followed his eyes. He turned back to her after a while, apparently satisfied.

'We'll camp here for the night.'

'D'you think my father might be here?'

'Let's go for a stroll, shall we?'

They walked towards the cluster of tents, Helen feeling her gut clench in hope and fear.

'How d'you think he might look, your father?' asked Connor. Helen paused. She turned to Connor, her eyes on his, but distant as she tried to see her father, how he might be now.

'About six foot, thick hair, grey, wavy. He might have a slight limp, he had arthritis in his knee even years ago. He has kind blue eyes, sort of drawn together, like mine. You know I can almost see him, sitting by a campfire, drinking his strong, milky tea, listening to Glenn Miller. He always loved Glenn Miller.'

Connor studied Helen's face, trying to step into her vision.

'OK. That's a pretty good start. Let's go look.'

As they joined the throngs of trekkers, Helen raked her eyes from face to face, searching for a familiar voice amongst the chatter.

Connor greeted most of the porters, chatted to them in the same strange language he had used on her father's housekeeper.

Connor smiled at Helen's puzzled face. 'Quechua,' he explained. 'Language of the country people.'

'How d'you manage to learn it?'

'I've spent months out here, over the last few years. Had to pick up a smattering.'

'Sounds more than a smattering to me. Find out anything?'

'No sign of him yet. I take it you didn't spot anyone who might have been him?'

Helen shook her head.

'Early days, Hel. We'll start the trek tomorrow. That might be more promising. Know how to pitch a tent?' he asked to distract her.

She smiled. 'I'll give it a try.'

'Great.' He carried their gear to a spot right in the middle of the field, surrounded by other tents.

'Safety in numbers?' asked Helen.

'Yeah. Something like that. I'm just going to drop off the keys with Ernesto's aunt. Won't be long.'

Helen had the tent up, the foam mattresses and sleeping bags down, and was boiling river water on the stove by the time Connor returned fifteen minutes later.

He sat down cross-legged on the dry ground and took the cup of tea she offered him.

'Where d'you learn all this?'

'I always kept a pack with a tent and cooking stuff on board with me at sea. When we docked somewhere and I had a few days off, I'd go camping.'

Connor grinned and took a swig of tea. 'You're full of surprises, Helen Jencks.'

Almost involuntarily, Helen ran the tip of her finger down his face.

'Why's that?'

'I've never met a woman who could pitch a tent in five minutes, beat up a couple of thugs without even messing up her hair, and is as beautiful, wilful and gentle as you.'

Helen smiled. She rolled away from him on the grass and stared up at the sky. They lay side by side, inches apart. For a long while neither spoke. Helen gazed upwards, playing her childhood game, seeking palaces in the clouds until the river and the mountains turned purple in the dying light and the first stars flickered.

Helen went to bed soon after a supper of meatballs and rice. She took off a few layers and crawled into her sleeping bag. The down warmed quickly, but the air felt chill on her face. She lay still, listening to the roar of Primus stoves and the low murmurings of conversation, broken by chords of laughter, coming from the surrounding tents. She could hear Evan moving around outside.

When, a little later, he slipped into the sleeping bag next to her, she imagined that she could feel the heat of his body. She lay in silence, eyes closed, pretending to be asleep, painfully conscious of his body next to hers. She listened to the murmur of his breathing, deep and slow and rhythmic, waiting in vain for it to lull her to sleep. She tried to conjure her father's face, wondering how life would have marked him over the past two decades. She fought to hold on to his image, but it flickered and dissipated on the canvas above her head, driven out by sudden fear. It was so thin, that layer of canvas, stirred by the wind. So fragile – just a few knife strokes and her hiding place would be ripped apart.

CHAPTER 69

Helen awoke at dawn. She was alone in the tent, but she could hear Evan whistling outside, accompanied by the gentle roar of the Primus stove. She pulled on extra layers of clothes, and her hiking boots. She moved slowly, preoccupied. She seemed to remember words, sounds, from the night before, but the memory slipped away, leaving a vague unease that was forgotten in the beauty of the morning. She unzipped the tent and stepped out onto the wet grass. She looked beyond the other tents, still silent with sleeping trekkers, to the encircling mountains, towering above her like the citadels of a great empire. The rising sun gilded the snow-capped summits to the west. The valley lay in shadow, cool with the morning dew.

'God, it's beautiful.'

Evan stood beside her, following her eyes.

'Wait till we get to Machu Picchu.'

'Tell me about it,' asked Helen. 'What's it like?'

Connor smiled. 'It's almost impossible to describe. It's like some fantasy place from your childhood dreams. Shangri-la.'

'The lost kingdom of eternal youth.'

'Only if you're sacrificed do you gain immortality, according to the Incas.'

'Maybe I'll give that a miss. Come on, at least try to describe it for me.'

'All right then. It's the lost city of the Incas, part of the largest empire in the New World. It was built during the height of the Inca empire, between the mid-fifteenth and early sixteenth centuries, probably as an estate for the Inca King Pachacuti, to celebrate his successful campaign against the Chancas. It was part of a complex of sites in the area, all remote, accessed by the Incas' trails, all set amongst the most staggering scenery. It was built to an incredibly high standard, huge hunks of stone weighing hundreds of tons set together with others with the most amazing precision. No one knows how they managed to move the rocks, let alone carve them so finely. It was abandoned a few years after the conquest of the Incas in 1532. No one knows why. It was "lost" to the world until 1911 when Hiram Bingham discovered it, although the local peoples probably knew of its existence all along. Parts of it have been rebuilt, but quite a bit of it, up to the roofline, remains intact from Inca days. That's the spiel, but nothing I say can prepare you for it. Wait till you see it yourself. No photograph can capture its beauty, or its mystery. If you believe in magic, you'll find it there.'

Helen wondered for a moment if they would ever get to Machu Picchu. She pushed the thought from her mind and sat down to the huge breakfast Connor had prepared: beans, bacon and toast. The sun rose as they tucked in, its rays flooding down the mountainsides towards the valley.

'Eat well,' said Evan. 'Today we have about fourteen kilometres to do. Not too hard, but you've a heavy pack and the altitude might bother you.'

Evan was worried about how Helen would fare, how fast she could go, how long she could keep going, if they needed to flee. She was fit, by city standards; she could hold her own in a gym, but that didn't count for much in the mountains, and *soroche*, or altitude sickness, was no respecter of fitness. Helen nodded, saying nothing. She looked at Evan, strong and lean, his eyes glowing. His pack weighed over eighty pounds. He shouldered it as if it contained nothing more than a down sleeping bag, and walked as if it were not there.

They followed the banks of the Urubamba river, over the bridge, and began to curve their way upwards. They walked through forests of eucalyptus, where the shadows fell upon them, scented with the balm of the leaves. They emerged into dazzling sunlight, to banks of cacti, tiny star-like pink flowers, glowing orange berries and flame golden petals. A hidden flautist seemed to be following them. Helen turned around and scanned the mountainside, but the flautist remained invisible.

'It's a bird,' said Connor. 'It always catches people out.'

'It sounds like a spirit,' said Helen.

'The *campesinos* think it is.'

A world of colour, smell and birdsong. Of magic. It beguiled her. She could see in the visions flickering across Connor's face that he had long been bewitched. She felt herself walking away from her world and stepping into the Inca kingdom.

This was the Peru that Maldonado had spoken of: wild, mysterious and beautiful. He had promised her too that if she stayed long enough in his country, she would experience the other side, the price it exacted, the violence. Had it been a curse he was laying on her, even then?

As they gained height, the Urubamba grew distant, but wilder, and its roar stayed with them, a churning violence, like a message of warning.

'See that track down there, beside the railway, by the river?' asked Connor.

'Yeah?'

'Pizarro went that way when he was looking for more Inca villages to rape and pillage. This trail we're on remained hidden, and thank God too or he might have followed it all the way to Machu Picchu.'

Helen looked down at the track below and imagined Pizarro and his armoured horsemen advancing up the valley. She imagined the fear that the Incas must have felt when they saw horses for the first time, the sparks flying from their hooves, the armour-plated warriors astride their prancing backs.

The roar of the water filled her ears. She imagined it pierced by screams. Where would they have run to, the Incas, trapped between the river and the mountain? How many murdered spirits haunted these valleys?

She had a sudden vision, as if she were ten years in the future, looking back, seeing herself as she was now, walking through the cacti, the sun hot overhead, the sky dazzling, the sound of the river, the birdsong, an illusion of tranquillity, while the descendants of Pizarro waited for them around the next bend.

She felt Connor's hand on her shoulder. 'Are you OK?'

She was sweating heavily, breathing hard. She shook her hair from her face, caught it up in one hand and lifted it away from the back of her neck. 'I'm fine. A bit hot, just getting used to the altitude.'

She felt him lifting her pack from her back. 'Sit down, rest. All good armies stop for five minutes on the hour and we've been going fifty-five minutes.' He took out her water bottle. 'Drink, you'll need a lot.'

She sat down cross-legged on the trail and drank, her eyes on the bottle, trying to shake off her sudden fear. Connor kept his hand on her shoulder, then took the bottle from her and put it back in her rucksack. She looked up and smiled.

'Thanks, Evan.'

He must have seen the traces of fear in her eyes, for his suddenly clouded over, and he looked from her to the countryside beyond, scanning, searching, then returning his gaze to her, calm, but unsatisfied. She sensed that he'd seen in his mind the vague outlines of the premonition in hers.

'Come on,' he said gently, helping her up. 'Machu Picchu beckons.'

They climbed the side of the valley, past tiny villages of smiling children with mud-striped faces and mischievous eyes who were tickling tiny black-haired piglets which squealed in delight. The children stopped their game to greet them with high-pitched *holas* and requests for *caramelos*. Connor dug into his shirt pockets and dished out a handful of sweets. The children grinned like demons.

Connor stopped every hour to feed Helen snacks from his rucksack. Dried fruit and nuts, apples, water. After four hours' walking she began to feel weak. There was a patch of sweat on Connor's back when he took off his rucksack, but that was the only sign of effort. Where the track was wide they began to pass small groups of tourists, sitting sweating in the sun. They looked innocent, happy, innocuous. They were not her father. Helen and Connor greeted them, trying to veil their disappointment, and walked on. Where there was space, Connor walked alongside Helen.

The track grew narrower as they began to ascend a steep hill, and Connor dropped back behind Helen, allowing her to set the pace. As they approached the crest of the hill, walking single file along a narrow path, they encountered a man wearing a hard hat. He stopped, blocking the path, and spoke to Helen.

Connor moved past her, put his body between hers and the man's. '*Sí?*'

He and the man spoke for five minutes, then Helen saw Connor hand over money. The man nodded, glanced around, then let them pass.

'What was that all about?'

'That was an official, checking tourist passes. We should have bought ours in advance, but no problem, he just sold us some.'

'Seemed expensive.'

'Keeping him happy was expensive.'

They walked in silence, Connor preoccupied. He stopped after a couple of hours to make camp by a river. They were alone, the other tourists still some way back down the trail. Helen pitched the tent next to a tree covered with deep-purple orchids while Connor cooked a late lunch. As they ate sausages and rice, Connor seemed happy enough but Helen could sense his unease. She wanted to go to him and ask what it was that troubled him, but she could feel his reticence. When lunch was over she stood and stretched.

'I think I'll be really indulgent and go and have a sleep.'

He smiled. 'Good idea.'

While Helen was sleeping, a large party of trekkers arrived. Connor waited until the porters had got their party settled, then he walked over to them. They were eating lunch in the open, alongside a luxurious mess tent in which the trekkers were discussing the rigours of the first day's trek.

He greeted the porters, two of whom, Alejandro and Jesus, he had worked with and knew well. He sat down cross-legged in their semi-circle.

'*Hola, flacos. Qué tal?*'

They swapped news of tourists from hell, and the odd, gorgeous, lissome Scandinavian girl who more than compensated. There didn't seem to be anything unusual about the trail so far as Connor could gather from listening to their gossip. No strangers asking questions, no search parties. That gave Connor no comfort. Maldonado was known for the subtlety, ingenuity, and ruthlessness with which he gathered information, or pursued his campaigns. If he wanted to move invisibly, he could. Connor changed tack. He leaned forward on his elbows and spoke softly.

'I need your help.'

They waited.

'I'm looking for a man, a friend of a friend. He's an archaeologist; some of you might have worked with him here or at Machu Picchu.'

'What's his name, *amigo?*'

Connor paused. 'Arturo Leon.'

The porters looked from Connor to each other, suspicion in their eyes.

'I mean him no harm.'

Alejandro and Jesus relented slightly, now only puzzled, but there was still hostility in the eyes of the others.

'What's he like, this Señor Leon?' asked Alejandro, who was the senior porter.

Connor tried to see what Helen had seen. Part of him rebelled against something so non-scientific, but what was he left with if he stuck to science? Age and height. Age was just a number, not a precise description of how someone might look, and even height was unreliable; inches could be lost to a stoop. He had a sudden presentiment of how it must feel to grow old, and how much worse too if you were robbed of the identity of your youth. Who could he reminisce with, this ageing man, if he was still alive? There would be no one who remembered his beauty, or his strength, or his potency. They would see him only as an older man. He would have to rely on lonely memories, tarnished. They had loved him, Helen and her mother, and when he remembered their love he would conjure their pain too, so there could be no comfort for him even in the memory of love.

'He's an elderly man,' said Connor slowly, 'with grey hair, thick grey hair and maybe a grey beard. He's about six foot, heavy body, but not fat. He has blue eyes, kind eyes, but sad too. He's friendly, but he doesn't talk much about the past, not the recent past, only about what happened hundreds of years ago. He has no past, no family, he seems to have been here for ever, working on his digs, exploring, trekking, perhaps not so much now. He might have a limp, in one knee, but he loves to dance, and to listen to music. He likes Glenn Miller.' He scanned the listening faces as he spoke and he thought he saw then a flash of something in the eyes of one of the porters, but he could not be sure and the man said nothing.

'You love him?' asked Alejandro.

Connor turned to him in surprise. He loved his daughter. The sudden consciousness of that should have shocked him, but, simple as a fact, inevitable as sunrise, it didn't.

He felt as if he knew the father, could begin to imagine the man's loss, loneliness and pain, his sense of injustice that he had done what he did from love, not from its absence.

'Yes,' he said. 'I would love him.'

Alejandro watched him, puzzled, and then spoke, as the senior porter, for the group. 'We will think, try to remember, and we will ask questions. We will find you if we hear anything.'

Darkness came and Helen and Connor ate dinner. Connor told Helen of his conversation with the porters.

'You saw no one?' she asked.

Connor shook his head.

'Let's have another look,' suggested Helen. They cleared dinner away, washed the plates in the river, then walked around the campsite. There was no one who could have been her father. Helen returned to their tent, eyes downcast.

As the moon rose, Helen and Connor crawled into their respective sleeping bags. Helen lay next to Connor, listening to his breathing. He seemed to be awake too, and, like her, feigning sleep. She could smell him, in the heat that rose from his body. He smelled like sweet cider, like honey. She longed to put her lips to him and taste him. Only inches away, to reach out and touch him, to touch his chest through his unbuttoned shirt. He, like her, slept with his clothes on. She could imagine the moonlight, filtering through the tent, carving his face into planes of white marble, smooth and beautiful, cold to the touch, and hot, like ice on tender skin. Why didn't he touch her? He just lay there, as if he were immune to her, while she lay trapped in sleeplessness.

Some time later she felt movement and watched him get up,

pull on his boots and jacket, quietly unzip the tent, and step outside. She lay still for a while, feeling the tension that he'd left behind, until she too got up, pulled on a jacket and boots and walked outside into the moonlit night.

She saw him some way off, down by the river, his back to her. She approached him silently. As she drew near, she could hear his voice, low and smooth, above the dull roar of the river. She took a few steps closer, and suddenly he turned.

He seemed shocked to see her, angry almost, and his eyes seemed to be travelling back to her from a great distance.

'What are you doing?' she asked gently.

He looked defensive. 'Saying a prayer.'

'You mentioned my name.'

'Mine too. I was asking for safe passage.'

'From whom?'

'The mountains, Ausangate and Salcantay. I learned it from the porters. Praying to the mountain gods goes back to the Incas. The porters always have a special ceremony at the beginning of every trek. They mention all the names of the trekkers, ask the mountains to protect them.'

'How lovely.'

'It is lovely. The porters invited me along to join in their prayer ceremonies a few times. It was a great honour, they hardly ever let outsiders in. I was trying to remember their exact words, in Quechua. I don't think I got it exactly.'

'Don't worry.' She touched his arm. 'I'm sure the mountains will still protect us.'

In silence they made their way back to the tent, and climbed into their sleeping bags. They lay together, side by side, still separated by the gulf of inches. He turned his face towards hers.

'Try to sleep. You'll need all your energy tomorrow, for Warmi-wanusca.'

'Warmi what?'

'It's a Quechua name. It means Dead Woman's Pass.'

CHAPTER 70

When Helen awoke, it was to hear the whistle of the kettle, and, seconds later, Connor's cheery 'Morning' as he ducked into the tent with a cup of steaming *mate de coca*.

'Laced with sugar,' he said, squatting down beside her. 'And I've got porridge, followed by pancakes, waiting outside.'

'Wow!' Helen sat up and took the tea with a smile.

She emerged from the tent five minutes later.

'I'll have the pancakes first.'

'No, you won't, you'll eat your porridge, then have the pancakes as a reward.'

'I'll be sick. There's no room for all of that.'

'There is. You'll burn it up.'

'I don't like the sound of this Dead Woman's Pass.'

'If you take it slowly, eat and drink enough, you'll be fine.'

She surprised herself by finishing her porridge and still managing to put away two pancakes dripping with honey. Connor had already finished his and was packing up their kit and putting away the tent. She got up to help. 'You're spoiling me, you know,' she said, stashing tent poles.

'It's easy.'

They set out as the sun was chasing shadows from the encircling peaks. They left the sleeping camp behind them, eager to make time, to begin their search again further down the trail. They walked beside the river, which flowed aquamarine pale, smooth like rippling silk. The sweet, plaintive sound of birdsong followed them. They walked slowly, Connor letting Helen go first, cautioning her to go at what seemed like a ridiculously slow pace.

'Snail could beat us,' she said. When she tried to go faster, she would feel his hands snake around her hips and pull her back.

They followed the valley, walking in the shade of a forest of bright orange trees.

'Quenoas,' answered Connor when Helen remarked on them. 'Only grow in the Andean heights.'

Orchids wound themselves around the branches of the trees. The track was bordered with yellow flowers like tiny daffodils. In the undergrowth delicate porcelain-blue flowers glowed like bluebells. After a while they came to a bridge.

'This is the happy bridge,' said Connor. 'The valley is named after it. Cusichaka.'

'Perhaps it'll bring us luck,' said Helen.

They crossed the bridge, then turned away from the river, weaving their way along a narrow track up the mountainside, under the brilliant sun. A raucous squawking made Helen look up.

'Wow, look at that!' Hundreds of green parrots flew overhead like a flock of jewels, their wings flashing emerald in the sun. The parrots flew down the valley, and landed in the canopy of the cloud forest below, audible, but invisible.

Soon Helen was soaked with sweat. She stopped by a stream which plummeted across their path, dipped her hands in the chill water, splashed her face, and trickled handfuls of water down her chest and over her head. Her hair was slicked back, curling wildly, and the V of her chest, exposed by her low-cut T-shirt, was slick with sweat. Her chest rose and fell exaggeratedly with the effort of breathing at altitude. Connor watched her, just two paces away from her. She was smiling at him, pleased with herself, enjoying the effort, unknowing as he gazed at her. He thought of women he knew in London with painted nails and mascaraed eyes, their hair perfectly blow-dried in the latest style. Helen was covered in sweat, her face streaked with dirt, her hair sticking to her skin. He had never seen anyone so desirable. He wanted her with an urgency he had never felt. He forced himself to remember the lecture he had given her. Only three things mattered: surviving, finding Helen's father, and getting out of Peru, alive.

'Keep moving,' he said hoarsely. 'It's hard to start up again if you stop for too long.'

Helen pushed on. After a while they left the bare mountainside and entered a forest of white-barked, moss-covered trees with branches curved and distorted like pleading arms with crooked arthritic fingers.

'Will you lead for a while?' she asked. 'It's easier sometimes to follow.'

'Sure. Just want to get something out of my rucksack. Hang on a sec.' He sat on a rock, took off his rucksack, dug around in a pocket and pulled out a small bag of leaves.

Connor handed her a wad of them. 'Here, chew these.'

'What on earth are they?'

'Coca.'

'Coca? As in cocaine?'

'Mmhm. Raw material, but like this it's more beneficial than harmful. It gives you energy, acts as a painkiller, helps with tummy bugs. It also happens to be legal in Peru, and sacred to five million people.'

'Sacred?' Helen gave him a dubious look.

'It's been sacred since the Incas, if not before. The coca leaf's been given a bad name by the narcos. It's the shit they do with it that makes it harmful. Throw in some sulphuric acid, liquid petroleum, cement powder, sodium carbonate, permanganate, ammoniac, ether, add a dash of hydrochloric acid and stuff it up your nose. Recipe for a great life.'

'Sounds like you could knock up some of your own.'

'I'd rather stick to the leaves. I've gone on three-month ex-peditions in the jungle and survived pretty much on yucca, water and coca. It's incredible stuff in its natural form.'

Helen pushed the leaves into her mouth and began to chew.

'They taste disgusting.'

'Got to be good then, haven't they?'

Connor walked in front of Helen, slowly, but without effort. His breathing was even. Hers sounded like a trumpet in her ears. She wanted to catch hold of him from behind, to reach forward her arms and encircle his waist, to pretend to slow him down, as he'd done to her, but her arms stayed fixed by her sides.

One, two, three, four. Count to a hundred, keep your head down, then stop, rest and start again. Maybe the coca leaves were helping, but this was still agony. They approached the top of Dead Woman's Pass. If Maldonado's men appeared now, there was no way she could get away. She forced the thought from her mind and concentrated on her steps.

She couldn't look up, it was too depressing to see how distant the pass remained. Look down and count, stop and breathe. She felt sick, not ill sick, but in pain. She had a sudden vision of Clarke's, where she used to go for breakfast. God, wouldn't it be heaven to be sitting in Notting Hill now, cool and clean, with lungs full of breath, drinking coffee, eating pain au chocolat, reading about other people slogging their way up mountains? Far from this mad, beautiful, violent place. Safe in her old life.

One final burst, Helen's lungs screaming, and they reached the summit.

'Well done,' said Connor. 'Four thousand, two hundred metres.'

'Awesome,' gasped Helen, bending over, hands on knees, sucking in deep breaths of the thin air.

Connor threw open his arms, she went to him and he gave her an extravagant hug.

'How are you feeling?'

'Fantastic,' said Helen, her face glowing. Sick as she felt, the sense of achievement was heady.

Together they gazed down over the route they had just climbed, at the harsh, bleak landscape of the pass. Helen turned to the other side. A cascade of brilliant green valleys fell away below her.

'The Valley of Silence,' said Connor. 'Look, in the distance you can see the silhouette of the rainforest, and beyond that the Vilcabamba range.' The towering mountains seemed to mark the end of the world.

A group of porters glanced at them as they hurried past and began to run down a stone stairway as wide as a street that seemed to descend to the heart of the earth.

Down to Pacaymayo. One and a half hours of descent, down back-jarringly-deep steps. Below them in the valley were trees and bushes, but on the path they remained exposed. The wind whipped Helen's sweat-soaked hair, cooled her, then, inch by inch like creeping ice, chilled her. When she could take her eyes from the path she gazed around, distracting herself. When she saw a cluster of tents, she looked at Connor hopefully. He checked out the campsite, and their fellow campers before they pitched the tent.

'Camp. Home for the night. I looked for your father. No sign.' He squeezed her arm. 'We'll look again in the morning. We have to be closing on him. Old bugger must be fitter than I thought.'

Helen gave a weak smile. Part of her was too exhausted to worry about much else besides her aching body. The other part, the indefatigable yearning deep in her heart, was beginning to quicken with excitement, as if, as Connor suggested, they were gaining on her father, and it was just a question of time. She prayed they still had enough time, that they could get to her father before Maldonado got to them.

Connor stroked her face, to offer comfort, as if he had read her mind.

'You did bloody well today, Hel. That was quite a fast pace we set.'

'Just as well,' said Helen, looking up at the feathery white clouds. 'Mares' tails. Bad weather coming.'

'Yeah, I reckon so,' said Connor, impressed. 'It's supposed to be the dry season, but that's never a guarantee against rain.'

They'd finished a late lunch and were sitting outside the tent, watching tired trekkers straggle into the campsite, when the wind came up and storm clouds began to gather. Connor studied the skies. 'I reckon we've got about ten minutes, what d'you think?'

'Sounds about right.'

'Let's get into the tent, roll up in our sleeping bags. We can play cards, while away the rain.'

The rains came twelve minutes later: huge drops against the side of the tent, like the arrows of an attacking army. The wind battered the canvas like ghosts trying to rip their way in. The cloud blacked out the sun and darkness fell early.

Connor suddenly looked up from his cards. 'Are you all right?' Helen had gone quiet.

'I'm a bit cold.'

'Here. I put some hot tea in the thermos.' He poured her a cup and took a bottle from his rucksack. 'Have a nip of brandy too.'

He sat and watched her carefully.

'Christ, you're shivering. Right. Only one way to warm you up.' He unzipped his sleeping bag, then hers, then zipped them together. As she lay watching him, he got in beside her.

'Take off your clothes.'

'What?'

'Take them off.' She could feel him manoeuvring beside her as he took off his own clothes.

'What are you doing?'

'I'm going to keep you warm. You won't be able to feel my body heat through layers of clothes, and you need to have your skin close to the down for the sleeping bag to work properly, so' – he said it more gently this time – 'take off your clothes.'

She laughed, tried to undress, slowed by cold fingers.

She left on her knickers, and Connor his boxer shorts. He wrapped his arms around her and pulled her into his chest. He rubbed her skin with his hands, brisk movements. Slowly she began to stop shaking, as his warmth sank into her skin. His hands began to move more slowly over her, and he pulled her tighter against him. She felt the length of his body, she felt him harden beside her, unmistakable, demanding, painful against her thigh. She held onto him. Suddenly, he pulled away.

'Helen, I'm sorry. I don't want this to happen.'

'Why not?'

'I'm supposed to be looking after you. I won't be much good to you with my trousers round my ankles.'

'You're not wearing any trousers.'

'You know what I mean.'

'I do,' she said, and began to move her fingers over his skin. He was warm, his skin smooth, like silk over the hard curves of his muscles. The scent of him was intoxicating. 'But I think the mountain gods are on our side. They'll give us a few hours' protection.' She paused, tracing her fingernail down his stomach. 'But if you're not sure . . .'

He pulled her back to him, and began to kiss her. She could feel his yearning like a wind roaring in a tunnel. She could feel it catch and pull at her body, her heart, and her mind, and she opened them all to him.

CHAPTER 71

Helen woke in Connor's arms. Her face lay against the curve of his chest. She breathed him in, his smell, warmth, and strength. She'd felt his energy as he'd made love to her, an incredible, reined-in power. She'd wondered at its ferocity, how it would feel, completely unleashed. There'd been sweetness too, and a mesmerising tenderness. She remembered the tins of Lyle's Golden Syrup that she kept lined up along her kitchen shelf: gold and green, the lion lying with its belly open, bees flying from it, the biblical quotation beneath: 'Out of the strong came forth sweetness.'

She felt Connor stirring. He opened his eyes, smiled and touched her face.

'How are you?'

'I'm pretty good.'

'Not cold any more? No headache, stomach ache, altitude sickness?'

'Well, since you ask, I'm a little bit dizzy, but I'm not sure I can blame the altitude for that.'

He laughed and then kissed her long and slowly.

'Are you sure you're not just a little bit cold?'

'Well, I could be warmer . . .' She smiled, her eyes narrow and voluptuous as she drew him down upon her.

Later, lying peacefully, they could hear the world waking around them, first the birds, then the cooks, then the porters and trekkers from the neighbouring tents. The porters spoke softly, while the tourists noisily checked on who was the stiffest, who had slept the best, who had the best bites and who had had the strangest dreams.

'God, someone's having bacon, can you smell that?' asked Helen.

'Mmm. I can,' said Connor. He extracted himself from the sleeping bag and pulled on his clothes. 'Stay here, rest a bit more. I'll get breakfast together, and give you a five-minute warning so you can get dressed.'

She lay back and luxuriated in the warmth he'd left behind. She pulled the sleeping bag around her and sighed contentedly, too happy to be wary.

She emerged from the tent fifteen minutes later.

'Where d'you get that bacon?' she asked with glee, staring down at the sizzling frying pan in Evan's hand.

'Americo. He's the cook for that party over there.' He nodded at a large group of tourists gathered round a table eating hungrily.

'He's a mate, we've worked together quite a few times. They're on some de luxe tour. They've got so much food they could feed us for a week and not notice the difference.'

'Yum, and eggs too. The perfect breakfast. But don't I need to eat another few pounds of oatmeal or something?'

Connor smiled. 'Easy day today, and so beautiful. I can't wait to show you how gorgeous it is.'

'There was no sign, was there?' Helen asked, eyes straining as she examined the scattered groups.

Connor had done a thorough search for her father amongst the different trekking groups, and he had quizzed Americo without success. He shook his head.

They packed up, walked past the de luxe tourists who were still eating, and exchanged waves. The tourists watched them go, looking wistfully at the joy that seemed to radiate from them.

'We're on the original Inca stones now,' said Connor. 'The earlier part of the trail, up to Dead Woman's Pass, was used as a smugglers' route by moonshiners in the eighteenth and nineteenth centuries. Their mules' hooves destroyed the trail.'

'How many roads did the Incas have?' she asked. 'I remember my father telling me they had a huge empire criss-crossed by trails.'

'They did. They built at least twenty-five thousand kilometres of highways across what's now Peru, Ecuador and Bolivia, as well as parts of Chile, Argentina and Colombia. Many of them are still there, hidden by the undergrowth.'

Helen had a brief image of Inca warrior ghosts, walking the path before them. She was consumed by the trek that day. It was like a dream, a fantasy of an enchanted journey. Ruins, mists and trees hung with moss; orchid-filled forests writhing with poisonous snakes. The mists wheeled around them, veiling the burning sun, cloaking the mountains, suddenly exposing towering tors of granite. Following them always was the distant roar of a river that could never be seen, but which flowed somewhere beneath them, through the sheltering forests.

They crested another pass, of just under four thousand metres. This time Helen found it less of a strain. Her body was adapting rapidly, delivering the extra fitness she needed. Connor watched her growing strength with relief. At any moment, should they have to flee off the trail and into the wilderness, Helen would have to call on every last reserve of strength and then more. With his SAS training, the prospect of extreme endurance held no terrors for Connor, but his fears for Helen were intense. His only hope was that the strength of Helen's will would get her through where her body would otherwise fail. Or, even better, that they would somehow elude Maldonado.

They walked down towards the jungle canopy: a thousand greens, oranges and ambers, the sudden shock of purple orchids hanging from the trees. Black butterflies flew around their heads as the trail neared the snake forest.

'Stay on the trail,' warned Connor. 'You go in the snake forest, you'll never come out.' He glanced around, supremely alert. If Maldonado's men were waiting for them, this was the perfect choke point. There was nowhere for them to run to, nowhere to hide. In a spectacular feat of engineering, the Incas had built up the trail on walls of stone, so that the snake forest fell away to one side, with steep walls of granite on the other. The further they walked, the higher the wall became. A careless step, and they would have dropped hundreds of feet to their death.

Helen paused to gaze down. The trees were like Japanese line drawings, their moss-covered contours indistinct like running paint. Birds sang to each other like men whistling out a secret code. It felt like a lost world. When they stopped talking and moving, there was complete silence broken only by the lithe and plaintive birdsong.

Helen remembered a story her mother used to read to her when she was very young, about an enchanted valley, and the man who must walk through it, surrounded by hazards, to find his destiny. He walked through forests of trees where the leaves were made of gold, and the fruits that rained down into his hands were diamonds, rubies and emeralds. The man was safe from all the hazards of the secret valley because of the cloak he wore, which made him invisible. The mist that swathed her and Evan was like a cloak of invisibility. It seemed to deaden all sound, even their own footfalls. It felt to Helen as if they were surrounded by myths and spirits, as if they, in their silent passing, were spirits too. The mist moved about them, whispering as it passed with the cold touch of a ghost.

As they descended, the path disappeared into a tunnel carved into a huge leaning slab of rock. Connor stopped some way away and whispered into Helen's ear.

'Wait here.' He went on ahead, vanishing into the darkness of the tunnel. He reappeared a few minutes later and beckoned to her. She walked down to him and followed him into the tunnel. The sun lit the first five steps, then for the next thirty feet they were plunged into darkness. Evan pulled Helen to him and kissed her as condensation dripped down their necks. When they pulled apart and walked out, footsteps followed them. They wheeled around, but there was nothing in the darkness, save the echo of their own passing.

They walked over another pass, of three thousand eight hundred metres. That night, they camped above the clouds. There was still no sign of Helen's father. She began to fear she might never find him. They watched the darkness come and the sky clear. After dinner they stood outside their tent and gazed at the brilliant glow of the Milky Way, at the dust of a billion stars.

The next morning they broke camp early, and set off on the trail through the sky.

'Today,' said Connor, 'we arrive at Machu Picchu.' In his eyes Helen saw excitement, and warning.

The clouds parted and the first rays of dawn fell on a snow-covered mountain that dominated the horizon.

'The north face of Salcantay,' said Connor. 'The name means wild, uncivilised. Six thousand two hundred and seventy-one metres of it.'

'The sacred mountain?' asked Helen. 'The one you prayed to for safe passage?'

'Yeah, one of them.'

Helen wanted to say: it seems to have worked, but with every step closer to Machu Picchu, she felt growing excitement, and dread. They walked down through the melting clouds, past ruins cut into the precipitous mountainside.

'Phuyupatamarca,' said Connor. 'It means *Cloud-level Town* in Quechua. Could have been a ceremonial site, could have been a fortress.'

Helen studied the tumbling terraces set around domes of granite, imagined heads smashing like melons on the hard stone.

They walked down for ever, thirteen hundred steps, a one-thousand-six-hundred-metre descent into the cloud forest. The jungle thickened and warmed around them. The landscape seemed to become more abrupt and exuberant with every turn in the serpentine trail. The air was still and heavy, cloying like chocolate. Higher up it had slipped down their throats like white wine.

As they lost height, the mountains seemed to grow around them, encircling them, like fortresses of the gods. Range lay behind range, the green ebbing to snow-capped blue on the far horizon. Above them, wisps of cloud glittered silver against the brilliant sky. It was as if an artist had been profligate with his paint, for the leaves of the trees were silvered by the sun, the forest path was dappled with a hundred shades of gold, and boot-shaped flowers glowed yellow in the undergrowth. Even the air itself seemed to glitter. Helen and Connor's eyes shone with the colours. Black, white and vivid orange butterflies danced around them.

Connor stopped and turned to Helen.

'We're approaching the Sun Gate. The Incas meant it as a choke point. There's no other way into Machu Picchu.'

'You think Maldonado's men might be there?'

'It's possible, but there'll be lots of other trekkers around. They won't make a move in such a public place, but if they're there, they'll tail us.'

'What do we do then?'

'Play it by ear. Maybe we'll be lucky.'

'Yeah, maybe we will. The Sun Gate. It's such a beautiful name. Hard to believe anything bad could happen there. What is it exactly?'

'It's meant to be a place of transformation. The Incas worshipped the sun, it brought life, change. It could also bring death, by its absence. There's supposed to be something magical about the Sun Gate. All sorts of powers are said to be concentrated there. It magnifies good and bad and sets one against the other. The most powerful force will triumph. The Quechua say once you've gone through it, you'll never be the same again. It's like the Rubicon to the Romans. Once you've gone through it, there's no going back.'

'Maybe that's what happened to my father,' said Helen.

The path wove along the mountainside, climbing now, twisting upwards, till they came upon a staircase that seemed to reach into the sky. As they stood below it, they could see nothing save infinite blue beyond the last step.

'The Sun Gate's at the top,' said Evan. 'Are you ready?'

Helen smiled, then ran up the steps. Up she went, heart pounding, breathing hard, all in one burst, not wanting to stop. She reached the top. The Sun Gate stood before her, a gateway of hewn stones. She walked up to it, looked about her, and, very deliberately, walked through.

Beyond was a world of intoxicating lushness: rich green moss-covered mountains stretching out for ever, a foaming river way below. And at the centre, balancing on the saddle of a precipitous ridge, the ruins of Machu Picchu.

They appeared to grow from the mountaintop. In all their subtle symmetry they formed part of the beauty that surrounded them. Helen felt the onset of tears, brushed them from her cheeks, and gazed at the miracle below her. This is what they would have seen, centuries ago, the Inca travellers: a view of incomparable beauty that rushes into your soul like a river. This is what her father saw. She moved about slowly, touching the warm skin of the stones of the Sun Gate, feeling for his fingerprints.

She stood, caught in time, her eyes lingering over all the different visions below.

'The most beautiful view in the world,' said Connor.

'I don't know if I can leave,' said Helen. 'I could stay here for ever.' They stood, shoulder to shoulder, staring out at an unknown world that stretched hundreds of miles, over the ranges and beyond, to Amazonia.

They could see no sign of threat. Rucksacked trekkers milled around, but Connor dismissed them. Inwardly, he felt sure Maldonado's men had to be here somewhere, that, as he had told Helen, it was just a matter of time. He said a silent prayer, asking that, if Helen's father were here, they would find him soon. He had a keen sense that their time was running out.

He tried to push the fears from his mind, while keeping super alert. They walked down the carved stone, past llamas grazing on the narrow path. Down towards the citadel, towards the peak of Wayna Picchu, which towered behind Machu Picchu, watching over it with the stillness and implacability of a guard.

CHAPTER 72

Helen had feared that it would be an anticlimax, that the beauty and magic of Machu Picchu that Connor had evoked would in reality be smaller than the dream. But what towered before her now was greater than anything Connor might have conjured. Photographs were as ashes to a live body. Nothing captured Machu Picchu, a kingdom ruined but alive. The power was not just in the configurations of stones, but in the awesome setting. A thousand feet below, the Urubamba river churned through the gorge that cut around the base of the mountain. Surrounding them a circle of snow-covered peaks and green ranges soared into a dazzling sky. The citadel stood at the centre.

'It's like a hidden kingdom,' said Helen. 'You're right. It is like Shangri-la. Inaccessible. Protected by the mountains, and by that river.'

'It's so Inca to build it like this, among all this beauty,' replied Connor. 'They believed in a great harmony between man and nature.'

'They certainly captured it here. How could you ever fight nature when you look out on a view of paradise every day?'

A sense of harmony flowed through the trapezoidal stone arches, through the temples and up the staircases. Everywhere she walked, Helen felt herself drawn on naturally, upward all the time. Connor let her wander as she pleased. He followed behind, seeing the glory through her eyes. They walked through the royal sector, where the construction was so fine that it was impossible to slip sheets of paper between the perfectly fitted stones. They looked down at the precipitous terraces.

'What did they grow here?' asked Helen.

'Corn and coca leaves.'

Helen passed through a stone entrance into a three-walled space, the top wall of which curved back on itself.

'The Temple of the Sun,' said Connor, 'known as the Torreon.'

Helen gazed at a carved boulder.

'It looks like an altar,' she said.

'It probably was, and used for astronomical observations too. In the early eighties, archaeo-astronomers discovered that the window over there' – he pointed to a rectangular window which looked out onto the gorge below – 'was perfectly aligned to the sunrise at the June solstice. And the Pleiades. The sun rises above the Veronica mountain range, and the first rays cut through the window and hit the altar stone.'

'Tomorrow,' said Helen, 'we'll see it. I wonder if it was ever used as a sacrificial altar?'

'We don't know. The Incas did go in for human sacrifice, generally of children as perfectly beautiful as they could find. They believed that those sacrificed became immortal, and would be their ambassadors to the gods.'

'I don't feel it,' said Helen. 'Not here. It seems so peaceful.'

'Perhaps you're tapping in to the female spirit. Hiram Bingham thought Machu Picchu was a woman's sanctuary. One legend suggests it was the last refuge of the Virgins of the Sun. Another that it was a university of idolatry, where the priests and high priestesses were trained. The Incas left no written records, so no one really knows what Machu Picchu was.' Connor smiled. 'It's anything you want it to be.'

Helen walked on up into the citadel until she came to the highest point. A stone structure stood at the centre of an open space. It was about six feet high. It seemed to Helen like an abstract representation of Wayna Picchu, the almost pyramidal peak which towered behind it. Instinctively, she stretched out her hands and touched the warm stone.

'It's carved from living rock,' said Connor. 'It's part of the mountain we're standing on.'

'It feels alive,' said Helen, her eyes glowing.

'It's meant to be the most powerful part of all Machu Picchu,' said Connor. 'The Intihuatana stone, the hitching post of the sun.

Many of the observations tomorrow will be done from here.'

Helen had an image of the Incas trying to lasso the sun with a golden rope. The image was replaced suddenly by one of herself bound to the Intihuatana stone. She wondered if that would bring her father to her.

'I want to get you out of sight, lie low for a bit,' said Connor, as if seeing the image in Helen's mind. 'I know a place to camp, just outside the citadel. It's well hidden, and we can get back into the citadel for the ceremony tonight without tickets. That's our best bet, Hel; your father's bound to be there tonight.'

Helen nodded slowly. She took one last, lingering look around, scanning the hordes of tourists, then she turned and followed Connor.

They pitched the tent under an overhanging rock, on a small flat space on a steep hillside. The tent was green, well camouflaged.

'Camping here's illegal,' said Connor. 'The last thing we want is to be picked up by the tourist police.'

'What would they do?'

'Hand us over to Maldonado. We have to assume SIN have circulated your picture and description countrywide. Look, Hel, I need to go and get more food. We might have to make a run for it tonight, and we'll need extra provisions. You stay here. You're well hidden.' He kissed her and turned to go.

'Don't be long.'

'I won't. Stay out of sight, keep alert. If there's any trouble and you can run, see that clump of trees down there . . .'

'Yeah.'

'Make for there. There's a small cave just below. Hide there and I'll find you.'

'You expecting trouble?'

'Rule number one, always have an emergency rendezvous.'

'You didn't answer my question.'

'Yes, Hel, I am expecting trouble.'

He saw in her eyes that she could feel the same presentiment of danger closing in.

CHAPTER 73

Connor eased round the side of the mountain, out into the mêlée of tourists gathering in the forecourt of the Machu Picchu Ruinas hotel. He headed for the groups of porters, dazzling against the stone in their red ponchos. They were chattering happily. They'd just been paid, now most of them were looking forward to a few days' well-earned rest. Connor greeted them in Quechua, chatted for a while, buying what little supplies the cooks had left after four days on the Inca Trail. He swung round as he felt a hand on his shoulder. Alejandro stood behind him, his face grave. He beckoned Connor aside.

'I've had no luck, my friend, trying to find the man you sought. But I have something else for you. There have been men asking about a man that sounds a lot like you, and a girl. They say the man is with this girl.' Alejandro took a folded newspaper from inside his poncho. He opened it up and showed it to Connor. A photograph of Helen stared back at him from the pages of the *World*.

Connor handed Alejandro twenty dollars.

'You never saw us.'

'No, *jefe*, but others have and they talked.'

Connor slipped from the crowds and found the shelter of the forest. He hurried back to the tent. Before going in, he watched the area for fifteen agonising minutes, checking it was safe. When he'd satisfied himself that it was, he gave a low call to warn Helen he was coming in, then crawled into the tent. Helen's stomach lurched with fear at the trouble she saw in his eyes. Connor opened up the newspaper, spread it out on the ground. There were two articles under the byline, *Rod Clark*. He and Helen read in silence.

Global investment bank Goldsteins International has launched an internal investigation following financial irregularities believed to have been committed by one of its traders. Sources indicate that the sums involved could be as great as fifty million dollars. Unlike Barings, these losses are alleged to be lost profits. The trader concerned is believed to have made these profits from illegal trades in the vast derivatives market, misappropriating the profits from these trades, thereby depriving the bank of profits which are lawfully theirs. None of the traders who work on the derivatives desk had any comment to make.

The article then set out to explain the derivatives markets and to detail the major frauds that had been committed in those markets. In the next column was the second article by Rod Clark.

Helen Jencks, a trader who works for Goldsteins International, is being sought by friends and family. Goldsteins say she is on an extended holiday. Jencks was expected back in London after the bank holiday break, but never reappeared. Jencks is the daughter of rogue financier Jack Jencks, who disappeared in 1976, the day after it was discovered that twenty million pounds of client funds had gone missing from Woolson's where he was a director.

The article then elaborated on Jack Jencks and his alleged fraud and disappearance.

Helen's face smiled out from a photograph alongside the article. She stared at it, her fists clenched in rage.

'The bastard. Everyone can see the implication. I'm the guilty trader. When I get back to London I'm going to make him pay for this. I swear to God I'll destroy him.'

'We might never get back there, Hel. Maldonado's men are here. They're looking for us, and they've been tipped off that we're here. We have to go now.'

'What? Give up now?'

'Or die.'

'That's not writ in stone. There's still a chance. There has to be a chance.'

'There's no chance. Unless we leave now. It's not as if we've even seen a glimpse of your father. None of the porters I've spoken to know him.'

'Perhaps they're covering up. Perhaps he goes by a different name. Perhaps we described him wrong.'

'And perhaps his housekeeper lied. Perhaps he never came here. Perhaps he was in his house hiding all along.'

'No. That's impossible. He's here. He has to be.'

'Wishing won't make it so. Not even all the yearning you feel can conjure him if he's not here.'

'He is here, dammit all to hell. And I'm going to stay now and look for him tonight. I've come all this way. He's just within my reach. Nothing's going to stop me now. Not Maldonado. Not you. It all comes down to personal safety with you, doesn't it? You mustn't make love because of the risk of being caught with your pants down. You mustn't go after something you've dreamed of all your life because it could be dangerous. Why'd you join the army? Why do you live if everything you do is governed by an obsessive desire to cut the risks? Why do you see phantoms everywhere?' Her voice rose with the edge of desperation. Desperation for him to see what she meant. 'Don't you see? This isn't a sterile laboratory, it isn't war games in a sealed room. You see phantoms everywhere and you invoke them.'

His voice cut through hers. 'You don't know what you're talking about.'

She laughed with anger. 'Oh, I do. It's you who doesn't understand what I'm saying. You think you can control everything, quantify everything, that it all comes down to staying alive.'

'If I didn't think that, I'd be dead ten times over.'

'We're not in a war zone now.'

'You don't think so? Let's see, shall we? You want to go ahead, hang around here today, then go to the ceremony and look for your father.'

'That's what I am going to do. You can leave now, just tell me how much I owe you.'

He spun round and gripped her bare arm. 'I don't want your money.'

Everything he said made sense, and everything she said made

sense, and yet somehow they found themselves on opposite sides of an abyss that grew with every word. She knew already that it was too great to bridge.

'Just go. Get out. Leave me.'

Connor seemed to sag, then he turned abruptly, picked up his rucksack and disappeared through the mouth of the tent.

Helen stared at the canvas, as if she would be able to see him through it, like a fading X-ray, as he walked away. How had it happened? Three minutes of words, words which trapped them, making retreat impossible, however much they might have wished it. There was always a point of no return. She hadn't expected to go beyond it now, of all times. This felt like her father's desertion, though this time she had seen the man she loved walk away. She had sent him away.

Still she stared at the canvas, until the tears began. She brushed them away savagely, and began to laugh, wild and angry, disbelieving, as if the biggest cosmic joke ever had just been played.

'What else can you do?' she asked, quietening, as the laughter burned out.

Connor walked out into the forest. He walked until he felt alone, until there was silence.

He almost bled anger. He hated Helen, hated himself, yet he knew he was right. She was in mortal danger, even if she chose to ignore the threat so that she could continue to chase her dream. Like most people, she believed in her own invulnerability. That she had foiled one attempt on her life must have fuelled her fallacy. He'd seen too many corpses to harbour any illusions of immortality. This was his territory, yet Helen attacked him with it. But he couldn't be both things, sensitive lover and protector, when the two were in conflict and the outcome would be life or death. Images of Helen swam through his mind. He saw her smiling and triumphant at the top of Dead Woman's Pass. He saw her wild and shaken, walking away from the two men she had beaten up. He saw her vulnerable and joyful as he made love to her. And he wept. Whatever Helen pretended, Connor knew that, save a miracle, she was living the last hours of her life.

CHAPTER 74

Helen took refuge in her tent. She couldn't eat. Nor sleep. She yearned for Connor. She wept for him. She yearned for her father. Through it all, she felt the grip of terror as she imagined Maldonado's men, waiting in the dark. At midnight, she set out.

The night seemed so vast and invulnerable, cloaking the looming mountains. She could almost feel their contours. Little by little as her eyes grew accustomed to the darkness, she could detect the faint gleam of snow on distant summits. Her path was lit by the moon, one quarter full, and by the starlight which filtered down from the glowing galaxies in the skies above. She climbed the hill, went over the wall, and gained entry to the citadel. A man stood alone, high in the ruins, playing the Pan pipes. The sound drifted down, insidious and haunting. Knots of people walked through the ruins, gesturing in the dark, their voices low with suppressed excitement.

There were hours to go before the ceremonies started. Most people, she supposed, would arrive in the early morning before dawn.

She scanned faces. Looking for Maldonado, looking for her father. If her father were here, would he recognise her twenty-three years on? Would she know him, or would they pass like strangers? Strangers nodded to each other this evening, united by the thrill of being there. Would father and daughter nod and pass? She almost recoiled as her mind formed the words: father, daughter. Her sense of herself as a daughter had died when her father left, but he, somehow, retained the title 'father', even though she had begun to wonder what that meant. Two decades ago it had meant being there, being strong and right and gentle. Being together through the passing of time. She felt weighed down by the past. It always seemed to define her more than the present ever would. Could she never throw it off? And now here she was searching for it in the faces of strangers, while a sentence of death hung over her. She paused beside a learned-looking group listening avidly to a white-haired woman at their centre. Her voice carried as if she were standing on a podium addressing a lecture hall.

'Viewed from the Intihuatana, it would seem significant that sacred mountains align with the cardinal directions. The Veronica range lies to the east, and the sun rises behind its highest point at the equinoxes. Wayna Picchu is due north. The line of snow-capped peaks of the Pumasillo range is to the west, the sun setting behind the highest summit at the December solstice and the equinox line crossing the northern end. The massif of Salcantay lies to the south, its highest summit being at an azimuth of precisely 180 degrees. The Intihuatana was, therefore, at a central point from which sacred mountains were in alignment with the cardinal directions, and where significant celestial activity took place.'

Her words floated through Helen's mind as she scanned the group of listeners. Several sensed her scrutiny and turned to glance at her. She held their eyes, her breathing suspended, then rejected them. She walked deeper into the citadel, a figure alone, caught in the moonlight.

Connor hugged the darkness like a hunting animal. He walked through the ruins, watching, searching. He had stowed his rucksack in the cave under the boulder in the Temple of the Sun. Without its weight he felt lithe and fast. He didn't think of Helen now, save how to protect her. If he couldn't feel as she wanted him to, at least he could act. What a fool to think that he could feel. That part of him which had still been able to feel after his mother's death and a childhood of his father's neglect had atrophied during the years of action. Helen refused to see that you could not simply switch from one mode to the other at will.

He saw her, walking up to the Intihuatana stone. A few paces ahead of her was a man. She seemed to be watching him. She did not look down to check her footfalls on the uncertain path. The man was tall, with thick grey hair. He walked with a limp.

Connor glanced down to the foot of the steep stone staircase. Two men were climbing slowly, eyes fixed upon Helen.

Helen watched the old man reach the top of the stairs and pause for breath. Then he walked up to the Intihuatana stone and touched it with both hands. He stood there for a long time, just holding the stone, eyes closed. He seemed to be oblivious of her presence. After a while, he released the stone and sat down on the low wall that edged the precipitous terraces below. Then he turned to Helen. She found herself staring into the eyes of a man she had seen a million times in her waking dreams.

Helen looked at the man who was her father and could not speak. His legs were thin and when he sat his trousers rode up to reveal bony ankles encased in wrinkled socks. He was sitting forward, hugging his knees. His face was drawn, the skin papery brown; his eyes were a paler hue than the dazzling blue she remembered.

Jack Jencks gave Helen a polite smile and began to look away. Something in her eyes stopped him. He glanced back. She was still looking at him. Something in his mind conjured a girl of seven running into his arms, her eyes innocent and bright. This woman knew too much of the world. He understood too well the cost of the wisdom, compassion and rage that burned in her face. But in the pinpricks of light in those dark eyes, in the body of the woman who stood before him, he could see his daughter. He looked at her as if he had seen all the secrets of the world in one glimpse into infinity. Wonder, horror, amazement, joy and sorrow chased each other through his eyes.

'Oh, Helen. Is it really you? I must be hallucinating.'

He spoke with the voice that had haunted her dreams.

'Yes, Daddy.' Her voice broke on the word. 'It's me.' She took a step towards her father, then froze.

'How touching,' said a voice behind her. She wheeled round to see Victor Maldonado standing at the top of the stairway. He looked from Helen to her father. His face, lit by the moonlight, was drawn in a grimace of mockery. Behind him was a thin, grinning *mestizo*.

'Spy meets spy. Father meets daughter. Sorry to interrupt, but Helen and I have a little unfinished business of our own,' intoned

Maldonado, walking closer. She could feel the menace in him. She flinched as he touched her, and shook off his arm.

'Why'd you do it, Helen? I took you in and you spied on me, beat up and shot my men.'

'You tried to kill me.'

'What choice did you give me, eh? I can't have spies running around my home.'

'I'm not a spy. I never was.'

'Ah, it was just coincidence that you came. Just coincidence that you knew how to beat up some of my best men, disarm one of my best assassins, and shoot him; just coincidence that you becalmed my killer dogs and ran away.'

'I came here to escape from London. I never had any bad intentions towards you.'

'Ah, the set-up. Financial fraud, a fugitive. We all remember when that story was used last, don't we?'

'Helen . . . my God. Why are you here?' Helen jumped as her father called out. He unclenched his arms from his knees and unsteadily stood up. He took a few faltering steps towards her. His words echoed round Helen's brain. His voice was deep. It had always sounded as if it came from the depths of the Welsh valleys, but there was a river in it now, as if his words were drenched with sorrow. They were not crisp and clear, but slow, water-bound.

'She's a spy, Jack. Maybe even an assassin, sent to kill me. Now she's going to come with me. Sorry to break up this little reunion.'

'How can you be this?' asked Helen, taking hold of Maldonado's arm, leaning towards him, searching in his eyes for the good part of the man. 'What have you turned into?'

'He turned a long time ago,' said Jack Jencks. 'He took the gold. Always did have a weakness for it, didn't you, Victor, even when we were first friends at Cambridge, you, me and Dai; do you remember, you loved money, never had enough? I always wondered how long you'd last, but none of us knew what tragedy was waiting for you. It turned you, and God knows it might have turned us all. But you don't need Helen.' His voice broke on her name and it was a few moments before he spoke again. 'Whatever she's done or hasn't done, leave her out of this. You have enough. You've done enough for a thousand lifetimes.'

Helen could see her father's words working on Maldonado. The coldness flickered, she could see shards of pain and it felt to her as if the whole mountain were balanced on the flow of his voice. They could tumble, all of them, into the gorge below if just one word was wrong.

Angel walked up to Helen's father, stood before him and spat into his face. Helen watched as the spittle ran down over his eyes, over his skin. The violence and the loathing flared in her, she could feel it coursing round her body. *Weigh it up, watch, calm, analyse, then act.* She could hear her sensai's voice.

Her father took a ragged handkerchief from his shirt pocket and wiped his face. He spoke to Maldonado as if Angel was not there two feet from him. 'It's the scum behind you that I despise; they were always waiting for their chance to turn you, while they fed you poison. Scum like him.' He looked at Angel. 'If you could leave them behind . . .'

Helen could see Angel's response in the making. She could see the muscles clench in his arms, could see the sinews move as he drew back his hand. She could almost feel the blow that would smash into her father's face.

'Kiai!' She leapt towards him, raising her arm, palm towards his face, as if to immobilise him with the force of her spirit. Off balance, he grabbed her and they both fell over the wall down one terrace. Angel landed on his back, Helen on top of him. He let out a groan and Helen could see he was winded but he grabbed hold of her throat with both hands and began to squeeze. She forced her knee down into his stomach until he let go, then she tried to throw him over the next terrace. Just as he was falling he swung his legs so that they swept her feet from the ground and she fell. He grabbed her and together they crashed over the terrace, landing eight feet down on the next level. Helen leapt up, feeling fire in the shoulder she'd landed on. Angel straightened up, reached inside his jacket, took out a pistol and moved to point it at Helen.

With the speed of a striking snake, Helen caught his wrist, turned under him, and threw him in kokyu nage. The pistol flew from his hand. He landed heavily on his back. Helen grabbed the gun. Angel lunged at her. She wheeled out of range. Carried by his own momentum, denied a target, Angel plummeted over the next terrace. He landed on his neck. Helen heard a crack and she had to fight back vomit. She stared down at him, but he didn't move. She watched his inert body until she could bear to look no more, and was in no doubt. She began to climb back up the terraces, her nails tearing the earth. As she neared the top she heard voices. She peered over. Connor stood before her. He was holding Maldonado in an armlock. For a moment, she felt a dizzying joy to see him standing there, next to her father. Then the horror once again claimed her. She climbed up the last terrace, over the wall, and walked out into the open space beside the Intihuatana stone.

'What happened down there?' asked Connor.

'One of Maldonado's men,' said Helen.

'And?'

'Dead.'

Connor could see the onset of shock in the stiffness of her body, in her unnaturally bright eyes.

'We have to kill him too,' said Connor, nodding at Maldonado.

'No,' said Helen, looking into Maldonado's eyes. 'Leave him.'

'He'd kill you, in your place, believe me,' said Connor. 'And if we don't kill him, we'll never get away. He'll have his men on us in ten minutes.'

'I'll keep him here,' said Jack Jencks. 'Give me the gun and I'll buy you time.'

Helen stared at her father, reeling.

'Leave you? After twenty-three years? Do you know how I've looked for you?' She was weeping now, her words fighting with her sobs. 'I've travelled half the world searching for you. Have you any idea what it's been like? Now you say go, leave me.'

She saw the tears course down her father's cheeks.

'I would give the world to keep you here. There hasn't been a day go by when I haven't thought of you. I speak to you in my dreams. I've got so much to say to you, so much to ask you, I –' He faltered, racked by a sob. He struggled for composure, regained enough to continue. He nodded at Maldonado. 'You don't understand who you're dealing with, Helen. I don't in God's name know how this nightmare came to pass, but I know enough to see that he's planning to kill you. I heard rumours of a search, of a hunt to kill. A man and a woman. Never did I think it might be you. If you stay here, you'll die.'

Helen rushed forward and grabbed her father's hand. 'You could come with us.'

He gestured to his leg. 'I can hardly walk. Arthritis. I'd slow you down. Maldonado's men would catch us in minutes.'

'But you were supposed to be doing the Inca Trail. You must be able to walk.'

'Who told you that?'

'Your housekeeper.'

'Ay, Patria, protecting me. I came by train. I couldn't walk a kilometre.'

Helen dropped his hand and doubled up, her body convulsed by spasms. Her father caught her arm, gently eased her up till she stood straight.

'You have to go. Otherwise you die. I can hold Victor here at gunpoint. We can hide down on the terraces. Your friend' – he nodded at Connor – 'can help get me down there. No one will see us. I can probably get you an hour's head start.'

Connor took the pistol from Helen. He levelled it at Maldonado. 'The best thing would be to kill him,' he said.

'Please. You can't,' said Helen, with infinite softness. 'I know you should, but you can't.' She turned to Maldonado. 'Remember this. We're sparing your life. A blood debt. You owe us. You have to protect us.'

'He'll never do that,' said Helen's father. 'There's precious little honour in him.'

'Then he'll kill you,' shouted Helen.

'No. He won't kill me. We go back too far,' lied Jack Jencks.

'Enough of this, Christ almighty,' hissed Connor. 'Stand back, let me kill him.'

'No,' said Helen. 'You have to let him live. Don't ask me why. I just know there'll be a payback. Some time, somewhere. Please, I'm begging you, don't kill him.'

Connor kept his eyes on Maldonado. In his ears he could hear his training, the low calm voice of reason, and then it was drowning in a howling of something that ambushed him out of nowhere, the soft voice, promising something he had never seen in his life.

341

Slowly he lowered the pistol and handed it to Jack Jencks, who pointed it at Maldonado's knees. Connor turned to Helen.

'Your only chance is to take your father's offer.'

Helen looked from Connor to her father. 'I can't go. I can't leave now, not without him.'

Helen's father took hold of her. 'Go, please. Do you think I could stand here and watch you die, or be led off to be killed? This is the only way I can save you. Nothing can ever make up for what I did to you, but at least let me do this.'

'You had no choice when you left,' said Helen, through her sobs. 'I know that now.'

'You have to go,' said her father. Helen could feel the agony in his voice. 'I left and I broke your heart, and mine. Now you have no choice. You have to go.'

'And break our hearts a second time.'

'It's that or die. Let me save you.'

Helen felt that she was losing her heart in a torrent of agony. Then there was a dullness as if she were dying, and her body was giving her its last gift to erase the pain that was killing her.

She looked at her father, hugged him to her. Connor forced himself to wait the lost seconds that could hold their death.

Suddenly Helen dragged herself back from her father, drank in the image of him, and with a cry turned to Maldonado.

'If you harm him, if you touch one hair on his head, if you do not let him go free, I swear I'll come back and kill you. I will curse you with every drop of my blood, with all the blood you've ever spilled.'

'You think you could harm me?'

Helen, eyes glittering, stepped closer to Maldonado. 'You know I could. I could kill you now, with my bare hands, break your neck with one move. I'm an agent, remember, your own words, an assassin. I'll find a way to come back here. You've got enough enemies who'd be glad to help me. I'll destroy you, bone by bone.'

Maldonado looked into her eyes and turned away. Connor watched her, spellbound by her savagery. Helen moved back to her father.

'Daddy, we'll meet again. I promise.' With a sob, she wrenched herself away. Connor forced Maldonado down three terraces, helping Helen's father down at the same time. He left them, hidden in the darkness, climbed back up to Helen, gripped her arm and ran with her towards the flight of steps.

'This way. We can't leave by the main exit. Maldonado's men'll be all over the place.'

They retrieved Connor's rucksack, then set off down the precipitous mountainside. Connor took Helen's hand and led her down the terracing, ten terraces down, leaping and landing with a blow from the eight-foot drop. She ran with him over tripping stones and past stinging branches, their way lit by the brilliance of the moon and stars.

Ahead of them lay a slanting field, then forest. They ran across the open ground, and stopped in the shelter of the trees. Helen sank to the ground, breathing hard.

Connor sat down beside her. Her eyes were wild with agony.

'Oh God, Evan. What are we going to do?' she asked, her voice breaking.

Connor gripped her hands. 'We're going to survive, that's what. You're going to keep your promise to your father. If you're ever going to see him again, you've got to fight with everything you've got. You can't break now. Do you understand?'

Connor stared into her eyes, trying to fight down his panic. The madness he saw in her seemed to be winning, then he felt her coming back to him, the slow burn of survival fighting off the insanity of her grief. She nodded her head. 'Yes. I do.'

'Good.' Connor kept up his pressure. 'We've got two choices. I reckon we've got half an hour before Maldonado and his man are missed. Then there'll be a dragnet. If we can move fast enough, we should run now. I know a route we can take that they won't know, but it's at least three hours away. We might not make it that far. In our favour, it's probably in the opposite direction they'd expect us to go. Or else, we find somewhere to hide, and hole up here for a few days, maybe a week, until the hunt's passed by. If we're found, we'll be killed.' He spoke coldly, but this time Helen recognised in his apparent dispassion the desire to lay bare the truth, and to keep the emotions of it at bay.

'I don't think I can stay still.'

'OK, we'll run.'

'Where to?'

'We'll head for the jungle. To a place near Boca Manu. A friend of mine has a lodge there, with an airstrip. He's always buying and selling planes. If he's got a big enough one, I'll fly us to Colombia.'

'You can fly?'

'Learned in the army.'

He could see the doubt in Helen's eyes, the flickering agony. He started to wonder if they could go on, but almost as if she could read his fears for her, she got to her feet and her eyes hardened.

'Let's go.'

Dizzy with shock, she just moved with him, as if by silent consent, fighting to recover the surface of herself, enough to function, like an accident victim learning to walk. Delicate, delicate, each step, the air around her full of straining breaths. The death they had left behind felt like the echoes of a distant earthquake, something that shook them and passed by. Connor was inured to sudden death. It was a part of him, as familiar and unfathomable as life itself. For Helen it was dwarfed by finding, and losing, her father.

'Why did he do it?' Helen's voice rasped through the night. 'Why did he stay?' As she moved through the forest, the trees drew blood from her face, mixing with the rain of her tears. Connor stopped, took her into his arms and held her. He felt her breath coming in great gulps as her chest heaved against him. He held her until her struggle eased and her breath began to return to normal. Then he gently drew away and gave her his water bottle.

Helen drained half the bottle, gazing off into the darkness as if trying to see through it. Connor touched her arm, and they began to move again. The silence felt as thick as a prison wall. The words he spoke were to distract, and to keep them alive.

'Do as I do, silently. If I run for cover, follow me. If I throw myself to the ground, lie alongside me. We want to avoid being seen, but if we can't find cover, then act perfectly normally, but think of everyone we pass as a potential informer. We'll walk as far as we can, sleep during the day, then move again at dusk.'

She was nodding silently, drawing in his voice, filling her mind with his words.

'We'll follow the valley down to the low jungle. There's a route hardly anyone knows about. We'll get on that and walk for a few days, then we should hit the Cusco jungle road. We can walk along that, maybe hitch a lift on a cargo lorry.'

'Then what?'

'Find my friend Alvaro, get him to lend us a plane, fly into Colombia, make our way to the embassy in Bogotá. They'll get us back to the UK.'

'You make it sound so simple. Just a little stroll into the jungle, and a hop across the border, with half the intelligence services of Peru looking for us.'

'It is simple. We do it, or we die.'

CHAPTER 75

They walked through the night. After three hours, they branched off into almost impenetrable jungle. They forced themselves through battling branches. After about forty yards, they came to a path.

'Is this what you meant,' asked Helen, 'the path Maldonado won't know about?'

'Yep,' said Connor. 'We've just moved the odds infinitesimally in our favour.' He didn't need to add that the odds were still overwhelmingly against them.

They walked on into the dawn.

'We should really stop and lie up now it's light,' said Connor, 'but I want to put some more distance in, if you can keep going.'

'I can keep going,' said Helen, grimly.

The day was a mockery. The sky grew bright as a diamond against the green mountains. The air danced a fine frenzy against her skin. She felt life keenly as never before. The enormity of her pain wept from her, and with it twenty-three years of wishing, wondering and yearning. To find her father, to lose him again, and to see through her own pain his agony. The weight of it unbalanced her so that she felt she would fall over. But she walked, pace by pace, with Connor beside her, guiding her.

There is something mesmerising about walking long distances. The body seems to move up into an unknown gear, and settle into a rhythm which liberates the mind. They walked down through the gathering heat of the day, insidious and relentless. They stuck to the trees when they could, but every so often they had to cross bare hillside or open fields. On and on. Feet bruised on the stones, ankles turning and holding, on and on to the unassailable beat in her mind, through tiredness, into the haze of exhaustion. By late morning, the beat became subconscious. Helen found stray thoughts homing into her mind's void, half-remembered conversations from years ago, and, slowly, as the miles rolled away, came Roddy, Wallace and Rankin, their faces soft, insubstantial, almost blending. When she thought of them, fat in their armchairs, back in London, she felt like laughing. She found herself wondering where it came from, this savage laughter, so raw, so near the surface. It was like a weapon, hard and fine.

Connor led her into a deeper part of the forest, off the track. The branches reached for her hair and scratched her arms. Connor stopped beside a slight mound, skirted round to the far side, then took off his rucksack. He rummaged around inside and pulled out two apples and a tin of bully beef. They feasted on the fruit and meat, washed down with purified stream water. Then Connor took from his rucksack a large green string hammock which he strung between two trees. He held out his hand to Helen and together they climbed into it and lay down, wrapped around each other. Connor kissed her. She looked at him with graveyard eyes, and closed them against the world. Sleep came to her like a lover.

Helen awoke with a start after a few hours. She looked around but she could see nothing moving in the thick foliage. Her eyes scanned the jungle, slowly reassuring her that no human outlines were flickering through the hundred trembling shades of green. Her breathing crept back to normal. She turned to look at Connor as he slept beside her. The palms of his hands lay open. They were large, his hands, disproportionately so, like Michelangelo's David. Rough and hard. They could touch her so gently, or pull her to him with a force she felt could break her, but they seemed so defenceless now, those open palms. His whole face looked vulner-able: the slightly parted lips, the crease in his forehead that drew his eyebrows together even in sleep. There never was for him the escape of being wrong. His life was a rockface, one mistake would be fatal.

She kissed his forehead with the softest touch, eased free of his arms, got out of the hammock and went a little distance away to pee.

Pulling up her jeans, she froze. In an echo of what had woken her moments before, she heard a quick clatter of voices, perhaps just thirty yards away. She headed back to Connor, moving almost like a hunting animal, sinew by sinew on silent feet. Connor lay in the hammock, fully awake. He looked at Helen and she took his meaning, and stood motionless against a tree. They stayed like figures frozen in a masquerade until the voices passed and faded into the quiet of birdsong and animals snuffling and leaves whispering like silk in the forest around them. For fifteen minutes after the voices had passed they did not move, or speak. Only then did they feel as if they could breathe fully again. Helen got back into the hammock beside Connor.

'Do you think it was Maldonado's men?'

'They were making too much noise. Village men. But they'll have been warned to keep a look out. I know how it feels out here, like you're the only one alive. It's so distant, inaccessible. One hour into the jungle and you think you're untouchable. But the jungle's alive with danger. Snakes, falling branches, tarantulas, a thousand eyes watching. I'm not the only one who knows my way around. Maldonado's men'll be spinning a web – tribespeople, villagers, hunters, SIN's jungle force, the terrorists. MRTA and the Shining Path hole up in the jungle. And the narcos. Maldonado'll make it worth their while. They'll all be looking for us.'

Helen gazed upwards into the green light. 'A search party of psychopaths. Can we go now? I'm not sure I can stay still any longer.' Her whole body felt needled by thousands of shocks of adrenaline. Connor glanced at his watch. 'Five more hours. We move at dusk.'

How many weeks had he lain up, still as a log, waiting and watching? So much easier to be the hunter than the hunted. He took Helen's hand, and pulled her closer. 'Imagine you're a tree, sleeping gently.' He held her lightly, and whispered to her until she fell asleep.

Connor lay awake beside her, alive with silent thrill. When she awoke hours later he seemed to her like a young boy who had discovered the secret of how to flirt with the suicide of speed: so alive, so close to the prospect of death.

Darkness fell around them. The birds shuffled, murmured their good nights and fell silent. The animals of the day burrowed down into the spongy floor and took cover, or hid in the enfolding canopy high above. Helen and Connor untwined and rose slowly from the hammock. Connor untied it from the trees and packed it up. He gave Helen his water bottle, she took a few long gulps before handing it back. The water was brownish, rasping with chemicals, but it cooled her against the closeness of the night. Connor gave her a granola bar which she ate in two mouthfuls.

'You could survive out here for months,' said Connor, reading her thoughts, 'with curves like that.'

'And what about you,' she asked, 'with your sleek hard muscles? How would you survive?'

'I'd eat you,' he said, approaching with intent, 'starting here.' She stifled her laughter as he began to nuzzle her breast.

'Save your energy,' she said with a fierce smile. 'You might have to carry me before tomorrow.'

They set off through the thickness of night under the canopy. Connor led, picking his way slowly through the trees, along a rough path. Helen could hear the quick intake of breath when he was bloodied by thorns.

'Can't we use your torch? Surely no one will see us here.'

Connor shook his head and Helen visualised the net of Maldonado's men spreading out around them.

'Train your eyes,' said Connor. 'Imagine the darkness is speckled with holes of light, and feel your way. Try to see with your mind.'

Slowly, her eyes grew accustomed to the darkness. She felt as if she moved through a dark pool, making ripples that spread and faded, then the water closed behind her leaving no trace of her passing.

After half an hour, they left the forest for the open fields and dirt tracks. The sky was huge and clear above them. They walked by starlight. All around them the night was rich with the smell of the eucalyptus trees that lined their path. Their leaves were tinged bronze by the great orange moon that rose from the clouds. They walked without speaking, almost mesmerised by the beauty of the night. All they could hear was the rhythmic fall of their feet, and the sporadic barking of dogs, breaking the silence of the night as they passed.

They walked downwards, almost falling through the darkness, until they came to a vast plain. The long grass undulated in the breeze. They moved as if through a dreamscape. In the memory of dreams, there is never sound, only images. Helen thought that at some time in the future, if she survived this, she would look back on this night as if it were an episode in someone else's life, for she felt she would never be able to recall the silent beauty of the moon-tinged grass that moved like a calm sea around them, nor the silver-capped mountains whose gaze swept over them and beyond, to the mysteries of Amazonia. She and Connor walked side by side, enchanted. She wondered how she was able to be like this, so intensely alive she could feel the night breathe, while, inside her, the wound left by losing her father haemorrhaged. Pain, longing, despair and fear were so close, hovering like phantoms around her, occasionally swooping down, threatening to over-whelm her. What kept them at bay was the raw elation of survival, and the strange magic of the night. Helen looked at Evan, at his eyes taking in the wonder, and knew it was the same for him.

'Do you think we shall ever see a moon like this again, you and I together?' she asked him.

'Where would you like to see it?'

'On the Marlborough downs, ten miles from Dai's house. There's this little copse of five beech trees at the highest point. I'd see it from there, on a midsummer's night.'

'Then that's where I'll see it too.' Connor smiled, took her hand and together they walked across the sea of grass. It took them all night to cross the plain, and when they hid themselves to sleep for the day, they lay in the hot air that seeped up from the jungle below.

CHAPTER 76

Helen and Connor lay together in their copse of bushes, above the cloud forest. Helen gazed down at the canopy, an unreadable mass of foliage, miles below. The sun was setting, burnished orange over the endless green. Soon they'd have to start walking again. They'd been on the run for two days now, and Helen could feel her body, racked by emotions and the rigours of flight, beginning to weaken. She wondered how long it would hold up.

She turned to Evan, took his hand, and squeezed it gently. He looked inquisitively into her eyes. He seemed so trusting, waiting in silence for her question, so ready to answer, whatever it was she had to ask. He showed no crack, no impatience when she had to stop for rest, no greed as he gave her most of his food, and he showed no fear, just an omniscient calm.

'Will we make it to Colombia?'

He had not expected that, and the surprise showed momentarily in his eyes, but then he smiled and squeezed her hand back. 'Of course we will.'

'What are our chances?'

His eyes couldn't lie so quickly a second time. He knew she had seen the hesitation.

'Don't worry,' she said. 'I've always been a gambler. It wouldn't be the first time I've beaten the odds.'

Her eyes shone in her dirty face. Connor had never wanted her so much. He fought down his desire. What lay ahead would drain every last reserve of energy from Helen, and then demand more. He pulled her head to his chest, and stroked her hair, holding her while she gleaned a little more sleep from the dying day.

They started moving again an hour later. They walked off the plain, down a thousand steps, through scattered shrubs, which became bushes, then trees. As they went further down, everything seemed to grow. The trees rose from head height to twice that, and the forest grew denser around them, slowing their progress. The thick impenetrability of trees could harbour a hundred watching faces. Helen shuddered as she imagined terrorists or SIN crouched and waiting for them.

Connor was wary, as always, stopping every ten minutes to listen. Any crack of a twig, any patch of darkness that moved could be their unseen pursuers. He never dropped his vigilance. His sharp eyes, constantly searching, kept alive the spectre of pursuit.

'Don't think because we can't see them they aren't waiting in the darkness. They'll be behind us, searching for our trail, if not pacing after us. They'll be ahead of us, waiting at choke points. At bridges, along the Cusco jungle road, at airstrips,' explained Connor. 'They know we'll turn up sooner or later, if we're still alive. All they have to do is thin out and wait.'

'So how do we get around them then?' asked Helen, hard-eyed with fury at his calm in the face of what was, in his logic, the inevitability of death. 'What am I missing?'

'We have to be better than them. We have to think like them and be cleverer, we have to move faster than them, not just more quietly, but silently. We have to use the cover of the wind, of the night, of the jungle, and we pray that we're lucky. And we have to want to live more than they want to kill us.'

That's what it came down to, thought Helen, with each step into the territory of fear and exhaustion. The instinct for survival was like passionate love. No step was too far.

They walked on through the night, hour after hour. At 4 AM, after nine hours of walking, Helen could sense Connor searching for something beyond pursuit. He consulted his compass, stopped to study large stones that they passed. He changed the angle of the route they were taking a few times.

'What are we looking for?' asked Helen.

'An Inca route I discovered with some explorers when we were searching for Paititi. Watch out here.' Connor led her through a patch of particularly dense undergrowth that left streaks of blood on her face. They emerged onto a narrow track that looked as if it had been recently cleared. Slabs of stone were just visible beneath the ground foliage.

Helen wiped away the blood on a grimy handkerchief.

'What's Paititi?'

'El Dorado, the lost city of gold. It was the last refuge of the Incas. In 1536 they rebelled against the conquistadors, then withdrew to Vilcabamba in the jungle. They stayed there for thirty-five years before they were finally defeated. After that, Vilcabamba itself was consumed by the forest and "lost". There are supposed to be vast treasures of Inca gold there that the conquistadors never found.'

'I presume you didn't find it?'

Connor smiled. 'Thousands of people have died searching for it. Legends suggest it's guarded by warriors expelled from the Machiguenga tribe, psychopaths.'

'That's reassuring,' said Helen, picking a black-and-yellow-striped spider out of her hair, wondering if it bit and if it was poisonous. 'Has anyone ever seen it and lived to tell?'

Connor blew the spider from her fingertips. 'Nasty-looking, but harmless.' He decided not to tell her it was a baby tarantula.

'There are all sorts of stories about people getting lost, falling asleep and waking up in a temple of gold. They pick up something – I've heard tell of a child's golden hand – and wander back into the jungle, but no matter how much they search, they can never find Paititi again. Those who try almost always end up dead.'

'So there's a curse on it, like the Moche tombs.'

'Could be. In Guarani, one of the jungle languages, Paititi means anguish, sadness, affliction.'

'So perhaps it's as well you never found it. Whereabouts is it? Are we near?'

'It's meant to be somewhere between Machu Picchu and Manu, in the jungle, at about five hundred metres' altitude. Could be anywhere around us.' Connor smiled. 'Who knows, might even stumble on it, since we're not looking.'

'And get killed by Machiguenga psychopaths. A more poetic end, I suppose, than being shot in the back by Maldonado's men.'

Helen's thoughts veered back to her father. She tried to feel him in the heat of the jungle, wondered if he had walked this path, searching for Paititi, chasing legends, while back home, in her

353

dreams, she chased him. She felt as if she could see his eyes gleaming in the darkness.

He won't kill me. We go back too far, he had said of Maldonado. The yearning in her swelled up. She replayed the scene on Machu Picchu, conjuring her father, the sound of his voice, the brief moment when she hugged him to her. His eyes, racked with pain and love. So good, so brave, selfless. Was he giving his life in exchange for hers when he stayed to keep guard on Maldonado? Was he doing penance in the only way he could? To have found him after twenty-three years, only to kill him. The cruelty of it was almost beyond enduring. She felt she would drown in her grief. Part of her wanted to fall to the jungle floor and give in, let the madness claim her. In horrified reaction, the survival instinct rose within her. Her death would solve nothing, save break her father's heart if he managed to survive. And betray Evan. Every step of the way, he had risked his life for her. He could have turned and walked away a long time ago. He could have left when she screamed at him to go, to leave her, but he came back, and now he was saving her life. Where could she have run to in this wilderness without him to guide her? How could she ever hope to keep her promise to her father to see him again, without Evan? Through all her pain, she felt her admiration and her love for him growing.

'It doesn't scare you at all, does it, this wilderness?'

'I know what to eat and what not. Where to get water, what to watch out for. I know I can survive out here, but for some people it can be one of the most frightening places on earth. All they see is leaves and trees and the horizon never further than twenty feet away, until they come to a river. Some people go mad with the claustrophobia. To other people, the jungle's neutral. To me it's a kind of friend. I just forget that the outside world exists. This becomes my world. Time seems to stretch for ever as if you'll never die, or maybe it's just that you stop worrying about it. I get this incredible sense of peace.'

'You sound protective of it.'

'I am. It's a kind of paradise. There are over five million species of plants and animals here and probably at least ten per cent of those science hasn't identified. Can you imagine what might be out there, just waiting to be discovered? They've already been developing this incredible new anti-inflammatory drug from the bark of a tree called uña de gato, cat's claw. It's being used to treat rheumatism, arthritis, Aids, cancer. It's probably one of the drugs of the century. And, at the same time, every year an area the size of Switzerland is cut down and destroyed.'

At 6 AM, Connor slung the hammock between two ficus trees. He gave Helen a packet of peanuts, his water bottle, a third full, half a stick of pepperoni and three boiled sweets. He took a few sips of water and the other half of the pepperoni. He hunted around in the jungle and picked ten ficus fruits which he washed with purified water and shared out between the two of them. A pathetically inadequate meal. He wondered how much longer Helen could keep going. In the fifty-odd hours they had been on the run, she had already gone much further than he would have thought her capable of on feeble rations and a diet of fear that would have immobilised many.

They fell asleep holding each other. Connor would have preferred to keep watch, but he weighed the odds and decided to risk sleep.

Helen awoke nearly twelve hours later. Her body ached and her throat cracked with thirst. Connor gave her what was left of his second water bottle, five ficus fruits and another bag of peanuts.

They were on the move as dusk fell. Connor led Helen off the rough trail and into the thickness of the jungle.

'We've got to get some water. There's a pool near here if I remember rightly.'

The branches seemed to resist their progress. The roots conspired to trip them. Helen felt her coordination going. Her body shook with a violent tremor.

'What is it?' Connor took hold of her arm.

'This place is so immense. If I take four wrong steps I'm lost.' She could imagine herself trapped by thorns, writhing bloody, imprisoned, as Connor disappeared into the distance.

Connor stopped and took both her hands in his. 'You won't get lost. You'll stay with me. I know the jungle, I know how to move around.' He pulled her against his chest and held her silently until he felt the terror leave her body. He soaked up her pain, and her fear, knowing all the while he could not show a crack in his confidence, or a single doubt. He'd been trained for this in the SAS. Escape and evasion, jungle survival. He'd even been trained how to quell the fear and grief of his men, but Helen's agony cut through all his defences. He tried to force it down, to concentrate on staying alive.

They walked on, Helen calmer. After twenty minutes they came to a large clearing with a small pond in the foreground and clay-coloured walls rising up beyond. They drank the last of their water and Connor refilled his two bottles adding purifying tablets. They sat for a while, watching the gathering twilight, listening to the snuffling of animals settling down to sleep.

The air was rent with a screech. Helen looked up to see a pair of macaws flying overhead. The birds landed on the clay walls. Helen and Connor paused to watch as another pair flew in, then another, and within minutes the air rang with the cries of macaws and the sky glittered with flashes of red, turquoise, gold and green.

'It's a clay lick,' explained Connor. 'I wanted you to see it, to see something beautiful.'

'It's incredible,' said Helen, turning to kiss him.

'They pair for life,' said Connor. 'There's a lovely legend about where macaws get their colours. The blue ones bathed in a lake where no river flowed in or out. The red ones bathed in a lake of blood from the child of the Kadiueu tribe. The brown ones bathed in mud. The green ones rubbed against the foliage, and the white ones were those which never moved.'

The image of the parrots stained with the colours of the jungle, flying into the sunset above the silhouette of the rainforest, and the sound of their exuberant screams, would stay with Helen for the rest of her life.

CHAPTER 77

After a while, they came upon a dirt road. Connor stopped beside it, looked up and down, and listened for a long while.

'The Cusco jungle road. We'll make good ground, but be ready to take cover.'

Helen nodded. Connor set off at a cracking pace. He was silent, as usual. He walked his long, loping walk, devouring ground. They went for four hours like that, trance-like along the road, bordered by the dark shadows of the jungle. Mud slid beneath their feet. Crickets chirped as they passed. Insects buzzed and drank their blood. The sweat ran down them in rivers as they walked through the hot night. They heard no one, saw nothing, save the way ahead.

Connor suddenly stopped abruptly, stood listening. He motioned to Helen to get off the road. She felt the cruel prick of fear, and started to move. Something seemed to be almost paralysing her. She wanted to move, faster, off the road, get away, GET AWAY. All her instincts were screaming.

There was a crash of sound to her left, then a fury in the jungle. Two men leapt out onto the road. She saw the glint of metal. Two pistols were pointing at her face. Connor had spun around, started to move towards her, and frozen as he saw the guns levelled against her head. Two more men came at them from the left, pointing their pistols at Connor. The men spoke in Spanish in low angry voices. Helen wanted to lunge, lash out, knew that this time there was no fighting the odds. Connor's eyes were on her, she looked into them, and gave him a smile of infinite sweetness and regret. Connor's face was implacable with anger, but in the seconds that she stared at him, she saw the anger fade until there was nothing, and she didn't recognise the face that stared back.

'Who the fuck are you?' said an American accent, low with rage. A tall, thick-shouldered man approached them. He was dressed, like all the others, in jungle camouflage and a black balaclava.

Anger showed in the other balaclavaed eyes, and a strange impatience.

'Doesn't matter to you,' said Connor. 'Just let us go and you can get on with your business.'

One of the men holding a gun to Helen's head gave a small shift of contempt, and pushed his pistol into her skin.

'I asked you who the fuck you were,' the American demanded.

Connor took an educated guess that would either ensure their murder or, just possibly, their release.

'Let's just say Blair O'Patrick is a good friend of mine.'

The American glared at Connor. 'You with the Brits?'

'The Regiment actually.'

'And who the fuck's this?' The American nodded at Helen.

'Woman officer,' said Connor quickly. 'Training.'

'That what you call it. You better be who you say you are.'

'How else would I know O'Patrick's name?'

'Give me another.'

'Gus Jamieson,' said Connor, 'but you might not know him. He's lower down the ranks.'

The American turned on his heel and walked a few paces into the jungle to consult the men who Connor knew would be hiding there. He returned after an agonising wait.

'You're lucky, buster. You and your girlie fuck off out of here quietly. And tell your fucking CO to check for compromise next time you feel like *training*.'

The men holding pistols to Helen's head withdrew with looks of regret.

'We're on our way,' said Connor and began to move off. Helen forced her legs to follow him. She walked past the big American. He was so close, she nearly brushed his face. She could almost feel him smelling her and the rancid fear that rose from her skin.

Pace by pace, silent in the night, she followed Connor, arms almost rigid with terror, unable to reach out, to touch his back and urge him to speak. If she was walking she was alive. Her back ached. It still trembled an hour later, every cell imagining the feel of a bullet ripping into her shoulder blades.

Connor stopped. He took his water bottle from his rucksack, gave her a sip. She took it with unsteady hands, and at last found her voice.

'Who were those people? Why did they let us go?'

'DEA,' said Connor. 'They were lying up for an ambush. We walked into the middle of it. I knew something was wrong. I could feel it, and we walked right into it.'

Helen touched his arm. 'How could you know?'

He threw off her hand. 'It's my job to know. We're lucky not to have been killed, shot as we walked. It was pure luck we had a chance to speak.' He cursed himself, he hadn't meant to frighten her, but when she spoke her voice was calm.

'We weren't killed. You said the right thing, whatever the hell it meant, and they let us go.'

'I said the name of one of the top undercover DEA guys. Only another drugs boy, or perhaps a top narco, would have known it.'

'Couldn't we have just asked them to take us in? To get us to the American embassy or something?'

'Not quite so simple as that. There'd have been Peruvians on that job too, and they may or may not know about Maldonado. I'm hoping they'll have been lying up here for days, concentrating on the job in hand. I don't think they can know about Maldonado, or they'd never have let us go, but they will, soon, then they'll have to report that they've seen us. They'll give out our last location. We're going to have to move like rockets now, Hel.'

'How far is it to your friend's place?'

'Twenty hours of walking, perhaps more, and we can't stop until we get there.'

She felt wails of exhaustion rip through her. She took his water bottle from him and drank deeply. She handed it back with a faint smile.

'Better get going then.'

CHAPTER 78

This time there was no stopping with the dawn, or with the morning. Connor led the way as if he drew Helen forward with an invisible thread.

The air grew thick and heavy around them. It felt like honey as it slid down into their lungs. After walking for fifteen hours, Helen could feel herself begin to hallucinate. Her mind turned to a place called London, so far away, unreal. If she didn't think about it, it wouldn't exist. Here all sound was muted by the sheltering forest, and you never could see beyond twenty yards in any one direction. The animals alone spoke. The air was rent by the cries of macaws, and by the mocking laughter of monkeys. The birds could fly, they were emissaries, messengers, their cries told of the world outside, of knowledge, but the monkeys screamed with the hot-house hysteria of claustrophobia. They lived in the canopy, venturing down to the forest floor only rarely. To them, the canopy was as vast and unyielding as a sea; it stretched out for ever. At peace the monkeys were the most beautiful, dream-like creatures as they stepped gently through the trees, but when they shrieked Helen felt the proximity of madness. It worked on her like the sound of breaking glass, a splinter of insanity and destruction. She wanted to stand in the naked jungle and scream back at the invisible monkeys.

Her father appeared to her in a waking nightmare, then he began to dissipate in her hallucinations as even her grief and yearning were subsumed by exhaustion.

They stopped at noon. The heat gripped them, the sweat soaked their clothes and streamed into their eyes. Connor took a few sips of water and let Helen finish it. There was nothing to eat. Connor produced a packet of coca leaves he'd been saving for when the food ran out and exhaustion began to cripple them. He gave Helen a small handful.

'Thanks.' She took the leaves, wrinkled her face against their bitter taste. She looked at Connor. He appeared tired, but steady. Helen could feel the waves of exhaustion shake her.

'How much more?'

'Seven hours to Shintuya. That's the end of the road. We pick up the river just before there, cross, then another hour to the Villa Carmen.' Connor pulled her to him and she could feel herself swaying against his chest.

'Nearly there, Hel, you're doing so well. I don't know any other woman who could do this, even some of the specialists in the army would have trouble.'

'It's better than dying.'

They rested for half an hour, then moved on. As the hours passed they heard their first truck. Its rumblings were discernible from several miles away. They had plenty of time to steal into the jungle, lie flat on the floor, faces turned down to conceal their dirt-blackened skin and glittering eyes. More trucks came and went, then dusk fell and their headlights snaked along the dust road. As they passed Helen felt sure that the eyes of their passengers must be upon them.

'We need to be careful here, Hel.' She found herself smiling at his understatement. 'We're getting close to a choke point.'

'Where is it?'

'Shintuya, about four miles away. I'm going to get us off the road as soon as I can find a break in the jungle.' Connor studied Helen. He could see her fighting exhaustion. Walking on the road was so much easier than battling through the jungle, but infinitely more dangerous. He kept on the road until he could bear the risk no longer.

They veered off into the jungle and struggled through the dense undergrowth. Helen fell and staggered back to her feet three or four times, before the trees thinned out and they began to walk downhill. The air freshened, then they saw the river.

It was huge, deep chocolate brown in the starlight, rippling and eddying, bearing away the occasional huge tree, half its branches reaching up to the sky as if pleading for rescue.

'We need to get hold of a dugout,' whispered Connor. 'There's a small village of Piru tribespeople a few miles downriver. They'll give us a lift.'

'Can we trust them?'

'The Piru? They'll look and stare and giggle at you, especially the children, then they'll help.'

They found the village an hour later. Helen glanced at the luminous dial of her watch. It was eight o'clock. They had been going for twenty-six hours, with less than one hour's rest. She touched Connor's shoulder as he walked in front of her. He stopped and turned to her.

'Evan, I don't think I can go much further.'

'It's all right,' he said gently. 'You won't have to. Not much further. We'll get a canoe, then cross the river, then just one more hour, and either we fly out, or we rest. I promise.'

Connor did not want to go near the village, but swimming the river with Helen was unthinkable. Exhausted, she would drown in seconds in the swirling currents.

Helen closed her eyes for a moment, her body beseeching her to just slide down to the floor and sleep. She felt as if she was dying of tiredness, as if everything that was inside her had long since run out, leaving her with the hollow of death. She conjured her father, recalled her promise to him. She forced her eyes open, gazed at Connor, drank in her love for him, and followed him as he walked towards a village of reed huts. Under cover of the jungle, he stopped and crouched down. Helen lay down beside him, and passed out. Connor watched the village for half an hour before waking her.

'I'm going to go into the village, try to get a canoe. I won't be long. Don't sleep, I need you to keep lookout.'

Helen nodded, pulled at her eyes to keep them open. Connor kissed her face, then walked up to one of the huts. It was built on stilts, accessed by a wooden ladder. He said a word of greeting, then climbed the ladder. Helen watched him disappear. Her vision was blurring. She rubbed her eyes frantically, but it didn't seem to help.

She could smell smoke and hear bursts of laughter amidst the dry rumble of conversation. Then there was a sudden silence and she could imagine Connor speaking to a watchful audience. She couldn't hear his voice. Often, when it was important, he spoke so quietly she would have to strain to hear him. She heard a low, contemplative voice, and moments later a sharp grunt, then Connor appeared with two men. Together they walked down the wooden steps and came up to her. The men wore mud-coloured robes, striped red. They had broad attractive faces, dark as the river. Quick eyes appraised her, smiling warmly.

'They'll take us across the river,' said Connor, helping Helen to her feet. She smiled, held on to Connor and shook the men's hands. They turned and beckoned for Helen and Connor to follow.

Then the night exploded. Gunfire roared, and soldiers bearing rifles ran out from the jungle a hundred yards away. The Piru hurled themselves to the floor. Connor threw off his rucksack, and grabbed Helen's hand. Her mind and body sprang to life. She ran with Connor across the open village to the river's edge.

Together they plunged into the turbulent water. Helen went under, thrashing for the surface, losing Connor's hand. The current caught her, she felt something heavy smash into the side of her head, she took a breath. The water filled her mouth and flooded her lungs. It weighted her clothes, dragging her down. She began to see stars, felt herself losing consciousness.

I'm dying, she thought, with a mixture of strange objectivity and unbearable sadness. She thought of her father, of Dai, of Evan. How she loved them. Suddenly she felt a rage of energy. She struggled violently against the roiling waters, thrashed again, broke the surface, coughed and took an almighty breath. She stayed up, searched the darkness for Connor. She saw him a little way down the river, eyes fixed on her, swimming towards her, borne off by the current. Shouts came from the river bank. She could see the soldiers crouching, lifting their rifles to their shoulders. She heard the explosions as they fired. The water next to her thundered and sprayed. She let herself go under, heard the explosions again in her underwater world, then she struggled for the surface, lungs bursting. Now she was moving faster, into the midstream where the current was most powerful. She could see in the distance the soldiers getting into a dugout canoe. She gasped as a hand grasped her hair.

'It's OK, I've got you,' said Connor. She felt him kicking, fighting the current. Inch by inch, he pulled her towards the far bank until they were almost there. She felt her feet sticking to the mud of the river bed. She floundered and slipped. Connor picked her up and carried her to the shore, on into the scrubby bushes of a small beach. He lowered her gently on the sand. She lay still, her heart roaring, as the soldiers struggled for control of the canoe caught in the midstream current. Then they passed.

Connor lifted Helen to her feet, searched her eyes with his. She tried to move, started coughing, the river was coming up, she felt her world spinning, feared for a moment that the blackness creeping around her eyes would overwhelm her. She shook her head, a jolt of pain cleared the blackness, she put one foot before the other, found herself moving again, following Connor as he beat a path, listening to his words drifting to her slowly from a long way off.

'Not far now, keep going, almost there, Hel, good girl, my love, keep going, that's right, nearly there.' She collided with the trees, felt a warmer wetness mix with the river water that was running off her. She tasted the sharpness of blood in her mouth, heard Connor curse. Still they struggled through the trees. She had no idea how much time passed before he found the path he was searching for.

He walked with his arm around her waist, supporting her. 'Easier now, my love, on the path. Come on, Hel, not far now.'

Into the blackness they walked, on and on, until, through the impenetrable trees, they saw a distant glimmer.

They stumbled towards it and the light grew larger. There was a building. Connor was weaving round to the back, into the kitchens. Helen felt herself sink to the floor. The last thing she heard was Connor talking fast and low to a man wearing a chef's hat.

CHAPTER 79

A pool of blood spread out around the back of Helen's head. Another gash leaked blood from her cheek. Alvaro rushed forward and grabbed hold of Connor with the panic so often elicited by blood.

'Evan, *qué ha pasado*? Let me call –'

Connor bent down, parted the bloodied mass of Helen's hair and checked the wound. Just scalp. It'd have to wait. He stood up.

'Do you have a plane? Do you do still have an aircraft?' Connor felt the first tremors of panic and shut them down, closed everything down.

'Why? What are you gonna do?'

'Fly out. Now.'

'At night, without clearance? Are you mad? You wanna be shot down? Do you know how many planes have been shot down flying out of Peru into Colombia in the past year?'

'Over ten. Not such bad odds. We'll be killed if we stay here.'

'You'll be killed if you go up now.'

'Maybe. Maybe not.'

'They've got radar, they've got a kind of AWACS, they've got satellite lookdown. You think you can hide up there?'

'What do *you* do? Pay someone to turn it off, look the other way?'

'There's too many eyes up there, man.'

'You know as well as I do, there's less than a one-in-twenty chance they'll come after you, even if they wanted to. They haven't got the resources.'

'If they don't get you, you'll crash anyway. When was the last time you did any night flying?'

'I've got four hundred hours' night flying. I'll take my chances. Christ, Alvaro, just tell me what kind of plane you've got.'

'King Air. C90SE.'

'Yes,' yelled Connor.

'Cost eight hundred thousand dollars, man.'

'Easy come, easy go.'

'You can't just take my –'

Connor grabbed Alvaro by the neck with one hand. 'I don't want to hurt you, my friend, but I'll kill you if I have to. You'd better believe it.' Connor tightened his grip. Alvaro flailed his arms in the air. Connor held on for another pulse, then released him.

Alvaro crashed to the floor, forcing breaths down. He looked up at Connor, saw the uncontained violence in his eyes, believed him.

'All right, all *right*.' His voice went high pitched.

'Give me the keys,' said Connor, dragging Alvaro to his feet. 'Let's go.'

Connor marched Alvaro up the back stairs to his room. White-wash, mesh windows, an unmade bed, the smell of mildew and sex. Alvaro produced the keys from a beer can with the top sliced off.

'Charts?' demanded Connor.

'Where for?'

'Right up the continent.'

'You heading for Colombia, you'll be going right over Iquitos, man, bang over the radar.'

'Just get me the charts. I need low and high altitude, IFR and VFR. I imagine they'll be handy, well used. How many times you head up to Colombia?'

Alvaro took eight sets of charts the size of camel saddlebags from a wall cupboard. Connor flipped them open, one after the other. 'Big crease right on Leticia, yep. What a surprise.'

Connor hurried back to Helen, picked up her inert body and carried her over his shoulder.

'Where's the plane?'

'Out the back, in a hangar.'

'You go first.'

Connor followed Alvaro out into the darkness, across a field, to the hangar.

'Open the door.'

Alvaro unlocked the padlocks on a series of heavy bolts, pulled back a large sliding door and hit a light switch. Overhead fluorescent strips lit up a white twin-engined prop plane about thirty-five feet long, with a fifty-foot wingspan. Three round windows were grouped in a cluster along the fuselage behind the cockpit, with another, smaller window just before the tail. The legend OB1330 was marked on the tail.

Connor nodded at the marking. 'OB, good, glad to see you got Peruvian ID. HK and we might get shot down.'

'You think I'd fly with Colombian ID?'

'No, you'd paste a sticker over it, I guess. Open the door.'

Alvaro took out his keys and opened the door at the back of the plane, Connor lifted Helen inside, carried her up to the co-pilot's seat and strapped her in.

He got back out and began to pace around the plane, doing a visual inspection. 'Tell me you've got full tanks,' he said.

'Always keep her tanked up.'

'I'll bet you do. Needed a few quick getaways yourself.' Connor checked the nacelle tanks by the engines, and the wing tanks. All four were full. He checked the landing gear, the wings, tail, propellers, windows, screens and oil. He came back to Alvaro, satisfied.

'What's normal cruising speed?'

'Two-thirty knots at eighteen to twenty thousand feet.'

'Range?'

'Gonna be round eleven hundred fifty miles, with thirty minutes' fuel reserves.'

Wordlessly Connor calculated the approximate distance to Bogotá: twelve hundred miles.

'I assume you got Global Positioning System.'

''Course I have.'

'Got a spare, hand-held?'

He saw the evasion in Alvaro's eyes. 'Get it. And grab us some food and drinks. Hurry.'

Connor waited, checking the plane over again. Every minute

Alvaro was away brought their pursuers closer. But if he got this wrong, lost them in the skies, they'd be dead. He struggled to stay patient. Alvaro finally returned and gave him a hand-held GPS and a bag of food.

'Landing distance?' asked Connor.

'Four hundred and thirty yards. Where you headed?'

'I'll let you know when I get there. You can come 'n' pick up your baby.'

'Not gonna be any baby left,' muttered Alvaro. Connor slammed the door on his words.

He checked the door was secure, took his seat and strapped himself in. Helen lay unconscious beside him. Connor opened the first chart, took out his plotter, calculated his first coordinates and fed them into the plane's GPS and into Alvaro's hand-held set which he would use to cross-check. Then he took the pre-flight check list from the ceiling flap and went through the rundown. It was two years since he'd flown a King Air. He forced his mind to concentrate through biting tiredness. He checked the battery charge, then hit starter switch number two. The turbines started to turn, he checked the propeller was moving, checked the yellow engine light was on, then hit the condition lever. He monitored the turbine temperature, then put the start switch to 'off'. He switched on the generator, waited for the battery to boost up, then switched on the start booster for the number one engine and went through the start-up process again. He checked his lights, air conditioning, radar, GPS, pressurisation tanks, booster and transfer pumps, the annunciator panel and the trims. He pushed forward the power, propeller and condition levers, and the plane began to move forward. He stopped, checked the brakes, and went through the line-up check. He glanced around, ensured the runway was clear, then accelerated up to one hundred knots and took off into the darkness.

He scanned the forest below him as the plane rose. The lights of the Villa Carmen faded behind them. They were free. He resisted the urge to let out a great whoop as they soared upwards.

Positive climb, landing gear up, reduce power, climb check list. He climbed to eighteen thousand feet, ran through his cruise check list, and added new coordinates to his GPS.

368

He turned to Helen. She was drifting in and out of consciousness, but at least the bleeding had stopped.

After an hour, she forced her eyes open, looked out of the cockpit window and saw a river, brown and distant, lit by the crescent moon, running like blood through the jungle below. She was in the air, flying over Amazonia.

Connor heard her stir beside him. He dug around under his seat, pulled out a battered first aid box.

'How are you?' he asked.

She smiled, stroked his face with butterfly fingers. He could see her spirit shining through.

'Here.' He handed her the first aid kit. 'Should be some iodine and cotton wool. You've got a bit of a head wound. And your cheek's gashed. Better bathe them.'

'Thanks.'

Evan saw her flinch as she bathed her wounds. When she had finished, she pushed the first aid box under the seat and turned to Connor.

'We made it.'

He leaned across and kissed her.

'Yeah, Hel. We made it.' He reached into the bag of food and shared out packets of biscuits, apples and bottles of Coke. 'Dinner time. Eat as much as you can.'

'Wow. What a feast!'

Connor glanced at Helen while she ate, trapped as she was between exhaustion and hunger. He caught the Coke bottle which dropped from her hand as she fell asleep again. She'd performed a miracle, fighting her way through the jungle for four days with little food or rest. Now he'd have to perform his. How could he warn her, tell her that they might still be shot from the sky as a narco plane on an unregistered flight, or else, if the authorities decided to stay within the law, that they could be escorted down from the air by the Peruvian air force? If they were lucky, they'd end up in prison. Then, when Maldonado got to them, they'd be spirited away and killed. All he had to do was fly them twelve hundred miles north, across Amazonia, up the spine of the Andes, through a darkness that hid hazards from him, but shielded him from no one. The heat of the plane's engines reflecting off the metal fuselage betrayed their passing to the watchful night. AWACS, satellite lookdown, and ground-based radar scoured the air.

CHAPTER 80

Alone in an unravelling world, Connor's eyes scanned the black distance as he caressed the controls. He studied his charts, checking the fuel gauges. In a straight line, he calculated that, if the winds were behind them consistently, he would have just enough fuel to get them close to Bogotá. He would land at Peters's airstrip, take the consequences when he got there. But a straight line took them right into the two-hundred-and-fifty-mile range of the radar at Iquitos. He couldn't afford a detour anything like that big, or they'd never make it to Bogotá. If he landed anywhere else, he couldn't be sure of his reception. Most airstrips in the area would be owned by the narcos. If they saw a strange plane landing in the night, they'd shoot it down, ask questions later. Also, he wasn't sure just how badly hurt Helen was. He'd seen people die from less exhaustion and shock than she was suffering from. Add to that her head wound, the water she'd ingested from the river Manu, and with that the possibility of dysentery at best, cholera or typhoid at worst, and her prognosis wasn't good.

Connor decided he had to take the straight line. Two hundred and fifty miles from Iquitos, he brought the little plane down till he was just two hundred and fifty feet above the canopy. Any lower and he'd risk crashing into the jungle. The odds of being picked up by radar were much lower at this altitude, but it was still possible. He could only hope that some other illicit planes were in the sky that night, that the radar would be turned off to accommodate them. The moment he felt his concentration go he'd have to take them up, take his chances.

They flew so close to the canopy Connor could almost fancy he saw the eyes of the wakened monkeys glowing up at them in terror. He turned periodically to check on Helen. She veered between sleep and wakefulness, when she would gaze out of the window, her body limp.

Connor had been flying for over two and a half hours, with one hour of that skimming over the jungle canopy. Now he was powerless, a defenceless target, able only to pilot the plane with all the skill he could muster, and pray that luck was on their side. Death could come any time. He imagined cresting the canopy, the plane's underbelly ripped out by the trees. Or else shot down by FAP, the Peruvian air force. Blackhawk helicopter gunships, that's what they'd use. Shoot them down in a torrent of bullets. They'd tumble to the ground in a ball of fire. How long would he have? Would he live for a second in the inferno? Christ, get a grip, rein yourself in. He brushed the sweat from his forehead. He checked the GPS. They were flying the closest they would come to Iquitos and the radar – seventy-five miles due east.

They flew on. Another twenty miles, fifty miles, a hundred miles. With each mile Connor felt hope creeping with the breath into his lungs. Two hundred and fifty miles, out of range. Just pray now that there weren't other dishes turning, tuning in to him, that AWACS and lookdown were looking the other way, and that the resource-stretched FAP would just watch their screens impotently while he flew away.

Flying this low he was using too much fuel. He took the plane up. Here he didn't have to concentrate quite so hard, didn't have to scour the jungle for any outcrops, rise up suddenly, then dip down again, but his eyes still felt as if they were burning up. They were beginning to flicker and blur.

They flew high above the distant trees, over the dark ceiling that looked to Helen like the floor of the world. By the light of the moon, she could see the forest kingdom stretching out for ever. Now and then there would be a flash of river, coiling through the green. She shivered when she saw the rivers and turned away.

'Where are we?'

Connor turned round sharply. He checked the GPS.

'Over Colombia. Just flying over a place called Puerto Leguizamo.'

'Then what?'

'We're about three hundred and forty miles from Bogotá, about another hour and a half.'

'We land in Bogotá?'

'Yeah.' He hoped so. If they made it that far.

Helen lapsed back into unconsciousness. Connor flew on towards the Cordillera Oriental. He took the plane up from eighteen to twenty thousand feet. His charts showed a mountain called Cerro El Nevado, marked at over fifteen thousand feet. He checked the annunciator panel, eyeing the fuel dial. They'd been flying for four hours fifteen minutes. Soon they'd be getting low. Enough for another seventy miles, give or take. Peters's ranch was about seventy-five miles away.

He flew over the *páramo*. He reached across and touched Helen's shoulder. She gave no response.

'Hel, wake up.' He shook her.

'Uh, God, what's happening?'

'We'll be landing in the next twenty minutes or so. I'm going to need your help spotting the strip.'

'Christ, it's pitch black out there. We won't spot a thing. Don't you have coordinates?'

'It's not Heathrow. It's an unmarked landing strip on a private ranch. It's not marked on charts. The nearest marked place is ten miles away.'

'Oh shit. It's like looking for a man overboard in a storm.' She dragged her hair off her face and stuck her nose to the window. 'If we don't find the strip, can't we land in a field?'

'We're over the high plains, it's rough ground, full of boulders and trees. In daylight we'd have a chance ...'

Daylight was over five hours away. He reached out and took her hand. 'We'll land, we'll find the ranch, or we'll find somewhere decent to put down. I promise you.' He kissed her hand, she squeezed his and smiled. He wondered if she knew he had just promised her the impossible. She knew about navigation. She'd know the odds. For a moment their eyes lingered on each other. For that brief time, love blocked out fear.

They flew on, over the unrelenting darkness. Connor took the plane down to five hundred feet. He felt his life beginning to pass into the wilderness of fortune. He imagined running out of fuel, crashing down amongst the rocks on the *páramo*. This wasn't the fear of being shot down, of the awful release of sudden death. This was a long-drawn-out torture, like drowning. With every passing second, they came closer to death, or death, stalking them, drew nearer. This time was worse too, because they held their fate in their own hands. They had the power to see and to search for bare land, and they had the power to miss it.

'We have to land in the dark,' said Helen.

'Yeah. The place must be thirty miles away. We'll be in the area in under ten minutes.'

He glanced up at the annunciator panel. The 'no fuel transfer' light flashed red. The wing tanks were empty. Only the nacelle tanks had fuel, and precious little there. Connor felt his pulse begin to race. He stared at the light, gripped by fear.

'Must be around here, now, coming up on the horizon.'

They flew for three minutes, four, five, six minutes. Helen snaked her eyes back and forth. There was nothing, no break in the interminable darkness. Connor brought the plane around, searched with a cold intensity, yearning for a speck of light, for the gleam of a window in the moonlight. He checked the fuel gauge. Soon the plane would have used up all the reserves. They had one minute, maybe two. They would lose power rapidly; at around eighty knots they would stall. He made up his mind, he began to take the plane down. They'd just have to land on the rough ground. Each bit looked as good or as bad as the next. He needed around four hundred and thirty yards to stop. Four hundred and thirty yards without a boulder, without a tree, or a ditch, or a building. On a wing and a prayer, he thought.

'Bend over, hug your knees,' he said to Helen. 'I'm going to try to land.' He reached out and gripped her hand. For the first time, she saw death in his eyes.

She looked away, out of the window and screamed out.

'Over there! We passed something, on the right. Looked like an airstrip.'

'Better bloody be. If I turn around and there's nothing there . . .'

'Turn around. Do it. I saw something.'

Helen's stomach lurched into her mouth as Connor banked steeply and hauled the plane around.

'Where? Where is it?'

'On the right, further back, just a bit further and it'll be there. I saw the moonlight glint off metal, and there was a space, a darker black, like a strip. I'm sure of it, I –'

'Oh Christ, I'm losing power. We're going –'

'Wait, it'll be there, just a bit further, a bit more to the right.'

They couldn't breathe. Their life went into their eyes, into the search.

'It's there,' Helen screamed.

'I see it. I see it. I'm going straight in.'

A landing strip stretched out below them. Fifty yards away Connor could see the faint outlines of the ranch buildings.

'OK. Landing. Get ready.'

Connor approached the strip in darkness. He prayed there were no obstacles, no sleeping cows or parked tractors. He lowered the landing gear and the wing flaps, and crossed himself. The nose dipped, they felt themselves falling sharply, they were bumping and flying and bumping to earth again. The plane shook, Connor jammed on the brakes and they began to lose speed. They juddered to a stop at the end of the runway.

Connor turned to Helen with tears streaming down his face. He threw his arms up towards the sky in a salute to the fates. Helen kissed him, tasted the salt of his tears, mixing with hers. He gripped her hand, they gazed at each other in silence. Then he went through the shutdown procedure.

Suddenly he stiffened. Two men were approaching, carrying machine guns, with dogs at their heels.

'Follow my lead,' said Connor quietly. 'Whatever role I give you, play.'

'We get out?' asked Helen.

'In a minute. This place belongs to a friend of mine, but I don't think he'll be too happy about my dropping in from the sky.'

'Why not?'

'He tries to keep a low profile. We might have been tracked here by radar.'

The men stopped outside, levelling Uzis at the cockpit. With relief, Connor recognised Pepe and his son. He waited until they had recognised him, then motioned that he was going to get out.

'Come on.' He took Helen's arm and pulled her from her seat. 'No sudden movements.' They moved down to the back of the plane, Helen holding onto the seat backs to keep herself steady. Connor opened the door, threw down the steps, picked up Helen and carried her out.

'Señor Evan,' said Pepe, his voice incredulous. 'What are you doing here? What's going on?'

'Emergency,' said Connor. 'My friend's hurt. I've got to get her to Bogotá and a doctor. Will you help?'

'We have only one jeep,' said Pepe, uncertain. This man was a friend of his boss, trusted with the ranch. He knew the Señor would be angry with the way he had just flown in, but he would be even angrier if Pepe failed to treat Señor Connor as a friend.

'One's all we need. Get it now. Would you? Please.'

For a moment Pepe said nothing, then he seemed to make up his mind.

'Comó no?' Why not? He and his son turned and walked towards the finca. Connor and Helen followed.

'How are you, my love?' He held his arm tightly around her waist, supporting her as she walked.

'Alive.' She smiled.

Pepe went briefly inside the house, returning with a set of car keys. He nodded to a red Suzuki jeep parked in front of them.

'Better to wait a few hours,' he said, 'until dawn. There are terroristas in the area. It's not safe to travel during darkness.'

For a few hours they slept. It felt as if it had only been a moment when, at six, Pepe wakened them with omelettes and coffee. Helen fought down nausea, ate as much as she could. Connor devoured everything on his plate in five minutes. They thanked Pepe and his son, hid the plane inside an empty hangar, then left in the jeep, with a tank full of petrol, three bottles of Coke, some bread and two jerseys borrowed against the cold. Helen gripped the dashboard of the jeep to try to smooth out some of the most violent bumps on the rough road. Every part of her body seemed to ache.

She found herself almost hallucinating about a hot bath, crisp white sheets and clean clothes.

The sun rose over the surrounding peaks, casting long rays over the plain, taking the chill from the morning air. They drove down into a valley of pastoral greenness, grazing llamas, gentle rolling hills and chalets.

Helen leaned towards Connor. 'How much further?'

'About an hour to Bogotá.'

The traffic thickened as they drove on. They were regularly overtaken by huge four-wheel-drive cars, which surged by with a contemptuous roar, and left in their wake the dull thud of a beat, played full volume.

It didn't seem real, coming into this modern metropolis after so long in the wilderness. How long was it? Time had become an issue of living or dying. The passing of hours, minutes and days was subsumed by moments which seemed to have the capacity to stretch for hours or else pass in a whisper.

Helen watched the city growing around her, the tall buildings, the bustle, the traffic, the elegantly dressed women walking along the pavements, the exclusive shops, and, at various intersections, long-haired men with the eyes of preying animals. Helen could only imagine what she must look like, as the men swept their eyes over her, then looked quickly away.

She turned to Connor. 'How the hell will we get into any embassy looking like this?'

'I know the ambassador. He knows who I am. Don't worry.'

The residence of the British ambassador was a two-storey colonial structure on Calle 87, deep in the leafy suburbs of Bogotá. They pulled up on the corner outside a high wall.

'Don't get out yet,' Connor said to Helen, 'or they might think there's a bomb in the jeep. Lots of car bombs here,' he added in explanation.

He got out, walked up to a pair of ornate, heavily guarded gates, addressed a few quick words to one of the three guards. Helen could see the suspicion in the man's face.

The guard disappeared into a control booth. Helen saw him talking into the telephone. After five minutes another man came, he looked quickly at Connor, probingly at her, before shaking Connor by the hand. Connor returned to the jeep, jumped in, grinned at Helen, and drove through the opening gates, up a sweeping drive, round cool green lawns.

They parked beside a gleaming green Range Rover. Connor helped Helen from the jeep, taking her arm as they approached the residence.

Bougainvillea tumbled down white walls. A dog barked deep inside the building, the smell of bacon frying scented the air. They walked up a flight of steps, through a carved wooden door, into a high-ceilinged reception area, hung with oil paintings and strewn with deep rugs. They were shown into a characterless office where they sat for a while, just looking at each other, weary and elated with survival.

A man walked in. He was about six foot, with a ruddy complexion, thick-set with huge hands. He wore a navy suit with extravagantly wide pinstripes. Connor got to his feet, shook hands with him and turned to Helen.

'Helen, this is Peter Ingram, the British ambassador. Peter, this is Helen Jencks.'

The ambassador took her hand in both of his. His voice was reassuringly gruff. 'Helen, welcome to the residence.'

She almost laughed at the incongruity of it all.

'Thank you, I'm glad to be here,' she answered.

Ingram's eyes ran over her with an ironic smile. 'Yes, I'll bet you are. Perhaps you'd like to have a bath and a bit of a lie-down.'

Helen almost swooned. 'That'd be great.'

The ambassador called out into a side office. A homely woman of about fifty appeared. She was wearing low sensible shoes, a blouse with a bow, and a gathered mid-calf-length skirt. She gave Connor a motherly smile. He winked back at her.

'Hilly, this is Miss Jencks. She and Mr Connor will need a couple of rooms. Perhaps you could take care of them. Miss Jencks can go with you now.'

Hilly gave them both an approving smile, as if she were oblivious of the mud, the blood and the torn clothing. She reached out her hand to Helen. 'C'mon, love, follow me.'

*　　*　　*

Up a marble staircase, under the glistening chandelier, onto a carpeted hallway, her bruised feet cushioned, her footsteps silent, a door thrown open and a gracious smile.

'Righty-ho. Call me if you need anything. I'm on extension four on the intercom. Have a good rest. You'll be nice and comfy here.' Hilly smiled and disappeared.

Helen looked at her room: a double bed with white sheets, a warm patterned quilt, four pillows, plump and soft. Through a connecting door was her own bathroom, cream marble, a huge deep bath, a mirror above the washbasin. She approached the mirror from the side, stepped before it, confronting herself.

Her hair was matted with blood and mud. Her face was streaked with both. A gash ran jagged across her right cheek. Her eyes were bloodshot, her cheeks sunken. She stared at her reflection, at the stranger she had found within herself. She looked until her shock began to wane. She searched in her battered features for her father's face, trying to conjure him, fearing that she would never see him in the flesh again. She wept with the loss of him, until all her tears were cried and the sheer joy of being alive began to rise again within her.

A brisk knock on the door interrupted her. Hilly was waiting outside with a bottle of water, a pot of tea and a plate of sandwiches.

'Looking a bit peakish. Thought you could do with a little snack.'

'Oh, you're an angel. Thank you, you're so kind, I –'

Hilly ushered her into the room. She put the tray down on a table beside the bed. 'Go on. No nonsense. Eat all this up, have a bath and a kip, you'll feel right as rain. Oh, and I brought you some alcohol and antiseptic cream. Nasty cut you've got.'

'Thanks,' said Helen. 'Don't suppose you've got any of the drinking variety around.'

'Alcohol? Good gracious, yes. We're practically swimming in it. What would you like?'

'Brandy please,' said Helen. 'Lots of it.'

'I'll bring you the bottle, you can do what you like with it.'

'You're a life saver. Can I ask you one more thing?'

'Shoot.'

'I need to get a message to someone. My godfather. I want him to know I'm safe.'

'Give me his name and his number, and I'll see what I can do.'

'Dai Morgan.' Helen gave his telephone number and Hilly wrote it down on her hand.

Hilly came back two minutes later with a bottle of brandy and a cut-crystal glass.

'Here you go. Just off to call your godfather. You get some rest.'

Helen drank the tea and devoured the sandwiches – smoked salmon and cucumber. She washed it all down with a full glass of brandy, shuddering as she sank the last drop. That should kill off any bugs from the river Manu.

She went through into the bathroom, ran herself a bath, stripped off her clothes and stepped into the steaming water. Exhaustion came at her like a fever. She shook involuntarily. She bent her head over her knees, took a few deep breaths to ease the trembling, lay back, soaking her hair, letting the water run over her face. Every cut it touched stung with pain. The water dripped, weak red, back into the bath.

CHAPTER 81

The ambassador took Connor through into his study.

'I can't sit down in here,' said Connor, gesturing at his mud-caked clothes.

Ingram nodded at a green leather chair.

'Sit in that. It's seen worse. Want something to drink, whisky, water, coffee?'

'Thank you. Coffee. And water.'

Ingram rang through his order on the intercom. Three minutes later an aproned woman brought in a silver pot of coffee and a jug of iced water. She served the ambassador and Connor, then retired silently.

Ingram sipped thoughtfully at his coffee.

'I'd been warned to keep an eye out. Seems to be some kind of flap on. In a little while, I'm going to give you the phone and you can call your lot back in London, but you and your little fugitive have come bleeding into my turf, so you can start off by telling me what the hell's going on.'

Connor took a long pull of water and began to speak. The talking was almost worse than the running.

Ingram freed him two hours later, having had his vanity flattered and his curiosity indulged by hearing what he believed to be an acceptable approximation of the inside story. He took Connor to a secure phone from which he could ring London, then left him alone.

Connor rang Carlyle.

'Yes.'

'What kind of a greeting is that?'

There was a moment of silence and then Carlyle's outraged joy.

'Bloody hell. Where are you?'

'Bogotá, at the embassy.'

'And the girl?'

'Here too.'

'What's going on? There's a DEA report that cites seeing you and the girl or else your doubles looking like shit in the Peruvian jungle. DEA says you're being hunted by SIN.'

'I'll tell you later. Just get us out of here. First plane out. Get Farrell to call Ingram. I don't want any problems.'

'He'll be delighted to pass you on.'

'Probably. I expect we'll be on the night flight. See you at the airport?'

'I wouldn't miss it. Oh, and Evan?'

'Yeah?'

'Well done.'

'For what?'

'Staying alive.'

'You'll get the noon flight,' said the ambassador, coming out of his study after speaking to Ian Farrell. 'Less time you spend here the better. I can probably lie as well as you if I have to deny your presence here, but I'd rather not have to.'

Connor nodded. 'I'll go and wake Helen. What about passports? We lost ours.'

'I'll get you out on diplomatic papers, won't take long. The plane's scheduled to go at twelve thirty. Be ready to leave in two hours.'

'Perhaps someone could show me where Helen is, and if I might ask you for a bath? I don't quite look the part of a diplomat.'

The ambassador summoned his assistant. 'Hilly, show Mr Connor where you've put Miss Jencks, would you?' He turned to Connor. 'Bathe in her rooms, I'm sure that won't be too much of a hardship.' He walked away. Connor watched him, wondering at the change in Ingram's attitude. He smiled to himself and followed Hilly up the stairs to Helen's room.

Helen was lying in bed, the sheets pulled up to her chin. She opened her eyes and smiled at him as he closed the door behind him. He sat down on the edge of her bed.

'We have to leave in a couple of hours, Hel. We're flying out at twelve thirty.'

Her eyes registered her exhaustion and she moved with effort into a sitting position. The sheets fell down to her waist as she did so.

'Christ, Hel, you've lost weight.' He smoothed her hair, stroking it, pulling her against him. 'I'm sorry,' he said slowly.

'Whatever for?'

'I shouldn't have allowed any of this to happen. I shouldn't have exposed you to this.'

She smiled at him and took hold of his hand.

'You still think you could've stopped me?' She got out of bed and swayed slightly as she stood, naked, cut and bruised, gazing down at her clothes in a heap on the floor.

'I'll ask the bloody ambassador for some clothes for you. His wife is a bull of a woman, I'm afraid. One of those well-fed, well-exercised county types. I don't remember going much for her taste.'

'It'll feel like couture after this lot. What about you?'

'Ingram'll give me something. We're flying out on diplomatic papers, so they'll have to make a bit of an effort with us.'

'Why so sudden? I thought perhaps we might spend the night here.'

'They probably feel it's safer to get us out of the region as soon as possible.'

They were driven to the airport in the green Range Rover. The doors slammed with the dull thud of an armoured vehicle. The bullet-proofed windows remained permanently locked. The air conditioning felt like an arctic winter.

The British Airways flight had been held for them. They walked on, took their seats, turned to smile at each other, hands locked. The plane pulled back from the gate, taxied onto the runway. With a last burst of acceleration, they were airborne, flying from mayhem towards home.

CHAPTER 82

It was dark, just before dawn. Helen could see nothing in the blackness below her, but she fancied she could feel the moment when the plane left the great anonymity of the seas and flew over English soil. She tried to calculate how long she'd been away. It had been almost a month. Those few weeks felt like a trick of the light. She had lived a life in that time and come home a different woman. She'd found her father. She'd seen his face. She knew that he loved her, and he would have known too that she loved him. That she'd lost him, probably for ever, was an unhealable wound that she would have to learn to live with. She had learned what it was to face death, and to fight with everything in you to survive. And she had fallen profoundly in love with Evan Connor.

When the plane touched down at Heathrow, Connor took her in his arms and hugged her. He buried his face against her. Her hair fell over him, she could feel his lips warm against the skin of her neck. She held him to her with a fierce strength.

'We'll be all right,' he said into her shoulder.

She pulled back and looked into his eyes. 'We'll be fine.'

'We'll be met by some of my people,' he said. 'You'll be asked a lot of questions, what you did, and about me. Tell the truth, Hel.'

'What will happen if I do?'

'I don't know, but it's better to start off telling the truth.'

'I'm not saying I won't, but why d'you bring it up?'

'Because if you don't, they'll break you until you do give them the truth. Don't make the mistake of thinking they can't. You've been through one kind of hell, but they can give you another.'

He could resist them, the knowledge that he could showed in

his eyes and in the fathomless coldness she'd sometimes seen in him.

'Don't worry. Your people don't bother me. Wallace, Rankin, Roddy Clark, Goldsteins, the police, the whole damn lot don't trouble me. How can they hurt me after what I've gone through, finding my father, losing him again?'

'Are you just going to let them get away with it, the people who set you up, that bloody journalist?'

'No, I'm not going to let them get away with it, Evan.'

'What are you going to do?'

Helen gave a wild smile. 'I'm a butterfly. I'll flap my wings.'

'What are you talking about?'

'It's called chaos theory. Revenge. I promised myself when it happened that I'd even the score, I was just waiting for the right time. That time's come.'

A small woman, no more than five foot two, waited for them in the arrivals hall. She stood apart, looking at them, determined, curious, unsmiling. Her features were cast yellow by the overhead lights, giving her a jaundiced complexion. Her eyes roamed Connor's body, then flicked onto Helen Jencks. Jencks looked quite different from the photographs of her: pared down, thinner, wiry. Her skin was deep, weathered brown, the contrast heightened by the blonde hair curling down her back. Her walk was fluid, powerful, vaguely predatory. There was something almost menacing about her, the ragged cut that bisected her cheek, the hardness in her eyes.

Tess Carlyle stood quite still as Helen and Evan approached. As they drew close, her face seemed to undergo a subtle transformation, a brief softening of her angular features – a mother to her son, a lover to her beloved – and then the sensuality was gone, replaced by an anger that seemed to Helen almost proprietorial.

She nodded but did not touch Connor.

'Evan.'

'Tess.'

Lowered voices, a meeting of eyes, hers probing, Connor's robust. She turned to Helen.

'Helen Jencks, I presume, or is it Williams, as in your passport?'

Her voice was powerful, low as lead. She rolled her r's slightly. In another incarnation she might have been Eartha Kitt.

'Jencks,' answered Helen levelly. Then, in the faintest parody of Carlyle's apparently casual tone of inquisition: 'And you are?'

'Tess Carlyle,' she answered, a small flicker of amusement in her eyes.

They shook hands, Carlyle's small and bony, like a bird's claw. Not a robin or a finch, despite her size. Nothing tame. A hunting bird, a little killer, a peregrine falcon. Killer's eyes too that roamed over Helen. No mercy in that glance.

'Come this way.' The bony hand extended behind her back. Helen could almost feel the force of it, though Carlyle didn't touch her. Helen saw, as she moved, a couple of men move with them. She walked alongside Connor. His face was inscrutable, perhaps the slightest hint of grim amusement showed in the set of his mouth.

They were taken to the car park, to a Land Rover Discovery prickling with communications antennae. One of the silent men opened the rear passenger door and nodded to Helen. She got in, the man after her. Tess Carlyle went in the other side, flanking Helen. Connor got into the front passenger seat. The other silent man drove.

They sped through a dawning London. Although she would never see it, or anything, with the same eyes again, the old buildings, the hidden order, the sense of familiarity hadn't changed. But it didn't seem real. After the sweltering heat of the jungle, after the maddening closeness of a million trees, seething earth, swollen rivers and a billion crawling insects, this city of stone and concrete and leaden air seemed unreal. The motion of the car, the pedestrians heading for their offices, the order of traffic lights seemed like a mockery. This was life, this was normal, yet all the while something inside her screamed with what she had seen, what she had done. There seemed to be no linking the two worlds. She had crossed the divide of nice, sane, painful life and couldn't ever imagine crossing back again. She thought with a flicker of irony that perhaps the legend of the Sun Gate was true. She, for one, would never be the same again.

CHAPTER 83

In the car, no one spoke. Helen felt Tess Carlyle watching her. Occasionally, she looked back, met a pair of appraising eyes, returned the scrutiny.

They pulled up at a house in a forgettable street south of the river. Carlyle commandeered Connor, guiding him into a room off the floral-carpeted hall. He gave Helen a quick, reassuring smile as Carlyle closed the door on them. The driver gestured for Helen to go upstairs. He showed her to a bedroom.

'Should be everything you need. I'd sleep while you can.' He gave her a look as he turned to leave, a fleeting sympathy, then his face became passive, anonymous, a grey man whose features she would be unable to recall when she tried, years later, to remember all the details of her return.

She closed the door. She heard him lock it behind her and walk downstairs. She crossed the room to the window. It was covered by bars.

'So, tell me, what have you managed to do?' Carlyle poured herself a coffee from a thermos provided by the driver, then raised a questioning eyebrow at Connor, who nodded. She poured him a cup, moved across the room to him, her high heels silent on the carpet. Graceful, extravagant of gesture in the moments when she let go, as far as she ever could, otherwise, as now, restrained, every word and gesture measured, paring herself down that she might listen and observe.

'What were you running from?'

'We got close to Maldonado, too close. I can confirm, if you still want or need it, that he's as dirty as a festering dog. He tried to kill Helen. We ran, he found us. I had to kill Angel Ramirez to get away.'

Carlyle studied him for a moment and he could almost feel her burning the truth from his bones.

'If that was your intention, you made an uncharacteristic mess of it. Angel Ramirez isn't dead, he's a quadriplegic.'

'Oh, God.'

Carlyle saw the wound. The one thing men like Connor feared more than death was crippling injury.

'How d'you know?' he asked, despite himself.

Carlyle gave him a contemptuous look.

'You're not my only asset in the region, Connor. They tried to cover it up. Word seeped out. There was an assault. Big manhunt for the perpetrators. They'd have cut you into a hundred pieces if they'd caught you. What the hell were you playing at?'

'What do you think? Trying to put a little meat on paper instructions that come from nice clean air-conditioned offices. You never plan for the dirt, do you, the shit at the execution end? It's just an instruction and a goal. Well, you've got your goal, now you want to hear the dirt, and pass judgement. All of you with your grave, disapproving faces, because I broke a few of your precious rules.' Connor knew what was coming. The reprimands, the warnings, the black marks on his record, the censure of grey-faced civil servants who fought for nothing more than a seat on the 8.20 into Waterloo. They would quibble over his expenses, argue for his dismissal, sit fatly while they tried to make him beg for his job. And all along, he would be seeing Jack Jencks's face as he said goodbye to his daughter, or Helen's face as she ran from him. Twenty-three years of agony because Jack Jencks had done his bit for the Firm which had now happily forgotten him and his sacrifices, which would never understand why Connor had broken the rules for Helen and would do so again.

'Get out there,' he said to Carlyle, his voice low with controlled anger. 'Live that side of life. See how far your rules take you. Or else just program robots to follow your every wish.'

'Come on, Connor, it's not what I do or don't want. You know the game. There have to be rules.'

'Bugger the rules and the game. I've had it. I want out. Your

388

office politics bore me and the lure of the field is pretty tarnished. I've flirted with death enough times to know I don't want to do it any more.' Though he'd never tell Carlyle, falling in love with Helen had changed his perspective. Living and loving had now become infinitely more exciting than his old dance with death.

'It's not that simple and you know it. If you ever want to extricate yourself without a whole heap of shit sticking, you better play straight.'

Connor laughed. 'You know me better than that. Do you really think I'm going lose sleep worrying about the kind of shit storms you and the Firm can stir up? I'll tell you, Tess, because I took the job on and I intend to finish it. Then, as far as I'm concerned, you can all go to hell.'

CHAPTER 84

They spoke until darkness fell, then at 10 PM Carlyle gave Connor a room. She rested for two hours, then went to Helen's room at midnight, unlocked her door and switched on the light. Helen woke, forced herself up through clouds of exhaustion. Carlyle could see the effort, could see the will in this woman, as she pushed herself up from the bed, stroking back her hair from a face swollen with sleep.

'Give me a minute.' Without waiting for a reply, Helen went into the connecting bathroom and splashed cold water on her face, then she went downstairs with Carlyle. They sat at a dusty table and Helen felt the exhaustion come at her again. She gathered herself, and faced Carlyle.

'Tell me everything, from the beginning, in your own words,' instructed Carlyle, leaning back in her chair, eyes never moving from Helen's.

'How else do you speak?'

'Well, you could speak in lies, which would be futile, or you could be evasive, which would waste your time, and mine –'

'I've had the spiel,' interrupted Helen. 'You'll break me in time, so tell the truth from the beginning.'

'Let's hear it then.'

'You're pretty sure, aren't you, that you could break me?'

'I have a reasonably efficient machine to call upon.'

'My approximation of the truth . . .' Helen pulled her hair back into a ponytail, exposing her angular face and the ragged cut across her cheek. She leaned across the table towards Carlyle. 'Ask away.'

'Why did you run?'

'First, because Maldonado tried to kill me. Then, because I killed one of his men.'

'Angel Ramirez?'

'Yes, I think that's what Evan said his name was.'

'You killed him?'

Helen gave a grim smile.

'Connor claims he did,' said Carlyle.

Helen said nothing.

'How did you manage that?'

'Your intelligence didn't stretch that far?'

Carlyle wore a serene smile. She betrayed no sense of being ruffled, but Helen could feel a sudden quickening in the air.

'Would you like a demonstration? I do aikido. I'm a black belt, second dan.'

She spoke until the first grey streaks of dawn broke the orange-tinged blackness. Answered questions, cuttingly clear. Goldsteins, the set-up. Maldonado, her deal with Connor, her search for her father, finding him, losing him, her last image of him pointing a gun at Maldonado, his eyes on her, harrowed and yearning as she turned and ran away. Only then did she feel herself close to breaking.

'I'm sorry about your father,' said Carlyle. 'It doesn't bode well.'

'Don't you speak to Maldonado? Couldn't he tell you where my father is, what's happening with him?'

'He wouldn't tell us. We've no way of forcing that information from him. He'd simply deny all knowledge. What's in it for him?'

'You must have some bargaining counter.'

'We'll do what we can.'

'I don't have much faith in your remedies.'

'Stay out of it. Enough damage has been done.'

'Oh, I know. I brought this on my father. Seeking him out. Should have left him to his peaceful retirement, left him to die in his own time. It was emotion, not calculation. You've never acted on it?'

'Too frequently.'

'For a control freak, I suppose, one lapse is too much.'

'What will you do now?' asked Carlyle, levelly. Helen had an image of her barb bouncing off the hide of protection this woman wore. It wasn't that she had constructed a facade of equanimity, more that she had been forged from pains that inured her to everyday life. The mortification of the saints . . .

'What will *you* do now?' asked Helen. 'Your people made it necessary for him to go there in the first place, don't you think you have a duty to get him out? Or doesn't duty matter? Is it irrelevant here?'

'Duty to what, or to whom?'

'Clever answer. I'm sure you have duties to many things and to many people, but I have just one now.' She paused and gave what seemed to Carlyle a rather sinister smile. 'No. Make that two.'

'You escaped with your life. Wasn't there a lesson in that?'

'Absolutely.'

'We could probably hold you, the Serious Fraud Office at least, on suspicion of fraud at Goldsteins.'

'Not for long. Anyway, I think you overestimate your power. Goldsteins won't want me anywhere near the SFO. I wouldn't fight the City, if I were you. They've as much to hide as you people, and better reason. Money. Billions of pounds. That's a stronger reason than any of your watered-down duty.'

'What did you do?'

'I was born with the wrong name. I ran away when I could have stayed. I took a decision I'd take again. I implicated myself, I made it easier for the people who set me up. I did nothing criminal.'

'So what are you hiding?'

Helen wanted to laugh. The awful power in Carlyle's eyes, the lure of the confessional, might have been irresistible.

'Have you ever been close to death?' asked Helen.

Carlyle looked pleasantly surprised. 'You have, and the experience has hardened you, and you're not going to answer my question.'

'It's not relevant.'

She'd been talking and answering questions for six hours now. She had been given nothing to eat or drink, save coffee. Carlyle paced around, wired. Helen thought it must be over soon. Her body started to fall into fractured, exhausted sleep when she was pulled back by Carlyle's mellifluous voice.

'So how did you make all that money, at Goldsteins?'

'What money?' Christ, her voice was starting to slur now.

'The papers suggested up to fifty million dollars.'

'You believe what you read in the papers?'

'How did you make it?'

'I didn't make it. I didn't make a penny illegally. Look, why don't you just get on with breaking me? Try it, get it over with, huh? Do whatever it is you do, you'll get the same answer you get now, but can I make a suggestion?'

'Go ahead.'

'Do it to Hugh Wallace and Andy Rankin. If that's what you're interested in. Christ, what does it matter?' She pushed herself up from the table, and her chair crashed to the floor behind her. She flinched and for a moment Carlyle saw beneath her rage and exhaustion. She was the woman who had maimed Angel, the man who, in cahoots with Maldonado, had been responsible for killing one of Connor's friends. Had she been sentimental, Carlyle told herself, she would have had to mark that down as a good thing. For now, she saw that she had dragged as much as she usefully could from Helen.

'We might have to talk some more, but I'll arrange for you to be driven home now,' said Carlyle, surprising Helen. 'Is there someone you'd like to call?'

'Thank you. My godfather. I'd like to go to him. I assume you know where he lives.'

'It's probably unrealistic to suggest you don't talk to him about all this, but I wouldn't let it go beyond him. You never know, it might prejudice your father.'

'You'll play any emotional card, won't you? What d'you think Maldonado's next move'll be?'

'When he finds out you're back here, he'll know he's been compromised. He'll be at his most dangerous then. Not necessarily to you, I don't think he'd try to take you out on British soil. It's Angel Ramirez I'd worry about.'

'I thought he was dead.' Helen could hear the blood pulsing in her ears.

'No. You didn't kill him, Helen. You paralysed him. He's a quadriplegic.'

Helen swallowed a vomit of horror.

'He's still active, still masterminding business, I hear, from his hospital bed. He could reach over here in an instant.'

'Maldonado, Angel Ramirez and all their henchmen have tried to kill me three times, and they've failed three times.'

'I'd keep a low profile if I were you. There's always fourth time lucky.'

The car was waiting for her outside.

'Where's Evan? Is he still here?'

'Yes.'

'May I say goodbye to him?'

'No.'

CHAPTER 85

She would not sleep. Though exhaustion claimed every cell in its falling grip, she kept her eyes open. She wanted to see every inch of her homecoming in the light.

She sat in the back of the car as a silent driver sped her away. They crossed Vauxhall Bridge and headed along the Embankment, lined first with offices, then council houses. They drove through Chelsea. Grand houses looked down on them as they passed. Helen gazed across the river, dappled blue by the rising sun which gleamed off the roof of the pagoda in Battersea Park. She rolled down her window. She could smell the seaweed of the tidal river, the freshness of the trees that formed an avenue along the Embankment, the dry dust that spoke of a rainless week, and the lingering car fumes.

The smells of London stayed with her as they pulled onto the M4 motorway, fading only as fields began to replace factories and the air quickened. They drove west through green pastures and the Wiltshire downs. The sun continued its long, lazy arc into the sky. She could feel its heat and smell the grass as she gazed out at a landscape she had once thought she would not see again. She had dreamed of this.

Finally they turned off the little side road into the long avenue that led down to Dai's house. He and the dogs appeared at the top of the steps when the car was still some way away. Helen was out of the car before it had come to a final stop. The dogs leapt and barked, she was in Dai's arms, hugging him, crushed by his embrace.

Dai tried not to register the shock he felt at seeing her bloodied face, the weight she had lost, the look in her eyes; wild, determined, implacable. Together they brushed away tears that neither could hide.

They went to his study, sat in the old familiar chairs. The sun slanted in through open windows as a breeze blew in and danced around them. The dogs, having welcomed Helen with a frenzy she had never seen in them before, now lay in blissful contentment at her feet, every sleek muscle fully relaxed for the first time since she had gone. Occasionally one would open an eye and gaze at Dai, just to reassure herself that her master was better now, that the crippling tension they felt in him had really gone. Derek came in, hugged Helen, then went off, red-faced with emotion, to get breakfast. He brought Helen plates of scrambled eggs, cups of coffee, glasses of orange juice and perfectly tanned toast with marmalade. She ate and smiled. Every moment was balm.

When he could put it off no longer, Dai asked what had happened. He listened with thrill and horror as Helen spoke. She could see him searching her for damage. He asked her more questions until there was nothing and everything left to say.

'Are you all right, Cariad?' he asked finally, leaning forward to touch her chin, not understanding the absence of the damage he feared he would find.

'I don't quite know how to explain this. I'm exhausted, I haven't slept properly for days, I'm covered in bites, cuts and scratches, I feel half starved, I feel torn apart when I think of my father, I yearn for Evan Connor, even though we've only been apart for twenty-four hours, but I feel this incredible wild joy that's more powerful than anything I've ever felt before.'

Dai looked at her, his head slightly to one side, marvelling at her, remembering how it felt to survive.

CHAPTER 86

Helen slept for twenty hours, the deep, apparently dreamless sleep of the exhausted. She awoke slowly, stretching luxuriously, feeling the first flickers of strength return to her body. She showered and dressed in old jeans Dai brought down from the attic. She hadn't been able to fit into them since she was fourteen. Now they hung loose around her waist. She walked down the long carpeted hallway. Sunlight streamed in through the open mullioned windows, dust particles dancing along the beams. She could feel the summer breeze against her skin, it carried with it the smell of the first hay harvest, a cooked, musky summer smell that bathed her in a fleeting tranquillity.

She walked downstairs, out through the open front doors, stopped at the head of the worn marble staircase that led down to the driveway. Beyond was the avenue of trees she had seen so often in her dreams in Peru. Now it stretched before her, ancient oaks, each one a monument, diminishing in perspective as her eyes roamed, until all she could see in the distance was a sea of green, suspended eighty feet in the air. Waiting to bear her away again.

She ate breakfast with Dai. Lapsang souchong and kedgeree, only half a plate. Her stomach had shrunk during her escape. Dai gently urged more on her. Her cat Munza reigned in the dining room. The Dobermans were solicitous, tried to keep out of his way. Scoldingly, he jumped up onto Helen's lap, tail lashing, and allowed himself to be petted for five minutes before jumping down without a backward glance. Supercilious green eyes, abandonment beneath the pride.

The newspapers were laid out, as always, on a side table: *The Times*, the *Daily Telegraph* and the *Daily Mail*. Helen picked them up, flicked through them, put them down again. The irrelevance of other people's news when your own story was still unfolding.

'Any plans today?' asked Dai with transparent casualness.

'Delicious breakfast with my favourite godfather' – Helen smiled as his eyes wrinkled deeply – 'then a long walk with the dogs.'

'What are you plotting, Cariad?' His voice was sharp-edged with care, suspicion, and the wariness of respect.

'I can't leave it like this, can I? My father's lost again, his life probably hanging in the balance thanks to me, if he's not already gone. And I'm supposed to lie low, watch my back, not venture into polite society, where I'm a little fraudster, thanks to Wallace and Rankin, and Roddy's articles. Daddy's heiress, a ready-made criminal . . .' She laughed. 'If only they knew.'

'You could have gone after Wallace and Rankin when you first found out about the fraud. Spared yourself all your agony in Peru.'

'No, I couldn't, Dai. I did the only thing I could, and I'd do it again. I had to search for my father. I didn't care then what they'd done to me, next to the chance of finding him. I promised myself then I'd deal with Wallace and Rankin when I got back. And I will. Just got to add Roddy to the list.'

She walked the dogs to the copse of trees at the top of the downs. She stood for a long time, gazing at the green countryside, rolling away below her to gentle hills turning blue in some unfailing trick of the horizon light. The dogs chased each other with wild abandon. The sun rose high in a cloudless sky. A perfect day. *Where would you be, if you could be anywhere now?* she remembered asking Connor while they fled through their jungle world. She had chosen this place, high on the Wiltshire downs, and Connor had chosen to be here too, with her. She tried to invoke him. Taste, like honey, sweet cider, musky and strong; the sound of his voice, low, smooth, vital, full of humour. The contours of his body, his silken skin, the hardness of his muscles. His lips, the lips of a sensualist. His eyes, tempered by the knowledge of death, burning with the rage for living that survival brings to all but the determinedly amnesiac. Now she had it too. The power of survival.

CHAPTER 87

S he switched off her emotions to say goodbye to Dai and Derek. Derek looked bewildered, accusing. Dai understood, and there was balm in that. She could see him trying to suppress the questions and cautions that leaked from his eyes. He had wisdom and love enough to let her go.

She collected together the remnants of her life in London – Munza and her keyring. Her house keys, and Roddy's, jangled on it. She stepped into her father's car, smelled the warm leather, sank back into the bucket seat. She imagined him sitting here, his worn hands on the steering wheel. She felt tears rush to her eyes, and struggled to banish them. It was not the time to cry, not now, while there was still hope, however faint. She turned on the CD player she'd installed. Nina Simone sang out 'House of the Rising Sun'. There was something of the outlaw in her plaintive voice, a caution for loss, but a pure implacability; she would have done it all again.

She drove within the speed limit. What she had to do now was too important to risk being stopped by the police for something as petty as speeding. She didn't have a complete plan yet, just the outlines, just enough to nudge the fates in the right direction.

She glanced out of the window. Fields of green, Friesian cows grazing, sheep dotted like confetti on distant hills. Horses flicking languid tails, coats gleaming in the sun.

She stopped at the service station just before London. As she queued in the shop, she was aware of undisguised scrutiny. When she returned to her car, she studied her face in the driving mirror, fingering the unhealed cut that ran jagged along her cheek. For a moment she remembered the searing pain, the river in the jungle, the shots exploding in the water around her, the current bearing her away. The shadow of it showed in her eyes. She turned the keys in the ignition and drove off.

It was lunchtime when she arrived at Campden Hill Square. She found a space for her car, making no attempt to park it any distance away, to be surreptitious. She watched Roddy's flat for a while. He should have been at work, but she wanted to make sure. After ten minutes, she walked down the steps to his door and rang the bell. No reply. She took out her keys. They turned smoothly in the lock. She pushed open the door and walked into the flat, closing the door softly behind her. Books and gin. With the familiar smell, the memories raced back. Good and bad. Helen pushed them down, all save the photograph he had taken on a summer afternoon, the photograph in the *World*.

Into the bedroom, open the wardrobe, part the rows of suits, the ironed jeans. Her fingers on the safe, caressing the combination lock, trusting that he hadn't changed it. He had told her the number, instructed her, with her facility for numbers, to memorise it, in case he ever forgot. Another attempt to pull her into his life, like giving her his keys, all done under the guise of insurance. Helen laughed out loud as the safe clicked open.

Another insurance policy of his was never leaving sensitive back-up material with the *World*. *Might fall into the wrong hands.* Her fingers explored the two lead shelves. Papers. She checked them. No interest. No money. Never kept it long enough to fill a wallet, let alone spill over. Her fingers roamed deeper. Two tapes. She pocketed them, locked the safe, padded out of the bedroom, locked up behind her and drove home.

Dawson Place gleamed in the sunlight. She paused for a moment, drinking in the sight of her home, the sense of joy rising within her. The roses were in full bloom. Mrs Lucas must have been giving them her usual five-star treatment. Manure from the Hyde Park stables by the smell of it.

She let herself into her flat. She opened the cat box and released Munza. He paced around, tail erect, forming a question mark. Home, security, a normal life, seasons of memories. It felt different, but still exquisite to be back. She walked through the rooms, stopped to stare at her bed, lingered in the kitchen, imagining lost smells. Then she played the tapes.

Zaha Zamaroh's voice rang out. As Helen listened, her eyes widened in shock, then she began to laugh, great convulsions.

'Yeah, Zamaroh, take him apart.'

It was all there: Zamaroh's exposure of Wallace and Rankin's crime, of how they had set up Helen Jencks; Wallace's admission of guilt, his transfer of fifteen million dollars into Zamaroh's account. Proof of her innocence ... An idea began to form in her mind. She went to her stock of wine, pulled out a bottle of Puligny Montrachet, uncorked it and poured herself a glass. She sat very still, cross-legged on a silk Bukhara rug on the drawing-room floor. A shaft of sunlight turned her hair to fire. She looked unseeing out of the window, oblivious of the cries of children playing, the baying of dogs. Careful, knowing with every sinew the consequences of success, she wove her calculations.

She picked up the telephone, and rang Victor Maldonado. Carmen's voice, alert, menacing. Helen spoke, heard breath down the line, then nothing, as Carmen held herself in.

'Doctor Maldonado. Now. *Espero.*' I wait.

She waited for several minutes, fancying that she could see down the telephone lines into the hallway where the telephone lay on a carved wooden table beneath the fierce gaze of Paso horses with noble faces and cruel hooves. Maldonado, staring down at the receiver, as if he were seeing a ghost.

'Helen.'

His voice made her jump. It was heavy, slow, regretful, as if they had both suffered the same tragedy. Accusing too in its slight edge, in the silence.

'You think I betrayed you,' she said. 'I didn't. I hope you didn't betray me.'

Maldonado gave a great shuddering sigh. 'Why did you ever come to Peru?'

'To find my father.' She waited in silence.

'You found him,' Maldonado said finally.

'And lost him again.'

Another silence. Helen could hear the grandfather clock chime in Maldonado's study.

'Why are you ringing me?'

'To ask you for my father.'

Maldonado laughed, a bitter, regretful, almost self-mocking sound.

'You think I have him? You think he's alive?'

'He said you couldn't kill him,' said Helen, straining to keep her voice from breaking. 'I don't think you could.'

'But to let him go . . . Assuming I had him, why should I?'

'Remember what I said to you on Machu Picchu.'

'You threatened me, I seem to remember,' he said, his voice distant, as if it were all academic. 'Are you threatening me again?' he asked, amused now.

'I'm offering you an exchange.'

'What could you possibly offer me?'

CHAPTER 88

Helen went to W.H. Smith on Notting Hill Gate and bought six ninety-minute blank tapes. She returned home and made three copies of each tape she had taken from Roddy's safe. She sellotaped one set to the underside of a chair, put another set in an envelope, and the third set in her handbag. She telephoned a motorcycle courier service and arranged for them to come to pick up the envelope which she double-sealed with tape and addressed to Dai. The courier arrived half an hour later. Black leather, a powerful walk, dark hair curling out from beneath his helmet. Helen handed him the envelope.

'It's off junction fifteen,' she said, taking the time to give him detailed directions.

'Thanks, darlin'. Save me a lot of time that.'

'No problem.'

'Nasty cut that,' he said, eyeing her cheek. 'How d'you get that then?'

'Hit by a tree, in a river in the Amazon, escaping from a bunch of drug runners.'

'Yeah, luv. 'Course you were.'

'Mind how you go,' said Helen, shutting the door with a smile.

She waited for sunset, then she consulted her Goldsteins directory of home telephone numbers and rang Zaha Zamaroh.

'Zaha. It's Helen Jencks here.'

'Well . . . Helen. What a surprise.'

'I'd like to come and see you, Zaha.'

'I think you'd better come in to Goldsteins tomorrow. With a lawyer, if you have one.'

'I don't think so, Zaha. I don't think you'd appreciate a lawyer.'

'I'd appreciate . . . ?'

'AZC. CILD, Antigua. Account number 2483 –' Helen interrupted herself. 'Would you like me to continue on the telephone, or in person?'

She had occasionally wondered how Zamaroh lived. Fifteen minutes later she had her answer. Onslow Square in South Kensington. A penthouse flat, bleached wood floors, Scandinavian painters on the white walls, a fragment of a carpet framed and hung – a delicate lattice work overlaid with profuse blossoms and foliage. Helen walked up close to it.

'A Shah Abbas. Beautiful.' She studied the rugs covering the wooden floors. 'A Saruk, a Seraband and a Ferahan. That pale green is so fine, like sunlight on the rainforest.' Helen gazed down at the carpets in rapture.

Zamaroh stared at her in amazement. 'Where d'you learn about Persian carpets?'

'My godfather's an Arabist, a collector. I learned from him. Heirlooms, or did you buy them with your ill-gotten gains?'

Zamaroh glared at Helen for a moment, then broke into a smile. She was wearing a floor-length jellaba, intricately embroidered with gold thread. Gold earrings flickered against her brown skin. She looked more like a goddess than ever. But here she was all quiet dignity, the bombast she displayed on the trading floor left there.

'Would you like a drink?'

'You asked for vodka, I seem to remember, and you drank to easy money. Easy come, Zaha, easy go.' Helen opened her bag and handed Zamaroh the two tapes. She sat on a low white sofa. Chopin's *Nocturnes* played in the background. Zamaroh silenced them, lay back on a long, pale, canvas-covered sofa, played first one tape then the other.

She looked around the room as the disembodied voices rose to fill it. Her eyes lingered on her paintings, on calm seas with cold pure light, on beech trees shimmering in a wind you could almost feel, on cornfields golden against a blue sky, on empty shingle beaches. Her totems, her peace. When her own recorded voice died away and the tape ran silent, she turned to Helen. She looked as relaxed as a snake, contemplating the best angle from which to strike.

'I don't have a jugular any more, Zaha,' said Helen as if she had read her mind, 'nor an Achilles heel.'

'What happened to your face? What happened to *you?*'

Helen smiled, remembering the motorcycle courier's reaction when she answered his question.

'You wouldn't believe me if I told you.'

Zamaroh got up to pour herself a whisky. 'You?' She gestured delicately with the bottle. Helen shook her head.

'I'll have the tapes please. And don't get any ideas, I've got copies stashed away.'

Zamaroh held the tapes with the tips of her fingers, as if they were contaminated. She handed them to Helen and resumed her seat. A Persian cat wound around a corner, ignored Helen and jumped up onto its mistress's lap.

'So why don't you tell me what you want?' asked Zamaroh, stroking the smoky-grey fur of her pet.

'All of the money you collected from Wallace and Rankin.'

'Fifteen million dollars?' Zamaroh's voice rose and a fragment of her trading floor personality cut through. 'Are you mad? Why on earth should I just hand that over to you?'

'Because if you don't, I hand in the tapes, to Goldsteins, and the SFO.'

Zamaroh nodded. Helen could see her replaying the tapes in her mind. She could see a faint embarrassment colour her face, imagined that it was caused by Zamaroh's speech to Wallace, the personal disclosures of what it meant to her to be a non-white woman in the City. That embarrassed her more than theft. The myth Zamaroh had created, that nothing touched her, was shattered by that speech, her own public image of herself betrayed.

She glared at Helen in a quick anger that faded as her intellect reasserted control.

'Clever game, Helen. Wallace and Rankin set you up. Were you setting them up all along?'

Helen smiled. 'That would have been something, wouldn't it?'

'What will you do with them?'

'Same as I'm doing with you.'

'You're very confident that we shall all comply.'

'A few years in an open prison, end of your career? All the money confiscated?'

'It might never go to trial. You know how impotent the SFO is.'

'I don't think it's a risk you'd be willing to take. It's the end of your image too, isn't it? A soiled heritage for an Iranian princess.'

'You bitch.'

'Nothing personal, Zaha.'

'Then what is it? Why do you want the money? I always had the impression it wasn't very important to you.'

'You're right. It's not. But it is to other people.'

CHAPTER 89

Helen knocked loudly on Hugh Wallace's door, relying on his customary taste for solitude. She heard footsteps, then silence. She could imagine him scrutinising her through the peep-hole. She could almost feel his hushed breathing, see his colour rising, nervous fingers yanking at a grimy collar. She looked ahead levelly, meeting his unseen eyes.

'Open the door, Hugh. Or would you prefer I kicked it in?'

Helen Jencks's face was inches from his. He checked his double bolts. He wanted to turn, pad silently back to his den, his can of Heineken and his computers. But there was something irresistible about the force on the other side of the door.

'I'll do it, Hugh. Ten, nine, eight –'

One by one, he drew back the deadbolts. He edged open the door, filled the gap with his body, as if this would keep her out. Helen smiled at him.

'What do you want?' his voice was taut, almost a whine. His wrist rested on the doorpost. Helen played for it, caught it, doubled it back, walked him inside.

'Curiosity killed the cat, huh, Hugh? Never could resist it, could you?' She smelled his fear. His hand turned slippery with sweat. She released him in the drawing room. He edged away from her, to the other side of the brick sculpture. Helen followed him round, pushed him down onto a sofa. He sprawled, ungainly, then drew himself up tightly, knees together, arms folded.

'Your face seems to have healed up nicely. I hear you were mugged.'

Wallace flinched. Helen stroked one of the four speakers in the room.

'Bang & Olufsen. Surround sound. I've got something you might like to hear.'

She slotted the first cassette into the machine. The sound of voices flowed around them, perfectly recreated, concert quality, every inflection, every suggestion picked up. Helen lay back on the sofa opposite Wallace. She never took her eyes from his face which sagged and hardened as his ego fought against reality in a grotesque display of realisation and disbelief, fear and rage, impotence and posturing. Seeing him before her, she felt no great thirst for revenge, but, in case the craving came upon her at some time in the future, she committed to memory these paroxysms of disintegration.

She played with the remote control, lowering and raising the volume until Wallace contorted his face and covered his ears.

'Shut if off!' he screamed. 'Someone will hear.'

Helen turned down the sound. 'Yes, they will, unless you do exactly what I want.'

CHAPTER 90

Helen awoke the next morning to the sound of rain. She pushed herself out of bed and looked out onto a rainbow. She remembered the double rainbow she had seen with Connor, in Cusco. Had it been a good omen or a bad one? Half the sky was black, the other gleaming bright and blue. She went in search of her address book, rang Damien, her bank manager in Jersey, and had a brief conversation with him. Then she pulled on shorts and a T-shirt and pushed her feet into running shoes. She didn't wait to stretch but ran out into the sun shower. The rain coursed down her face, the sun flickered on wet pavements. Into the park, onto the wet grass she ran, until her strides became fluid as the rain itself.

The shower burned itself out in the June sun. The grass seemed to be steaming. She ran home, took a bath, put on clean jeans, a white T-shirt and trainers, and walked off to Europa to buy supplies.

She had just finished a breakfast of mangoes and Colombian coffee when the doorbell rang. She padded into her bedroom and craned her head around the curtains. Roddy Clark.

The anger burned at her, like a flame that blazed then guttered. She went to the intercom, pushed the buzzer, heard the surprised click of the door as Roddy pushed it open. Harsh steps on the parquet floor of the hall, then he stopped outside her door. She flung it open. He stepped back.

'Helen!'

'Who were you expecting, Lucrezia Borgia?'

'I . . . er . . . it was just a routine call. See if you were back.'

'Here I am.' She folded her arms across her chest. 'You didn't think your drivel would keep me away?'

'Come on, Hel, let's not –'

'Get personal? Is that what you were going to say?' She laughed. 'Your missing trader angle seems a bit fanciful now, doesn't it? A factual inaccuracy. All your implications of wrongdoing might seem rather self-serving.'

'What are you getting at?'

'Oh, you're worrying I might sue you. Defamation of character. I wonder how much that's worth?' She saw the flicker of fear in his eyes. He knew in advance that he had lost. 'Get out, Roddy. You never had a clean heart. All your scribblings are tainted. You and everything you write are an irrelevance, always were, always will be.'

CHAPTER 91

Notting Hill was alive with summer, brown skin and sweat, exotic scents, cappuccino on the pavement, Pimm's in the garden squares. An air of languor concealed suppressed excitement. Courtship on the streets. She watched it all as if through a lens. She didn't want to talk to Dai, she couldn't face Joyce, not while she was in this limbo of waiting.

She had taken her gamble. Maybe she was right, maybe wrong. Time would pass sentence. The weekend came and went. Dai rang, worried. Mrs Lucas came up to see her, welcomed her home, insisted she come down for tea, a chat and some cake to build her up. All the while, Helen waited, staring from the high-ceilinged cool of her flat out onto the brilliant green of oak leaves, dappled with sunlight. On Monday morning Damien rang from Jersey, breathless with respect.

'You asked me to ring you when any payments came into your account. We received two this morning. We –'

'What's the total?'

'Twenty million dollars.'

She waited a while longer, trying to calm herself with the comfort of meticulous routine. She ground fresh coffee beans, filled the percolator with water, shook coffee so fine and fresh it seemed like dark scented air, packed it down into its little receptacle, and put it on the stove to simmer. She turned on Nina Simone, listened to the hideously carefree 'My Baby Just Cares For Me'. On the cooker, the percolator spat hissing coffee. Helen poured out one small, wickedly strong cup and carried it through to the telephone. She waited while the coffee cooled slightly then drained the cup.

A gust of wind blew in through an open window, stirring the heavy curtains, whispering at her hair. She picked up the telephone. Her hand shook as she gripped the receiver, and rang Maldonado. Carmen answered. Interminable wait. Then the deep voice. Injured, unforgiving, curious.

'Helen.'

'How much is my father worth?'

'Helen, what are you –'

'There's a brisk business, isn't there, in this kind of thing? Kidnap. For ransom. Let's say Angel got hold of my father . . .'

'What are you saying?'

'He'd release him, wouldn't he, for the right price?'

'Why are we having this conversation?'

'I'm a fraudster, remember?'

'Are you?'

'Let's say I am. The papers think so, don't they?'

'They imply that.'

'Is he alive?'

'Why are you torturing me, and yourself?'

'Is he, is he alive?'

Maldonado said nothing.

'Banco de Panama. BD 1564 831 9929,' said Helen, reciting the number of the bank account she had discovered in Maldonado's desk. 'Is that correct?'

'Where did you get that?'

'Just answer me, is it correct?'

'Yes.'

She rang Damien.

'I'd like you to make a transfer, electronic wire, to be processed today.'

'Certainly, Helen. Just give me the details. I'll need written confirmation later, if that's all right.'

'That's fine.'

'OK. What'll it be?'

'Payment to Banco de Panama, account number BD 1564 831 9929.'

'Name?'

'No name.'
'Amount?'
'Twenty million dollars.'

CHAPTER 92

Helen rang Joyce. She got the answerphone.

'Joyce, hi, it's Hel. I'm back. I'm just about to go to Wiltshire. Give me a call.' She could imagine Joyce's face when she picked up the message, fox-like features pursed with anticipation.

She rang Dai, told him she was driving down to stay with him. She began to throw clothes into a bag. The ring of the intercom surprised her. She paused, holding a T-shirt aloft. She dropped it to the floor as the intercom rang again. Very softly, she moved around her bed, skirted the wall, and peered out through her bedroom window. A man stood outside, tall, thick-set, wearing an ill-fitting grey suit. He had thin sandy hair, combed back. Something about him was vaguely familiar.

'Shit. I'm not going to hide for ever,' she whispered, walking quietly to the intercom.

'Yes.'

'Miss Jencks?'

'Who were you expecting?'

'Miss Jencks, if that's you, my name's Michael Freyn. I'm head of security at Goldsteins.'

In answer, Helen pushed the buzzer, unlocking the front door. She opened her own door and watched Freyn approach. He walked with the awkwardness of one bearing bad news. Helen smiled at him.

'Show me your ID.'

He looked somewhat surprised, then reached into his pocket.

'Slowly,' said Helen, taking a step towards him.

Moving in slow motion, he showed her his pass.

Helen checked it, then nodded. 'All right. Come in.' She walked with him into her drawing room. 'Sit down, please.' She watched

414

him choose a straight-backed chair where he sat square-kneed, facing her head on. She moved around the room.

'Coffee, tea, water?'

'Water, please.'

Helen went to the kitchen, poured two glasses of sparkling water and carried them through. Wordlessly, she handed one to Freyn, and sat down.

'What happened to your face?'

'Walked into a door.'

'Right.' He gave a small sigh. 'I'm going to have to ask you a few questions, if that's all right. Your disappearance from Goldsteins worried us.'

'It was a personal matter. I had to go abroad. I should have informed the desk. I have no excuses. I'm sorry.'

'That won't really do, Miss Jencks.'

Helen shrugged. 'It'll have to. How did you know I was back?'

Freyn smiled. His eyes seemed to say: I ask the questions.

'Why were you away so long?'

'It's not relevant to you.'

'I'd like to know.'

'Why?'

'It's an interesting subject. Even the *World* seemed to think so.'

Helen laughed.

'What's funny?'

Helen thought of bullets exploding into the river, of swimming into Connor's arms. 'People miss the point.'

'What is the point?'

'Why not ask the *World*?'

'Do you mind if I make a telephone call?'

'Go ahead.'

Freyn brought out a mobile telephone from his jacket pocket. He pulled up the antenna and dialled.

'Evangeline. Could I speak to James, please. It's urgent. James? I'm here with Helen Jencks. You said to call when I found her. Perhaps you'd like to talk to her yourself.' Freyn turned to Helen. 'Would you mind?'

She shook her head.

*　　*　　*

415

Savage arrived forty minutes later. Helen opened the door to him. He stood, elegant, pinstriped and sombre before her. Standing there in her jeans and T-shirt, one bare foot on top of the other, she looked to him like some kind of Amazon. She was honed down, great long, sinewy muscles ran beneath deep-brown skin, and her eyes glowed with a light he hadn't seen before. She looked to him as if she'd won a victory in a game he couldn't even fathom. She received him with a nod and acknowledged him by name, almost as if she were ticking him off against some hidden list. He followed her into the drawing room. He picked his way across her Persian carpets.

'Beautiful. Seems a shame to walk on them,' he observed.

'Doesn't sound like you,' said Helen, smiling, shaking his outstretched hand. For a moment his face was fixed, then he broke into his slit-eyed crooked smile

'You take liberties with me,' he said.

'In my own home . . .'

'Hm.' Savage turned to Freyn. 'Thanks, Michael.'

Freyn understood, reluctantly got to his feet.

'See you back at the office,' he said to Savage. To Helen he gave a small bow. She showed him out.

'How very civil,' she said, returning to Savage. He sank down into a sofa, crossed one knee over the other. She curled up in her sapphire-blue velvet armchair.

'What happened to your face.'

'My cat.'

'We found out about the mispricing.'

Extraordinarily, she seemed to brighten on hearing this.

'What the hell's going on, Helen?'

'Take off your clothes.'

'What?'

'You heard me. One by one, slowly, so that I can see.'

'Helen, I really don't think this is the time or the place. Much as I've always wanted –'

He paused as she doubled up with laughter. 'Oh, God, James. This isn't about sex. You want me to talk? Tell you what's been going on?'

'I do.'

'You might be carrying some kind of recording device,' she explained with meticulous patience.

'I can assure you I'm not.'

'Humour me.'

He got to his feet, took off his jacket and draped it across the back of the sofa. He bent down and began to unlace his shoes.

'If you insist.'

'I insist.'

Off came his shoes. Helen picked them up and examined them. Finely crafted black leather brogues, marked 'Lobb, St James's Street'.

'Hand tooled?' asked Helen with a grin.

Savage looked up, a navy sock in his hand. He gave her a murderous look. 'How do I know you don't have some video recorder running?'

'You don't. You'll just have to trust me.'

He snorted and threw down his sock. He took off his tie and dropped it beside the limp socks. Cufflinks, gold, not too discreet, gleamed from the coffee table, his shirt, white, slightly creased now, he laid over the back of the sofa. All the while, arms crossed, Helen watched him, looking every inch a Roman queen sizing up a slave at auction.

Savage unbuttoned his flies. His trousers slid down to his ankles with a hiss of silk lining. He stepped out of them and laid them across his jacket. He stood before her in a pair of blue-and-white-striped boxer shorts. His breasts were beginning to sag with age. His skin was pallid. His knee bones over-protruded. The flesh hung limply from his upper arms where once there must have been firm muscle. He should have looked vulnerable, but the ferocity in his eyes rebuked her.

'Satisfied?'

'Mmm . . . I'd have expected silk paisley,' she said with a smile, eyeing his underpants. 'You can drop them too.'

'Don't be ridiculous.'

'Who knows what you might be hiding down there.'

'You're enjoying this.'

'Absolutely. Drop 'em.'

Savage pulled down his underpants, kicked them off, and pirouetted before Helen.

'There, that wasn't so hard now, was it?'

'You're pushing your luck, Jencks.'

'That's what you hired me for.'

'True. Shouldn't you do the same now, slip out of those jeans, in the name of sportsmanship? Who knows what *you* might be carrying.'

'Nice try, James. Nothing more than an agenda. Get dressed.'

Savage put his clothes back on. As he did so, Helen slipped on a pair of trainers.

'Are we going somewhere?'

'For a stroll.'

They walked to Kensington Gardens, and sat down on a bench opposite Millionaires Row. A great oak shielded them from the bright sun. The cries of children sporting in a playground rent the air. Rollerbladers scythed by. They sat, a few inches apart, staring forward like lovers trying to fathom one another in the lull of an argument.

'What have you found out?' asked Helen.

'Mispricing of KOSPI options. We calculated we're probably down about fifty million. Thirty of that is lost profit to Goldsteins, twenty actual losses. Not too greedy. Pretty difficult to spot. Clever. Your signature on every dodgy trade.'

'And?'

'And? You fled.'

'You've no more hard evidence?'

'Only suppositions.'

'You think I did it?'

'What am I supposed to think? You disappeared.'

'And now you want the truth?'

'That'd be nice.'

Helen laughed. 'You either won't believe me, or you'll try to have me committed.'

'I want to hear it. I'm here to listen.'

'I don't have your kind of truth. This is outside everything you've ever known.'

'Try me.'

'You'll wish you never asked.'

Helen spoke for half an hour. Savage said nothing. He shifted around on the bench, leaning forward, clenching his knees, grasping his temples with his fingers, his eyes shifting from Helen's face to a spot on the wall of one of the houses on Millionaires Row.

He sat up straight when Helen had finished talking. He waited for some time, as if fearing more revelations. Then he punctured the silence with a great long exhalation until it seemed to Helen that his lungs must collapse.

He turned to face her. 'So, the long and short of it is that twenty-five million dollars of Goldsteins' money is with AZC, around five or so with Wallace and Rankin, and twenty million dollars is in the hands of some bent intelligence drugs king in South America.'

'Yep, that's about it. And if you ever tell anyone my side of the story, they'll think you're mad. I'll never corroborate a word.'

'Jesus Christ.' Savage held his head in his hands, looking up at Helen with quiet fury. 'What's happened to the one point five mill in the Banque des Alpes account?'

'Banque des Alpes? What's that got to do with anything?'

Savage studied Helen's eyes. They looked back steadily, cool and clear, utterly puzzled.

'Good God. None of this is happening. It's too . . . absurd doesn't even begin to describe it.'

'I said you'd wish you'd never asked. What happened to me in Peru is another story, but what went down on your own trading floor shouldn't surprise you. What did you expect? The whole place is seething with brilliant, avarice-riddled minds and giant egos. You unleash these people on the markets with the explicit aim that they savage the competition. Their job is to be as creative and as ruthless as they can in making money. When they do, they're treated like medieval kings and queens. They think they're untouchable. Is it any wonder when they turn around and savage you? Gouge away some of Goldsteins' fat profits. It's your night-mare, isn't it? Yours and every chief executive in every bank from here to Tokyo, that one of his hungry young things will feed from the wrong trough. You're lucky at least. You can swallow the loss before breakfast and not feel it. The *World* got onto it, but I've a feeling there won't be any more articles about it now. You've got an even chance to cover it up, save Goldsteins' reputation, and your career.'

'And in the process, save your skin too.'

'Do you honestly think, after what's happened, that I give a damn for my own skin? It's alive. That's what counts. I'm not frightened of the Serious Fraud Office, nor of exposure. I've been exposed when I was innocent, d'you think I'd care now that I'm guilty.' She leaned right up to him. 'And what am I so guilty of? Stealing from thieves to try to save the life of my father . . .'

Savage got to his feet. He stared at the pain, hope, love and yearning in Helen's face

'I can only hope it works.'

CHAPTER 93

Savage returned to his office at six o'clock. Freyn was waiting. He looked anxiously at Savage's pinched face.

'What did she tell you?'

'The subject is now and will be for ever closed. Helen Jencks has resigned. Andy Rankin will become Hugh Wallace's research assistant. The two of them will invent products we'll never use. Over the course of the next six months, they will leave us, quietly. Neither of them shall ever work in the City again. I'm going to put the word out on AZC, a few whispers here and there. In three months no respectable outfit'll touch them.'

'What about Zamaroh? Didn't you suspect she might have some hand in all this?'

'If she did, Helen decided for some reason to spare her. Zamaroh stays.'

'What'll you tell Compliance?'

'That's my own private nightmare.'

'Why not tell them the truth? Tell them what Helen told you?'

Savage gave a bitter laugh.

'I don't think they're quite ready for that. Nor will they ever be. This episode is over, the investigation closed. Everything's back to normal. Got it?'

'Er, yeah. Got it.'

Freyn left, puzzlement mixing with the loyal obedience on his face. Savage stood alone in his office, staring out at the City skyline. He had, as Helen said, an evens chance of pulling it off. Like her, he was a gambler.

CHAPTER 94

Helen set off for Wiltshire in her father's car, the evening sun slanting low into her eyes. She drove through Shepherd's Bush, into the rush-hour traffic. It took nearly an hour to get out of London onto the M4 motorway. She pressed her foot down on the accelerator, felt the surge of power, changed from third to fourth gear, accelerated again till the speedometer climbed to one hundred, then she eased into fifth and cruised. The car still handled like a dream. She pushed down further on the accelerator and laughed at the prospect of a speeding ticket as she scorched past the slow lane where the cars seemed almost stationary.

She arrived at Dai's at eight. In the driveway, dominating the crescent before the house was a forty-ton truck. Unlike most of the monsters on the road, this one gleamed with care. Chrome shone against the red bodywork. Helen got out of her car and walked up to the lorry. Handpainted in italics on the driver's door was the word *Beast*. Helen knew that if she opened the door the scent of Chanel No. 5 would ease out into the evening air. She walked up the steps and rang the bell. Through the thick oak door she heard voices.

'Hey, I think it's the beige beauty.'

The door burst open. Joyce ran out with a scream.

'Aah. I don't believe it.'

Helen hugged her. 'I thought it might be you. There's only one person I know drives that kind of monstrosity.'

Joyce pulled back. She studied Helen's face, frowning at her cut.

'Leave Beast out of it.'

'She looks good.'

'So do you,' said Joyce, 'sort of good and bad at the same time.'

'Well, that's as much as I can probably hope for,' said Helen, smiling. Dai appeared behind them. Helen went to him and hugged him.

'Any news?' he asked her.

'Nothing.'

'Come 'n' have a drink.' He put his arm around her, Joyce linked arms with Helen on the other side, and together they walked into the drawing room.

'Joyce has been regaling me with road stories from Cornwall to John o'Groat's,' said Dai. 'Sounds as if she's been on the road for weeks.'

'Stopped long enough to administer a little rough justice,' said Helen, with an admiring look at her friend.

'You bet I did. Sensai'd be ashamed of me. Too bad. Aikido's about justice. Thought I'd dole out a bit of my own.'

'Good on you, girl.'

'Yeah, right. Now I wanna hear what's been going on. Dai clammed up, said it had to come from you.'

Helen touched her arm.

'Tell it over dinner, Hel,' said Dai. 'Let's just talk, the three of us, as if everything were normal, for an hour, as if you'd never been away.'

Helen smiled. She was beginning to learn how to allow one part of her to be happy, while other parts lay in pain. She'd thought she'd learned that lesson years ago, but then she had simply numbed all feeling. To relish the pattern of joy in a life, to accept the strands of pain that wove through it, now seemed to her, not just possible, but the only way to live. Her fears for her father were like a gash in her heart. Connor's absence was a seeping wound, but she would smile through them.

They sat down to lamb roasted with rosemary and garlic, golden potatoes with burnished skins that cracked against her teeth and succulent mangetout from the garden.

'I think I'll need a month of dinners to tell my story,' said Helen, 'and it hasn't even begun to end yet.'

Joyce listened with horrified fascination.

'You remember that lunch we had, just before you went away?

You said you were going to look beyond the ranges, something odd like that, look for a little chaos? God, girl, you certainly found it.'

'Yeah, I did, didn't I?'

'What you gonna do now?'

'Wait.'

'You? You've always been hopeless at waiting.'

'Still am.'

Joyce and Helen stayed up late drinking brandies, getting drunk, Helen remembering and trying to forget at the same time. Her father, Evan, loving, yearning, and mourning.

Joyce stayed the night. She left after breakfast in a great roar. Dai freed the dogs and they chased the articulated lorry all the way up the mile-long drive.

As Helen and Dai returned to the house, James Savage rang. Derek took the call.

'Hold on a second, would you please, Mr Savage.' He walked into the hallway.

'Hel, Mr Savage?' he asked with a questioning lilt.

'I'll take it.' She walked into the library and picked up the phone. 'James.'

'Helen. Listen, you ought to prepare yourself. I've started legal proceedings against the *World*. I have to know what they've got against us, drag it into the open now. If they still have something, another copy of your tapes, which I have to assume is likely, I want it out now. It'll destroy us sooner or later. If it's to happen, better it be sooner.'

'It needn't.'

'No, not you, but me. It would destroy me. I'm not going to be held to ransom by the fates like that.'

'So you're summoning them and all the furies to your table.'

CHAPTER 95

Roddy Clark faced Roland Mudd across the editor's desk. 'Small technical problem,' said Mudd. 'Goldsteins are suing us. Defamation of character. Theirs and Helen Jencks's. You got it wrong, Roddy. Jencks is back in town. Apparently, she'd simply gone on an extended holiday. Stress, executive burnout, that sort of thing. Our implication that she was running from her involvement in something fraudulent stacked up only as long as she stayed away, or as long as Goldsteins were prepared to distance themselves from her. We got that wrong, too. They're right behind her, suing us on her behalf, with their very considerable resources, which, in case you can't do the sums, are just a tad larger than ours. We have no case against Helen. We took a gamble on her, we pushed the legal boundaries 'cos it made a great story. We lost. Fine. It pisses me off, but that's the game. Now, Goldsteins – we should trounce their overpaid arses in court, shouldn't we, because we have the tapes incriminating them up to here? Problem is, we don't have the tapes. Records state you signed them out two weeks ago. Mind telling me why you did that, and where they are now?'

Clark shifted in his seat. 'You know my feeling about source material. I like to keep it myself. I don't always trust it might not fall into the wrong hands.'

'Ease off the double negatives, will you? Makes you sound shifty.' Mudd got up and started to move round the desk to Clark. 'You have both tapes, I presume?'

'At home. In my safe.'

'Go and retrieve them.'

*   *   *

Clark felt a strange sense of unease as he took the tube to Holland Park. A law suit wasn't that rare. The *World* probably had a couple a month. It was bad form, unnerving, but many of the best stories pushed the legal limits. How many times had the *Washington Post* been threatened with law suits over Watergate? News was a battle ground, with journalists on one side, lawyers on the other. Occasionally, the press pushed too hard, got it wrong. Miscalculated. Roddy couldn't understand why Goldsteins hadn't ditched Helen. With her incriminating name, the last thing Goldsteins should have wanted was to enter the public arena of courts and newspapers to defend her. What was even less explicable was Goldsteins' suing over defamation of their own reputation. With the tapes, the *World* would win, so why on earth were Goldsteins suing? They might not know of the tapes' existence, but the *World*'s article had been sufficiently detailed to imply first-rate source material. And why sue now? It must have something to do with Helen's return.

Roddy began to feel sick as he opened his safe. He reached in, scrabbled around with his hand. The tapes were gone. He knew at once who had taken them. She had his keys, she knew the combination, she hadn't even needed to break and enter. Her revenge was complete.

'Gone! What do you mean gone?' shouted Mudd an hour later.

'They're not there,' said Clark dully.

'Were they stolen, did you misplace them, did they vaporise?'

Clark looked away.

'Jesus Christ!' Mudd hurled his mound of plasticine at the wall. It made a dull thud and slipped to the floor. 'You never noticed anything?'

'I haven't been into my safe for over a week.'

'No signs of burglary, I presume?'

'No.'

'So Helen Jencks stole the tapes?'

'How could she? She doesn't know the combination.' He didn't know why he lied, some strange legacy of feeling for Helen.

'Somebody did.' Mudd paced round his office. 'Shit. No bloody case at all. Moses knows how much we'll have to cough up. It's

426

not even the bloody money bothers me most. It's knowing they're getting away with it. This should've been a great story. Now we'll have to print an apology, an unequivocal retraction. Goldsteins'll go round smug as hell and everything'll be nice and clean and proper in the City, meanwhile some bugger's waltzing round with fifty million dollars.'

'Not Helen.'

'Not Helen. She just made the perfect fall girl. No one'll know the truth now.'

'So what do we do?'

'Our lawyers call theirs. We trade horses. We cough up and print a retraction and an apology. You piss off for two weeks' unpaid until I can bear the sight of you. If I ever will be able to again.'

Mudd got to his feet and stood nose to nose with his journalist. 'Well done, Roddy. The bastards win again. Another great City cover-up is hatched.'

CHAPTER 96

Helen took the Dobermans for a long walk before lunch. It gave her a chance to be alone, away from the loving ministrations of Dai and Derek.

She ran with the dogs, chasing them, turning and running, letting them chase her, rolling with them in the grass. They were the first to see the lone figure walking towards them. They ran back to Helen, pointed themselves in the direction of the stranger and began a low growling.

'It's all right, girls, quiet now. Let's go and see who it is, shall we?'

Nothing could ever happen to her here at Stonehurst. The place was a fortress. She was free and safe within the estate walls. Dai had always looked after her, always protected her, until those times when she shunned protection and sought danger. She had her aikido, and four trained Dobermans forming a cordon around her. She walked towards the stranger. That's what you do.

The growling of the dogs grew louder as the figure came into range. There seemed to be something familiar about his walk. Helen stared at him intently: blue jeans, a long loose stride, a broad chest, powerful shoulders. He was near enough now that she could pick out the details of his face, his smiling lips, his creased blue eyes, the scar at his right temple. She laughed with joy. Tears wet her cheeks and she tasted salt. The dogs looked up at her, stopped growling. Their muscles relaxed in pleasure at her happiness.

'Sorry I'm a bit late,' said Evan Connor.

'It's all right,' lied Helen. 'I wasn't expecting you.'

Connor laughed, took her in his arms, held her so tight she could almost feel his thoughts. When they drew apart there was joy in their eyes. He held her at arm's length, studying her, then he pulled her close again, mouth to mouth, kissing her until she felt her blood would turn to smoke.

They walked back together to the house. Dai appeared with Derek. He looked at their joy, at the energy that seemed to flow between them, at a bond that transcended their obvious physical attraction. Their love radiated all around them.

He approached, smiling. 'Let me take a wild guess. You must be Evan Connor.'

Connor smiled, and shook hands with Dai and Derek.

'How d'you do. Sorry to turn up unannounced.'

'You're not sorry at all,' said Dai. 'None of us looks particularly sorry. From what I hear, you and Hel are lucky to be here at all.'

'Yeah, we had a bit of a time of it.'

'I know how pig-headed that girl is.' Dai glanced at Helen. 'I know you couldn't have stopped her when she made up her mind. I've just got to thank you for getting her out in one piece.'

'She got herself out too. You don't see courage like hers often. And will. I don't think I've ever met anyone with a stronger will.'

'She always had that. Even as a little girl. You'll join us for lunch of course?'

'I'd love to.'

As they sat down to eat, Dai studied Connor. Helen could feel how quickly they warmed to each other. She knew Connor had passed all the tests Dai might have had for him and more.

James Savage rang just as they were finishing lunch. Helen took the call in Dai's study.

'The *World* has offered to settle, remarkably quickly, I must say.'

'Remarkably,' agreed Helen. 'I thought these things took months.'

'Normally they do. Apparently there was some problem with their corroboration. A key piece of evidence went missing.'

Helen giggled. 'That's too bad.'

'They didn't even have a copy, would you believe it?'

'How unprofessional.'

'They tried to put a value on your career, which of course is now ruined by their defamation. I informed them that your total package at Goldsteins was worth at least one hundred and fifty thousand pounds a year, depending on bonuses. I argued that you had at least another five years as a trader. The *World* tried to say you'd get married, have babies and do a maximum of another two years. You are, after all, the ripe old age of thirty. I told them they were being sexist bastards.'

'I'm impressed.'

'They offered three hundred and eighty thousand pounds.'

She smiled. 'Tell them I'll take it.'

'Happily.'

'I hope the furies'll stay away now.'

'I hope so. What about you? Any news?'

'Life gets better. Still a way to go.'

Helen returned to the dining room.

'Good news?' asked Dai, studying her wide grin.

'The *World* apparently had a problem with some missing evidence. They offered to settle out of court.'

'You accepted?'

'Yep.'

'Good settlement?'

Helen nodded.

'What'll you do with the money?' asked Dai.

'Buy a boat and sail away. I'll call her *Freedom*. Invite you all.'

'Where to?' asked Connor.

'Does it matter?' asked Helen.

'Not remotely.'

After lunch, Helen and Connor took the dogs and walked up to the copse of beeches at the summit of the downs.

'This is the place I told you about,' said Helen. 'Remember? You asked me where I would choose, if I could see any place again, be any place.'

'It's beautiful,' said Connor, lying back on the grass and staring up at the clouds. 'Did you ever think you'd see it again?'

'I never stopped believing,' said Helen.

'Even in the river?'

'Maybe I had a few doubts in the river.'

Connor remembered her eyes when he'd helped her from the swirling water. He'd seen the look before, of someone who feared imminent death. He took her into his arms and made love to her.

'What happened with Carlyle and co.?' Helen asked Connor later, lying beside him, stroking the hair back from his face.

'I spent five days with them in the country, debriefing various people.'

'They're satisfied?'

Connor shrugged and Helen felt his shoulder move against hers.

'Who knows. They got all I could give them. My cover's blown now. My usefulness to them is over, at least in that part of the world. And I've no desire to work for them anywhere else.'

'Why not?'

'I've done it for long enough. The thrill's gone. It'd be nice to just have my own agenda for once.'

'What do you want to do?'

Helen felt him move closer. He put his arms around her and pulled her into his chest.

'Sail around the world with you.'

CHAPTER 97

The next morning, seated at breakfast, they read the retraction and apology in the *World*. Alongside the article was a photograph of Helen, who, it said, was now taking a vacation at her godfather's house in Stonehurst, Wiltshire. The paper was pleased to point out that there had been no fraud at Goldsteins, and wished to apologise to Miss Helen Jencks for any suggestion that she might have been responsible for any wrongdoing. The paper acknowledged that it had paid substantial damages to Goldsteins International, and to Miss Jencks, to compensate for any damage to their respective good reputations. Helen read it, laughed and made paper planes of it. She and Connor finished breakfast and set off with the dogs to the beech grove.

In the arrivals hall of Heathrow airport, shaking hands flicked through the *World*. The old man had forgotten the pleasures of British newspapers, better than anywhere in the world, despite their games. He'd flown into Heathrow two hours ago, landing at dawn. It had felt as if the world was awakening around him. So much was different, it was alien. He had looked around for something to reassure him and found nothing. He had changed some dollars for pounds at a foreign exchange bureau, bought the *World*, the *Daily Telegraph* and the *Financial Times*. He found refuge with his papers in the arrivals coffee bar. Sitting alone, sipping a frothing cappuccino, he read about a country that became in parts more familiar and more alien as he read on. Then he saw the photograph. The shock turned to a smile. He drained his coffee, folded up the *World* and got to his feet.

Disorientated, full of hopes and doubts, he headed for the taxi rank. A black cab pulled up. The driver hopped out to help the man with his battered case.

'Where to, guv?'

Helen was upstairs taking a shower after her walk with Connor and the dogs. She didn't notice the taxi pull up on the drive outside. She didn't see the stranger get out and walk to the imposing doors.

While she was drying her hair there was a knock and she opened the door to a grave-faced Dai. He seemed to be struggling under the weight of a great emotion. He searched for words.

Helen dropped her hairbrush and took hold of him. 'Dai, what is it?'

'There's someone to see you. He's waiting in the study.'

'Who is it?' she asked

But he would only shake his head and turn away.

Helen walked downstairs, pushing the wet hair from her eyes. Connor and Derek were standing in the hallway, watching her. The study door stood closed before her. She looked at it, tried to imagine what lay beyond, but in her mind there was blankness, and an awful fear.

She knocked twice, then pushed open the door. The stranger stood in the room, smiling hesitantly, the old man with her father's eyes.